Richard J. O'Brien

The People's Republic Of New Arkaim

Red Grit
Books

Copyright © 2021 by Richard J. O'Brien

Cover Design by the author

Red Grit Books

First Edition: August 2021

The Red Grit Books name and logo are trademarks of Red Grit Books.

ISBN: 978-1-7377027-0-2 (paperback)

Printed in the United States

For all my fellow travelers.

Contents

Once they notice you, Jason realized, they never completely close the file. You can never get back your anonymity. It is vital not to be noticed in the first place.

~Philip K. Dick, *Flow My Tears, The Policeman Said*

PART I

When a man in a modern army is broken from field grade to private, it is likely that he will be old for a private, and that his comrades in arms, once they get used to the fact that he isn't an officer any more, will, out of respect for his failing legs, eyes, and wind, call him something like Pops, or Gramps, or Unk.

~Kurt Vonnegut, *The Sirens of Titan*

Chapter 1: Grunt Funk

My fifty-fourth birthday had just passed when I learned the army wanted me back. Surely, I thought, someone had committed a grave clerical error. Uncle Sam had me confused with another and decidedly younger Caleb Aloysius Paladin from New Jersey. If not, the army brass at the Pentagon had lost their goddamn minds. They had to know that my original enlistment ended thirty-two years ago. One thing they didn't know was that when I was forty-four years old I suffered a mini-stroke. I got lucky. It wasn't that bad. Sometimes, though, it takes me a while to think of the right word. For instance, I might want to say the word pie and I would use the word pole instead. It only happens to me when I am speaking. Sometimes the mistaken word wasn't even close to the one I needed, alphabetically speaking. Anyway, the mini-stroke turned out to be small potatoes.

I also had a heart attack while getting three stents put in when I was fifty-two years old. Did the army know that? Doubtful. Here's what happened: I suffered a widowmaker heart attack during a routine stent procedure. That's when the left anterior descending artery gets close to or totally clogged. Blood stops flowing into the left side of the heart. In my case, this brought on the heart attack. My cardiologist said if I were at home instead of on his operating table I would have died. My demise may have turned out to be good news for my wife, but we'll get to her soon enough. Lucky for me, there was minimal damage to my heart. My cardiologist recommended exercise: running, weight training with free weights or machines, that sort of thing. He said it didn't matter. My cardiologist was a lunatic. Did he think I was Rocky Balboa training to fight Ivan Drago? I became a walker instead. I told myself that I would hold out until I reached my sixties before I started walking around the local mall early in the morning before it opened for business like all the other senior citizens did wearing their Velcro walking shoes and nylon warm-up gear.

Where was I? Oh Christ. The army. That's right. It was hard to imagine, given the world's connectivity in the twenty-first century, that no one at the Pentagon knew these things about my health. What the hell did they want with me after all this time?

The government was slick. It knew what it was doing. To them, it didn't matter that every guy from my original infantry unit was at least my age, if not older. I kept in touch with a few. From those few I learned about the others. Some of us were in poor health, ranging from coronary disease (like yours truly) to hip replacements, from cancer to diabetes. Others were already dead. I couldn't run up a flight of steps without getting winded. And there were guys worse off than me. One guy from my old unit was already a great-grandfather. The recall made no sense.

Confusion was nothing new to my old infantry unit. Back in the 1980's they pumped us full of various vaccines almost every quarter. When we asked, we were told not to. When we pressed the issue, it was always the same: the flu, cholera, and the like.

When we were out on maneuvers, the entire unit—privates, noncoms, and officers alike—experienced lost time. Back then we chalked it up to fatigue. No one dared to talk about UFOs or anything like that. Each of us was afraid in our own young impressionable way of being tagged as that nut job who believed in nonsense or, worse, broke completely from reality, resulting in a lengthy stay in the mental health ward of the post hospital before receiving a general medical discharge.

The lost time thing could be explained through the aforementioned fatigue which worked in strange ways. Sleep deprivation was known to cause hallucinations. More often than not, however, it boiled down to some schlub on point during a night movement through the backwoods of Fort Campbell that got turned around after forgetting how to navigate terrain using a compass and a map. In the infantry, shit like that happened all the time.

There was this one guy in my unit, Bartholomew Henry Kidd from Newark, that we used to call Fly Kidd back in the 80's because when we were off-duty he used to dress in all of the latest hip-hop fashions. Fly continued to suffer bouts of lost time even after being discharged. I heard through the grapevine that he'd just disappear, sometimes for weeks on end, eventually show back up, and have to patch things up with his wife. It was always the same story. He got lost in his own neighborhood and suffered long blank spots in his memory.

Fly and I never had much in common, even during our enlistment. I found out about the lost time incidents after his enlistment ended once we friended one another on Facebook. I messaged him once and told him to go under hypnosis. He wrote back and basically told me that he didn't truck with the devil. We remained Facebook friends, but I never spoke to him or even messaged him again after that. I did learn though that he had also suffered a heart attack just a couple of months after I did. So now we had both in common: New Jersey and heart attacks.

In the years following my enlistment entropy did her best to undo Fly, me, and our fellow cohorts. The majority of us had survived so far. For me, things started looking up, health-wise at least. Just when I thought I could start counting my blessings again along came Uncle Sam to screw up the works.

I should have known it would turn out this way. The nightmares I experienced since my original discharge couldn't have been a coincidence. As I got older, the dreams occurred with less frequency, but they never completely went away. It was always the same nightmare: an early morning run with the infantry company, just before dawn, in the humid heat of a Kentucky summer, the awful funk of grunts sweating off the alcohol consumed the

previous evening, when out of the dark came a floating aircraft
carrier with a gold hammer and sickle crisscrossed with a red star
over them painted on the hull. I was momentarily able to glance at
the giant craft before it opened up on us with its turret guns along
the hull's bottom. Fifty caliber rounds chewed up the street as the
unseen gunners strafed the entire area, killing nearly all my cohorts
before I could wake up.

In the years following my enlistment, I became acutely aware of
army recruiting ads, both on television and on the internet. Be All
That You Can Be. An Army of One. Army Strong. The slogans
had changed over time. In 2018 came Warriors Wanted. They
weren't even sugarcoating it anymore.

Sometimes, in recent years, I came across recruiting ads online.
Experience Makes the Difference was one ad I saw on numerous
occasions. I only saw it at home on my laptop or desktop computer,
never at work. I googled the slogan one night and found no
evidence of the army using such an ad. Another recruiting ad was
Fight Smart, Not Hard. That one appeared on my television one
late night. Grainy footage of soldiers in a desert fighting giants that
stood twelve feet tall flickered on and off as a male voice announced
in Latin: A Terra Ad Novum Mundi. After that the commercial
always ended with a black screen. I asked around. No one I knew
recalled ever seeing an ad like that on their television. I was
beginning to think I was cracking up, but the government was slick.
It knew what it was doing.

Official notification of my recall to active duty came hand-delivered
by an army courier. The envelope it came in with perforated edges
resembled the kind you get with your W-2 form or a final paycheck
that got mailed to you after getting shitcanned from a job for being
such an asshole and your now former employer didn't want you
showing up on the premises to pick up your final pay for fear of
retaliation. I have been there, for sure, but I digress.

The army didn't send just any S-4 jerk to deliver my orders.
They sent a Special Forces sergeant who knocked on my door with
all the urgency of a sheriff about to serve a warrant. When I opened
the door, the sergeant—despite his class A uniform, jump boots,

and iconic green beret—looked like a young cop, one of those young men you see around your neighborhood that you convince yourself is a twelve-year-old boy, rather than accepting the fact that you are getting that old.

"What's this?" I asked when he held out the envelope after he asked me my name.

He didn't bother to reply. The sergeant's expression remained neutral as he looked me in the eye.

"I need you to say your name," he informed me.

"Cal Paladin," I said. That's when his expression soured. "Paladin, Caleb Aloysius. Serial number—"

"We know your social security number," he said. "You don't need to repeat it now."

"So what is this?" I took the envelope from him.

"None of my business," the Green Beret said, rendering a salute.

I returned the salute, one of those over-exaggerated John-Wayne-style types from the movie *The Green Berets*.

The sergeant executed an about-face after he lowered his salute. He descended my porch steps and strode to a waiting black sedan at the curb.

I went back into the house and tore open the envelope.

US ARMY
Department of Off-World Operations Command (OWOC)
420 Army Pentagon
Washington, DC 20310-420

23 April 2020
Re: Special Reactivation

Dear Specialist (Ret.) Paladin, Caleb A.,

You have been selected for reactivation. Pursuant to Separation Orders 2211212-198920, you are hereby ordered to report to OWOC Station 8877, Fort Dix, NJ on 4 June 2020. Failure to report for duty will result in arrest and forfeiture of property and identity.

Please obey base rules at the joint military base to include but not limited to speed limits, military protocols regarding drug and alcohol usage, and general personal safety. Further instructions will await you upon completion of in-processing.

After that there was a closing paragraph detailing all the legal action that could be taken against me if I failed to comply. Then a "Sincerely" followed by a name: Jedidiah Hanson Leister, MAJ GEN, US ARMY OWOC.

If it hadn't been for the sergeant in uniform at my door, I thought it might be an elaborate hoax. The language in the orders sounded close enough to what I'd seen when I was a soldier. Of course, back then everything was typewritten in triplicate with carbon paper and later mimeographed. They had computers. They even had Arpanet, which was a precursor to the internet. What the Department of the Army didn't have was a good fire sprinkler system in its records warehouse in St. Louis where, in 1973, a fire destroyed over sixteen million official military personnel files that dated between 1912 and 1964.

Twelve years after that fire, my enlistment began. When I was discharged four years later, I had already learned about the fire in St. Louis. In those days, I was paranoid that all records of my military service would be lost just like so many service members who had come before me.

There were no more fires, to my knowledge, that wiped out personnel records. Even so, I made several copies of my DD-214, my discharge papers, distributed them to my parents, my in-laws, who frowned upon that portion of my life since they were Quakers, and my older brother Todd because he had a safe deposit box at a local bank, and my Aunt Rita who lived in Northeast Philadelphia. Aunt Rita died in 2001, just two days after 9/11. She was my mother's sister. My father died in 1995, ten years after I joined the army. My mother followed him a decade later. My brother Todd developed esophageal cancer and died in 2012. He left behind a wife, Marianne, who returned my discharge papers to me before she went to Nevada to join a religious cult.

"The Lord works in strange ways," my father-in-law Moe (short for Moses) Bartram said when he learned of Marianne's journey to the Nevada desert.

"She just wasn't ready for a personal relationship with God," said Annie Bartram, my mother-in-law.

My sister-in-law Marianne had blown a gasket after my brother died. The Bartrams were kinder than me. They talked incessantly about how some people move farther away from God. I thought Marianne had slipped off her trolley. My in-laws thought they were right. So did I. My wife Emma, to whom I'd been married for twenty-three years, got tired of playing referee. She didn't side with her parents. She didn't show favor to me. Instead, she left everything behind and went off to live with Marianne on the compound owned by The Radiant Angels of Zaphkar.

Chapter 2: Carla's Estranged Gorilla

I called my congressman about the army reactivation notice. People were always going on about that. If you have a legitimate beef with your government, start with a phone call to your congressman. So, I did. My congressman was not available. I left a message.

Three days passed with no return phone calls.

On the fourth night, I went to a local diner. In the autumn of my life, I had already become what I feared most. I dined alone before 5:00 P.M. in order to get the early-bird special price. What made the experience at the diner even more pathetic was that the entire waitstaff knew the story between my wife and me. It began one night when I was in a bar down the road from the diner. I was bleary-eyed, drunk, maudlin, all of the above.

Carla was her name. She had a Joan Jett haircut, a tattoo of Woody Woodpecker on her left breast, and another tattoo on her lower abdomen just above her pubic mound that read Trough in Cyrillic script.

The lovemaking was awful. I took full blame since I wasn't quite over my wife leaving me. In my drunken state, I blubbered about how Emma had left me to join The Radiant Angels of Zaphkar, the cult out in Nevada.

"Are they those guys who worship an angel as God?" Carla asked.

"No, well yes," I corrected myself. "The worshippers consider themselves angels in human form. Zaphkar is also an angel, albeit a higher one, and their deity."

"If I didn't have a kid, I would totally join something like that."

"That would be awful," I said. "You wouldn't want to live with a cult."

"You know you can't stay the night, right?"

I figured as much. For one, she was at most thirty years old. At the time I was forty-five. She saw me as a pity fuck. I saw her as a tattooed local. It would have never worked out. Secondly, the small living room in her apartment was littered with children's toys. Her ex-old man, a regular gorilla judging by the photos Carla kept on display even though they were separated, was scheduled to drop off the kids later, which was early Sunday morning.

"Jimmy normally keeps them until Sunday evening," said Carla, "but he's got to meet his anger management therapist."

She didn't elaborate any further. I didn't pursue it.

When I got home that morning, a couple of hours before sunrise, I felt lousy about sharing my problems with Carla. She seemed cool.

During my next visit to the diner, Carla and her coworkers treated me indifferently. Maybe it's a fluke, I thought. They gave me the cold shoulder the next time as well.

One afternoon I was in there eating a burger and her estranged gorilla came in raising hell about a pending court date. Two big Mexican cooks came out of the kitchen brandishing Berti white-handled carving knives and suggested that Carla's gorilla leave. He did. I never saw him again.

The years went by. Life went on. Emma did not return.

Four nights after I received the army orders I went to the diner for my early dinner. Carla was working the counter where I sat.

"You're never going to guess what happened to me," I told her.

"Your wife quit the cult and came home?" Carla said with only the slightest sarcasm.

I told her about the army orders. She thought I was making it up. Later, right before my dessert, when I got to the part about calling my congressman Derek Northrop, Carla suggested I talk to Tammy.

"Who's that?" I asked.

"She works for Congressman Northrop," replied Carla. "What I mean is she's an intern."

"Does Tammy come to the diner often?"

"She works here part-time," she replied. "She's here tonight."

Carla nodded at a nervous-looking blond girl who looked too young to be in college let alone interning for a congressman. I started to get off my stool, but Carla stopped me.

"Just wait," she said like I was some kind of stalker. "She's working right now."

Tammy Wescott, the diner waitress cum Congressman Northrop's intern, sounded like a young Republican on crack. She went on a mile a minute about border security, Marxists masquerading as Black Lives Matter protesters, the absence of Jesus in the public school system, and the decline and fall of white culture in America. I don't know what schools she had gone to in her life so far, but she had it all wrong.

Back when I was in college I used to hit on girls like Tammy and try to bed them. Getting a Jesus freak yuppie conservative into bed was a surefire guaranteed memorable romp. Girls like that, with God as their co-pilot, were up for pretty much anything.

How Tammy, teetering between John Birch Society fanaticism and Tea Party madness, ended up interning for a democratic Congressman was beyond me, but in the end she promised to slip him a note about my situation concerning the army. I had to endure her rap about Jesus and small government, but at least she left out Ayn Rand.

The Congressman's office didn't call me until a week before Memorial Day. I didn't get to speak to the congressman. For all I know, I could have been talking to Tammy's father or her uncle. Yes, the armed forces reserved the right to call up individual ready reserves in a time of crisis. What was the crisis? I wondered. The congressional aide who had telephoned didn't know.

"Doesn't an act of war have to be declared by the president and approved by Congress?" I asked.

"That's a gray area," he said, sounding a trifle too enthusiastic over the prospect of the president starting a war on his own.

After the call ended I was struck by four separate truths:

1. The congressman was useless.
2. I had less than two weeks before I was due to report to Fort Dix.
3. Surely, I wasn't alone in receiving the army orders calling me back to active duty to a unit in the U.S. Army I'd never heard of.
4. If thirty-odd years out of uniform taught me anything, it was that military service was a call answered by both patriotic baboons and hard luck cases.

There was only one way to find out if I was alone in receiving the orders. I doubted that discovering whether former members of my unit also received the same orders would have lessened my anxiety, but at least I wouldn't be among strangers.

I was in my mid-fifties, out of shape, and in my spare time I daydreamed about renouncing my citizenship and moving to somewhere like Costa Rica or Greece. What possible good could I offer, at my age, to an army outfit that, to my knowledge, didn't exist? Did they send all the pencil pushers into combat and were now in need of replacements?

Chapter 3: The Wildegalax

"At first, I didn't believe it," said Paul Stanislavski when we talked on the phone.

Paul had been in my infantry platoon. During basic training, the drill sergeants nicknamed him "Sunshine" for two reasons:

A. Paul never looked happy.

B. The Drill Sergeants could never correctly pronounce his last name.

In the early years following our respective enlistments, we stayed in touch, even visiting one another as time went on. He came to New Jersey a few times. I drove out to Ohio twice a year while I was in college.

At one point before he turned thirty, Paul was engaged to be married. He told me that the wedding was off after his fiancée accused him of cheating on her. He never offered any details, but I suspected that another woman wasn't the problem.

There were rumors during my initial enlistment. When Paul became my roommate I soon got caught up in the rumor mill, not as a gossip, but one of the players in the sordid tale that unfolded concerning my roommate. No one ever said anything to our faces, but some of the guys treated us differently. Sidelong looks and abrupt conversations in the communal showers were enough to let us know how our fellow soldiers felt.

Paul reached a point where he could no longer take it. He requested a transfer to another company within the battalion. Our company commander, one of those Moral Majority shills who preached a bit too much for even the most religious company members, turned Paul down for the requested transfer on account of the COHORT[1] contract that my roommate, and the rest of us, had signed.

In the end, our company commander did move Paul to a different platoon. After that, the rumors about Paul being gay or bisexual, depending on who was telling the story, died off.

When Paul moved to the second platoon, a guy named Kirk Shetland became my roommate. Kirk came from Trinity, Texas, the birthplace of writer William Goyen.

"I ain't never heard of him," Kirk admitted.

Fellow soldiers may have quit gossiping about Paul's sexual orientation, but they found another target in my new roommate Kirk Shetland. Soldiers know the value of music with regard to maintaining their sanity. Some guys in my old unit had amassed quite a collection of vinyl. Kirk was different. He owned just two albums: The Greatest Hits of Hank Williams and The Magic of Judy Garland, a six-album box-set. He played the Hank Williams album sparingly, believing that it would one day be a collector's item. As for Joots, Kirk only played her music when he was inebriated. It didn't help our situation that he liked to parade around in a short red chiffon robe that he told everyone was his smoking jacket. His penchant for smoking Djarum Supers with a long cigarette holder during off-duty hours, a prop that, along with the chiffon robe, made him look like a flapper transvestite, did not help either.

I heard from Paul a couple of years after we left the army that Kirk Shetland ended up killing himself. Paul seemed especially

---

[1] The COHORT unit was the army's diabolical attempt to send a group of soldiers through basic training and then onto their military occupational specialty (MOS) training before shipping the lot of them to a regular duty station. The army thought it would help with morale and ensure what the army called *unit cohesiveness*. That was a fancy way of saying the army sought to lessen friendly fire incidents during wartime since being a member of a COHORT unit we would become bosom buddies. There were a number of problems with this reasoning. For one, there was no war in the mid-1980's. Another challenge was that not many of us became best friends. At best, at least for those of us who didn't go AWOL, our experience was that of asylum inmates who managed not to murder one another. The U.S. Army COHORT option, as you may have guessed, turned out to be a disaster.

saddened by this news, but he never mentioned Kirk's passing again.

By the time he reached forty years old, Paul had moved around a lot—California, Nevada, and New Mexico, mostly—before returning to Cleveland where he had grown up. We'd seen each other only once since then. I wouldn't say our friendship was strained, but it wasn't as close as it used to be.

To his detriment, Paul wanted to be many things—an artist, a writer, a doctor, a truck driver—but he wasn't willing to commit to one thing. Worse, he lacked even the slightest conviction in any endeavor he undertook, as if by skipping across the surface of various pursuits something might stick to him.

"What are you going to do?" Paul asked.

"Go to Fort Dix, I guess," I replied.

"What if we all just sat it out?"

"I'm sort of curious."

"They probably just want to interview us."

"About what?"

"Maybe about the mystery surrounding the efficiency of a fixed fighting position," he replied. Then, "How should I know?"

We talked about other things after that, but my mind kept going back to all that business about "off-world operations." I mentioned it to Paul. He was at a loss for words, which, for as long as I had known him, was a rare thing. By the time we said goodbye, I barely remembered the conversation. My obsession with the "off-world" business clouded my concern for nearly everything else.

Reverend Bertrand Bauerfang, Initiate Supreme and founder of The Radiant Angels of Zaphkar, was a charlatan of the highest order. He came from humble origins, as near as I could tell. His father was a Canadian foreign service nabob of some sort and his mother a Bahraini Jew who fled to India with her family when she was twelve years old.

Emile Bauerfang, Bertrand's father, met Sarah Sabar, his future wife, at a party held at the U.S. Embassy in Bombay. It was rumored that Emile Bauerfang fell down a flight of stairs after seeing Sarah's large pale green eyes.

Another story concerning Sarah Sabar's beauty, the one published in *The Autobiography of the Oracle of Heaven: The Initiate Supreme's Exposure to the Human Plane*, told of how when she was just sixteen years old, Sarah's beauty had caused a commercial freighter named The Makara to run aground at Juhu Beach. In the Initiate Supreme's autobiography, the account detailed the precise moment that the captain of the freighter, Ajay Mehta, espied the young teen through his binoculars and attempted to steer his ship closer to shore for a better look.

A third tale, the most plausible one, I discovered in a book published by Jay Lane Rice entitled *Confessions from Canaan: How I Left The Radiant Angels of Zaphkar and Lived to Talk About It*. Rice, who served as Vice President to the Initiate Supreme for a decade, chronicled a well-documented series of events that told of Emile Bauerfang's penchant for young Indian women.

Sarah Sabar, Bertrand's mother, was nineteen when she met the much older Bauerfang. By the time she was twenty years old she was pregnant. Her parents were ready to disown her.

Bauerfang worked some magic, pulling some diplomatic strings, and had the entire Sabar clan moved from Bombay to Toronto in the summer of 1960. The diplomat married Sarah Sabar just as she was starting to show. The future leader of The Radiant Angels of Zaphkar was born on an average winter day on December 20, 1960.

The early writings of Bertrand Bauerfang, those that he self-published before founding his order, were science fiction novels that could best be described as Nazis in space. In his books, German was spoken at the farthest reaches of the known universe. Human men and women addressed each other as Herr, Frau, and Fraulein. He self-published eight novels in his space Nazi saga. This was long before the advent of the internet and the birth of Amazon. Try as he might, Bauerfang could not get his books placed in brick-and-mortar bookstores, not even in the abundant independent stores that once dotted American cities far and wide.

When the internet first came online Bertrand Bauerfang was one of the first to establish a presence, gathering a disturbed and strange following as he published short stories on a website set in Wildegalax, his space Nazi saga universe. The name of the universe he had created was a play on the phrase wilde galaxie, or feral galaxy. Bauerfang thought himself quite clever. Sadly, so did a growing following.

Kooks, quacks, perverts, and supremacists of every stripe subscribed to his website. Suddenly, his book sales took off, which is to say that he steadily sold them to the outliers who liked his storytelling.

There were themed parties, orgies mostly, in which attendees dressed up in Wildegalax uniforms comprised of black spandex with fabric around the genital and chest areas cut away for ease of access. In Bauerfang's novels, humans in the Wildegalax universe were raised with their tits and bits exposed.

Bauerfang once argued in a rare pre-Radiant Angels interview at a science fiction convention in the 1990's that he was fascinated with Germany's frankness and openness about sexuality, hence the skin-tight clothing on his characters with cutaways strategically placed.

The interviewer went on to ask Bauerfang if he could justify the vivid descriptions in his novels of pre-pubescent sex organs on boys and girls. Bauerfang could not. The interview was published in Fantasy and Sci-Fi Romper, a now-defunct rag published in New York.

Bertrand Bauerfang soon pulled the plug on his website. The abrupt action was followed by a brush with both paranoia and the paranormal. An entity that called himself Zaphkar told Bauerfang that he was to peddle smut no more. That was the first visitation. Eight more would follow that year in 1998.

After the first visitation, Bauerfang burned the remaining copies of his self-published novels. Six weeks later, he petitioned the court to legally change his name to Razon (with a long "a") Spiritus Sancti.

The judge presiding over Bauerfang's case was Silas Bowery. He was a card-carrying member of the far-right 13th Hour Revelation[2],

---

[2] Among other tenets, the 13th Hour believed that Jews were Satan's servants, and that intermarriage was Satan's triumph over the earthly plane. The 13th hour feared what most white supremacist groups did, a changing American landscape in which Caucasians would soon become a minority. In their view they saw white suburbia turning into something police dogs, fire hoses, and, later, gated communities failed to stop: a

a group founded by a Houston businessman and an evangelical minister of The Christ Church of Rapturous Glory, a megachurch located in the suburbs of Houston.

Judge Bowery took one look at the petitioner with his olive complexion and kinky dark hair and had his bailiff take Bauerfang into custody. The petitioner was then committed to a mental hospital for psychiatric evaluation.

Bertrand Bauerfang resurfaced in 1999 when he used some inheritance money to purchase land in the Nevada desert.

A decade passed. In that time, he published his Nine Visitations online and garnered a sizable following, each one desperate for spiritual fulfillment.

Among the initial flock that moved to Nevada to be with the Oracle of Heaven were Tammy and Tracy Bowery, the twin twenty-year-old daughters of the judge who had the spiritual leader committed. Bauerfang considered this a minor victory in his quest to share the word of Zaphkar. Judge Bowery did not. He hired mercenaries and sent them to extract his children from the compound. In those early days, Bauerfang's first apostles totaled sixteen. That number would grow.

The reason no one ever heard of the rescue was because the Oracle of Heaven forbade guns on the compound. Theirs was to be a movement of peace. Bauerfang handed over the Bowery women to the mercenaries without a fight. He feared not the mercenaries, but the harm that might come to his unborn children Tammy and Tracy each carried.

A year later, Tammy and Tracy Bowery returned to the compound along with the dozen mercenaries her father had originally hired. The Bowery women had with them their infant children, girls named Lilith and Eve after the first two women ever created. As for the mercenaries, Tammy and Tracy had worked a

---

multi-cultural haven that bolstered local economies and promoted empathy for all humanity. The 13th Hour wasn't having any of it. They used convoluted understanding of biblical passages and other documents as window dressing for their hate, like most frightened and weak white supremacists did.

sort of divine glamour on the dozen men. The mercenaries buried their guns in the Nevada desert and joined The Radiant Angels of Zaphkar.

I scanned local news online from time to time searching for information about the Radiant Angels compound in Nevada. Each time I did I hoped to glimpse a photo of my wife Emma. I wanted to read about how the members of The Radiant Angels of Zaphkar had come to their senses, escaped from Bauerfang's sway, and sought aid from people in the nearest town. I never found such news.

Chapter 4: The Hooker Who Tried to Shank a Lawyer

The closer I got to my report date at Fort Dix, the more I thought about The Radiant Angels of Zaphkar. By then the Initiate Supreme's followers numbered three-hundred-thirty-three, which included Emma and my sister-in-law.

I had it in my head that I wanted to kill Bertrand Bauerfang and if not, then at least destroy what mattered most to him. Still, I knew that such action would not bring my wife back.

Almost seven years had passed since she had left, I had written letters to the closest town (Elko) marked with her name and "general delivery." I also put in parentheses at the bottom of the envelope the phrase "Radiant Angels of Zaphkar Compound," but I never heard a word from her. It wasn't out of the realm of possibilities that mail, if it got there at all, was monitored and in some cases simply discarded. None of my letters were ever returned to me. Whether they had reached the compound or sat in a dead letter office, I never found out.

Though Emma never once reached out to me, I continued to write her letters. We didn't have a formal divorce, my wife and I. After five years of her absence, I had thought seriously about filing anyway since we had surpassed the eighteen months of separation required in New Jersey. I tried a few times. I even told a lawyer all about how my wife had run off with my dead brother's wife.

"Are they lesbians?" the lawyer asked. His name was Johnny Barbarese. He stood maybe five feet six inches tall and weighed close to three hundred pounds.

"I didn't say they left together," I told him. "My sister-in-law left first—"

"Are they lipstick lesbians?" Barbarese asked. Then, before I could answer, he added, "Which one is prettier? Your wife? Or your sister-in-law?"

"I just want to know what my options are."

"You say your brother's dead?"

"Seven years now."

"Do you think there's any reconciliation in the future for the three of you?"

"You mean—"

"I always wanted to be with lesbians," Barbarese admitted. "Or at least two bi girls. One time, I paid two hookers in Atlantic City to go down on each other. When I whipped out my cell phone to film it, one of them tried to shank me. You believe that shit? A hooker trying to stab a lawyer? It sounds like the beginning of a bad joke. Marone! What's this world coming to?"

When he laughed, Barbarese snorted like a pig and his tongue stuck out like an exhausted kitten gasping for breath.

Lucky for me, it was an initial consultation. Barbarese offered them free for potential first-time clients. He called me many times after that visit. It was brutal in the land of law practices. Solo acts like Barbarese competed with not only firms but independent lawyers like him as well. The first four times I told him that I had reconsidered and no longer needed his services weren't enough. He kept calling. Finally, I had to tell him to go fuck himself. The lesson I learned was this: some lawyers had no business practicing law; others, like Barbarese, deserved to be stabbed by prostitutes.

Chapter 5: Jesus and the Space Force

Max Kunstler was the only army buddy that I still talked to every six months or so. In basic training, everyone called him "Trotsky" because the drill sergeants thought anyone as smart as Max had to be a communist. Or maybe it had to do with Max's Van Dyke beard and the glasses he wore upon his arrival to Fort Benning. After a post barber gave him a crew cut and shaved off his mustache and beard, and he was issued BCGs[3], Max no longer looked like Trotsky. The barber had done him a favor. The nickname did not stick.

Currently, Max lived in Providence where he ran a small avant-garde theater called Beckett's Bus Stop. His wife taught American literature at Brown University. Max's dual college degree was in philosophy and theater. He sort of fell into managing the theater a few years back after the original manager and co-owner died after choking on a veggie burger. The former manager's name was Wilcox Broughton.

"The pay is shit," Max confessed the last time we caught up in person, "but some of the performances make it worth it."

---

[3] Birth Control Glasses: An unofficial moniker given to the thick black frame eyewear issued by the U.S. Army that pretty much guaranteed zero chance of getting lucky. The BCG replaced the earlier and not so politically correct RPG or Rape Prevention Glasses which carried with it obvious negative connotations.

The last time I drove to Providence it seemed like an entire day had passed before I got through Connecticut and arrived at last in Rhode Island.

Max was a good guy, but he was forgetful. Three months after my wife left me to join The Radiant Angels of Zaphkar, Max and I spoke on the phone one night. He asked me how Emma was doing. I could tell by his tone that he'd completely forgotten that she left me to live in a cult commune. We didn't talk about it afterward. And Max never mentioned Emma's name again.

When I telephoned Max he didn't waste any time getting around to a subject I would have just as soon avoided.

"I talked to Yodel last night," Max told me.

Yodel was a guy named Orval Gurley Taylor who'd been in our platoon. He came from Ouray, Colorado. During basic training, he made the mistake of telling our platoon drill sergeant that Ouray was the Switzerland of America.

"I'm going to call you Yodel," Sergeant Fisk decreed in his Louisiana bayou drawl. "From now on, you answer to Yodel. You got that?"

Sergeant Fisk spent that first week doling out nicknames to everyone in our platoon. It was your ass if you confused them or forgot them.

"Did Yodel get his orders too?" I asked.

It was no secret that I had little tolerance for Yodel. Behind his wholesome good old boy demeanor was a guy who was as mean as a rabid dog, a guy with at least two faces despite proclaiming how good a Christian he was. The religious right did a lot of that. It was like when a parent felt compelled to tell others how good a parent they were. The opposite was in fact true. They just needed to convince themselves the same if not more than their audience. Anyway, Yodel's kind were everywhere, pretending to do God's work, as if advancing a white-centric agenda was a divine commandment.

"You know Yodel," Max reminded me. "He's probably packed and ready to go."

"What about you?" I asked.

"I'm supposed to report to the Air National Guard base in North Smithfield," he said.

"I'm thinking about not going."

"Don't be foolish."

"No, I'm serious."

"So am I," he said. "Look, we're closing in on the underside of sixty years old. This is probably just a formality, an exercise for the pencil pushers. Budgets have to be justified. Don't go to jail over it."

The cardinal rule was this: ever since Yodel visited me in 2005 and told my wife that Quakers weren't real Christians, I chose to block him from my life. No more phone calls. No more social media contact. No more acknowledging his borderline white-power Christmas cards every holiday season that depicted Mary, Joseph, and Baby Jesus as fine Nordic stock with their blue eyes, their blond locks, and their skin as pale as a white picket fence post.

Despite distancing myself from him, Yodel Taylor did his best to get me to acknowledge his existence after he had offended my wife and me. In his eyes, my being raised Catholic was worse than being a Quaker. Yodel and his evangelical ilk considered my kind Papists. In his eyes, we were as far removed from Christ as the Jews were, even though the messiah was one of their own. A lesson Yodel never learned. As a Catholic, my kind were third on their Klan-influenced list behind blacks and Jews. Anyway, despite Emma's hasty departure, my life (to say nothing of my health, both physical and mental) improved once I cut Yodel out of it.

Don't get me wrong. There's something to say about Yodel's tenacity, misdirected though it was. He continued to send Christmas cards. The first few Christmases I felt bad about depositing those cards directly into the trash, mostly because of the wasted stamp. By 2009, I didn't care. I moved that year, and I changed my phone numbers: both cell and house phones. Then I gave Max strict orders not to share that info with Yodel.

I introduced the aforementioned preamble for one reason here: after I spoke to Max about the army orders, I broke the cardinal rule. I called Yodel the next day.

"I got them, too," Yodel offered when I mentioned the orders I had received. "My guess is, and I'm just speculating here, that the military is spread so thin around the globe they're going to need us older soldiers to provide security for the new Space Force."

Space Force, I thought. Jesus Christ.

"I don't know, man," I started to say.

"Look, brother," he cut me off. "I've been praying on this really hard and your phone call just proves that the Lord Jesus Christ works in mysterious ways. We were pre-ordained through God's grace to serve our beloved president—"

He was still going on about Jesus, the president, and Space Force when I hung up on him.

Chapter 6: The Poor Pencil Sharpener

Herb Kaufman was my manager at Morley's Health Guide in Philadelphia where I worked as an editor. Herb's official title was Editor-at-Large. What that really meant was that he spent a lot of time away from the office wining and dining potential advertisers for the medical professional quarterly founded in 1922.

A week before I was due to report to Fort Dix, I showed him my orders.

"What is this?" asked Herb. "Are you trying to be funny?"

He squirmed in his seat behind his desk. Herb Kaufman's notorious stomach ailments would have felled lesser men long ago. Not a day went by when poor Herb was on the brink of shitting his lungs out. Sometimes you could hear it stirring in his intestines the way you do thunder while the approaching storm was still just out of view over the horizon.

"It's not a joke, Herb," I told him.

What I liked to do, and please don't think me cruel, was to keep Herb at his desk for as long as I could just to watch him squirm. Eventually, he'd pull rank and hightail it out of his office and speed-walk to the lavatory in the hallway. Somewhere around the lunch hour Herb's condition would subside just long enough for him to run over to the deli on Walnut Street where any number of ingredients on his hoagie might trigger a second wave of intestinal discomfort.

"And I'm supposed to do what with this?" Herb asked.

"I'd like for Human Resources to see what my options are," I told him.

"What do you mean?"

"If it turns into something," I said, "I need to know that my job is secure until I return. It's only fair."

"Fair?" he bellowed. "You want to talk to me about fair? My guts feel like they are being pressure-washed from the inside out—"

"Maybe you should lay off the dairy?"

"It's not that," he said. "It's hereditary."

One day, Herb brought his two boys Avner and Eli to the office. Avner was eight years old, Eli was twelve. Whatever bug that afflicted Herb had been passed down to his sons. He took them to lunch that day to his favorite deli. Herb and his sons weren't back at the office for more than thirty minutes before each of them jumped around like chimps on crack, gripping the seat of their respective pants, as they made their way to the hallway lavatory.

Three guys from proofreading who did not see the Kaufman contingent enter the lavatory soon followed, unaware of what grotesque gaseous machinations were at play inside. A chorus of curses could be heard that afternoon up and down the hallway along with fervent pleas for courtesy flushes.

One of the proofreaders, before retreating to the elevator to carry him to another floor in the building, suggested that Kaufman and his boys "just kill themselves" rather than inflict another moment of such offense. He was new. Herb fired him the next day.

"Be that as it may," I said of his hereditary woes, "I am serving my country and the law says I can't be fired for that."

Herb leaned back in his chair and farted when he did. He immediately sprang forward, clutching his gut as he tooted a second time.

"You're not a lawyer!" he cried. "What could you possibly know about any of this?"

He waved my orders like a kerchief, as if he were a Georgian belle attempting to stave off the vapors as Sherman's army approached.

I reached out slowly and took the paperwork from him.

"It could be a day," I said. "It could be longer. No one's telling me anything."

"Go see Estelle in Human Resources," he advised me.

Going to see the human resources manager was my least favorite thing about the job. It was always a production in a literal sense.

Estelle Silverman was the eighty-year-old human resources manager who paid no mind to the company's 1950's-inspired conservative dress code policy. She wore embarrassingly short skirts and ridiculously high heels with defiant pride.

No one liked to go to Human Resources, mostly because no one could endure Estelle's tales of her youth when she was a Radio City Music Hall Rockette in the early 1960's. One time I had to sit through her spiel and watch as she performed the famous Rockette kick. She got some height, but she also kicked a pencil sharpener off the edge of her desk and sent it sailing at the window. The pencil sharpener bounced off the glass and struck me in the head.

"Oh thank God," Estelle cried.

"I'm all right, thanks," I told her.

"That poor pencil sharpener." She went to the window. "I thought for sure it would break the glass."

After I spoke to Herb that day I was relieved to find that Estelle was out to lunch. I made a photocopy of my orders and left them on her desk along with a note explaining how I had been called up for duty.

Around three in the afternoon that day my extension rang. Estelle was on the line when I answered.

"Caleb," she said, "I have Herb here with me on speaker."

"What did you find out?" I asked.

"We can hold your job for up to five years."

"That seems excessively long—" Herb broke in.

"Shut up, Herb," Estelle said.

"Thank you, Estelle," I said.

"I'm done," Herb announced. "You fucking veterans get all the goddamn perks."

"Language," Estelle said to Herb.

I heard a door close.

"He's so mad," said Estelle. " It's not healthy to act like that all the time."

"He's not feeling well," I said.

"He's going to have a heart attack."

"Estelle," I said, "I should get back to work."

"Aren't you a little old for combat?"

"I don't think it will come to that," I assured her.

"All the same," she countered, "you be careful over there. If you get scared, doll, just think of my long legs kicking—"

"Thanks, Estelle," I said and hung up.

She meant well, Estelle did, but it grossed me out.

Chapter 7: The Parable of the Snowball

The Reverend Bertrand Bauerfang once wrote:

The notion that the mind is somehow woven into the fabric of the soul is a false one, though it is a sentiment taught to many in the world's religions. No matter the good times and the bad we experience in human form, we take no memories with us when we are born again anew in light.

He went on to describe a soul that met the souls of his parents, but they no longer recognized one another. The slate got wiped clean for each of us when we died. Later in *The Book of Ziyarae*, dictated to Bauerfang by the angel Zaphkar, the Initiate Supreme used various parables to illustrate how souls, stripped of mind and memory, still recognize each other, but not in the way people think.

It's true we are the stuff of stars, the Initiate Supreme wrote in his autobiography, but our existence is light-based rather than carbon-based. Bertrand Bauerfang had been an average student in school with abysmal grades in the sciences. The ideas he presented in his autobiography were a testament to that. Yet, even an idiot, like a broken clock, can be right now and again. Somewhere along the way he picked up various morsels from Gnosticism and Manichaeism, mostly the parts about the soul being held captive in matter. Bauerfang's twist to this belief was that Zaphkar had been dispatched by the True God far removed from our present reality to deliver a revelation to the Initiate Supreme.

Bauerfang's parables were meant to reveal that the souls of individuals were not separate entities, but rather fragments of a greater whole. One of the parables Bauerfang penned was "The Parable of the Snowball." In it, he briefly described a small patch of snow getting kicked by a mountain goat. The snow patch rolled over and over, gathering mass, as it descended the mountainside until a giant snowball the size of a house reached the bottom.

The mountain goat was meant to represent Zaphkar, the angel of liberation. The snow that gathered into one gargantuan ball symbolized the soul fragments that, through Zaphkar's aid, rejoined themselves into a complete spirit large enough to punch through matter and escape what Bauerfang referred to as the reality prison.

It was quite the closed system that Bauerfang had developed. In the closing chapters of his autobiography the Initiate Supreme offered several criticisms of what he called new faiths like Scientology as well as modern spiritual guides like The Urantia Book. Bauerfang's biggest problem, however, had to do with the notion of previous lives. The Initiate Supreme also devoted several pages to a refutation concerning Scientology's idea of the "clear mind." Bauerfang, and more importantly, if one were inclined to believe the man's writings, the angel Zaphkar, maintained that the soul inhabiting a human body could never attain its ultimate potentiality which was reuniting with other soul fragments without the aid of Zaphkar himself.

In the short span that The Radiant Angels of Zaphkar cult's existence, several academics from the field of comparative religion have published papers on Bauerfang's system. In one article published in the Fall 2015 issue of Cave & Cosmos, Dr. Helmut Woll at the University of Bonn speculated that the absence of emphasis on the Alien God so prevalent in Zaphkar's message to Bauerfang may mean that the alien, unknowable god is non-existent until some as-yet-undisclosed end-time when all souls are reunited. Woll hypothesized further that the joining together of soul fragments could, in fact, serve as the birth of the Alien God, much like cells that make up a larger organism. In short, Woll proposed that the Alien God scattered itself in matter, as a self-imposed imprisonment, to better experience and know itself. An interesting premise, but not one that would aid me in liberating my wife from Bauerfang's clutches.

Prior to my departure for Fort Dix I thought long and hard about Emma and the Radiant Angels. For years I laid in bed alone lingering on the edge of sleep and often fantasized about storming Bauerfang's compound like some action movie hero armed to the ears with automatic weapons, explosives, knives, and martial arts expertise. In my fantasies, Emma didn't exactly swoon at the prospect of being freed from spiritual servitude, but she didn't resist exiting the compound with me either through the breach I had created.

In the seven years since Emma's departure, I had accumulated books and literature from The Radiant Angels of Zaphkar. I always wondered if it was Emma who slapped the adhesive, laser-printed mailing label on the padded envelope that found its way to my mailbox. Would our address mean anything to her now? Would my name spark some dormant memory? I had no way of knowing.

The Radiant Angels of Zaphkar never directly charged for their books and literature on their website. They did, however, require a $20 donation for each book requested. Through the years, I handed over money to the very organization that brainwashed my wife and held her hostage. I worried that such a thing, financing her captivity to a degree, made me the worst husband in the world. Sometimes, I fooled myself into thinking that my small donation helped to keep Emma and other cult members fed, safe, and sheltered. That feeling never lasted long.

Chapter 8: Dilettante Misprint

"Name?"

"Caleb Paladin," I told the MP sergeant at the gate.

He glanced over my orders for a third time, skeptical about their authenticity.

"Pull over to the holding area," he instructed me.

The holding area was a small parking lot to the right of the post's main entrance. There were five other cars there. Inside each were drivers who looked bewildered and angry over not having gained access to the base.

Before I left the house, I packed an overnight bag—a change of clothes and toiletries. Inside the bag were Bauerfang's autobiography and *The Book of Ziyarae*. To say that I wanted to know the enemy was a gross understatement. At that point in my life I doubted I would ever get close to him.

Reading Radiant Angels literature, I liked to believe, brought me closer to Emma on some quasi-intellectual-psychic level. If it didn't, it reminded me of what the priests used to tell us about it being better to have believed and found out God does not exist than to have not believed and found out that He does.

The thing that gave me peace in all this was picturing Emma stopping whatever chore she had been performing and looking east as she wondered about me. Sometimes I pictured her sitting on a rocky outcrop at dusk, a feral look in her eyes as coyotes howled unseen in the distance.

A few minutes later, a different MP with a PFC rank approached my car in the holding area. He couldn't have been a day over nineteen years old. His name tag read: Salter.

"Mr. Paladin?" said PFC Salter.

"Hey," I pointed at his name tag, "any relation to the writer?"

Whenever I got nervous, I yammered on about my favorite writers. It was a quality that made Emma crazy. She accused me of being elitist and worse.

"Why can't you just read James Patterson or P.D. James for once?" she admonished me one day.

"Is P.D. James the one who wrote that sex book?" I asked.

"What? No. You see what happens when you turn into a book snob?"

I never recovered. What well-read person would?

"Who?" PFC Salter presently inquired.

"James Salter."

"No, sir."

"He was Hemingway's heir apparent, in the world of letters."

"Doesn't ring a bell."

"He flew a T-6 Texan into a house in Massachusetts during flight training."

"I don't read much, Mr. Paladin."

"Sorry to hear that."

"Hazards of the profession."

"Cops should be well-read. It helps to foster empathy."

"Right, anyway," PFC Salter proceeded to point at the main gate with his whole hand like a karate chop, "you're clear to enter the base." He handed me a printout with my route highlighted. "Follow these directions, Mr. Paladin, and do not deviate. Understood?"

"Loud and clear, private," I told him.

"The password is misprint," PFC Salter told me. "The challenge is dilettante."

"I got it," I said.

He made me repeat it three times. Then he pointed at the gate with his karate chop hand.

If Fort Dix had an ass-end, Uncle Sam made sure that he put me and the other call-ups right in the sphincter. The directions there were clear enough. I ended up at a WWII-era-looking open-bay barracks in the middle of the woods off Fort Dix Road.

Unlike its Second World War counterparts, the barracks façade was not whitewashed. Instead, it was painted in shades of O.D. green, brown, and black. Around the sides, the back, and over top the one-story barracks was a multispectral camouflage net.

In a small dirt lot beside the barracks a Humvee was parked. Next to the Humvee, an Audi A8 with Jersey plates.

"Dilettante," a voice nearby said.

I looked around. There was no one about. It was then I remembered that I had forgotten the password PFC Salter had given me.

"Dilettante," the voice repeated the word.

I turned a full three-hundred-sixty degrees, searching for the source of the voice. If it came from a wireless speaker placed somewhere, the sound was incredibly clear.

The voice challenged me a third time.

"I don't remember the password," I said.

Suddenly, a bush nearby rustled and a soldier armed with an M-16 emerged dressed in a Ghillie suit. More bushes came to life, four in all, each one in an identical Ghillie suit woven with pine twigs, maple leaves, and creeping vines. They approached slowly with their weapons pointed at me.

"Keep your hands where we can see them," one of them said.

"What are you doing here?" another asked.

"How did you find this place?" a third inquired.

"The MPs at the gate gave me directions," I said.

"Bullshit," a fourth one said. "Hey, sergeant. Let's shoot him and be done with it."

"Negative," the sergeant said.

"I have orders in my bag," I told them. "See for yourself."

They went through my things, found the envelope with the orders inside, and carefully read the document. Only one of them kept their weapon trained on me while the others in their Ghillie suits and camouflage painted faces conferred with each other in hushed tones.

"Misprint!" I shouted when I suddenly remembered the password.

The sergeant in charge of the Ghillie-suited guards placed my paperwork back in my overnight bag.

"Tomorrow, Mr. Paladin," he said, "the password and challenge will change. I suggest you start committing them to memory before you ship out."

"Ship out?" I asked, watching them fade into the foliated surroundings and vanish.

I almost hyperventilated when I thought about how close I had come to getting shot. That's when I heard a familiar voice, one that I had not heard in three decades.

"My brother from another mother," he said. "I see you met the help."

Fly Kidd looked the same as he did when I knew him in the infantry, even if his close-cropped hair had turned snowy gray. He wore a Van Dyke beard now, something soldiers were not allowed to do in our day.

"What the hell is all this, man?" I asked.

"This is some bullshit right here," Fly replied.

We shook hands and then hugged. For another minute or so we stood in the sun talking, but it was getting hot. Fly suggested we retreat into the barracks.

"Not exactly Sand Hill," he said of the barracks once we were inside, "but it's air-conditioned."

"How many of us are expected here?" I asked.

"I have been here for a couple of hours," he said. "They don't tell me shit."

"Are you still married?"

"Yes," he replied, "and I just became a great-grandfather again. You?"

"It's complicated," I said.

"Yodel emailed me once and said your old lady split to join the Branch Davidians or some shit," said Fly.

"Koresh was before I got married," I told him. "And Yodel should learn not to tattle."

"Do you hear from any of the guys?"

"Max Kunstler."

"You don't talk to Yodel at all?"

"No," I said.

"I tried to keep up with Plush Prince and all," he said, "but it's hard."

"Did you re-enlist when the Cohort assignment ended?"

"Nah, not me. One dance was enough. What about you?"

"The same. Home and then college."

"I got into the post office, " he told me. "Then I saved some money, and I went in on a club with some guys I grew up with."

We reminisced about the old days: Fort Campbell in the 1980's and all the madness we endured. After that, Fly showed me photographs of his family on his phone.

"I wish I knew what the hell this is about," I said at one point, concerning our being called to Fort Dix.

"Like I said," Fly announced, "I'm in the dark as much as you."

We decided we'd wait another hour. If no one else came, Fly and I agreed to leave Fort Dix, provided they'd let us go.

"We should probably ask one of the help, as you put it," I said, "where we are supposed to go to eat."

"If you can find them."

Fly and I stepped out of the barracks. I couldn't help thinking that we were part of some grand mind-fuck experiment, the details of which we'd never know.

Five minutes passed. Fly and I poked around in the woods in the immediate vicinity outside the barracks, but we couldn't find a single Ghillie-suited guard.

"Come with me," Fly said, at last.

I accompanied him to the other side of the barracks.

Fly unlocked the Audi A8 and reached into the well on the driver's side door. He pulled out a Glock .10mm pistol. Before I could say anything, Fly pointed the pistol in the air and fired it three times.

"That ought to get their attention," he said.

Fly put his pistol back where he had found it, closed the car door, and locked it.

For the second time that afternoon I thought I was going to get shot when two Ghillie gorillas came trotting around the front side of the building with their assault rifles at the ready.

"We heard gunfire," one of them said.

"I didn't hear anything," Fly said.

"A semi-automatic pistol," the other Ghillie gorilla said. "Maybe a Glock from the sound of it."

"Say," I said, "do you fellas know where we might get some chow?"

"You're both restricted to the barracks," the first one said.

"Is this because of the gunfire that didn't happen?" Fly asked.

"No firearms are allowed on post," the second gorilla said.

"In 2016, the Pentagon said otherwise," I announced.

"Ok," the first one said, eyeballing me. "But you do need the base commander's approval."

"We'll need to search your car," the second one said to Fly.

"I'm a civilian," Fly told him. "And I have rights."

The first one slung his rifle. "I will radio for a mess cook," he announced. "It's imperative you stay here. Strict orders, you understand."

"Do you know why we're here?" I asked.

"That's classified."

Both Ghillie gorillas retreated and went around to the front of the barracks. It was only then I spotted three more of their kind standing off in the distance and watching us with binoculars.

"That's just creepy," I told Fly, pointing at the Ghillie-suited observers across the road from the barracks.

"You think they saw me fire my pistol?" Fly asked.

"I'm almost positive that they did," I replied.

"Fuck it," he said.

Fly unlocked his car, removed his pistol from the door well, and placed the pistol through the belt at the back of his pants. Next, he opened the glove compartment and removed two loaded clips. Fly placed a clip each in his front pockets.

"I don't think this day is going to get any better," he said as he locked his car once more.

Chapter 9: Hurry Up & Wait

In every army unit there's one soldier with a finger on the pulse of the base. This individual is typically an enlisted soldier of a lower rank. How this individual comes across various information, and verifies it, would baffle most intelligence agencies.

At Fort Dix, that honor belonged to Specialist Broward, the cook assigned to our barracks.

SPC Broward knew more than he should have for a cook in a non-leadership role. For instance, he was the one who told us that the Ghillie gorillas were members of Delta Force.

"Look," Broward said, "you don't have to believe me, but it won't change the fact that it is true."

Broward appeared afflicted by that rare condition so prevalent among enlisted personnel: he looked aged beyond his young years. At first glance, he looked to be in his fifties. When he told me that he was thirty-five, I didn't believe him.

"I used to be 11-Charlie," he explained.

11 Charlies were indirect fire infantry. In other words he had been a mortar man.

"And you gave all that up to cook?" Fly asked.

"No, sir," Broward went on. "After basic training, I got my jump wings. A couple of years later, I got to go to Ranger School. During my second enlistment, I completed the Q course. I was a Green Beret for ten years."

"Then what happened?" I asked.

Broward worked a propane grill out back behind the barracks. There were a few steaks, some chicken, baked potatoes, and shrimp.

"I got into a thing in the Sinai Desert," he said. "A review board found that militarily I was in the right, but the political climate at the time did not allow for overlooking the incident.

"They said I couldn't be in Special Forces anymore," he went on. "The thought of returning to a line unit just ate me up. So, I told my commander fuck it, I'll become a cook. And the rest is history."

"Why didn't you just quit the army when your enlistment was up?" Fly asked.

"I want to retire with a pension," Broward said.

"On a specialist's pay?" I asked.

"I got busted down to a private for striking an officer," he revealed.

There was an innate sadness in his tone, a regret too genuine to be a part of some shtick.

"Why are we being guarded by Army Delta?" Fly wanted to know.

"You guys don't know yet?" Broward asked, turning over the steaks.

"No one's told us anything," I said.

"Typical of the army," said the cook. "Hurry up and wait. Last to know and all that."

"Is there someone we can talk—" Fly started to say before he was cut off.

"You're going off-world," Broward said as nonchalantly as if he had asked us to pass him some steak sauce.

"That—"

"Ain't no bullshit," the cook proclaimed.

"I don't believe you," I said.

Broward nodded at a man in fatigues and a green beret in an uncovered Humvee as the vehicle pulled into the parking lot.

"You don't have to," Broward said. He pointed at the Humvee with his tongs. "He'll tell you."

Officers in the twenty-first century were a whole new breed compared to the ones I knew back in the 1980's.

The first thing that seemed odd about the man who climbed out of the Humvee was just how much the vehicle had yielded under the officer's weight. It wasn't natural, as if he weighed two or three times as much as a man his size did.

He was taller than Fly and me by a head and built like an NFL linebacker. The other thing that appeared peculiar about him was his face. It looked as if it had been carved from white marble. His steely pale gray eyes lacked any hint of a soul. The name tape on his uniform read: Prescott. He wore subdued captain bars embroidered on his collar.

"Good afternoon, sir," Broward said. "Care for a burger? Maybe some chicken?"

"No thank you, Specialist Broward," the captain told him.

"He never does," the cook whispered to me, like there was a punchline but the joke had eluded me.

"My name is Captain Prescott," the Green Beret said. "I will be in charge of your re-assimilation and transport."

"Whoa, whoa there," Fly said. "What do you mean by re-assimilation?"

"Yeah," I said. "And transport where?"

"There's a briefing tomorrow morning at 0900 hours," Prescott said. "Later today, two more recruits will arrive—"

"Recruits?" I asked. "There must be some mistake. I'm fifty-four years old."

"I'm fifty-four years old, sir."

"Excuse me?"

"You will address me as sir," he instructed me, "or as Captain Prescott. Is that understood?"

"I'm no longer a soldier," I reminded him.

"On the contrary," he told me. "You have been recalled to active duty."

"I'm leaving," I told him.

I made it about three feet before a strong hand landed on my shoulder and spun me around. I used the momentum to deliver an overhand right against the captain's jaw. His head barely moved. My hand felt like it was broken.

Prescott wrapped his left hand around my neck and lifted me into the air.

"Hey now," I heard Fly say.

I glanced down as he cocked the hammer on his Glock. Fly held the barrel of his pistol against the back of the captain's head.

"Oh," Broward said as he backed away from us. "You don't want to do that."

"I will blow your fucking head off," Fly warned Prescott.

"You will do no such thing," Prescott said.

Fly pulled the trigger.

When Captain Prescott collapsed, his grip on my neck did not loosen. We fell to the ground together, lying on our sides as we faced one another. A warm liquid splashed against my face after the bullet tore through the captain's head.

"What the hell is that?" Fly said.

I wiped my face with my one hand, fully expecting to see blood when I looked at it, while I tried to break the captain's grip on my neck with my other hand. A pale bluish green substance with a consistency like motor oil coated the palm and fingers of my hand with which I had wiped my face.

Meanwhile the dead man gripped my neck tightly, impeding my ability to breathe. Just as I lost consciousness, all hell broke loose. The Delta Force security detachment in their Ghillie suits appeared with their weapons trained on Fly. They shouted at him to drop his pistol. Reluctantly, Fly did so. As they closed in on him, the ground around me shifted. I made a few feeble attempts to free myself from the dead man's grip to no avail.

As I slipped into unconsciousness I thought not about Fly who by now was on the ground beside me as a Delta Force member shouted at him to remain still, but about my wife Emma and the Reverend Bertrand Bauerfang. I wondered if she was happy in her new life. I wondered if—

"Who is she?" a voice spoke.

That was the last thing I remembered.

It felt like I died. It turned out the visions I saw were just weird dreams.

When Fly told me that I'd been unconscious for less than a minute I didn't believe him. Specialist Broward confirmed what Fly told me.

When I regained consciousness, the first thing I noticed was that Captain Prescott's hand was no longer around my neck, choking the life out of me. I rolled over onto my stomach and, with Fly's help, got back on my feet.

Four Delta Force members struggled as they carried Prescott's corpse to the Humvee. The four men counted to three and tossed the officer's corpse into the back.

"I hate those fucking things," one of them remarked as the four retreated from the Humvee now.

"You all right?" Fly asked.

"I'll live," I said. "Did they call for the MPs?"

"For what?" asked Fly.

"He'll be charged with destruction of government property," Broward announced.

"No offense, Fly," I said, "but you just murdered the guy."

"Your victim," Broward said, "has to be human for that charge to stick."

"What is he talking about?" I asked Fly.

"That thing wasn't a man," he replied.

"A synthetic person," Broward said. "Synth for short. There aren't but ten in the whole U.S. Army right now, but your friend here managed to kill one of them."

"What good is one of those things if you can shoot and kill one?" I wondered.

"Generals and kings have been asking the same thing about soldiers since the advent of gunpowder," Broward said. "Lucky for your friend Fly there, Captain Prescott will get a replacement head and be back in action in almost no time."

"We don't have that technology yet," I said.

"Don't be so naïve, Paladin," said the cook. "Where do you think all that black budget money goes? Radar development?"

"The government is into some fucked up shit, boy," Fly remarked. Then, he said addressing Broward and the Delta Force guys, "No offense, gentlemen."

Broward and the other four shrugged it off.

"It's cool," one of the Ghillie gorillas said.

"Androids?" I asked.

The Delta guys all nodded in unison.

"One day human soldiers will be obsolete," a Delta guy said.

"A sad day, indeed," one of his cohorts added.

Nothing made sense to me. It was like I was on some other planet. Or I slipped through some sort of leak, as Kurt Vonnegut referred to them in his novel *Breakfast of Champions*, and I somehow ended up in another universe. Androids? On top of the confusion, my head ached. I felt like I was going to pass out again.

Chapter 10: The Hyena Chorus

The following morning, promptly at 0900 hours, with his new head, identical to the previous one, seamlessly attached to his neck, Captain Prescott showed up for the briefing he'd mentioned right before Fly had shot him.

I felt bad for Fly. The security force had confiscated his Glock. Fly didn't seem too upset, though. I think he was more relieved that, given the mission ahead of us, the army chose not to charge him. I suspected that he carried more than one weapon in his car. Evidently, so did the guards from Delta Force. They had our cars towed in the middle of the night. Fly and I never heard a thing.

"That's because we don't use tow trucks or flat beds," one of the Delta guys said.

"We stole that shit," another confirmed.

The Delta Force members high-fived one another before commencing a complicated handshake consisting of various grips, slaps, and knuckle brushes.

"Don't worry," the first one told us. "The vehicles are in a secure holding area."

That was doublespeak for you will never see your cars again. Fly was furious. He loved his Audi.

During the night, before our vehicles were confiscated, a lone weary traveler entered the barracks. He took a bunk by the door. Though it was dark, the person's silhouette looked familiar enough, even if it was stooped slightly with age now.

"Paul?" I said.

"Hey, Cal," he said like we were still in our old infantry unit, and he'd just returned from the chow hall.

"They made you come here?"

"Just got in from Wright-Patterson," he said. "They wasted no time."

"They got androids here," I told him. I jerked my thumb at Fly asleep in his bunk. "Fly shot one."

"Go back to sleep, Cal," Paul said. "We'll talk in the morning."

Fly slept right through the whole exchange.

That night I had some strange dreams. In one of them, Emma was getting married to Bertrand Bauerfang. Actually, at least twenty or thirty women were all marrying the Initiate Supreme under a canopy of desert stars.

I was on a peak overlooking the compound. The moment I started down a hill dotted with dry scrub brush I ran into a half-dozen coyotes.

One of the coyotes cocked his head and said, "fuck it, man." A dozen or more hyenas on the desert floor, barely visible in the moonless night, snickered and repeated the phrase "fuck it, man," like a chorus.

My intent was to get to the desert floor from the peak overlooking the ceremony, but the coyotes kept trying to talk me out of it. I didn't know which was weirder: the talking coyotes or the fact that I dreamed hyenas inhabited the Nevada desert.

Eventually I made it to the compound, but I was too late. A veritable blanket of naked women writhed over Bertrand Bauerfang's supine body, among them my wife Emma. Just before she took Bauerfang's blessed rod in her mouth she mumbled the words Paul had said to me before I fell asleep again: I don't want to be here. What I didn't notice from afar was that women loving the Initiate Supreme rolled off him and under the enormous bed like plates in a tank track only to emerge on the opposite side and do it all over again.

In that dream I didn't wait for Emma to make a full cycle and return to Bauerfang. As I made my way out of the compound, I became acutely aware that the constellations overhead were not the ones I'd grown up with in the northern hemisphere. Stranger still was that I knew the names of all the alien constellations like The Splayed Horse, The Fruit Bat, The Infinity Loop, and others.

Another dream I had was one in which Paul Stanislavski moved about the open-bay barracks in the dark. He floated a foot or two above the floor, rounding the bunks a few times before retreating into the lavatory.

I tried to follow him, but a palpable darkness on the lavatory threshold kept me from doing so. It was no ordinary darkness. That darkness was a vast void. Its purpose was to obliterate everything the way it did Paul.

My vision was blurred with tears when I woke up. It was just before dawn, judging by the dark blue sky I glimpsed through a window beside my bunk. I had an urge to urinate, the way I always did every morning ever since I had turned fifty. I wiped my eyes and got up from my bunk.

The lights in the lavatory were off. I felt along a wall a moment before I found the switch.

Paul's serene expression revealed that he had at last found the peace he sought through most of his life. He hung from a rafter inside the lavatory. He had used two belts to do the deed.

A chair was tipped over not far from where he hung. For an instant, I had hoped it was a prank. At first, I would feel startled then relieved when Paul opened his eyes and smiled at me. Instead, he swung slowly in a counterclockwise motion for ninety degrees or so and then back in the opposite direction.

The only sound in the room was the creak of the leather belts secured in a knot.

I ran to wake up Fly. Then I shouted for the guards.

Two guards entered the barracks and turned on the lights. I showed them into the lavatory. Paul's pallor revealed what all of us knew just looking at him hanging there. That didn't prevent the guards from cutting him down and attempting CPR anyway. One guard kept blowing into Paul's mouth and doing compressions on his chest. His partner felt for a pulse. Then he put his hand on the other man's shoulder.

Paul was dead.

When Captain Prescott showed up for his 0900 hours briefing, it was just Fly and me there to listen to an artificial man reveal the real reason why we were there.

"Do you think he remembers you shooting him?" I whispered to Fly.

Fly shrugged. "Fuck do I care?" he asked. Then, "Maybe they scrubbed his memory or something."

"You wish to share something, Mr. Kidd?" Captain Prescott asked.

"Yeah," he said. "I was just wondering if you remember getting shot in the head?"

Prescott's expression never changed. No hint of recollection, no anger, nothing.

"What an absurd attempt at humor," the captain said.

They scrubbed his memory, I thought. I looked at Fly. He leaned close to me.

"Yeah, he doesn't remember shit," said Fly.

"Broward," said Prescott. "If you could dim the lights, please."

"Yes, sir," the cook responded.

Since the previous day it became evident that Broward's special operations status was very much still valid. I expected that one evening he'd slither out of his bed and low-crawl beneath the bunks until he reached Fly's. Then, in a most expedient manner befitting a seasoned operator, he'd slit Fly's throat and dispatch him from this world.

I hoped it wouldn't come to that. I think that Fly had considered such a scenario, too. He had grown up thinking that one day some white man or another would try to dispatch him from this life. His father was probably the same way as was his grandfather dating all the way back to when his people were still slaves in Mississippi.

"I got white distant cousins down there," Fly had told me the previous evening. "My wife gave me one of those DNA tests for Christmas a few years back. She wanted to see if we could find out where our people came from in Africa. Did you ever do one of those tests?"

I told him no. It wasn't that I was a paranoid nut job about it the way some guys were, unwilling to have their DNA sample in some database somewhere. I just didn't care. All I had to do was look at my parents' respective family histories to know that I came from everywhere. Sooner or later, the trail would run cold, and much sooner than Fly's did.

"You have been selected for a special assignment," Prescott began as I raised my hand. "Technically, you will not be part of the regular army...Mr. Paladin?"

I lowered my hand.

"You guys do know I have heart disease, right?" I asked.

"Yeah," Fly spoke up now, "and I had me a heart attack too. Also a transient ischemic attack when I was forty-three. That's a mini-stroke just in case it's not in your databank thingy in your head."

"I am familiar with the phrase, Mr. Kidd."

"I had mine when I was forty-five," I offered.

"For real?"

"Scary, isn't it?"

"Man, I thought I was a goner."

"Same here."

"What do they call that? Entropy?"

"Things fall apart."

"Exactly."

"Gentlemen," Prescott said. "This is a special and highly classified opportunity. Any health concerns will be taken under consideration."

"Easy for you to say, Mr. Roboto," mumbled Fly.

"What was that?" Prescott asked.

"Nothing, sir," he replied. "I'm just hungry. That's all."

The captain pressed a button at his lectern and a screen lowered from the ceiling. A PowerPoint title page read: Veknyria: Earth Analog.

"Veknyria," Prescott began, "is an Earth analog, which is another way of saying that it is a planet separate from Earth but similar to it. The discovery of Veknyria was made almost by accident when the Chinese Government tested a neutron bomb in the Gobi Desert."

Another slide showed a grainy black and white photo taken a thousand yards away of what looked like two colossal trees on the edge of a desert landscape. The branches of both monstrosities were dotted with what looked from that distance like one and two-story buildings.

As Prescott spoke, he flipped through a few more slides with images pulled recently from the internet, images of floating cities that looked photoshopped.

"Since then," the captain went on, "the veil, if you will, between Earth and Veknyria has thinned, as evident in civilians photographing floating cities over land and over the ocean."

"I thought they debunked that shit," said Fly.

"Me too," I told him.

"Shush," Broward hissed.

On another slide was a photo of an oil tanker on calm seas passing what looked like a portion of a city constructed out of bulbous skyscrapers connected by bridges.

Fly's hand shot up.

"Please hold your questions until the end," Prescott said. "Off-world Command understands that this is a lot to take in but be assured that the members of your new unit, all of whom you know, were picked, just as you were, because their aptitude proved that they were the most qualified candidates to travel to Veknyria."

"Stanislavski was picked," Fly said, "and look what happened to him."

For that, Prescott did not have a response.

Chapter 11: An Atom in a Body Infinite

The Initiate Supreme Bertrand Bauerfang, channeling Zaphkar, once wrote the following of Earth-like worlds:

Planets just like Earth exist. Some are larger than our world. Others have suns more advanced in age than the star that provides daylight for us. Of the many Earth-like planets in our universe and others, one constant remains: each is occupied by an intelligent species—some more advanced than others—and the idea that one world might colonize another is not only madness but fruitless.

The last part of Bauerfang's words via Zaphkar regarding colonization stayed with me. I remembered the passage just as Captain Prescott finished our briefing. Visions of various planets thriving with intelligent life filled my head (mostly, populated by people who would just assume kill me than strike up some interplanetary dialogue). Prescott spent an hour talking about the planet Veknyria, showing various slides as he did. When the presentation ended, I still didn't know what I was supposed to be doing.

"You believe that bullshit?" Fly asked later that night after we ate chow.

"I don't know what I believe," I told him. As soon as I had shared the Bauerfang quote with him, I felt like I had made a mistake. "All I meant to suggest was that the idea of Earth-like planets with intelligent species is not new."

"I wish we still had our cars," said Fly.

"You still think you can shoot your way out of here now that we've been let in on the secret?" I asked.

"No," he replied. "But I got some weed in my glove compartment that I save for such occasions."

"For being forced back into the army?"

"I meant it helps me think," Fly explained. "Especially, about big-ticket items like this one. That's what my father used to call this kind of talk. Big-ticket items. Like the whole of existence was a giant department store."

We sat outside the barracks in the dark. It was too early in the summer for fireflies. A good hour passed without so much as a single mosquito bite. In New Jersey, where the mosquito is the unofficial state bird, that meant something.

"How come I don't hear any insects?" Fly asked.

He was right, of course. The familiar summer night sounds were absent.

"Did you ever talk much to Stanislavski during our enlistment?" I asked, trying not to think about how quiet it was.

"Not really," Fly said. "You know how it was back then. Everyone kept to their own. You white dudes together. The brothers with the brothers. Recruiters told me that in the army everyone was equal. Shit. That wasn't true at all. When I got out, I tried a couple of semesters of college. It was the same way there. Everyone gravitated toward their own color and kind. Anyway, I shouldn't lay all that shit on you. What were you going to say about Paul?"

"He went home on leave for two weeks one year," I said. "While he was there Paul found this church near his neighborhood. Given what happened this morning and knowing what he told me over the years whenever we talked, he seemed to be on a spiritual quest of sorts. He always said that he felt like there was something missing inside of him.

"The church he found was a storefront one in the middle of a strip mall," I went on. "It had a couple dozen folding chairs arranged in concentric circles. He said the minister's name was Leland. Leland with no last name. Minister Leland talked enough about the bible, but what he believed, and tried to get his congregation to consider was that people and the planets and the stars might all be part of a larger living organism, no larger than protons and electrons in our bodies."

"The bible says there's false prophets everywhere," Fly noted.

"Maybe that's true," I said. "But Paul used to telephone this guy from those pay phones across the street from the barracks. You remember those? He really got into that stuff about us being atoms inside a body infinite, or it would seem if we ever got to view it. Anyway, Paul even wanted me to go home to Ohio with him on a long weekend to meet the guy."

"Did you go?" Fly asked.

"Later, yes."

"Whatever happened to this Leland dude?" he asked.

Paul was livid when he heard the news. Leland, I told Fly that night, had been arrested for soliciting sex from a minor.

"Goddamn," said Fly. "Isn't that always the way? The closer to God a man gets, the more he thinks he can get away with anything."

"After that he got into Buddhism," I told him. "When he didn't achieve nirvana after a few months, he moved onto something else."

Fly grunted. It was hard to tell if he agreed with me or if I had somehow offended him.

We sat there after that listening to the night's silence. I don't remember the hour when we decided to turn in, nor did I recall if it was Fly or me who confessed being tired first.

We were like a couple of children when it came time to use the lavatory. Neither of us wanted to go in there alone. It was big, a row of sinks along one wall and directly across from the sinks a row of toilet stalls. A part of Paul's belt was still attached to one of the steel rafters after the Delta Force guys had cut him down.

"Sorry about that," Broward said as he stood in the doorway, scaring Fly and me. We never heard him approach. "I should have had someone take that down."

When the future Initiate Supreme was a nine-year-old boy, his father Emile Bauerfang got it in his head that young Bertrand planned to make a move on his mother as soon as puberty would allow. For health reasons (read: cirrhosis), the elder Bauerfang had to leave foreign service. He divided his retirement days between reading, writing, and drinking. Mostly, he drank. In those rare sober moments of his life, he managed to put together one hundred pages of hand-written notes that he hoped, providing that he could stay sober long enough, would become a memoir.

It was around this time that the retired diplomat Emile Bauerfang experienced his own liquor-induced revelation: his son was spending entirely too much time with his mother, a result of what the good doctor Sigmund Freud had called an Oedipus Complex.

Young Bertrand had indeed become fascinated with his mother, most boys and men were. Unlike other male members of society who came into Sarah's orbit, Bertrand harbored no psychosexual yearnings for his mother. He was, despite his father's gin-soaked illogical fears, quite well-adjusted in that respect. Nevertheless, Emile Bauerfang maintained that his son exhibited what the former diplomat turned dipsomaniac took for open hostility toward him.

"He hates me," Bauerfang told his wife.

"You're drunk," Sarah concluded.

Bauerfang, deep in the throes of denial concerning his alcoholism, never once considered that his son's disposition was, in fact, a direct response to his father's deteriorating grip on reality.

To remedy what he took for direct competition, the father smashed his son in the face with a garden shovel, nearly killing him in the process. Sarah, upon discovering the assault, whisked her son to the hospital where he was properly treated for a broken nose and orbital fractures.

Two things happened after the assault: Emile Bauerfang was placed under arrest for attempted murder and Bertrand Bauerfang's left eye changed color from brown to blue.

Sarah and her parents took this as a good omen. Blue was the color of divinity. From such trauma came a blessing. No one knew for sure if young Bertrand was able to see God with his blue eye, but the injuries he sustained from his father's assault had left him partially deaf in his left ear. Family and friends who came calling mistook Bertrand's inability to hear out of one ear for a trance-like state. Before long, they felt a twinge of jealousy toward the boy who had become so intimate with God.

Ten years later, owing to his infirmities, the future Initiate Supreme would be turned away from Canadian military service. He was devastated. Little did he know at the time that other avenues would open for him.

As for Emile Bauerfang, he spent the rest of his life—exactly 17 months and 23 days—in a mental health facility. When he died, neither Sarah nor Bertrand attended Emile's funeral.

A week after Paul Stanislavski hung himself, Captain Prescott, Specialist Broward, Fly, and I flew from McGuire Air Force Base to Kirtland Air Force Base in New Mexico. They put us in a hangar converted to a company-sized barracks.

Four hours after our arrival, the surviving members of my old infantry company, among their number was Max Kunstler, showed up laden with prescription medications and a few CPAP machines.

As my old cohorts got settled, I kept thinking about Bertrand Bauerfang and his father's attempt to murder him. I wondered if Emile Bauerfang had been successful in killing his son would my wife still be with me? What butterfly effect may have been avoided if the nine-year-old boy with one blue eye, the divine eye, never got struck in the face with a shovel?

In *The Autobiography of The Oracle of Heaven*, Bertrand Bauerfang wrote:

> *God most definitely possesses a sense of humor. Sadly, we humans in our present form, handicapped by our earth-bound languages, lack the vocabulary necessary to comprehend the divine punchline.*

When I read that I thought of the line in Genesis about the Spirit of God hovering over the waters. If He did have a sense of humor, maybe he would have reconsidered. Maybe, instead of creating the world and all its works, God would have decreed, "You know what? Fuck this shit." Instead, he gave us multiple universes, the platypus in macrocosm, and littered them with habitable planets. What was He thinking?

Chapter 12: Bumpkin the Magic Man

Max Kunstler looked like he hadn't slept in a week. We talked only briefly before the lot of us were corralled onto a bus and taken to a building a mile or so from the hangar where we were staying.

Aside from Max, I got to talk to Hick Haywood. His real name was Silas Gantry Haywood. He brought his nickname with him into the army. It was the only one our drill sergeant did not change.

"Boy," Sergeant Fisk said, "that one sure suits you."

"Thank you," said Hick.

"It wasn't a compliment," he replied.

Hick was from southern Georgia, a small town called Attapulgus in Decatur County to be exact: population <500. Attapulgus was the birthplace of civil rights leader Josea Williams who had been allegedly run out of town by a lynch mob when he was just thirteen years old. Hick seemed perhaps too proud of this slice of history, which was why guys like Fly had plotted to kill Hick via friendly fire if we ever went to war.

When he joined the army, Hick was twenty-four years old. Prior to that, he worked part-time as a small engine repairman during the day and at night he drove a forklift at CBTG Chemical, a company which employed most of the adults in town. He had a stutter back when I first met him. In the thirty-odd years since I last saw him, he had yet to fully conquer his impediment.

Toward the end of our brief conversation, Hick got excited about the prospect of serving his country again. Unlike the other guys, Hick bought into the myth of America, that poor guys like us were somehow obligated to support and defend the Constitution against enemies both foreign and domestic. The thrill of serving Uncle Sam again caused his stutter to return.

"So we're going to be fuh-fighting aliens and shuh-shit?" Hick wondered.

"Hopefully no," I said.

The first time around I joined the army for the college fund. I returned at fifty-four years old because I didn't want to go to jail.

Hick Haywood was different. But he wasn't alone in his blind patriotism. Yodel Taylor was another one. The moment a guy like that picked up a rifle purchased by Uncle Sam he envisioned himself a great American hero. Neither Hick nor Yodel understood that when they were dead and gone, and their bones reduced to dust, no one would remember their valor or their cowardice, much less their names. War did that. It erased names from history dating all the way back to Sargon the Great in Mesopotamia nearly five thousand years ago and it would do the same in the future.

It was weird being back in uniform. During his briefing, Captain Prescott revealed the penalty for not going along with the call-up.

"Your former cohorts who chose to ignore the orders," said Prescott, "are being gathered by law enforcement as we speak. Once in custody, they will be given an option."

Fly raised his hand.

"Excuse me, sir?" he said.

"What is it, Mr. Kidd?" Prescott asked.

"What kind of option?" asked Fly.

Prescott didn't answer. Instead, his expression appeared confused at first then angered, human-like, as if he'd suddenly remembered getting shot by Fly.

"Captain Prescott," I raised my hand. "May I ask what would have happened to me if I did not comply with the orders I received?"

Kill them with kindness, my wife Emma used to say. You attract more flies with honey than vinegar.

"If you chose to ignore the orders," Prescott said. "You would have been given the option to comply or be remanded to Leavenworth for no less than twenty years."

"Guh-guh-goddamn," Hick Haywood mumbled.

"So that's it," Fly whispered to me.

"What do you mean?" I asked him.

"You have to address the thing directly," he said. "Like a computer."

He'd taken to referring to Prescott as "thing" that day, as in "I just know that thing's going to kill me."

"I hope that sufficiently answers your question, Mr. Paladin?" the captain said.

"Yes, sir," I told him.

"Good," he said. Then, "Now, I'd like to introduce you to your unit NCO, Sergeant First Class Hector Romero. Sergeant Romero?"

A short, heavyset man with a high-and-tight haircut and sparse mustache stepped forward from the back of the room.

"Holy shit," Hick said. "It's like Sergeant Sanchez resurrected."

Captain Prescott didn't laugh, but the rest of us did.

Sergeant Sanchez had been a drill instructor at Fort Benning more than three decades ago. He was a skinny little Puerto Rican from some shithole block in the Bronx. He always acted like he had finally arrived. No one ever bothered to tell him that the army was the place guys like him went to avoid prison. Sanchez was the only NCO I'd ever seen who was allowed to wear double-soled jump boots, elevator boots we used to call them behind his back, to increase his height. If he hadn't dedicated his life to serving Uncle Sam, Sanchez would have made a good second-story man. He was too small for anything else.

To make up for being so short, Sergeant Sanchez used to threaten to knock out recruits.

"I'll fucking punch your lights out," he used to shout if someone so much as looked at him cross-eyed.

One time, in a classroom where we learned all about orto-chlorobenzylidene-malononitrile gas, or CS gas for short, a guy named Rueben from the third platoon drew a picture of Sergeant Sanchez as The Dead End Kid from Bugs Bunny ("I wanna an Easter Egg, I wanna an Easter Egg!"). Rueben drew Sanchez's head on the little infant's body and tiny elevator boots on the baby's feet. He added a speech balloon like in the comics that read: "I'll punch your lights out! I'LL PUNCH YOUR LIGHTS OUT!" The drawing got passed around.

Before long, the caricature of Sergeant Sanchez was intercepted by another drill sergeant. No one would admit to drawing the caricature. The drill sergeants threatened to PT us (army lingo for force us to exercise) until we died. That's when Rueben stepped forward thinking he was a man's man and admitted to drawing the pic. Sergeant Sanchez and the other drill instructors didn't care about his confession.

Normally, the chemical weapons training day ended like this: you entered the gas chamber, and someone yelled "GAS!" which was the cue to don your gas mask as CS gas filled the room. Then you were ordered to remove the mask and breathe in the gas. Breaking the seal, they called it. This part of the drill was designed to make you a bad-ass, to make you Be All You Can Be™, to use Big Green's recruiting parlance of the time. It didn't make you bad-ass. It turned you into a snot-dribbling, temporarily blinded, dry-heaving mess. Like so many things in the army, breaking the seal served no purpose. It was moronic. Naturally, it became tradition.

Rueben was the last one through the gas chamber that day. He ended up getting a good dose of tradition. Once the room filled with CS gas, they made him remove his mask. Instead of letting him replace it after so many seconds, they started dogging him. All the drill instructors but Sanchez were inside. All of them shouted orders through their gas masks. Sergeant Sanchez marched in a circle outside the gas chamber with his hands clasped behind his back like some banana republic revolutionary observing a tank battle from afar. Inside the gas chamber, Rueben was made to run in place, perform squat thrusts, push-ups, and jumping jacks, whatever suited their sadistic fantasies. This was referred to as corrective training.

In the end, the corrective training proved too much for Rueben. The drill instructors carried him out like the trash and deposited him on the ground. Rueben's uniform was covered with vomit. Snot formed an intricate web between his fingers, his nostrils, and his mouth. His eyes were teary, red, swollen from the effects of the gas.

Sergeant Sanchez squatted beside Rueben when the recruit started dry-heaving. "Next time I'll punch your fucking lights out, private," he shouted at him.

For the rest of basic training, Rueben never drew another caricature. He went on to Fort Campbell with the rest of our cohort unit. A year into his enlistment, he was medically discharged for being overweight. Rueben went on to become a comic book creator. You may have seen his work. *Sergeant Punchy* it was called. It was published by Orgy Campfire, an adult comic book publisher. Rueben spent a career getting back at Sanchez by putting his comic book character, loosely based on the drill instructor, in all sorts of hilarious scenarios, most of which involved lumbering redneck recruits who were short on paying attention and long on ambushing the little sergeant when no one else was around or large, powerful women who beat up Sergeant Punchy for his money outside of nightclubs. The last I heard, a movie based on his comic book was in development.

As for Sergeant Sanchez, by the time basic training ended the drill instructor fell into a deep depression and had to be hospitalized. The other recruits and I all thought it was because Sergeant Sanchez never got to knock anyone out. It turned out that army regulations regarding height requirements had changed. Sergeant Sanchez, who had devoted twelve years of his life to the army, was being medically discharged because he was too short to be a soldier.

Sergeant Romero's sole concern that month was putting us into some sort of shape. Hick Haywood refused to quit smoking, which went right up Sergeant Romero's ass since Hick jogged in formation with a cigarette dangling from his lips.

"Put that shit out!" Sergeant Romero said.

"You're guh-going to have to kuh-kill me," Hick told him.

Sergeant Romero let the matter rest.

Our uniforms looked pretty much like the regular army ones, only the operational camouflage patterns utilized different colors, six to be exact: red, orange, pale yellow, white, pink, and black. They issued us regular PT uniforms which consisted of black shorts and olive drab t-shirts with no insignia. It was just as well we didn't sport any markings revealing who we were. Top-secret mission or not, we made a pathetic sight attempting to run in formation each morning.

They took mercy and didn't bother to force haircuts on us like new recruits.

"Hey, sergeant," Yodel said one morning about two weeks after we arrived at Kirtland Air Base. "Why are our uniforms so different from the regular army?"

"You'll find out when you get to where you are going, Mr. Taylor," Sergeant Romero replied.

The following day, we were issued weighted suits. They were old-fashioned army chemsuits, the kind with charcoal lining between the layers, that were retro-fitted with steel plates. The first week they went easy on us. The suit only weighed forty pounds. After morning PT and chow, we were expected to walk around in the suits. That lasted a week. The following week we turned in those suits and they issued us sixty-pounders. The week after that the suits were upped to eighty pounds each. With each increase in weight came an increase in the amount of hours we were supposed to wear the weighted suits. It was torture. Then came a few marches with weighted rucksacks.

"This will give you some indication of what gravity on Veknyria will do to you during the first week or so," said Sergeant Romero as we went about our daily tasks wearing those heavy suits.

As if some sort of compensation for torturing us with steel-lined suits, the army, in its secret and infinite wisdom, had decided that we'd all be given the rank of chief warrant officer. It didn't matter if we had college degrees or not. For some of the guys like Hick and Yodel, the pay was more than they were making back home before they had been called up.

"Hey, I just realized something," Hick told Sergeant Romero one morning. "You have to salute each of us and call us sir."

"Warrant officers don't get saluted," came Romero's reply.

We were assured that our families and employers had been informed that we had been chosen for highly sensitive work that could not be revealed in the interest of national security and all that. It was good news for the guys with families. I didn't have anyone left. My parents and my brother were gone. When I told one of the S-4 clerks charged with in-processing everyone that I was the last of my name, she didn't look impressed.

"You're going to start a family now?" the clerk asked, sardonically.

Her name was Dunbar.

"That depends," I told her. "Do I have to marry you?"

"Next!" Dunbar shouted.

The army didn't care if my family name didn't carry on. If it did, that Green Beret sergeant would have never showed up at my front door.

I didn't bother Sergeant Romero too much the way some of the other guys did. Jody Pickett, for instance, one of Fly's old crew from our infantry days, tested Romero's patience every morning by making the sergeant guarantee that the letters Pickett wrote each night were getting mailed.

"Goddamn, Pickett," Sergeant Romero said each morning following his inquiry, "do I look like the United States Postal Service?"

Jody "Magic Man" Pickett was an interesting guy. He hailed from Birmingham, Alabama. His parents had met in March 1965 at the Selma-to-Montgomery March. In basic training, the drill sergeants bequeathed the nickname "Magic Man" on him after the Wilson Pickett song. It did not stick. In recent years, Jody ran a typewriter and computer repair shop. He dressed like a Yuppie in pleated pants and cardigan sweaters during off-duty hours and in three decades his casual wear had not changed. When I saw him after all those years he looked like the preppie that time forgot. He wore his whitish-gray hair in a kinky textured style, and he kept his matching goatee impeccably trimmed. For our purpose, and to Jody's relief, he was permitted to keep his beard, as were some of the other guys. When we were young men, Fly sometimes referred to Jody as "Brother Bumpkin" since Jody was from the South. In Fly's eyes, anybody born below the Mason-Dixon Line was a bumpkin. Jody tolerated Fly, but he secretly thought that Fly was too vain. For a religious guy like Jody, that just didn't wash.

"Every day I wake up and say to myself: What would Jesus do?" Jody told me one morning at chow shortly after our arrival at Kirtland Air Force Base. "Then I do what my wife tells me to do."

"Smart man," said Yodel.

"There's a man who will live a long time," Hick concurred.

"Hey, Cal," Jody said to me, "why do you think we haven't had any weapons training yet?"

The question surprised me. It was odd that none of us had seen a rifle since we became part of the army again.

"Maybe they're going to make us hand out fluh-flowers to the damned aliens," Hick offered, "like some kuh-kind of guh-goddamn hippies."

Chapter 13: The Desert of Earthly Delight

The Initiate Supreme and his Radiant Angels of Zaphkar practiced a principle known as prumashvallu. It comes from *The Book of Ziyarae*, the revelation of Zaphkar as told to the Reverend Bertrand Bauerfang. The basic meaning of prumashvallu is "something for something else." The concept is rooted in all we know; from the concept of matter never being truly destroyed to the consumption of plants or animals to create energy, it's not a particularly new idea.

Prumashvallu was one of the main tenets of The Radiant Angels of Zaphkar. Bauerfang wrote that if followers remembered nothing else except this principle, they would still be better off than most. Zaphkar forecasted to the Initiate Supreme that those seeking true knowledge in order to ultimately rejoin the great soul would be willing to give up something to have something else. In Bauerfang's estimation, it was not only the key to understanding the universe but the reason why humans existed.

Dreams also played a large part in this process of moving toward the great soul. Zaphkar explained in *The Book of Ziyarae* that no angel or daemon can hypnotize or otherwise brainwash a man or woman into seeking spiritual fulfillment, not as long as humans possessed free will. Even if free will never existed, duping someone into a spiritual path toward the ultimate liberation would not be prumashvallu. Zaphkar revealed to Bauerfang that without prumashvallu, the universe itself would collapse and force all the other universes as well toward oblivion.

Late at night, when the rest of the guys were asleep, I lay awake thinking about prumashvallu and how it applied to my current predicament. I did not consider myself a Radiant Angel. It takes more than reading a ton of publications from an organization to become a convert. If I wanted to be born anew as an actual Radiant Angel of Zaphkar, I had to make the pilgrimage to Bauerfang's compound outside Elko, Nevada, just like my sister-in-law and my wife did. There was no guarantee of instant acceptance. Joining up with the Radiant Angels was not like being born again in the Christian sense. There was no accepting Zaphkar as one's savior because that had never been his purpose.

In the early days after Emma left, I thought about quitting my job and going out west to join the Radiant Angels. At the time I still had over twenty thousand dollars in the bank. That would have been a small price to pay if it meant rescuing Emma and bringing her home. In reality, I had a better chance of growing wings. Investigative journalists reported that the Initiate Supreme Bertrand Bauerfang enjoyed earthly delights with the opposite sex. So much so, in fact, that he enforced a ratio among his followers: only one out of every four followers were permitted to be male. Of his three-hundred-thirty-three followers, including my wife and my sister-in-law, there were eighty-three men, excluding Bauerfang. Despite claiming in his autobiography that he remained in constant contact with Zaphkar, Bauerfang carved out plenty of time for the ladies, among them of course was Emma.

I needed an out. Some secret apparatus that would bring me to another planet did not interest me. A thousand things could go wrong. What mattered most was rescuing my wife from the clutches of that master manipulator Bauerfang. I wanted prumashvallu, but I wasn't alone.

Chapter 14: Plush Prince Goes Off Script

It was during the fourth week at Kirtland that my cohorts and I began to get loopy. Except for Max Kunstler and me, all of the guys in our group had families. They took our cell phones from us the moment we were airborne over McGuire Air Force Base. Hick, Jody, Yokel, and the others experienced the same thing from their original points of destination.

The most outspoken about a lack of communication with the outside world was Shevon Jones. If anyone would be willing to escape this lunacy with me, it was him.

Back in the 1980's, Shevon was known as "Plush Prince." Actually, drill sergeant Fisk had bestowed the nickname "Shortcake" on account of Shevon's height. He wasn't as short as Sergeant Sanchez, but he was damn close. It wasn't until we arrived at Fort Campbell when they started calling him Plush Prince. And by "they" I mean everyone whom Plush Prince hounded enough to get them to call him by his alter ego.

Shevon "Plush Prince" Jones came from Winstonville, Mississippi. When his enlistment ended, he re-upped and served in Germany and Korea before moving back to Winstonville. His family ran a funeral home in the neighboring town of Shelby. And it was to the mortuary he returned after giving Uncle Sam a decade of his life.

Plush Prince had dreams just like the rest of us when we were young and on the cusp of leaving our teen years behind. He dabbled in the guitar, and he could carry a tune. When he met Fly and Jody, the three of them formed a tight-knit group that called themselves

The Dope Grunts. When they weren't on-duty they sat around in the barracks dormitory room they shared with a fourth guy named Edgar Lee Hopkins, listening, in no particular order, to such artists as 2 Live Crew, Salt-N-Pepa, Kool Moe D, Public Enemy, Run DMC, and a host of other rap groups.

Plush Prince made no secret of wanting to become a rapper. He had a writing partner back home, a straight-up thug, according to Plush Prince, who sold weed and robbed convenience stores throughout the South. The writing partner, Earnie Wrangler, went by his rap alias Gritz-In-Da-Griddle. They'd known each other since grade school. If Plush Prince and Gritz didn't meet in the fourth grade, they might not have met at all, owing to how Gritz dropped out of school in the eighth grade. Their friendship and musical partnership would end after a home burglary committed by Gritz went awry.

By the time Plush Prince joined the army his friend Gritz had been handed a life sentence for murder. Plush Prince became a solo act. He didn't do much MCing while serving in uniform. The problem, Plush Prince admitted, was that he could not rhyme worth a damn. He did, however, find his voice in complaining about the infantry life every chance he got, sometimes with rhymes but most times without. My least favorite time of the year was when Plush Prince and I were assigned to the same fox hole during a field exercise. His swan song for the duration of his first enlistment was more of a lament that went like this: why they always fucking with me?

Once, during a battalion run, one of our sergeants, a new guy just in from the 82nd Airborne, called out different privates during the run to sing cadence. Most of us, when called upon to break ranks, stuck to the oldies but goodies, the tried and true cadences that wouldn't bring down the heat on you. Not Plush Prince. As soon as Sergeant Palmer called him out of formation to call cadence, Plush Prince knew it was his moment to shine. To the tune of "Momma, momma, can't you see? What the army's done to me..." Plush Prince sang a call and without thinking we provided the response.

Up before dawn I had to pee

(Up before dawn I had to pee)
Platoon sergeant started dogging me
(Platoon sergeant started dogging me)
Baby, baby, can't you see?
(Baby, baby, can't you see?)
The army's always fucking with me
(The army's always fucking with me)

The thing about cadence calling in the army is that it's designed not to motivate troops but to keep rubes foolish enough to sign up in the first place from thinking about home for too long. If you're tired enough, you will reply to any cadence thrown at you. For instance, if you're running formation and a soldier is called up to sing cadence he might, if he's disillusioned in the way Plush Prince had been, start cadence by singing, "Uncle Sam can go fuck himself." A soldier will utter a response to the call because he's been trained to do so. He expects some catchy phrases and rhymes designed to keep rhythm. Soldiers don't ask questions. They reach a point in their enlistment when they think, this must be ok if everyone's doing it. Nothing could be further from the truth.

Sergeant Palmer let one of the other NCOs take over calling cadence before he pulled Plush Prince to the side of the road. He wouldn't have been so pissed off if a cadre of medics weren't going by in the opposite direction, half of their numbers comprised of women. Sergeant Palmer made Plush Prince run circles around the battalion formation that day, much to the chagrin of the battalion commander Lieutenant Colonel Bradford Giles Powell, until the five-mile run had ended.

In thirty-five years, Plush Prince had lost none of his spunk. Max Kunstler chalked it up long ago to a Napoleon Complex. Plush Prince stood just shy of five feet five inches tall.

On the first day of his phone call campaign, Plush Prince confronted Sergeant Romero outside the chow hall following lunch. He cursed up a storm as he demanded access to his cell phone or at least a pay phone to call home.

"Do you hear that?" Sergeant Romero said, looking over Plush Prince's head. "Where's that disembodied voice coming from?"

"I'm right here, bitch!" Plush Prince screamed.

"Well, look at that," the sergeant said as he looked down at him. "Black hobbits *do* exist."

Plush Prince jumped the sergeant. It was a mistake. The problem with many men in today's society is that they watch televised mixed martial arts matches and feel that by some strange osmosis they are able to fight the same way the trained combatants do on television. Plush Prince subscribed to this faulty philosophy of martial prowess by osmosis. Sergeant Romero, having just come over from the 5th Special Forces Group, showed Plush Prince in short order the error of his ways.

"Goddamn, sergeant," Plush Prince wheezed, skipping around in a circle and clutching his lower back as he tried to catch his breath. "I think that last punch knocked my spleen into my lung."

"Just breathe through your nose," Sergeant Romero informed him. "It'll pass."

"Fuck that," he countered. He offered a few high-pitched wheezes before he spoke next. "I need to go to a hospital."

"There are pay phones outside the Base Exchange," said the sergeant. "You can go use one if you can make it there."

Plush Prince raised his right fist in a half-hearted Black Power salute. He took a couple of hesitant steps, then he fainted.

They brought us to a meeting room at one of the Air Force Inns on base. Plush Prince arrived a few minutes late. He had been hospitalized for a few days, not for the beating he'd taken at the adept hands of Sergeant Romero, but because of appendicitis. He took a seat in the back.

Captain Prescott introduced Col. Chester Morris Lester.

"Col. Lester just flew in from Washington today to address you men directly," Captain Prescott announced. "Please give him your undivided attention during his portion of the presentation."

"How you men doing?" Col. Lester said when he stepped up to the podium.

"Do they call you Moe?" Plush Prince asked.

His question went unnoticed by everyone except me since we put on a rousing if not disingenuous response to the colonel. Plush

Prince had his moments. Age had not slowed him down in that respect.

"Excellent," Colonel Lester said.

The multimedia presentation that day consisted of still photographs and short video clips of Veknyrian landscape. Throughout the presentation, the colonel assured us that we would be visiting Veknyria as observers.

"Uh, Colonel?" Hick Haywood raised his hand.

"Mister...?"

"Haywood, sir."

"What's on your mind, Mr. Haywood?" Colonel Lester asked.

That was the thing about ranking officers. Whenever they asked anyone what was on his or her mind they didn't really want to hear it. Hick, having never quite grasp so simple a concept, believed that the colonel was genuinely interested in what he had to say.

"I'm curious, sir," said Hick, "why the Department of Defense called back a bunch of fifty-something-year old vets for what seems like the mission of a lifetime?"

"Do you know Seneca?" the colonel asked. This was another ploy of educated officers. They asked the Hick Haywoods of the world if they are versed in ancient Roman writers. It was a sham, and Hick knew it because he quickly shook his head. "Seneca once wrote, 'Every new beginning comes from some other beginning's end.' What do you think that means, Mr. Haywood?"

"Beats the shuh-shit...I mean I don't know, sir," Hick replied.

"It means that men destined to do great things don't sit idle for long," Colonel Lester said.

"Goddamn right," Yodel woke up in the back long enough to clap a few times.

Max Kunstler turned and eyed me from his seat in the row ahead of me. He slowly raised his hand as I shook my head.

"Yes," Colonel Lester to Max. "You are..." his voice trailed off as he looked at the seating roster none of us followed. "Mr...Jones?"

"Not even close," Max said.

"I'm Jones!" Plush Prince cried out from his seat in the back. Then he mumbled just loud enough for us folks in the middle of the room to hear, "They always fucking with me. Always, man."

"Kunstler," Max told the colonel.

"I'd like to get through this presentation," Colonel Lester said, "so yours will be the last question until I'm through. Hooah?"

"Right," my old friend said. "Colonel, every one of us in this room is at least ten years older than you. You quote Seneca to make a point. And that's fine. I could quote Cicero and tell you that every man who has a library and a garden has everything he needs."

"Your question?"

"Hick there is almost sixty years old," said Max. "The rest of us are in our fifties. What I think Hick wanted to know is why call up guys with diminished faculties instead of using some crack platoon or two from the regular army?"

"Mr. Kunstler," the colonel said. "I could lie to you and tell you that after multiple cross-references and up-to-date background checks the army in its infinite wisdom chose you and your colleagues because of your natural propensity for original thought, for not following the herd, as it were.

"If I did," he went on, "I'd be lying. Instead, I will tell you right here and now that we just don't have the resources to stretch active duty and reserve units any further."

"In other words we're expendable," Max said.

"We're not at war with the Veknyrians, Mr. Kunstler," the colonel concluded, which was doublespeak for we're totally at war with this intelligent species from a parallel world, but if we tell the people of Earth then citizens all over the world will shit the bed.

"Suck it up, libtard!" Yodel called out to Kunstler.

"That will be enough of that," Colonel Lester announced. "When we go over to the other side we won't be Democrats or Republicans. We go as members of the United States Army of the planet Earth, and we will conduct ourselves accordingly. Is that clear?"

"Yes, sir!" everyone in the room shouted in unison.

Army officers of a certain pay grade like Colonel Lester were no different than cult leaders. Ranking officers, while outwardly disciplined, are paid, in part, to create chaos. Like cult leaders, these officers constantly create crisis situations, whether they are orchestrated in the form of a field exercise or flying off the handle if some poor private doesn't shout "At ease!" fast enough when said officers enter a chow hall. High-ranking officers like their cult-leading counterparts also possess a certain charisma. Wallflowers don't get to be colonels and generals. They don't get to be cult leaders either. Lastly, cult leaders and ranking officers often promise to change a person's world, for better or worse, as if they are gods themselves.

It didn't take long during the presentation for my mind to wonder. At one point, Colonel Lester suddenly looked like Bertrand Bauerfang. Then, as quickly as it happened, he changed back to himself.

When the colonel got to the part of the presentation about our method of travel, explaining something called a Frulx gateway, which, if I understood him correctly, was an interdimensional passage generator manufactured by a now-extinct alien race. Basically, the gateway folded spacetime back and forth until a rent was created.

"The Frulx gateway," Colonel Lester said, "was discovered in the American Southwest with a pre-programmed address that led us to Veknyria. We found evidence for another address once we reached Veknyria. It led to the home of the Frulx, but, as I mentioned, they were already extinct, the victims of a cataclysmic asteroid bombardment."

I raised my hand. "Sir?"

"Mr. Paladin is it?"

"Yes, sir," I said. "Could you explain to us in layman's terms how the gateways work with respect to landing in the right place?"

"Good question," said the colonel.

He spent the next five minutes revealing a possible escape plan if things went south and our numbers were diminished. It involved knowing the solar system designator, the planet designator, and the coordinates for longitude and latitude of a given place on a particular planet.

Colonel Lester concluded, "If you screwed it up, you could find yourself ill-equipped on Saturn."

Out of the original COHORT company I had served in during the 1980's, thirty-three of one hundred and eleven reported for duty at local bases.

Of the original one hundred eleven company members, eleven were dead, ten from natural causes and two suicides. Paul Stanislavski was the latest. Before him, in the late 1990's, a guy named Enrique Cordoba from Coleharbor, North Dakota drove his pick-up truck straight into Lake Audubon off 31st Avenue. The temperature dropped below zero degrees Fahrenheit that night. And while Enrique's truck came to rest just twelve feet beneath the lake's surface, the waters crusted over with an inch of ice by the next morning as a heavy snow fell. Before long, the ice in the lake thickened as winter progressed. Enrique's truck was not spotted until the spring.

As for the remaining sixty-seven members, twenty-three of them were deemed unfit for service, twenty-seven with serious physical conditions that included various amputations and six who were currently institutionalized. The remaining forty-four chose to serve their sentences, provided they were all apprehended.

It was hard to imagine that thirty-three of us were possibly going to war against an entire planet, even more difficult was that we were doing so without weapons. I could think of a dozen other ways to do away with aging veterans like us in order to save the Veterans Administration a few bucks. None of them included traveling to a planet in a parallel universe.

"No one is going to war," Captain Prescott assured us when Plush Prince brought up the subject.

"That is correct," Colonel Lester added, looking rather disappointed.

Colonel Lester told us during his briefing that Veknyria had a mass four times that of Earth and measured nearly forty-five percent larger in diameter.

Veknyria's sun resembled our own with only slight variations in size, age, and surface heat. The planet's host star compared to ours offered 18% more luminosity. As a result, daylight on Veknyria would appear much brighter.

Destrayama and Hiriruta were two moons that orbited Veknyria. The planet's population commonly refers to the latter as

The Withering Sister. Hiriruta had been damaged by asteroids long before life evolved on Veknyria. From the planet's surface it looks like a waning moon followed by odd-shaped clouds. The so-called clouds were enormous chunks of the damaged moon that have been locked into what's left of Hiriruta's gravitational pull. It was estimated by army researchers, based on the data gathered, that Hiriruta would eventually plunge into Veknyria in 1.5 billion years. Destrayama, the larger of the two moons and the farther one, was believed to be home to complex life, but no determination had been made as to the validity of such a claim since Veknyrians harbored no desire to develop conventional space travel. The treaty the U.S. Government established with the Veknyrians, Colonel Lester announced, prohibited us from bringing such technology to their world.

The orbit of Veknyria around its sun, being the third planet in its solar system, measured 377 Earth days, and the planet's orbital radius was 1.03 AU (astronomical units) compared to Earth's 1.0 AU. Gravity on Veknyria was 1.7 times that of Earth; in other words, I would feel like I weigh nearly twice my weight.

Colonel Lester informed us that the good news was we had already experienced something like it in our prior service days, if only temporarily, humping nearly one hundred pounds of gear and weapons around during field exercises. The gravitational difference was also the reason for outfitting us with weighted suits we were required to wear six hours a day.

"Theoretically," the colonel said that day, "if you spent enough time on Veknyria in that gravity environment, your bones would become denser, and your muscle mass would naturally increase due to your daily routine. It would feel like an intense workout every day until you got used to it. Upon returning to Earth, you could feasibly end up being twice as strong, but the effect would wear off as you acclimated once more to Earth's gravity."

Later that evening we were allowed to call home from landline phones that were monitored by army intelligence. They even gave us a script to use if a family member, friend, or loved one asked what we were doing there. The official line we were supposed to share was that we had been chosen for a long-term study for veterans over the age of fifty. I had no family left, but I did call Emma's parents to tell them that I had not forgotten about her. They sounded nonplussed by the whole affair, resigning themselves, as grieving parents do, to writing off their only daughter who lived beyond the scope of good taste and reason.

Pretty much everyone stuck to the script if a question arose. Then there was Shevon Plush Prince Jones. By the time they let us call home I knew I could no longer count on him to join me in an escape. He cracked a few minutes after his phone call began, unable to lie to his wife of twenty years.

"They sending me into space, Sheena!" Plush Prince cried out. "They always fucking with...Hello? HELLO?"

I felt bad. I wanted to tell him that we were absolutely being sent into space, just not the one Plush Prince, his wife Sheena, or the rest of us knew.

As for Plush Prince himself there was no reprimand for his actions. The powers that be had decided that the terminated phone call served as warning enough. Plush Prince did, however, have a come-to-Jesus conversation with the android Captain Prescott. I don't know what was said, nor did the Prince ever say what passed between them. All I knew was that when it was over Plush Prince looked calm, if not defeated. My guess is the android threatened to have Plush Prince's whole family terminated.

Around ten o'clock the next morning, one week after Colonel Lester's briefing, a charter bus pulled up in front of the hangar that had served as home for the last several weeks. Behind it, a deuce-and-a-half truck that would transport our gear to the location of the Frulx gateway.

"Ten dollars says the Prince dies accidentally on purpose," said Max Kunstler as we stood in line waiting to throw our gear on the back of the deuce-and-a-half.

"Wouldn't it be easier to discredit him when this was all over?" I wondered.

"You think this shuh-shit's going to end in a good way, Puh-Paladin?" Hick Haywood asked. "I thought you Yankee buh-boys were supposed to be smart?"

We stowed the gear on the back of the truck. Then we climbed aboard the bus that soon headed out on I-40 West.

Chapter 15: The Phony Savior

The sign read:

YOU ARE ENTERING ZUNI-LAND.
WELCOME.

The bus windows were tinted but judging from the long looks the reservation's inhabitants gave us as we passed it was easy to see that they knew we were military. The deuce-and-a-half following the charter bus was what clinched it for them.

It was hard to imagine that the Zuni people wanted us there. Old wounds and all. The uniforms may have changed, but we were still invaders, extrinsic usurpers to some degree or another.

"That's too bad," Sergeant Romero said when Yodel told him the aforementioned sentiment.

Yodel had his moments of empathy and compassion, but they were rare. Mostly, he was one of those patriotic morons who thought that white Europeans were the best thing to ever happen to North America. He was forever misquoting key historical figures to suit his needs. When he couldn't misquote something he construed as relative to his pseudo-argument, Yodel resorted to conspiracy theories as legitimate sources.

Currently, Yodel was agitated. When Sergeant Romero and Captain Prescott inspected our field gear before we packed it, Romero told Yodel that he was not permitted to bring a Holy Bible to Veknyria.

"Hey," Yodel readied himself for an argument, "I'm a Christian. That means I praise His name and spread His Word."

"Not to the Veknyrians you don't," Sergeant Romero said. "The orders are simple: observe and take notes."

"Sure, but what about—"

"This is not a topic for debate."

"Well, how the hell do you know that these creatures couldn't use Jesus in their lives?"

"For starters, they are not creatures," said Sergeant Romero. "They are an intelligent species with their own societies, their own art, their own songs and literature, and their own religious practices. They even have their own savior."

"If it isn't Jesus, it's a phony savior," Yodel cried.

"Mr. Taylor," Captain Prescott spoke up now. "While I would love to point out the holes in your line of reasoning, suffice it to say that there's to be no unnecessary influence on the Veknyrians. You want to go convert people, wait until you get back to go door to door. Am I making myself clear?"

"Yes sir," Yodel answered, deflated.

"Where are we going?" Fly asked.

"You will see when we get there, Mr. Kidd," said Captain Prescott.

"Sergeant Romero," Hick spoke up now. "What do they call their God?"

"His name is Zaphkar," Sergeant Romero replied.

I nearly fell out of my seat when I heard the name.

My last contact with Emma was a postcard with a photo of a ghost town on it. The message she wrote consisted of four words before she signed her name:

Made it (sort of)
~Emma

I did not know what "sort of" meant until I did some homework. I learned that The Radiant Angels compound was near Tuscarora, which was not far from Elko, Nevada. Emma had purchased her postcard from a service station that served as the Greyhound bus stop on Water Road. That much a Greyhound customer service rep had been able to find out for me.

"How does one get to Elko?" I asked the Greyhound rep on the phone. "Or Tuscarora?"

"Well, sir," the woman said. She told me her name was Claire. I never felt comfortable calling people I did not know by their first name. "I don't rightly know. I am answering your call in Toledo, even though I'm not supposed to tell you that."

"You don't sound like you're from Ohio," I said.

"No sir," she told me. "I'm from a little old town in the Texas Panhandle you probably never even heard of. Is there anything else I can do for you?"

Rescue me from my pathetic life, I wanted to tell her. Instead, I said no thank you and hung up.

By car it was another hour from Elko to Tuscarora. Did Emma hitchhike? I had always been the jealous type. After I got the postcard I imagined all manner of improprieties going on between my wife and whatever driver who picked her up. What was that old bumper sticker? Gas, grass, or ass. No free rides. It never occurred to me that Emma might have a phone number for the compound.

Emma had taken half our savings, $28,520, from a joint savings account where we had deposited money for over a decade. Our goal, when we reached retirement age, was to put that savings toward a small bungalow in a shore town, either Delaware or farther south.

Since Emma blew into Elko with over twenty grand, I had no doubts that the Initiate Supreme would send one of his flunkies to pick up my wife before she got cold feet wandering around a place she didn't know with a knapsack filled with cash.

With the exception of Max Kunstler and Yodel Taylor, I had not discussed my predicament concerning my wife with any of the guys from my unit. If I wanted everyone to know, all I had to do was bring Yodel up to speed. He would take care of the rest. I didn't, though, tell Yodel any more information, I mean, even when he asked, mostly because he would see it as a defect in me that I had lost Emma.

It bothered me when men spoke that way about another man's wife. I was not perfect, not by any stretch of the imagination, but I possessed empathy enough to know that talking about another man's spouse as if she were a set of Michelin tires or a DeWalt table saw was never a good thing. The world was changing. Guys like Yodel never got the memo. Yet, the army, in all of its foolish wisdom, decided, for reasons known only to those entities charged with decision-making, to let such a man represent planet Earth in a visit to a parallel world. Maybe that was the punchline in all this madness. The army knew what kind of man Yodel turned out to be. Despite obvious evidence, they were perfectly willing to let Yodel be his old nitwit self. It wouldn't take much, for an uncouth redneck like him hiding behind Jesus, to offend our humanoid neighbors in the universe next door and spark an interplanetary war.

Chapter 16: The Deer Clan

The bus pulled into a parking lot at the Pueblo of Zuni Tribal Government building. Sergeant Romero told us to off-load the bus but stick close. There was nowhere to go unless you needed stamps from the post office or felt the urgent need to wander into the desert.

Captain Prescott was the first one off the bus. As he headed for the entrance to the government building, Sergeant Romero caught up to him and gestured back at the bus.

"What the hell's that all about?" Kunstler asked.

"Maybe someone will realize he's fake," Fly said.

Kunstler knew the story of the captain being a synth. I wasn't sure if he believed that Fly had shot the android, but it wasn't my job to convince him. Let him think whatever he wanted about that.

Captain Prescott came back to the bus as some of us stood around with no shade to be found anywhere. He went back onto the bus and waited in the coolness inside.

Five minutes later or so Sergeant Romero came jogging back to the bus. He looked agitated.

"Everyone back on the bus, please," he bellowed.

We followed his orders. I was only too happy to give up the sunlight and get back into the air-conditioned bus.

It turned out we had to wait for a guide. Our destination, the Dowa Yalanne, a steep mesa visible from the Zuni Pueblo, was a sacred place of the Zuni. It is where ancestors of the present-day Zuni retreated when attacked by the Coronado Expedition. Dowa Yalanne is also associated with the "House of the Gods", and it is sometimes known as Thunder Mountain since Zuni myths say rain, lightning, and thunder are made there.

Fifteen minutes later, a short lanky old man with a slight stoop stood in the sunlight outside the bus. One moment he wasn't there, and the next he stood like he'd been there for centuries. The old man wore a light tan kilt and leggings with moccasins and a cream-colored shirt with a yellow sash around his narrow waist. On his head he wore a tan and black cloth headband.

"Sergeant," Captain Prescott said. "Go see if that's our man."

Romero left his seat and went outside. He spoke to the old man for a moment before escorting him onto the bus.

"This is our guide, Eddie Lonan of the Deer Clan," Sergeant Romero announced. "He's a priest. Please remember to show some respect for the customs and beliefs of our hosts."

Yodel mumbled something about Jesus. Hick Haywood punched him in the arm.

"Shut the fuck up, you ignorant son of a bitch," said Hick. "We on injun territory now."

"Knock that shit off, Mr. Haywood," said Sergeant Romero.

"Me?" Hick cried. He pointed at Yodel. "It was him."

"Just keep your mouth shut," he said.

Eddie kneeled in his seat to face Yodel and Hick. He raised a weathered hand as he said something in Zuni. Then he turned and sat down. He raised his hand once more and waved in a forward motion.

"Move on, driver," Sergeant Romero said.

The bus lurched forward. We left the parking lot and were on our way once more.

Captain Prescott shot out his hand across the aisle to shake the old man's. The priest ignored him, focusing on the road as the bus headed east.

The buses stopped along a dirt road half a klick from Dowa Yalanne. It was hot and we had to hump the short distance until we reached the shade at the base of the mesa.

Eddie Lonan looked particularly upset over the deuce-and-a-half that drove off the road and over the terrain until it reached the mesa base. His agitation worsened when Captain Prescott addressed him. The captain wanted to know if the entrance beneath the mesa was still secure.

"Sure," Eddie said.

He averted the captain's gaze a moment. Then, to everyone's surprise, the old guide took the captain's head in his hands and peered into his eyes. He muttered something and let go of Captain Prescott.

Eddie gave us a brief introduction to the Dowa Yalanne after that. Yalanne was the Zuni word for mesa or mountain, dowa meant corn. Eddie said that the Zuni identified their dead with clouds. It was not uncommon, he informed us, for a mother to tell her children that the "grandmothers" were coming if she spotted clouds in the sky.

"We will walk now," Eddie announced, "and ask the gods to reveal the kiva you need."

"What's a kiva?" Fly asked Sergeant Romero.

"A subterranean room used for worship on the mesa," he replied. "Usually, you get to them from the top."

Eddie the guide explained that we needed to trek counterclockwise around the base of the mesa. By then we had already offloaded our gear from the deuce-and-a-half truck that had followed the bus from Kirtland Air Force Base.

"Be careful of rattlesnakes," Eddie warned. "And the ghosts of Spanish conquistadors."

"Did he say snakes?" Plush Prince called out. "Man, I can't deal with no snakes."

"How do you think I feel?" Yodel said. "I think the old shaman put a curse on me."

"Thoughts and prayers, Yodel," said Fly.

"Y'all can go to hell," he replied.

"I just can't deal with no snakes, man," Plush Prince said.

"Oh my Lord," Yodel cried out. "Don't you ever shut up?"

"Look who's talking?" he countered.

"Plush Prince got you there, Yodel," said Fly.

"He does," I agreed.

"Fuck you guys," Yodel said.

"Hey," Sergeant Romero said as he walked at the rear of the formation. "At ease that shit. This is holy ground. You wouldn't show that kind of disrespect in a church. Don't do it here."

Walking around the perimeter of Dowa Yalanne was no easy feat. It was almost evening when Eddie told us to stop. He pointed to the line in the red-colored Entrada Sandstone, indicating a natural egress. The elevation of the mesa was over seven thousand feet. The place where Eddie pointed was a few hundred feet off the desert floor.

"Still glad you came?" Max Kunstler asked me when we were better than halfway up.

I did not see any conquistador ghosts or snakes. Nor did I glimpse any of the Zuni ancient ones that Eddie said liked to lurk around twilight. From where I stood, The Radiant Angels of Zaphkar compound was fourteen hours away. The quickest route, I had discovered, was through Utah. I filed that information away, hoping that upon my return I could go straight from Kirtland Air Force Base after my discharge to find Emma.

All thirty-three of us entered a large cave opening. Captain Prescott led the way and Sergeant Romero along with Specialist Broward took the rear. At some point during our final ascent, Eddie Lonan vanished in much the same way he had first mysteriously appeared.

The antechamber measured one hundred feet in diameter. It had a natural vaulted ceiling some sixty feet over our heads, the furthest reaches of it visible only by flashlight. The chamber walls had been painted over in turquoise colors with animals like birds and deer rendered in bright yellows and reds.

The main attraction was located toward the rear of the chamber. The Frulx gateway looked like it had been there for thousands of years. It was egg-shaped, a dark metal monstrosity that measured forty feet at its widest section. The machine had long ago fused with the cave floor and the chamber wall behind it.

Prior to our departure from Kirtland Air Force Base, our cell phones had been returned to us. I wanted to take a few photographs of the gateway, but that wasn't meant to be. They had kept our phones locked up for weeks. When they did give them back all of our original contacts, messages, photos, and the like were still on them, but the carrier had been changed to one created by Pulsargenix, one of the big defense companies. Pulsargenix's motto was "Designing strength and dominance for tomorrow today." The company logo was about as subtle as its motto. It depicted ICBMs on a parabolic arc above an ocean in a starry sky headed for what looked a lot like the continent of Asia. When I pulled out my cell phone, I discovered that all the functions had been disabled by Pulsargenix.

"I'm collecting cell phones," Sergeant Romero announced. "Specialist Broward will assist me."

Broward was used to the drill. He and Sergeant Romero produced what looked like cooler bags and started going from man to man to rid them of their phones.

"This is bullshit," Yodel proclaimed. "I'm a citizen. I have rights."

"You're a second-class citizen now, Taylor," Sergeant Romero reminded him. "It comes with the uniform."

"No cell phones are permitted to pass through the Frulx gateway," said Captain Prescott.

"What are we?" Hick Haywood asked. "Terminators now? Only living tissue gets through?"

"We could bring Abrams tanks if we wanted," the captain said. "Cell phones are prohibited in the other dimension as a matter of regulation."

"What if E.T. wants to phone home?" Fly asked.

"There's no cell phone reception in the next world," the synth said, missing Fly's joke.

"Uh, sir," Yodel spoke up now. "How do you send intel back here? We didn't even pack radios. How are we supposed to communicate with one another? How are we going to send a message back if we need help."

God bless Yodel and his ignorant ways. He didn't know that he was addressing an android: a walking, talking, sound and image recording unit designed for such work. Even if we didn't make it, Captain Prescott would get back to Earth and some egghead in an intelligence unit would download everything the synth had. It would not surprise me if they gave us back our phones on the other side so they could all link up to Prescott who would serve as one large recording databank.

Prescott, meanwhile, perhaps in an attempt to deflect attention away from his surveillance capabilities, launched an eloquent soliloquy concerning how information was transmitted in the old days before cell phones and computers. Telephones, as it turned out, were never secure, not even the Pulsargenix's closed loop network they had loaded onto our cell phones. Everything in our world could be hacked, the captain informed us. Intelligence gatherers in the past relied on dead drops and other forms to pass along vital information.

"You will gather intelligence the old-fashioned way," said Captain Prescott. "Upon your return, you will be debriefed."

"Aw, man," Yodel cried, "you mean I got to write shit down? What am I? Back in school?"

Sergeant Romero got in his face and quieted him down. I was hoping for another display of his efficient martial prowess, but Romero restrained himself.

"Sergeant," said Captain Prescott. "If you please."

Romero stepped on a metal pad about the size of the standard home plate in baseball. The Frulx gateway came to life. Pale blue lights around the face of the egg-shaped gateway lit up and then alternated flashing in a counterclockwise direction. What looked like steam jets shot out from the gateway's innermost side. Behind the gateway the chamber wall vanished, replaced by a fog that swirled clockwise like a slow-motion whirlpool.

"Motion sensor activated?" I asked Sergeant Romero.

"You catch on quick," he said. "The plate is like a start button."

"How come no one is guarding this? Can't anyone use this thing?"

"The real question is why would they want to," Sergeant Romero said over the low hum of the machine. "Interdimensional travel sucks big-time."

Captain Prescott was the first one to ruck up and move out. He gave us a classic *Follow me; I am the infantry* wave. Then he stepped into the spinning fog and faded from view.

PART II

You seldom see animals enjoying themselves in front of the slaughterhouse...

~Louis-Ferdinand Celine, *North*

Chapter 17: The Trip Flare's Red Glare

Overzealous, self-proclaimed patriots always shit their pants at the first hint of any real trouble. It happened to Yodel not long after we came through the fog on the other side. In his defense, he encountered an outlier about which no one had warned us.

Though the fog was thick you could still see the man in front of you and the man behind you if you kept less than five meters apart. Any farther away than that they became faint shadows.

The walk through the gateway didn't take long at all, less than a minute before definitive shapes of the Veknyrian alien landscape began to take hold.

Before reaching the other side, Yodel talked non-stopped about how he wasn't scared. He even went so far as to invoke the "ain't nothing but a thing" mantra. It was a phrase used in the army that began back in the 1960's. By the time of our initial enlistment a little over a decade after the Fall of Saigon, NCOs who saw action in-country were still using the phrase. Naturally, we adopted it.

We ended up inside a chamber similar to the one we left, only the walls and the ceiling were not painted. It was there that Sergeant Romero and Specialist Broward returned our cell phones.

"Keep them in your rucksacks," Sergeant Romero said.

The charging icon was on when he handed mine back, but the phone wasn't plugged into anything.

"Hey, sergeant," I started to say.

He nodded at Captain Prescott, indicating that the android was responsible for wirelessly charging our phones.

Once we reached terra firma outside the cave, it became apparent why our uniforms were colored varying shades of red, pink, white, and black. The rocky terrain in which we found ourselves appeared, at first glance, as pixelated as our uniforms.

"Hey,   Paladin,"   said   Yodel,   "you   look   like—YEEEOOOWWW!"

A winged creature as tall as a man swooped down, hooked his talon-tipped short arms beneath Yodel's, and hoisted him nearly twenty feet into the air.

The creature executed several loops as it held onto its prey. At some point during those loops, Yodel's intestines did a number on him. He soiled his pants. On its last downward arc, the monster used the force of its momentum to dash Yodel against the black-veined red rocks to our right. If Yodel was any more than fifteen feet in the air by that point, he may have experienced serious injury. The creature's intention, as Captain Prescott explained later, was to dash Yodel against the rocks, cracking his head open, and feast on his brains, for starters. Fortunately for Yodel, he was too big a prize for the monster.

"It would luh-likely starve and cuh-come buh-back for another of us," said Hick.

"Hey, fuck you Haywood," Yodel said, wincing as he worked his way out of his shit-stained pants.

"I'm just messing with you."

"You're lucky you weren't killed," Plush Prince chimed in. "Hey, Sergeant Romero, let's go back, man. I don't want no damned dinosaurs fucking with me."

"They're not dinosaurs," Captain Prescott said. "They're called parupanoon. And they're harmless."

"What?" Yodel cried. "That thing liked to kill me. Who's got toilet paper?"

"We're the invasive species," he countered. "It was just protecting its territory."

Jody Pickett, meanwhile, unslung his rucksack, opened the flap, retrieved a roll of toilet paper, and tossed it to Yodel.

"What the captain means is we're on his hunting grounds," Sergeant Romero said.

"Hey, sir," Fly Kidd said to Captain Prescott. "How did humans find out about this place?"

"Frulx gateways brought the first visitors to the New Mexico desert right after World War II," the captain revealed.

"You mean like Roswell?"

"No. That was something else," he said. "The visitors came through places like Nellis Air Force Base near Las Vegas and out at White Sands. In those days, there were mutual accords. The short answer to your query, Mr. Kidd, is that yes humans have been visited and technology and medicine was shared. From the 1970's on, however, relationships of that kind have become, shall we say, strained."

"Why is that, sir?" Jody asked.

"We have to keep moving," the captain announced. "Sergeant Romero, if you please."

"All right, gentlemen," the sergeant said. "You heard the captain. Let's move out."

"Hold up," Yodel pleaded. "I got to tie my boots."

"Well, hurry up."

"Hey, sergeant. What do I do with my soiled pants? Bury them?"

"No, Mr. Taylor," said Sergeant Romero. "You carry that refuse with you. We don't litter other planets."

Yodel stowed his dirty pants in a small plastic trash bag[4] and put it inside his rucksack.

---

[4] At Kirtland Air Force Base, each of us was issued these trash bags. The military had always been big on policing up after itself during field exercises. At Fort Campbell, everything we took out to the field during combat exercises was brought back to the rear, that included empty MRE bags and other assorted garbage. Sometimes we left trash bags on the sides of fire roads for pick-up. Other times we were tasked with hauling the garbage in ourselves on the backs of deuce-and-a-half trucks. Once in the rear, those trash bags filled with refuse were deposited in a dumpster behind the chow hall to the chagrin of mess hall personnel who took as an affront our dumping MRE wrappers in their dumpster (it is a testament to modern miracles in general that the army cooks charged with feeding us seven days a week just didn't poison us for the way we abused their sorry little dumpster). When it came to war, however, ecological conservation was a different story. Over a twenty-hour period during Operation

For the next few clicks, parupanoon circled several hundred feet above our heads. Six of them in all followed us. At times, I lost them in the sun's glare. Even with the military-issue wrap-around sunglasses they gave us, the light was brighter than anything I'd known on Earth.

To the east, Hiriruta, the Withering Sister, crested the horizon. Despite Captain Prescott's insistence that we keep moving, everyone quit marching to watch Veknyria's second moon Destrayama rise slowly from behind Hiriruta. Even the parupanoon appeared to be entranced as they quit flying in circles over us and darted off to the west.

We reached the top of a low mesa after the sun had already begun to set. The two moons appeared even more pronounced as they rose. From atop the mesa, it looked as if we were in the middle of nowhere. The climate was arid, but not excessively hot.

Colonel Lester was not joking when he spoke about the gravity on Veknyria and how it would seem like an intense workout. The only one who wasn't exhausted was Captain Prescott. That came as no surprise, given that he was a machine.

Sergeant Romero broke open a crate of trip flares he'd been hauling in his rucksack all day. It astonished me just how much he and Specialist Broward were able to hump in the new, stronger gravity, but they were Special Forces, after all, to say nothing of being younger than me, and used to carrying everything they needed.

"Mr. Paladin," Sergeant Romero said, "you remember how to set these?"

Frequent Wind, the final phase of the evacuation of Saigon, whole helicopters belonging to the Republic of Vietnam Air Force were dumped into the South China Sea to make room on U.S. carriers for other incoming aircraft. It was, after all, a one-way ride for South Vietnamese helicopter pilots and their passengers that day. With the People's Army of North Vietnam set to take Saigon, who could blame them? That day up to $10,000,000 worth of rotorcraft were relinquished to an underwater scrapyard. As an unwritten rule during wartime, environmental concerns were never high on the U.S. Military's list.

"Not really," I said. "It's been thirty—"

"Fine, fine," he said. "Pay attention. I'm only going to give this refresher course once."

"Should I write this down?"

"Don't be an egghead," he said. "This is your basic M49A1 Surface Trip Flare. She's an oldie, but a goodie. Here is your mounting bracket assembly with pre-drilled mounting holes—that's where you will secure it to a tree—"

"There are no trees on this mesa, sergeant," I told him.

"Get creative," he replied. "Use rocks."

He proceeded to show me how to secure the trip flare to rocks piled on one another using tripwire threaded through the flare's mounting bracket assembly.

"When you go," he said, "bring extra trip wire." He broke out a terrain map of the area. "This is us here. I need you to go down to the far end of the mesa here just before the incline that leads down to the desert floor.

"Set up a few of these trip flares from one edge of the mesa to the other," he went on. "Thread the trip wire through the trigger. Then make sure you twist it good like a bread tie, so it doesn't get knocked loose without triggering the flare. Now, you'll have to use other rocks to tie off the other end of the trip wire like I showed you."

"I got it," I told him.

"Pick one of your cohorts to go with you," said Sergeant Romero. "If you see anyone or anything on two legs headed up the trail toward us send that cohort back to me."

"What am I supposed to do?" I asked.

"Don't get captured," he said.

"I thought we're observers," I reminded him.

"Sure, sure," he said. "The climate has changed since my last trip. Anyway, take a half-dozen flares and go do your thing. Broward's got some stakes if you need them for the trip wire, but you'll have to camouflage them with scrub brush or whatever you can find."

We were in a desert that looked alarmingly like how I remembered the Mojave Desert from my prior enlistment all those years ago. The colors were all wrong, of course. And the two moons definitely told me that I wasn't in California, much less still on planet Earth.

When I asked Max Kunstler to accompany me he was lying on his back using his rucksack as a pillow. He had a beat-up paperback copy of Robert Heinlein's *Job: A Comedy of Justice* in one hand reading it while he absentmindedly twirled what looked like a root or a thin twig in his other hand.

"Didn't we read that book a hundred years ago during our first enlistment?" I asked him.

"Sure did," said Max. "This is your copy, by the way."

"No it isn't," I said.

"It most certainly is," he said. "It even has your name in it."

"I never wrote my name in any of my books," I told him.

"Damn," he said, "I almost had you."

"You had nothing," I told him. "Sergeant Romero wants me to set up some trip flares. I guess it's his idea of a perimeter defense."

"Great," Max said. "Since we have no weapons we will get to see our killers by the flare light."

It took Max and I no time at all to set up the flares where Sergeant Romero wanted them. By the time we returned to camp it was already getting dark.

Except for Captain Prescott, Sergeant Romero, and Specialist Broward, none of us were prepared for the alien constellations that revealed themselves as night came on. It was like watching a freeze frame of the greatest fireworks display I'd ever seen. No one bothered to tell us before departing that in addition to Veknyrian sun's intensity the stars and visible distant nebulae were so bright there was little chance of falling asleep, not without a blindfold or a shirt over one's face.

At first, there was a collective exclamation of sorts as we all stared in wonder. Then, the soft murmurs of wonder and awe wore away until each of us was left in his private and silent reverie.

I thought about Emma, about how long it had been since she walked out, and about how nothing in the Nevada night sky could come close to what I witnessed my first night on Veknyria.

Over the years, I spent my spare time writing stories and a few novels that never saw print. Actually, I had lost the will to send out any work once Emma left me. It was impossible to put into words the alien starry canopy that appeared close enough to reach up and scoop a handful of stars out of the night sky.

A watch roster was established. After that, Specialist Broward broke open the MREs and distributed them.

"No fires," he warned us.

I had not eaten a ready-to-eat meal, or a meal comma ready to eat, as the military catalogued them, in over three decades. I had almost forgotten just how lousy they were.

"Hey, Sergeant Romero," Yodel called out.

"What is it, Mr. Taylor?" the sergeant replied.

"That thing that scooped me up earlier," he said. "They don't come out at night, do they?"

"Negative," Sergeant Romero assured him. "They are strictly day hunters."

"That's good," he said.

"It's the *Gonggong* you got to watch out for at night," the sergeant announced.

"What the hell's a Guh-Gonggong?" Hick Haywood spoke up now.

"The Veknyrian name for them is *trallaspoolah*," Sergeant Romero said. "It resembles the Gonggong from Chinese mythology with its copper-colored head, its humanoid torso, and its serpent tail that measures seven to ten feet in length, both of which are colored vermillion. They have venomous spit and fangs that are two or three inches in length."

"For real?" Fly asked.

"Sure, sure," he replied.

"Man," Plush Prince cried out, "that sounds like the devil to me. I got to get the fuck out of this place."

"Relax, Mr. Jones," Sergeant Romero said. "They are not carnivorous, if that's what you are worried about."

"I'm worried about getting poisoned!"

"Don't go wandering into any caves at night," he warned, "and you will be fine."

"Got no guns or nothing," Plush Prince mumbled. "They always fucking with me."

"You gentlemen know the watch schedule," the sergeant said. "Specialist Broward will be around to let you know tonight's password."

As luck might have it, I was on first watch. Broward walked up and took a squat beside me.

"Pretty awesome, right?" he asked.

"I'm at a loss for words," I told him. That was the truth.

"Anyway, the challenge tonight is *ibid*," he said. "The password is *shoelace*. You got it?"

"Ibid shoelace," I told him. "I got it."

"Good," said Broward. "Captain Prescott is still out there. When he gets back he might have company."

"Who?"

"With him? There's no telling."

"What about the trip flares?"

"Oh," Broward said as he stood up, "Captain Prescott prefers to stay off the beaten path."

"How does an android do that?" I asked.

"They programmed him to make his own choices," he said.

"On everything?"

"Scary shit, isn't it?" he replied. Then, rather ominously he added, "Sleep tight."

A cloud cover moved in during my watch, turning the mesa dark. After my watch ended, I fell asleep. I remember thinking that I could smell cinnamon in the air.

The shouts of my cohorts woke me up a few hours later as one trip flare went off, followed by another and another. I was able to sit up just in time to see something zip past me, headed in the direction of the approach where I had strung the trip flares.

"Who was that?" I asked Sergeant Romero as he stood nearby.

"It was the captain," he said. "No one else moves that fast, not on this planet."

"What tripped the flares?"

"Veknyrian probe," he replied. "That's my guess."

I heard Yodel snicker from somewhere behind me.

"Something funny?" Sergeant Romero asked.

"Veknyrian probe," said Yodel. "It's funny because it's like 'alien probe.' You know, like when people get abducted, and the little grays poke and prod them."

"This is Veknyria," the sergeant reminded him. "We're the aliens here, you imbecile."

The red glow from the trip flares began to fade. The silhouette of Captain Prescott became visible now at the edge of the mesa. He stood there looking down as he searched for whomever was responsible for breaching our camp. The trip flares went out. I lost sight of the captain as the mesa went dark once more.

"Sergeant Romero," I said.

"Yes, Mr. Paladin?"

"You mentioned the Veknyrian god Zaphkar," I said.

"What about it?" he asked.

"Did you know there's a cult back on Earth," I said, "that call themselves The Radiant Angels of Zaphkar?"

"No, why?"

"The founder, a guy named Bertrand Bauerfang," I told him, "allegedly channeled messages from an entity he claimed was an angel named Zaphkar."

"What a coincidence," Sergeant Romero remarked.

"You don't think that's strange?"

"Mr. Paladin, what are you getting at?"

"What if Bauerfang is getting messages from here?" I asked. "Telepathically, I mean, between universes."

"All the data we have so far," the sergeant said, "supports that each universe connected by Frulx gateways are closed systems. Barring, of course, the gateways themselves."

"How many gateways are there?"

"Nothing gets in or out, if that's what you're wondering," he said. Then, he asked, "What was this cult leader's name?"

"Bauerfang," I said.

"You should tell this to the captain," he said.

"Do you think there's a connection?"

Sergeant Romero laughed. "I don't get paid to think," he said. "That's why we have officers."

Chapter 18: Max Kunstler Loses His Head

A day later we reached the outskirts of Riengmarnoon, a Veknyrian city built on the overlapping branches, some as wide as the Lincoln Tunnel, from twin colossal trees. From a distance, the giant branches looked as if they were packed with wasp nests the size of small buildings.

Colonel Lester explained in his briefing before our departure from Earth that the Veknyrians living in Riengmarnoon were able to manipulate the tree bark so that it became the exterior of living and commercial spaces. Interiors were built from materials often used by civilizations like ancient Rome, Turkey, and elsewhere that included mud bricks, plaster, and windows constructed from flat cylindrical opaque glass set in wood framework.

The first Veknyrian I saw was a lone one walking along the outside of a makeshift corral fence where the desert abruptly ended, giving way to sparse vegetation. He stood close to ten feet tall, and his massive shoulders were a good four feet apart. His upper arms were as thick as metal trash cans and his massive head seemed to grow straight out of his shoulders. He placed a weapon resembling a long-barreled rifle against a fence post, walked about fifteen feet from the weapon, and unfastened his pants before he squatted. The Veknyrian held one of his massive hands between his legs. He used his other hand to brace himself against the fence post next to him. His oblong eyes took up a good portion of his face. He appeared to be fixated on a spot on the ground just ahead of him.

I handed the binoculars back to Sergeant Romero who passed them to Fly to get a look.

Fly studied the scene a moment. He handed the field glasses back to the sergeant.

"Hey, yo," said Fly. "I am not going near that thing. He's built like The Incredible Hulk."

"He's female," Broward observed. Then, maybe for Yodel's benefit since he was always slow on the draw. "Not he, she."

"For real?" Fly said.

Max signaled Sergeant Romero. The sergeant handed him the binoculars next.

"Is he..." Max started to say as he looked through the binoculars.

"Having a private moment," Broward said.

"Right," said Max as he handed Broward the binoculars.

"She's relieving herself right there in the open like that?" Yodel cried. "Like a savage? These people need Jesus—"

"Shut up, Yodel," said Sergeant Romero. He signaled to Fly, Max, and me. "Let's move out."

Earlier that morning I got a chance to tell Captain Prescott all about The Radiant Angels of Zaphkar. I lied and told him that cults were a hobby of mine. Not belonging to them, I told him. I just wanted to know how they operated, how they lured people into their clutches, and how people managed to escape them without outside assistance like we heard about from time to time in the news.

I didn't bother to tell the captain about my wife Emma. I figured he knew all about my background already. If he didn't then someone farther up the pay scale certainly knew my life story thus far.

"And you're saying that this guy Bauerfang communicates telepathically with this entity?" Captain Prescott asked.

"That's the claim," I said.

"Interesting," came his reply.

We didn't speak of it again[5].

---

[5] Confession time: My hope had been that the android Captain Prescott would take my intel on The Radiant Angels of Zaphkar seriously enough for it to warrant further investigation. Here I was fifty-four years old and suddenly stricken with visions of my planet-hopping unit returning to

Fly, Max, and I separated from Sergeant Romero as we reached the bottom of the pass that led down from the cliff overlooking the plain. From there, we had a hundred yards or so between us and the Veknyrian woman relieving herself by the fence post.

The plan, though in hindsight rather idiotic, had been a simple one[6]. Unarmed, Fly, Max, and I would distract the woman giant while Sergeant Romero "rendered" himself invisible and stole her rifle.

"What about the treaty?" I asked.

"That doesn't say anything about stealing their weapons," Sergeant Romero replied. "Just let me concentrate now, so she can't see me."

As we closed the gap, Sergeant Romero went off to our left in an attempt to get to the rifle before the Veknyrian knew what was happening. The Veknyrian woman lost her balance and fell onto her back, her one hand rubbing herself. She wasn't peeing at all.

Earth and making a raid on the Radiant Angels compound, a walking wet dream of rescuing a wife with whom I had not communicated with in nearly a decade. Once they get their claws into you and fill you with fantasies of false bravado and heroism, whether it's in a movie like *The Green Berets* with John Wayne, a television show like *The A-Team,* or even television commercials in which heavily camouflaged soldiers appear out of damp, dense vegetation like well-armed ghosts spreading the gospel of democracy, you never quite get over it. Some small part of me still needed to grow up or, at the very least, go back into therapy.

[6] Sergeant Romero came from the new-jack mind-fuck school of Special Operations, the one that subscribed to esoteric nonsense from psychic warfare to meditation techniques for increased invisibility. As a special operator, he had been trained to go into a hot zone barehanded and find whatever weapons he could, if it came to that. On the way down to the mesa, Sergeant Romero gave Fly, Max, and me a crash course on the merits of invisibility on the battlefield. The gist was this: if you could project invisibility at your enemy, you would, for all intents and purposes, be rendered invisible in their eyes. In theory, say for a comic book character, it was good stuff. In reality, projecting invisibility was pure Big 80's ninja movie bullshit. Evidence of my critique, reader, played itself out soon enough, despite whatever Green Beret confidence Sergeant Romero mustered.

"What do we do?" Max asked.

"Make some noise!" Fly shouted.

The Veknyrian woman sat up. She arched her back and pulled up her pants. Meanwhile, Sergeant Romero looked like he was running in slow motion, owing to the planet's gravity. The Veknyrian rolled once, twice, three times to her right and was on her feet. In no time flat she picked up her rifle and pointed it at Fly, Max, and me.

Fly and I dove to the ground.

Max, who was a full head and shoulders taller than us, was slow to react. Too slow, in fact. He wore a sly grin, as if he couldn't believe that an inhabitant of another world was going to shoot at him.

The report of the rifle shot sounded. A single one. Somewhere Sergeant Romero was shouting in a language I did not recognize.

Max's knees hit the ground just when the rifle's round struck his face. His upper body snapped back a moment before his muscles contracted and he lurched forward, coming to rest chest down in the dirt. Everything above Max's lower jaw had disintegrated when the bullet struck him. His blood blended with the vermillion-colored dirt.

Sergeant Romero reached the Veknyrian just as she spun to point her rifle at him. He knocked the barrel aside as he drew a long knife from a sheath and drove the blade tip into the Veknyrian's big left eye.

Another round fired from the rifle. Sergeant Romero withdrew his knife and plunged the blade again and again into the Veknyrian's neck until she dropped to her knees.

"Come on," Fly said as he hit me on the shoulder. "Let's go!"

The Veknyrian fell forward on top of Sergeant Romero. She was still alive, despite her dark purple blood gushing from the wounds in her neck and the one in her left eye. She listlessly tossed the rifle aside and commenced pummeling Sergeant Romero with fists as big as bread boxes. The first blow cracked the sergeant's head open like an egg. The woman pulverized his chest and face for another few seconds before stopping. She straightened up, looked at Fly and me as we stood several yards away, and slowly rose to her feet. She took a hesitant step or two in our direction and collapsed.

A hand clamped down on my shoulder from behind, startling me.

"Christ," I shouted.

It was Broward. "Follow me," he said.

He didn't have to say it a second time.

The whole plan had gone to hell. We were one hundred yards or more from the dead Veknyrian when Broward stopped.

"You didn't grab the rifle?" he asked.

Fly and I looked at each other.

"You never said anything about it," Fly told him.

"What about Max?" I asked.

"Who?" Broward said.

"Kunstler," I replied. "And Sergeant Romero."

"They're dead," Broward said.

"What happened to not leaving a man behind and all that?"

"Don't start getting all righteous with me, Paladin," Broward said. He went on to catalogue all the campaigns he'd taken a part in back on Earth—Afghanistan, Iraq, and a few that never made the news. "Now, let's keep moving."

We made it back to the mesa where Captain Prescott waited patiently for us.

"What happened?" the captain said.

"Well, sir," Broward began.

"You weren't there," he said. "I want to hear it from these two."

Fly broke it down for Captain Prescott. The absurdity of Sergeant Romero's plan notwithstanding, I interjected in agreement with Fly when necessary.

"This is bad," Captain Prescott said.

"You think so?" Fly went off now. "That crazy bastard nearly got us all killed."

"Did we at least hide the bodies?" he cut him off.

Broward toed the dirt and then looked up at the sky as if interested in something overhead.

"Do you two have any idea of how bad a situation we're in?" asked Captain Prescott.

"Is that a rhetorical question or..." I started to say.

"Sir, look!" Broward pointed to the plain below.

A small contingent of Veknyrians, perhaps thirty or so on foot and another fifteen spread out between what I took to be two flatbed vehicles.

"They are early," Captain Prescott said.

It fell on Broward to gather us all and follow the captain down the pass to the plain below. When we got there I realized what I took for flatbed vehicles were giant creatures with round flat hard shell backs and six legs like a spider's. Their heads were t-shaped with no discernible ears, eyes, or nostrils.

All but one of the Veknyrians were armed with rifles similar to the one which the woman had fired at us. The head honcho among them carried no weapon at all. He stood atop the back of one of the creatures, towering over us as he addressed Captain Prescott in his native tongue.

As the captain and the Veknyrian in charge discussed what had transpired, the honcho's escorts eyed us closely. No one bothered to point a rifle at us. We were unarmed. Or so I thought.

Chapter 19: Loveless Mothers of Plumbers

Emma used to accuse me of going *ballistic* whenever I lost my cool during an argument. Looking back, I know I was a textbook case of passive-aggressive abusive behavior. Emma used to tell me that I scared her. She said she wasn't sure what I was capable of. She feared that one day I might snap, to use her parlance. In truth, she watched too many true-crime shows. Every disagreement between us she viewed as a prelude to murder.

Back then, and this is no excuse, I had issues. Mostly, I thought I should be somewhere in my life, that I should have achieved a certain station by a certain age, but I had not. When I was twenty-five years old, I wanted to write The Great American Novel. What recent college graduate with literary dreams didn't, right? In my late thirties, I accepted the fact that it probably wasn't going to happen. Then I set my mind to writing screenplays on spec, hoping that just one of them would open a door for me, I never sold a single one. I kept at it with fiction too, novels and short stories. My luck with those works proved somewhat better. I managed to sell a few stories over the years, but that was it. I was angry about that. I was angry about everything in my life. Emma caught the brunt of that anger simply because she was there.

The irony in this little confession is that the day she left me I quit writing. Nothing interested me anymore. Subconsciously, and this I worked out with a therapist, I chose to abandon writing with the slim hope that Emma would return and that without having anything else to write or fret over our lives would improve tenfold.

"That's the stupidest fucking thing I ever heard," my therapist Dr. Kyle Strauss told me.

His methods were unorthodox, to say the least. It was not uncommon for me to go to my weekly appointment and witness a patient leave his office in tears.

People go through a lot in life. Who was I to judge? I didn't need to. I had Dr. Strauss for that, like the time a young woman named Emily who was always scheduled before me exited Dr. Strauss's office balling like a child who had just fallen off her bike. When she ran out of the waiting area she nearly knocked me down in the process.

"Holy Moses," Dr Strauss muttered as I approached him. "You'd think she never heard the word 'no' before."

That day I spoke to Dr. Strauss about the word *ballistic*. We talked at length about what I experienced leading up to the outbursts that had pushed my wife to leave me and go to her parents' place. She stayed there three days. Then she withdrew half our savings while I was at work and lit out for Nevada.

"That's a whole different animal," the good doctor said. "Emma's retreating to childhood and all that."

"I know—" I started to say when Dr. Strauss held up a cautionary hand.

"If we're to continue these sessions," he said, "there's something I need you to do."

"What's that?"

"Stop referring to Emma as your wife," he said.

"I still have hope," I told him.

"That's the second stupidest thing you've said to me," he announced. Then, before I could defend myself, he asked, "How long was she receiving literature from this outfit?"

Dr. Strauss refused to use the word "cult." I told him that there were short booklets and pamphlets mailed to Emma by my sister-in-law.

"There were also letters," I admitted. "From my sister-in-law Marianne."

"Did you read them?" the therapist asked.

"No," I lied.

Of course I had read them. That's how I found out that Emma and Marianne had slept together a few times. From the tone of Marianne's letters, she was still very much in love with Emma. She also missed my dead brother, her husband. I thought that was weird, but I guess it happened, the being in love with your in-law of the same sex while longing for your dead spouse. As for Emma's feelings, I knew nothing. Whatever correspondence she sent she kept from me.

After that session, I didn't go back. None of us were perfect. Dr. Strauss called me at all hours for nearly two months trying to coax me into returning for more sessions.

"I don't think I need to come back," I told him.

"In my professional opinion," said Dr. Strauss, "I think you do. Besides, I like talking to you. Most of my weeks are spent with young women like Emily with daddy issues, soccer moms who are repressed lesbians, and plumbers whose mothers never loved them. At least we talk about books."

I wanted to go ballistic when he said that, but I didn't. Instead, I performed a visualization exercise Dr. Strauss suggested which went like this: I imagine myself blown to bits in thousands of small pieces coming back together to form a whole me. Sort of an explosion played backward. Whenever I did the exercise I always felt foolish. Still, it seemed no stranger to me than saying the rosary or counting backward when I was trying to fall asleep. The goal was to create a better version of me. I don't know if it ever worked.

The negotiation between Captain Prescott and the Veknyrian bigshot continued, Broward broke down what was going on between them versus what the Veknyrians feared most.

"They could tear us apart whenever they want," I told him.

"The mahoff knows the captain's a bomb," said Broward.

"I'm sorry," I said, sure that my ears were not hearing him right. "Say that again."

"Built into each android like Captain Prescott," Broward said, "is a limited strike thermonuclear weapon. The Veknyrians aren't technologically advanced enough to comprehend the devastation such a weapon could cause. The captain told the mahoff that he is a destroyer of cities. That's all the chieftain needs to know."

"Who pulls the trigger?" I asked.

"Detonate?" Broward asked. "The captain, of course. The protocol was developed to destroy gateways if any alien civilization tried to invade Earth."

"Any alien civilization?"

"Shit yeah. You think the Veknyrians are the only ones we're visiting?"

I had so many questions. Unfortunately, talks broke down, judging by the body language of the honcho Veknyrian.

"I need a volunteer," the captain announced.

"Right here, sir," Yodel blurted out.

It had always been his downfall. When we were young guys during our first enlistment, Yodel would volunteer for things without comprehending any of the consequences for doing so.

"Excellent," Captain Prescott said.

He signaled to the Veknyrian in charge who in turn grunted something to his soldiers. Two of them stepped forward, grabbed Yodel, and stuffed him into a giant sack. When Yodel began to protest, the two Veknyrians produced short cudgels and beat the sack until Yodel quieted down.

"What's all that about?" I asked Broward.

"Insurance," he said.

That night I awoke from a dream in which I floated over the Nevada desert. The details were not clear, once I was fully awake, but what I remembered most was being nervous about something I towed behind me. In the dream, a great dark mass blocked out the stars. Low in the night sky of my dream a red glow showed. A voice shouted. When I woke up, all hell was breaking loose. More trip flares were going off.

Captain Prescott shouted orders, something to the tune of *stand down* and *remain calm*.

"Y'all can go ahead and kiss my country ass," Hick Haywood said, firing his semi-automatic pistol.

"Hick's got a gun?" Fly asked.

"He must have kept it stowed in his rucksack," Plush Prince said.

"No good will come of this," Jody Pickett called out.

A Veknyrian ran toward him, stopping long enough to kick him and send him ass over tea kettle down the side of the mesa, before continuing on to the mesa's far end to make sure no one escaped that way.

Meanwhile, on the mesa itself chaos reigned. Three Veknyrians approached Captain Prescott and deflected the android's blows as he attempted to protect himself. They pounced on him. I thought for sure that they would tear him to pieces or, worse, Captain Prescott would self-detonate and take us all with him in a nuclear blast. Instead, he fought his way to the far end of the mesa, determined to get past the Veknyrian who had kicked Jody over the side. The Veknyrian kicked Prescott in the chest which sent him staggering backward. The android looked like someone who just stepped on a patch of ice and was struggling to keep from falling down. Prescott failed to keep his balance. He went over the side of the mesa. That was the last I saw of him.

"Goddamn," Hick cried when a Veknyrian swatted the pistol from his hand and, judging by Hick's scream that followed, broke a few of Hick's fingers in the process.

"Run," Plush Prince advised.

Strong hands held me down. A sack was placed over my head. I thought of my medication, oddly enough, which had been issued to me before we left Kirtland Air Force Base. If I were going the way of Yodel Taylor, would they be humane enough to let me retrieve my meds from my rucksack? Did the Veknyrians even have medicine? I wondered. The answer came soon enough.

A stick smashed into my face before my assailant beat me on the head until I lost consciousness.

Chapter 20: No God But Zaphkar

Another dream: I tumbled out of a womb into the world.

Hitting the cold hard floor jarred me awake. My head hurt, as did my back and legs. When I tried to get to my feet I got struck by a cudgel brandished by a Veknyrian guard.

"Bow before King Vragordash," a deep and harsh voice sounded behind me.

My lower back cramped. I could hardly catch my breath. My impulse, even though my body would not allow it, was to rush the guard and hope he'd put a swift end to my life. The option left the table, so to speak, when the guard gripped my head and shoved me toward the floor.

King Vragordash looked older than any other Veknyrian I'd seen thus far. He wore no crown, and I wanted to kick myself for putting such earthly notions on him, but his garments were much more colorful than his subjects. He wore what looked like a red silk robe with a cobalt sash that went over his massive right shoulder and around his waist. He wore an apparatus around his neck that looked like a ribbed vest of some animal skin with tubes attached. One tube was fitted to an earpiece that hung on the left side of the king's head and another tube was attached to what looked like a scuba regulator which sat an inch from his face.

When the king spoke into his apparatus a loudspeaker somewhere overhead translated his words into English. It was a peculiar accent, the English used in translation. If I didn't know any better I'd have bet on Philadelphia, maybe Boston.

"What manner of human are you?" the king demanded. Like the others, his large head seemed fused to his shoulders and chest.

"An ordinary one?" I asked.

The king pressed his giant fingers against the earphone over his ear.

"What about the one you call Yoh-delle," he asked via his unseen translator.

"It's Yodel," I said, before I thought to add, "your honor."

The guard flicked me in the ear with his big finger. The blow knocked me over on my side. I thought for sure he had deafened me.

"Where is your leader?" King Vragordash asked.

"Dead maybe," I replied, rubbing my ear.

"Do you mock me?" he asked, holding the earpiece on his head.

"No," I told him. "Why are you holding me?"

A collective gasp sounded in the court chambers. Strange torchlights burned on walls that looked like the inside of a tree. Court members of varying stature formed a horseshoe around me, stopping far short of the throne. More Veknyrians were crammed into two levels of seating built into the walls, balconies capable of holding twenty or more each. Everyone looked eager for the spectacle unfolding before them.

The king cupped his massive hand over the microphone and said something to his audience. Laughter ripped through the court until the king held up his hand.

"You want to know what I said?" asked King Vragordash. I nodded. "I said how can a species so fragile come this far?"

More laughter ripped through the court. The king held up his hand.

"What's going to happen now?" I asked. "Do you mean to kill us?"

"The army unit responsible for your capture determines your fate," he said. "I am but a humble servant of the people, protector of the land, and Zaphkar incarnate."

"You know Zaphkar?" I said.

"I am his incarnation," the king said. "Not unlike your Egyptian kings were Ra and others."

"How do you know about the Egyptians?"

The humble servant waved his suitcase-sized hand. "How long our worlds have been in contact is of no consequence to you now. But how does one like you know our God?"

"On Earth he's not a god," I said. Then I added, "Only an angel."

The king translated for his subjects.

Someone behind me shouted something in Veknyrian. Others followed suit, repeating the word. It took only seconds before the shouting reached the second and third-level balconies.

King Vragordash raised his hand again. The chamber quieted.

"My subjects think you blasphemous," said the king. "There is no God but Zaphkar. Before you leave my court, I will hear you say it."

"There is no god but Zaphkar?" I asked.

King Vragordash nodded to the guards who flanked either side of me. He waved in a dismissive manner, as if to say *get on with it.*

The guard to my left raised his cudgel. I punched him for all I was worth between his legs. For a moment, he stared at me with a bemused look like I had just tried to tickle him, then he brought his cudgel straight down on my head.

I woke up chained to a dungeon wall. The air was rancid and humid, the stone walls damp. Somewhere water trickled.

From a small, barred window to my right, I heard Hick Haywood and Jody Pickett give each other little pep talks now and again. I was alone in my cell. Every time I called out to Hick and Jody a guard bellowed something none of us could understand.

An identical barred window to my left offered nothing but the sound of someone sobbing. If I had to lay money on it, my guess was that the sobs came from Plush Prince.

The clincher came when I heard a guard open his cell door, a gargantuan wood and iron monstrosity big enough to accommodate our giant hosts without forcing them to stoop to get through. Two guards shouted at Plush Prince in their native tongue.

"I don't know what the fuck you're saying," Plush Prince shouted back.

"You give him hell," Hick cried out from his cell.

Among Veknyrians somewhere there had to be some exquisite poetry. Our jailers charged with keeping the king's dungeons were probably not known for being wordsmiths.

As Plush Prince ramped up his campaign, the guards grunted and laughed. They started singing as they unchained my cohort. The words to the song they sang sounded almost like cadence. Judging by the sounds in Plush Prince's cell, the guards had begun throwing him back and forth in a game of catch.

"I'm not playing," Plush Prince cried in a high-pitched voice at one point, "Quit fucking with me! Put me down!"

"Hey," Hick shouted, "put that man down and come over here if you want to pick on somebody closer to your size."

From what I had seen so far of Veknyria, the average adult inhabitant stood close to nine feet tall. Hick Haywood was only five feet ten inches tall. Even if our captors wanted to take Hick up on his offer, they didn't understand English and none of us, save for Captain Prescott who was MIA at the moment, knew how to speak the Veknyrian language.

There was no way to tell the passage of time in the dungeons. The guards eventually quit picking on Plush Prince, chaining him to the wall once more, and went about their daily routines.

The chains they used on us were thick. A metal band, presumably used normally on the giant necks of Veknyrian captives, had been fitted around my waist. Breathing was difficult enough on that planet. The guards warned us, in their own fashion, that we should not fall asleep with any length of chain atop us, otherwise we might suffocate. Or maybe they were encouraging us to make a quick exit by using those thick chains to pile them up on our chests and stop breathing. I sensed the guards rarely got prisoners. It was as if our presence was a nuisance beneath their dignity. Every so often Plush Prince recited the same soliloquy.

"They gonna kill us, man," he would mutter in his cell next door. "They gonna kill us and nobody gonna know. What I do to deserve this, man? Oh, man. Motherfucking God, come on. Why you always got to fuck with us? If you can hear me, save us. I ask this in the name of Jesus. Come on, man. Do something. I can't take it no more. Get me out of this hell hole. Please God..."

And on and on it went, sometimes for hours, until Hick Haywood had had enough and begged Plush Prince to stop. Sometimes it turned into screaming matches. When it did they never lasted long. The guards would visit their cells and give them both a beating. They even worked over Jody once just for being in Hick's cell.

There was no way to communicate with the guards. We were at their mercy when it came to food. What they served us was a cold gruel that tasted like oatmeal without all the fancy trimmings like cinnamon and sugar. I tried my best to keep a count of how many times I was fed that slop, but I lost count after the ninth time.

When it was quiet, which was not often, I thought about Emma and how things used to be before everything went to hell (read: before I took her for granted and then unloaded on her as often as I could because I wasn't satisfied with my station in life). They weren't all bad days between us, though. When we were first married...well, it's easy to imagine.

The one hurdle I had to negotiate at the very beginning of our relationship was her Quaker parents. When Emma first told me that she had been raised a Quaker I pictured her parents all duded up like William Penn and Betsy Ross. They looked nothing like that. Emma told me I was close-minded, prejudiced to a degree. I didn't argue. A man should know his limits.

When I slept, I dreamed. The worst nightmares were the ones in which I was living my life back on Earth, working my editor job, and avoiding any conversation that had to do with why I wasn't with Emma anymore. A close second to that nightmare was the one in which I dreamed Emma and I were together, it was in the near future, we were more or less the age we were when we first split. Emma and I were making love, missionary position if you must know.

"Oh Cal," my wife said just when we really got going, "you don't know what you are doing."

I wondered what Dr. Strauss would have made of that one. In hindsight, I shouldn't have even thought of my old therapist.

My dreams soon shifted to the ones in which my shrink was putting it to my wife. Emma was ecstatic. Dr. Strauss wore a gold

Star of David pendant the size of a bar coaster affixed to a thick gold chain. He had more hair on his back than he did his chest.

During intercourse with my wife, he utilized the worst euphemisms for sex. He said things that no self-respecting sixth grader would ever mutter on the school playground. The more he did so, the more Emma became aroused.

I thought this can't be happening. Colonel Lester mentioned that statistically speaking, if universes were infinite, there was a strong probability that if a person imagined himself as a different version then that someone was probably alive and well in one of the other universes. That meant that in Earth's universe Strauss wasn't really sticking it to my wife on the side. In another universe, the opposite was true. In other words, an affair between my wife and my shrink was happening and was not happening at the same time, a regular Schrödinger's tryst.

I was blinded by the light when they let us out. From the dungeon, the guards took us to a courtyard somewhere on the king's grounds. The Veknyrians did not have castles. King Vragordash's place mostly resembled a resort with its one-story abodes of varying sizes built on one of the city tree's branches that measured a half-mile wide and twice as long. What I took for wasp nests while surveilling the twin trees city turned out to be structures made from the trees' bark that had faded over time.

Colonel Lester told us during his briefing that the trees were called *sarlyu* trees. The Veknyrians, the colonel said, built their cities on and within that type of tree. There is no direct translation for *sarlyu* in Earth languages. The Veknyrian word loosely translated the word to *Destrayama's mistress*, owing to how the sarlyu's moss glowed at night when the moon Destrayama was full.

In the courtyard, several people gathered, some of them dressed in ridiculous colors to denote that they were members of the king's court and others dressed so blandly that they would have blended into the background had it not been for their intimidating size.

In short order, King Vragordash decreed that our little unit be separated and distributed to various families for further safekeeping.

"Until the fugitive Yoh-delle[7] is apprehended," the king spoke into his language filter apparatus, "Or such a time when the Earthling world honors its treaty and causes no more threat."

There were ecstatic utterances and shouts from the mob that numbered at least a thousand or more Veknyrians. I didn't understand the language, but it was clear that they were cheering their king. Someone shouted a word, almost as a mantra, that meant, I learned much later, *eat the foreigners*.

King Vragordash heard his subject's cry. He spoke into his translator to offer us humans a solace of sorts.

"There will be no eating of these humans," he warned.

Plush Prince was the first to respond. "Oh man," he said. "Just cook my ass, motherfucker. I'm done."

"Don't you mean turn you over you're done?" Hick Haywood offered.

I had to hand it to him. In face of such adversity, he managed to find some humor. Old Hick was either a genius or a fool, the line between the two no more than a ghost's veil.

Jody Pickett did not share Plush Prince's panic.

"I have a plan," Jody Pickett announced.

Jody's plan went like this: we'd rush one guard and the lot of us would be able to take him hostage. He hadn't been there when

---

[7] The Veknyrian word *yohdell*, I learned later on as a captive, meant "excrement of the parupanoon." It was also a word one Veknyrian might call another if they intended to insult him. According to custom, there was no recovering from being considered yohdell. Lifelong friendships were never repaired after one accused another of being such. Clans that lived in relative harmony in the tree cities went to war over such an insult. The reason for such animosity between parties was that the parupanoon were considered the lowest animal on the planet. Parents used the beast as a warning to children who misbehaved. If a child acted out of turn and the parents were at their wit's end, they invoked the parupanoon and threatened to leave windows and doors open so the creatures could come and snatch misbehaving children. To be attacked in the open by the parupanoon was said to be a life-long curse, turning the victim, provided he or she survived the encounter, into an outcast who was forced to live as a hermit. Brands in the shape of a parupanoon were burned into the faces of cursed Veknyrians so that clans from other parts of their world would know the circumstance.

Sergeant Romero got pulverized by the Veknyrian woman. Jody's plan was little more than a protracted suicide mission. None of us wanted any parts of his ludicrous plan. We might be divided up, held hostage in private homes, taken as pets even, but we'd still be alive.

"Don't do it, Jody," said Hick. "Even their children could crush us in a heartbeat."

"I'm with huckabuck on this one," Fly announced. "I say we make a break for it."

"I'd prefer to die on my own terms," I told him.

A couple stepped forward and bowed before the king. A formal exchange of words followed. Then the woman pointed at Plush Prince.

"You may take the runt," King Vragordash said into his translator.

"Runt? What the fuck?" was about all Plush Prince could get out before he was snatched up by a guard and presented to the couple.

The woman took hold of Plush Prince like a mother does a toddler and held him tight around his waist as he scissored her with his legs and wrapped his arms around her bull neck.

"Hey, man," Plush Prince called out as the couple took him away. "She smells good. I might have to tap that giant ass."

"That boy is certifiable," Fly announced.

Another guy in the unit, his name was Nate Willard, got picked next. In basic training, the drill sergeants simply called him Shit-for-Brains because he constantly screwed up. Anyone not interested in becoming intimate with the working end of a Louisville Slugger chose not to call Nate by his nickname. I didn't know much about him except to say that he came from Ledfinch, Massachusetts, a small town halfway between Lowell and not much else. There was a gas station in Ledfinch and a Dunkin' Donuts. Nate repeatedly robbed them both throughout his high school years, wearing some disguise or another whenever he did so. During his senior year he got arrested when the manager at the local Dunkies thought the bandit's dark skin looked odd. Nate also dropped his wallet in the parking lot. A do-good citizen on his way somewhere far from crime-ridden Ledfinch, stopping in for coffee before dark, turned the wallet over to the Dunkies manager since the license in it belonging to Nate had a local address. The police found black shoe polish in Nate's room when they searched his house. No one in the Willard family—not his former prostitute of a mother, not his current prostitute sister, not his incarceration-addicted father—owned a pair of black shoes. Nate lucked out when the judge, at his wit's end in Ledfinch and willing to take a public defender's job in Philadelphia just to get out of the town where citizens had a one in fifty-five chance of becoming a victim of a violent crime, gave Nate the option of entering the military. When we were young he was always in trouble at Fort Campbell. Guys like Nate took to the army like fire to gasoline. The drill instructors did what they could with him. Namely, they made sure he didn't kill anyone.

At his regular duty station, Nate's platoon sergeants picked up the slack in that respect, but Nate seemed incapable of adjusting to the life. If he wasn't in the drunk tank in Clarkesville for brawling, sometimes with college students from Austin Peay University, but mostly with the Clarkesville police officers whom Nate saw as worthier adversaries than college students, Nate Willard was forever setting the contents of trash cans on fire around the barracks. His favorite trash can was the twenty-four-gallon galvanized garbage can in the barracks laundry room. Soldiers disposed of all manner of flammable refuse in that can, ranging from dryer sheets to porn magazines so dated that they had lost their appeal. When scheduled field exercises drew near, Nate started fights with NCOs just to get out of going on them. Nate's logic was this: even the post stockade beat being out in the field, especially during cold weather training. Nate eventually got his wish after he beat up a sergeant from another unit at the enlisted club on post. The company commander called the MPs and had him locked up in the post stockade. When Nate was released after a few months, our commanding officer threatened Nate with a more accommodating living space at Leavenworth the next time he slipped off the path, which was officerspeak for the next time Nate fucked up.

Nate Willard wasn't having it that day in the king's courtyard. When he was presented to a family that would take him in, Nate made a break for it. Two Veknyrian children from the family gave chase. Nate did not get far. The children ran him to the ground. For good measure, and much to the crowd's pleasure, they broke

Nate's legs to make sure he would not escape again. After that, Nate changed his tune. He no longer wanted to escape. He wanted to die.

King Vragordash granted Nate his wish. He snapped his fencepost-thick fingers and pointed at Nate while the injured writhed and screamed. A guard hefted a giant mallet as he approached the spot where Nate lay. The Veknyrian children who had broken Nate's legs ran off in search of further adventure. They were bored. The guard stepped on Nate's hips, crushing them in the process, lifted the mallet high, and, as if putting down an injured dog, brought the mallet down on Nate's head that popped open like a watermelon dropped from a great height. Two Veknyrian men wearing long leather aprons came forward, grabbed Nate's broken legs, and dragged him away.

My turn came soon after that. I was presented to what looked like an elderly Veknyrian couple. Between the bright sun and the extra gravity I was not used to, I worried that I might pass out. The elderly couple ushered me into a waiting cart and off we went without so much as even a hello shared.

No sooner than we boarded the cart drawn by one of those disc-backed turtle creatures, the old couple donned giant goggles with lenses tinted nearly black. The disc-backed creature hauled us into a tunnel at the far side of the courtyard. When we were deep inside the tunnel the elderly couple removed their goggles, the better to see in the dark.

Chapter 21: It Doesn't Take a Genius

The couples' home was a modest one. It was positioned on the elbow of a massive branch a few hundred feet off the ground. From that height, the plains leading to the desert were visible. Like the king's palace, the exterior was fashioned from bubbled bark. Windows with opaque uneven glass offered a panoramic view of the branch that served as a thoroughfare as wide as a four-lane highway. The interior of the house had walls of adobe.

The old couple made sure that when we got to their home I removed my dirt-caked uniform. Then they walked me to a small pool that served as their bath. An intricate system of vines delivered water from a spring underground between the twin trees. The Veknyrians had bolt-action rifles, but they had no electricity. Before I waded into the bathing pool, both the old man and the old woman seemed fascinated by my anatomy. Compared to them, everything on me was relatively small. That didn't keep them from taking turns dunking me under water like a toy.

When I didn't do what they wanted me to do the man and the woman took turns batting me lightly on the head and pointing as they did so. Boom, eat this. Boom, lay down there and go to sleep. I knew what it was like to be someone's mistreated dog that dreamed of running away.

An escape opportunity presented itself one day not long after I became a captive in the elderly couples' home. Even at their advanced age, they would prove too formidable a foe given our size difference. It was one thing to use weight and speed to create power in a fight. It was something else entirely to battle giants, even old ones, capable of literally pulling your limbs off or, as that one woman did with Sergeant Romero, beat you until all of your bones were shattered, and you turned into minced meat.

The elderly couple weren't the only inhabitants inside the house. Their adult daughter and her mate lived there as well, along with three children who, even at such young ages as they were, towered over me. A few times the children decided to play a game with me, as if I were a household pet. It involved tossing me around and sometimes deliberately letting me fall. When they grew tired of this, they simply punted me around between the three of them. One of the children kicked me so hard I thought my ribs had cracked.

The day came when the abuse finally stopped. It was just in time because I had enough problems digesting the food they provided me which consisted mostly of a light-colored meat that tasted like chicken and yellow-colored vegetables that smelled like cabbage. What happened with the physical abuse cessation was this: guests from nearby visited the elderly couple to see the oddity which was me. They were cordial enough, the old couple's guests were, but they touched me all over, attempting to pull off my clothing until I bit one of them. I knew they were more than capable of killing me, even the elderly couple was, given the size, but by that point I no longer cared. After I bit the visiting male Veknyrian a row erupted between my captors and their friends. I didn't speak their language, but ultimately, after a few minutes, the guests left the house. I never saw them again.

On certain afternoons, a young Veknyrian woman came bearing thin books with drawings. These were children's primers with which she sought to teach me various words in their common language. My futile attempts at learning their language became a source of constant entertainment.

When the tutor wasn't there, I slept the way kittens do throughout the day. When I look back on that time, I realize that it stemmed not from exhaustion but from depression. There was nothing worse than not being able to go home again. The thought of never seeing another human being wreaked havoc on me. My keepers did everything they could to keep me engaged. They knew something wasn't right, but they didn't know what course of action to take. It didn't take a genius, no matter what planet you were from, to know when loneliness becomes unbearable.

Weeks later, I emerged from my depression obsessed with only one thought: escape. I didn't know all the branches of Riengmarnoon, but I knew if I kept the trunk to my right I would remain among the branches. It might have taken years to devise a way to get to the base of the trunk if the elderly couple hadn't taken me one day to an open-air market. When they did, the sight of another human being, one who did not look familiar at all to me, moved me to tears.

"What's with the waterworks, pal?" he asked me as we stood more than arm's length from one another.

He sounded familiar.

"You speak English?" I said.

"I should," he replied. "Born and bred in the city of brotherly love."

"You're not the voice of the King's translator by chance, are you?" I asked.

He looked stunned.

"There's a rumor that you guys crash-landed here," he said.

"No," I told him, wiping the tears from my eyes. "It was more complicated than that."

"My name's Michael Keegan," he said, offering me his hand. "They call me Sonny. Or they did, before I ended up here."

"Do you know how long you've been here?"

"Not a clue."

"I'm planning on an escape," I whispered.

"You don't need to keep your voice low," Sonny informed me. "None of them understand English."

"Will you help me?"

"Go where?"

"To the desert," I revealed. "There's a gate out there, one between worlds."

"No fooling?"

"Yes. How did you get here?"

"It was a government experiment," he explained, "that went wrong. Not by some secret gate. "

"It sounds preposterous, I know—"

"Not to me."

"Really?"

"Did we win?"

"What?"

"The war against fascism. The Second World War."

"We did," I said. Then I thought to add, "but fascism is still around. They call it neo-fascism now unless you're in America. Then it's called patriotism."

"The world sure did get strange. You make it sound like Hitler survived and made a comeback."

"No, the allies won that war," I assured him. "But sometimes you can't kill an idea once it takes hold."

"Meaning what?"

"A lot of Americans these days would accept a dictator if doing so made them safe from terrorists."

"What are terrorists?"

"They are like the Christian radical right," I replied. "Only, they tend to distort the Islamic faith they follow."

"I knew some guys like that," Sonny said. "They acted like diehard Jesus lovers, but they didn't think America belonged in the war because the Jewish Question wasn't our problem. People were stupid."

"They didn't get much smarter."

"That doesn't surprise me," said Sonny. "You sound funny. Where are you from?"

"2019," I said.

"Pull the other leg so they are both even length," said Sonny.

"Tell me about the experiment that got you here."

"I was a merchant marine working in the Philadelphia Navy Yard," he said, "helping load the remainder of gear onto a ship called the USS Eldridge. They were doing top secret radar stuff, allegedly, on that boat. Something to do with radar invisibility. All I know is once they kicked on their machines, rents were torn in the fabric of spacetime. I ended up here. Some guys, I'm guessing, weren't so lucky."

Like me, he wore a collar with a chain leash attached to it. In the primer the tutor used to teach me the Veknyrian language, there was an illustration of a male Veknyrian with a parupanoon fitted with a collar and leash similar to the one I wore. The word *hakshni* was over the Veknyrian man's head. Over the parupanoon which looked like a balloon as it hovered at eye-level to the man was the word *bokshni*. The latter was the Veknyrian word for "subject" or "possession." In its archaic form, bokshni meant "thing owned." Hakshni, conversely, meant "master" or "owner."

I was a fifty-four-year-old human male who had been forced into being the pet of an intelligent alien species. I never did find out what my earth age was in bokshni years.

If what Sonny Keegan told me was true, he was a living witness to Project Rainbow, the Philadelphia Experiment. Then again he might have been plain crazy. The trouble with parallel universes is that no one there can corroborate claims. Whatever the case was, it would have to wait. Our hakshnis were pulling us in opposite directions now.

I struggled against my leash. Sonny, conversely, went along willingly, as if he knew something about being held captive on Veknyria that I did not. Or maybe he was granted special privileges since he was the king's translator. In the open-air market crowd, I soon lost sight of him.

Chapter 22: The Withering Sister

It didn't take me long to learn simple phrases like "I'm hungry" or "I have to use the bathroom," both of which were considered impolite. In Veknyrian society, one never spoke of bodily functions.

The tutor still came to the house. She tried to make a game of my learning their language. Some days I was into it, other days not so much.

Now and then Iogul, the elderly woman, the matriarch of the clan, took me to the open-air market not far from her home. Her husband Narsogul accompanied us occasionally, but for the most part it was just the old lady and me.

When the weather started to turn, the bright nights turning cold, the open-air market was converted to a festival of sorts. Iogul's clan, the Korzeth, were an integral part in setting up the autumn festival. Iogul's daughter Sasbajel, along with her mate Jermol and their children, son Jutarq and their two daughters Ajutan and Zhamtan, were provided seats at a round table close to King Vragordash's table.

The Veknyrians of Riengmarnoon had no radio, no television, and no telecommunications owing to the lack of electricity. Likewise, there were no vehicles with engines—combustible or otherwise. The open-air market was the place to go for news. Paper currency[8] was exchanged there for goods and food, as well as information.

---

[8] Coins were non-existent in Veknyrian society. Aside from being a choking hazard for children (Veknyrian children were said to *rak vaveir gulh*, which in English loosely translates to "eat anything not nailed

The oldest books in the Korzeth household were bound with dried animal intestines, the covers constructed from a flat wood covered in a cured animal skin. The pages themselves were made from what appeared to be handmade paper. The primers used by the tutor were handwritten, the illustrations hand-drawn and colored with paints by some long-ago artist. Other newer books owned by the Korzeth clan offered the same hand-sewn binding and cover styles as the older volumes, but a uniform print on the pages suggested a printing press.

New and old books were purchased during the autumn festival that celebrated *Harjulhiri*: the death of the withering sister, the moon Hiriruta which, the tutor Jubajel Zabukni had explained to me, sunk below the horizon for the duration of the winter months. The book peddlers traveled far and wide to sell their wares. By the time the withering sister reemerged, marking spring's arrival, all the peddlers, my tutor explained, cleared out of Riengmarnoon, and the wealthier book peddlers traveled south a few hundred miles to make it to the southern hemisphere in time for its winter festival. Most of them sailed along the coast as the jungles[9] south of the arid plains where Riengmarnoon stood were all but impenetrable.

Though I learned much from her in our time together, it was difficult conversing with Jubajel. For starters, I kept reverting to English. The guttural sounds of the Veknyrian language set my teeth on edge, owing to the structural differences in our mouths. Despite this challenge, I continued to improve at writing out words in Veknyrian. That was how I largely communicated with Jubajel. In the beginning, I would write single words and point to each. An example might look like:

Harkju (What)   *Gergh* (Sacrifice)   *Zaphkar* (Their God)

---

down"), coinage of any sort were associated with the ancients, a people whom present-day Veknyrians largely considered a crude and superstitious lot that created and carried coins to ward off evil spirits (undoubtedly, the ghosts of children who choked on such talismans).

[9] Several histories, Jubajel informed me, told of gold mines in the jungles established by the ancients then abandoned once coins fell out of favor. The gold used for coins issued by the ancients was melted down and each tree city was said to keep its own store.

It would take considerable time for the two of us to work out in Jubajel's language that I meant *What do you sacrifice to Zaphkar?* Once we did, she snatched the parchment I had scribbled on and marched into another room.

That day I was persuaded, rather harshly, never to mention the god Zaphkar again. When I wrote down the Veknyrian words for "know" and "him," Jubajel dragged me through the house to a small courtyard dug into a portion of the branch where the Korzeth clan lived. There, away from the family's ears, she told me that since I wasn't Veknyrian I couldn't know him. In my broken version of her language I told her that a small group of people on my planet also worship Zaphkar. Jubajel told me it was impossible since *grexrid* like me possessed no soul.

A stunted yet heated argument followed—stunted on my part, at least—about the nature of the Veknyrians and grexrid. The word itself, grexrid, I would learn later had a variety of meanings: alien, soulless, and barbarian among them. In short order, they treated me, and their kind did the same to my cohorts handed off to other clans, as mere animals with no soul by which to know their god. It sounded a lot like an argument the local priests in my dioceses used to make during catechism. I had been reduced to Cal Paladin, simple beast.

I wrote the Veknyrian common tongue words for *how you know* for Jubajel to read. When her reply came I nearly fainted. *Zaphkar loves us above all others*, she wrote in Veknyrian under my words, because *Zaphkar tells us so. No soul, no higher love.* Not only was I a captive in a land to which I did not belong, I was being held and tutored by Zaphkar fundamentalists.

One day, when the arguments about Zaphkar were behind us, I wrote, *Veknyria many languages.* Oddly, Jubajel's kind never developed a written equivalent for the question mark. They asked plenty of questions. They wrote even more of them. As my tutor explained, it was all in the inflection if one was to write down a question. Anyway, Jubajel looked at what I had scribbled. Underneath the three words meant to ask about the number of languages on her planet, Jubajel responded: *What people would need more than one language.*

The autumn festival came late in the season and marked the onset of winter. Once the festivities began, I waited for Jubajel to drink a fair amount of nectar wine before I broke out my parchment and began to scribble.

Buy books, I wrote.

You cannot read, she scribbled her reply.

I learn.

Not with new books, Jubajel wrote. *Cost too much.*

In order to soften her up I played dumb about Hiriruta, the exploded moon. Jubajel had recently moved into the home of Iogul and Narsogul Korzeth. Aside from attempting to make me understand their language, the old couple's grandchildren had come of an age when their education was to begin. Jubajel enjoyed my genuine interest in the astronomy of their world. I sensed her days of teaching me were numbered since I had a hard time learning. Or maybe I was reading into Jubajel's tone that night.

My tutor wasn't completely inebriated but she was feeling good by the time I asked her about the armed scout I saw in the desert before we were captured. Jubajel acted uninterested, at first. Then, when she thought no one was paying attention to us, she wrote grexrid in small Veknyrian letters on a piece of parchment she tore off from the corner. Immediately afterward, she torched the scrap in a candle atop the table where we sat.

"Me grexrid?" I asked, pointing at myself.

Jubajel took a sip from her cup, then shook her head. She motioned for the charcoal pencil I held. I gave it back to her.

On the parchment beneath my illiterate question about the scout, my tutor wrote one Veknyrian word: *nerdrax,* the Veknyrian word for "other."

As soon as I read the word, Jubajel tore off that piece and burnt it as well.

Who, I wrote on another scrap. Jubajel looked confused. So I added, *nerdrax* next to it.

Jubajel considered the two words a moment. Then she wrote, *Northern grexrid come in metal sky boat. Kill many. Not see in a year.*

She shivered, rubbing her arms as she did so. In all my time among her kind I'd never seen an expression on any of their faces that resembled anything close to fear. Not even the female scout Sergeant Romero had killed showed any such emotion, even as she died. The Veknyrians were without question an incredibly strong people. What came to the desert from the north that needed guarding against, I wondered. My scattered group, as far as I knew, had been the only ones with access to a Frulx gateway. I pressed her about the metal sky boat. When I did an impression of an airplane with arms spread out as I made engine noises Jubajel laughed and slid her wine out of my reach. I reached for the parchment pad. Jubajel snatched it from me and sat on it. I was done writing for the night.

Chapter 23: Yodel the Pin Cushion

On the night of Harjulhiri, the symbolic death of the withering sister, I made my escape. It helped that the people of Riengmarnoon celebrated like it was Mardi Gras, New Year's Day, and the end of the world all rolled into one. Even the children were sloshed. I waited until they were all passed out snoring before I made my exit.

On the way out, I made a discovery in an anteroom off the kitchen that led to the rear courtyard. My old army uniform and boots were clean and placed on a low shelf. I used a beach-blanket sized dish towel to fashion a rucksack of sorts. Then I took the boots and the uniform and placed them inside it. After that I took a knife from the kitchen. The knife in my hands was the size of a short sword. I didn't care how large it was as long as I was able to cut off the leather-like band around my neck.

I must have looked quite the sight when I made my way out. A regular Frodo Baggins armed with Bilbo's Sting setting forth from the Shire. In truth, I had no idea where I was, but as long as I kept the tree trunk in view on the way down to ground level I knew I would be fine. The challenge was getting out of the tree city undetected.

I made it from the house of Korzeth down two giant branches before I sensed that something wasn't right. In most places the canopy was too thick to see the ground, what with the tree's leaves as wide as tennis courts and the numerous vines like subway tunnels between the branches that supplied the city with water.

After spending two seasons among the Veknyrians my body had grown accustomed to the planet's gravity. By the time I reached a fifth layer of branches during my descent, zigzagging my way down shoots and vines, some of them with handrails added to them, I saw the time in a shop window. Nearly four hours had passed. On Earth, I could have walked from Brooklyn to Manhattan in that time.

All morning long the nagging feeling I had first experienced once I was out of view of the house of Korzeth kept at me. At any moment, I expected to be confronted by Jutarq, Ajutan, or Sasbajel. That I was more of a curiosity to the Korzeth clan was made abundantly clear as I never once took my meals with the family. Instead, I was relegated to the anteroom off the kitchen. It would inevitably fall to the children to hunt me down since I was little more than an escaped pet.

Riengmarnoon didn't begin to stir with life that day until early in the afternoon. Along different branches were open-air markets and shops, but they all appeared closed. Here and there I passed various Veknyrians riding those flat-backed, turtle-like creatures known among the Veknyrians as the Harapanik. A few of them traversed rather steep inclines. When they did, the creatures feet shifted from round flat appendages like an elephant's to long pointed ones like a crab's walking legs. The creatures moved fast when pressed to do so by their masters.

In the early afternoon, I ducked into an alley behind a row of shuddered shops. Carefully, I sawed at the collar around my neck with the knife I had stolen. Every few seconds I stopped to feel if I had made any progress. It took me several minutes in this fashion, but I freed myself of that leash collar. I ditched the collar behind large barrels that smelled like sewage. I left the alley after that to continue my trek toward the ground.

I got hungry. Outside one house stood a basket with various dried meats and raw vegetables in it. I stole as many provisions as I could stuff into my makeshift rucksack.

At the end of the row where I had stolen the food I found a harapanik hitched to a post. I undid the rope and climbed onto the creature. Given the size difference between me and the average adult Veknyrian, I had to stand on its neck and cling to the bridle fitted around its head. When I tugged on the right side of the bridle the creature moved in that direction. It took some getting used to, but I managed to traverse several branches and a few hundred yards in my descent before the beast quit on me. It didn't matter by then since I could at last see the ground through the canopy .

At the base of the tree, I ducked into a crevice to change from the clothes my captors had forced me to wear back into my uniform. I had a vague idea of the route I needed to take back to the mesa from which I had been abducted. Once there, all I needed to do was to follow a straight path toward the rising sun for a few kilometers to the place where the gateway stood.

I needed water before setting out into the desert proper. East of Riengmarnoon were acres of farmland. It was this region that the scout Sergeant Romero had killed protected from the so-called nerdrax Jubajel spoke of the previous evening. There would be water for the taking once I reached the farmlands.

At the pace I was going nightfall would descend before I reached the mesa where my group had originally camped. I needed to find shelter for the night before continuing my journey.

The farmlands remained fixed in my memory throughout my captivity. When the Veknyrian soldiers took us from the mesa to Riengmarnoon we passed through several farmsteads. The Veknyrians had constructed an elaborate irrigation system that carried water from beneath the twin trees to the pastures a mile or so outside Riengmarnoon. If it hadn't been for those farms, I might have never known which direction to take in order to reach the gateway that would take me home.

My thoughts drifted as I walked down a road that led toward the farmsteads. A small copse became visible on my left. It was located just before a small canal and a footbridge. I recalled neither the canal nor the bridge when I was brought to the twin trees city. Judging from the sun's position, however, I knew I was headed in the right direction.

At the small cluster of trees, I turned to look back. No one had followed me.

A thicket grew at the edge of the road to my right not far from the footbridge. No sooner than I passed the thicket, a familiar voice called out to me.

"Yankee sumbitch," Yodel said from inside the thicket.

Before I could respond, he stepped out onto the road. He was still in his uniform. Affixed to his headgear and shirt were small twigs and branches, an apparent attempt at green camouflage that, in his pixelated red, black, pink, and white uniform, made him look like a derelict Christmas ornament.

Yodel walked up to me with his arms spread wide, ready to hug me. I slugged him in the face. He fell back right on his ass.

"What's the big idea?" he cried, rubbing his jaw.

"You fucked everything up," I said.

"What? Me? How?"

"The captain gave you orders," I told him. "You were supposed to remain with the Veknyrians as part of a deal since we killed one of them."

"Those giant sons of bitches weren't going to let me go," he argued. "Y'all were just going to leave me here to die."

"No we weren't," I said. "Sergeant Romero and Captain Prescott have been here several times already. They knew the terrain, the people. They knew what they were doing."

"Is the captain dead too?"

"No," I said.

"Why were you coming from the direction of the Riengmarnoon?" Yodel demanded.

"Because you got us all taken captive," I said.

"I was held too," he argued. "And I get punched for it?"

"They sent us to different houses," I said.

"Same here."

"Only now I lost track of everyone."

"Do you think they're dead?" asked Yodel.

"I don't know," I replied.

"Them sons of bitches treated me like a damned step-dog," he began.

Yodel's voice trailed off as his eyes went wide and his jaw slackened. I would have turned to see what had given him such a fright but over his left shoulder I spotted a couple dozen Veknyrian farmers and scouts headed toward the footbridge from a half-mile away or so.

"Hey," Yodel said at last, waving over my shoulder as he did so. "That's Hick Haywood."

I turned then to see Hick, Jody, and Plush Prince riding on the back of a harapanik. There were at least a dozen of the creatures in all. On some of them rode Veknyrians; on others were members of our alien delegation.

"What do you think they want?" I nodded in the direction of what looked like a vigilante group headed toward the footbridge from the opposite direction.

"Them?" Yodel asked without turning to look. His fair-colored face turned crimson as he blushed. "I might have fucked a farmer's daughter."

"How's that even possible?"

Yodel shrugged. "Don't read into it," he said.

"It's hard not to," I said, considering the differences between human and Veknyrian anatomy. "Since you're the 'step-dog,' would the farmers consider that a form of bestiality?"

"I don't know, buddy," Yodel said with a sense of pride. "Corking the onion is corking the onion, in my book."

As the opposing groups drew near, I thought about making a run for it. There was no way I'd get away with it. The Veknyrian farmers and scouts were armed, some with their giant rifles while others carried long javelins.

The caravan coming from the other direction, the one which Hick and my cohorts were part of, looked as if they would reach us first.

Yodel walked past me and headed off to greet Hick and the others escorted by their Veknyrian captors. He didn't get far. A strange warbling noise sounded overhead for a moment.

"Yodel," I cried, "look out!"

When he turned to face the angry farmers everything slowed down. Yodel looked my way, the slightest grin on his face. The first javelin pierced his lower chest and came out his back. He was still alive when the javelin tip burrowed into the dirt road behind him. Yodel held on to the cord grip just a few inches from the wound in his torso. If he let go, his body would slide backward, forcing the pole to reverse through him when his back hit the road. Yodel held on for what little life was left in him. He offered a bloodied, toothy grin, trying his best not to slide backward along the pole, when a second javelin sounded in the air during its approach.

"Close one, " Yodel said as the second javelin struck the road behind him. His body trembled. He gripped the pole hard as he vomited blood. "Don't let me die, Paladin."

I took a hesitant step toward him. "You're going to be fine," I told him.

Yodel knew well enough that it was a bullshit line the army taught a soldier to say to his buddy when the buddy was going to die.

"It ain't nothing but a thing," he grunted.

"That's right," I told him. "It don't mean nothing."

For a moment, his expression turned to one of temporary triumph. In that instant, Yodel exuded confidence, as if he might live through the ordeal, after all. That's when the warbling noise sounded a third time.

Yodel opened his mouth to say something else to me. When he did the third javelin tip hit home, shattering his front teeth before it pierced the roof of his mouth and exited through the top of his head. He collapsed onto the road. The javelins aggravated the wounds they had caused him, forcing his head into a grotesque, oblong shape as the hole in his chest tore open. For several seconds, the fingers on his right hand twitched. His eyes, forced at odd angles on his ruined face, regarded me a moment as his upper lip peeled back to reveal his bloodied gums. His eyes lost their focus after that. Yodel was dead.

Once Yodel was killed, I moved slowly toward the approaching entourage. If the farmers and scouts rained down javelins on me before I reached the group, so be it. They did not. Their beef had been with Yodel.

Within the caravan of Veknyrians and my cohorts, there was a smith who, when two of his countrymen held me down, refitted me with another thick collar. Someone else attached it to a thick chain. Next, the other end of the chain was attached to a collar the size of a bus tire one of the harapaniks wore. As quickly as I had become a free man, I was turned back into someone's property.

"Stay close," Hick advised me when I reached him.

"Is Fly alive?" I asked Hick.

"So far as I know," he said, "yeah. I believe so."

"But you haven't seen him?"

"When we first set out from the city."

"Plush Prince?"

"I don't know," he said. "The clan that took Fly in lived behind the one that held Plush Prince. If they let you get close enough to Fly, you can ask him what happened. He knows the details."

"Was Plush Prince killed by them?"

"No," he said.

"Tell me what happened."

"Well you know how he gets?" Hick asked. "I guess his host clan got tired of listening to him day and night." He nodded at movement behind me. "Here comes Fly now."

They had Fly muzzled in a cage like a rabid dog. Every so often one Veknyrian child or another poked him with a stick. Despite the muzzle, he was able to talk, the sound of his voice muffled.

The caravan came face to face with the farmers and scouts when Fly told me that Plush Prince's host clan got tired of hearing him crying about home.

"They cut out his tongue," said Fly. "Don't let them fool you. These people are savages."

"Where is Plush Prince?"

"Back there somewhere," he nodded toward the rear of the caravan.

The Veknyrians toward the front started shouting at the farmers and scouts. In turn, the farmers and scouts threatened the caravan members with their weapons. The kids who had been tormenting Fly left him alone to go see what the commotion was all about.

"Did they teach you their language?" Hick said.

"I know a few words," I said. "But not enough to comprehend what they are saying now."

None of us could piece together the argument. Judging from the farmers and the scouts among them I'm pretty sure they wanted to kill us all. The only word I could understand, one that Jubajel had taught me, was crakhaal, which meant "cursed." Blades, cudgels, javelins, and rifles were brandished at one another. They were willing to go to war over us.

The farmers and scouts were greatly outnumbered, but the city inhabitants looked uncomfortable with their weapons. The report of a few rifles sounded at once. The farmers and the caravan members close to them engaged in a brief hand-to-hand combat struggle. One of the Veknyrians close to where Hick and I stood was struck by a bullet. His head whipped back for an instant. When he turned to look at Hick and me a good portion of his head was missing. The Veknyrian collapsed dead onto the dirt road.

"Get down," Hick advised me.

We ducked beneath the harapanik that remained transfixed by the violence unfolding before him.

"The key!" Fly started shouting behind his muzzle. "The key!"

He pointed at the felled Veknyrian just a few feet from where Hick and I squatted beneath the flat-backed creature.

At the head of the caravan, farmers and scouts hacked their city brethren to pieces. I had to move fast. It took some effort, but I managed to get the key from the dead Veknyrian. I unfastened my collar first. Then got Hick free from his.

"Grab that javelin," he advised me.

There was one next to me sticking out of a different caravan traveler. It took some effort, but I managed to free it from the corpse's massive chest.

There was no key for the cage in which Fly sat. Hick wedged my javelin between the bars and tried to bend them. I gave him a hand. We managed to bend one bar enough for Fly to slip through. I still had the knife I stole from the Korzeth clan. So I cut the muzzle straps to free him of that humiliating apparatus.

The three of us retreated a dozen yards or so and ran into Jody Pickett. His keeper had kicked him in the leg, breaking it, in order to keep him from running before he went forward to join the melee.

"Just get Plush Prince," Jody said.

"Negative," Hick said. "Willard got his leg busted and then they put him down in a fashion not fit for an old dog."

"Leave me."

"You're coming with us, broken leg and all."

"I'll only slow you down," Jody warned.

We didn't give him a choice. We tried a fireman's carry with Hick under one of Jody's shoulders and me under the other, the two of us interlocking our arms to form a seat. The pain proved too much for Jody. He passed out, which made it easier to carry him.

"Keep moving," Fly warned.

At the rear of the caravan, we found Plush Prince leashed to a dead harapanik. The key I had didn't work on his leash. I sawed off the collar around his neck with the stolen knife.

"I need me one of those rifles," Hick announced. "Don't forget I attended sniper school."

"Thirty years ago," Fly reminded him.

"There!" Hick shouted, ignoring Fly's comment.

He gave over his portion of Jody to Fly and sprinted toward the front of the caravan. A long rifle lay in the road next to a dead scout. Hick grabbed the rifle. It was so heavy he ended up dragging it. Just when he reached the dead harapanik where he stood he managed to place the rifle on the flat-back and aim at the combatants forty or fifty yards away.

The ground shook beneath our feet. Turning, I spotted a flat-back on pointed feet scrambling at full speed toward us. The rider was Veknyrian, a familiar face I thought I had seen the last of when I left the house of Korzeth.

"Qualtaag!" shouted Jubajel. Stop!

Hick spun the rifle around on the flat-back, braced himself, and pulled the trigger. The recoil knocked him off his feet, but he was otherwise fine.

"Qualt—" Jubajel managed before the bullet tore into her shoulder and knocked her off the harapanik.

The beast she was riding continued its charge. It scrambled forward, barely missing Fly, Jody, and Plush Prince, and kept going along the side of the road until it veered off into the copse down by the footbridge.

Another rifle report sounded. A bullet bit into the flat-back corpse where Hick busied himself by turning the rifle around toward whomever had fired at him. He braced himself again and fired his rifle. This time he managed to stay on his feet. His shot hit center mass, causing the scout who had fired at him to fall backward onto the road.

A few other scouts advanced on us now, their rifles aimed at Hick.

"Don't," Fly cried out.

It was too late. The three scouts fired at once. By some odd alien miracle they missed Hick who, in turn, wasted no time in firing his weapon, hitting two of the three scouts. The third scout's weapon jammed. Hick aimed his rifle, bracing himself as best he could, and squeezed the trigger. Click! He was out of ammo.

"Four goddamn rounds?" Hick cried. "That's it? What a piece of shit! Find me ammo!"

It was too late. The third scout, all nine feet of him, hoisted his rifle like a baseball bat and started running for Hick.

I tossed Fly the knife I had. Then I picked up a javelin stuck in the road and ran up the back of the dead harapanik. The javelin was heavy but manageable.

The scout was almost on Hick when I came down with the javelin. Meanwhile, Fly slipped around the giant's legs and slashed him behind the left knee. The scout swung his rifle. Just as I drove the javelin through his right eye into his skull, he struck me in the hip with the butt of his rifle.

My first thought, as I sailed through the air, was that my hip was broken. I landed in a somersault on the side of the road, the back of my shoulders hitting the ground first, and tumbling a few times before coming to a stop in tall grass.

Chapter 24: The Machine Man

The next thing I remember was an angry Veknyrian grabbing me by my shirt with one big hand and lifting me into the air. In his other hand, he brandished a dagger nearly as long as my leg. He was all set to stick it through my abdomen when Jubajel called out: "Qualtaag!"

After that, everything happened at break-neck speed. Fly, Hick, Jody, Plush Prince, and I were lashed to thick tree limbs nailed together in an "x" shape. Then they laid us atop the remaining flat-backs.

Before pushing off toward the farmsteads, there was a heated discussion between the remaining farmers and Jubajel about the fate of Jody and his busted leg. That was decided by an elderly Veknyrian who met us at the footbridge. He looked like a shaman with a staff carved with intricate patterns and festooned with the skulls of small animals. He wore wild braided hair on his head. He pressed his thumb in various places along Jody's broken leg. Jody cried out and the old man pointed to the creek below.

Two farmers picked up the x-frame to which Jody had been latched and lifted him over the rail of the footbridge. They were all set to drop him into the shallow water below when a sharp thunderclap sounded.

None of us saw the initial flash.

The twin trees city stood on the horizon. The next second Riengmarnoon had been reduced to just the trunks that were bathed in flames as a mushroom cloud rose up toward the heavens.

It took no time at all for the wind and ash to reach us. The air wasn't as hot as I thought it would be, given the nuclear blast.

"Captain Prescott," Hick noted.

The walking nuclear threat had detonated.

After several seconds, the spell was broken.

The two farmers holding Jody tied to an x-shaped cross shrugged and tossed him over the bridge rail.

Fly, Hick, and I started screaming. From where I lay on the harapanik's flat-back, I saw Jody's x-shaped cross hit the water.

The creek wasn't that deep, just enough for the water to run several inches over Jody's face as he struggled against the rawhide strips that kept him bound to the x-shaped cross. As Hick and Fly cursed our captors, I watched Jody beneath the clear surface of the creek water. After a couple of minutes, he quit struggling, breathed in water, and gave up the ghost. I never saw anyone look so frightened.

Meanwhile, several women from the farmsteads paraded past us bearing shovels and other excavation tools. The battle on the farming road had been a vicious and brutal one. Aside from my cohorts and me, Jubajel, and what I took to be three of her brothers, there were no other survivors. The dead would be buried on the side of the road.

The shaman turned his attention on Jubajel. He ripped her bloodied shirt off and tossed it aside, leaving her bare from the waist up. Jubajel made no effort to cover her breasts. The shaman treated her bullet wound as it was a bee sting, picking up dirt from the side of the road, spitting in it, and rubbing it into the wound. Then he crumbled up some leaves from a plant and jammed them into the wound, one in the front part of Jubajel's shoulder and another in the upper back where the bullet had exited. He took two bullets from a pouch on his hip, removed the rounds of each from the shells and poured gunpowder into his hand. Carefully, he filled both the entrance and the exit points on Jubajel's wound. Then he produced a flint and ignited the gunpowder. A brief flash flamed as Jubajel grunted. The wound had been cauterized. The shaman wrapped the wound with cloth after that. Satisfied with his work, he went on ahead to catch up with the burial detail.

Jubajel patted the top of my head with her right hand. One of her brothers took off his shirt and draped it over Jubajel's shoulders. My tutor mumbled something to me as she winced. I couldn't understand everything she was saying to me, but I managed to piece together the following words:

Souls   *Offering*   *Zaphkar*

I wasn't sure if she meant the Veknyrian dead or us.

Before moving on, Jubajel said many things to her brother. In my pidgin Veknyrian, I understood that Jubajel was returning to her home on one of the farmsteads to tell her family of how what she called the *machine man* destroyed Riengmarnoon since King Vragordash had refused to free the humans.

My thoughts bounced between the protocol that gave an android license to destroy alien cities and Jody Pickett's lifeless eyes looking up at me from just beneath the creek's surface. I wished that the bomb had been big enough to wipe out the farmsteads, the road leading to the desert, and all of us with it.

That night they put Fly, Hick, Plush Prince, and me into a barn. I decided there in the dark that I would acquiesce and show Jubajel some remorse. It was important for me to win her favor again, no matter what the other guys said. It was the only way I would get to kill her.

It was next to impossible to sleep, strapped to a makeshift cross. Before they carried us into the barn, I glimpsed the desert that bordered the farmsteads. Beyond the sand and rock, a low shadow stood at the edge of the horizon. I knew that mesa. It was the one we had been abducted from, the one beyond which stood the gateway home.

Aside from the four of us, there were three harapaniks in large stalls. The barn reeked of harapanik waste. I tried not to think about it much, but it was there, in my face like Plush Prince's muted presence.

My old, mutilated friend managed to sleep off and on through the night. When he did, he must have dreamed he could still speak.

Different sounds came out of Plush Prince, but none of it was intelligible.

People who got caught up in a cult were often found to be easily led and influenced, if not easily manipulated. One psychiatrist's book I read mentioned that cult followers all had one thing in common: the need for validation and identity.

During the first two years or so after Emma left I blamed myself. Was it something I did that brought my wife so low during our marriage? Did I drive her to join up with The Radiant Angels? Over time, I had taken plenty of self-inventory. Dr. Strauss helped me realize just how much I took Emma for granted. Often, I drove a wedge between Emma and her parents. The same went for her and her friends. Emma's mother and father, however, kept after their daughter, reinforcing their purpose in her life as she got older. Emma's friends were another story. They stopped coming around. They stopped inviting her out to dinner and to the movies. Emma regretted it and blamed me. Of course, I denied I had anything to do with it. As a result, she came to despise me more than she ever did.

"You were a regular shit heel," Dr. Strauss had told me during one of our sessions. "Most spouses tend to be. Women can be just as much as men. The good news is you recognize it. You can manage it if you choose to do so."

He gave me a bunch of affirmations to write down. And a list of ten questions to fill out before our next session. Dr. Strauss didn't mean one or two word answers. He wanted me to really think about it and provide at least a paragraph. No editing was allowed. I had to write my answers in ink, and I wasn't allowed to cross out any mistakes. I don't remember many of the questions now except for one. If you could be anything what would it be? I wrote down a loving husband and I listed in five or six sentences the reasons why.

"This is bullshit," said Dr. Strauss when I read my responses to him. "Husbands are supposed to be loving. Otherwise, they shouldn't be married. You're like one of those guys who expects to be clapped on his back and congratulated for simply doing his job like the pilot who landed a plane full of people in the Hudson River—"

"Sully?" I asked.

"That's the one," he went on. "I can't pinpoint it now, but somewhere along the way we started giving kudos for expectations, whether it was job-related or something as simple as graduating high school. You don't have kids, so you missed out on that. The graduation thing, I mean. My girl graduated from high school two years ago. She's still complaining about not having been given a proper party. For achieving an expectation? I asked. It's the twenty-first century, for fuck's sake, I told her, not the 1930's. Everyone should graduate high school."

I fell asleep and dreamed that Emma and I were high school sweethearts. We were walking to school to take part in the commencement, each of us carrying a cap and gown.

A black van drove up along the curb and stopped just ahead of us. The side door slid open. Four guys wearing fraternity jackets piled out and snatched Emma. Each one wore a lanyard around their necks with a laminated card announcing them as members of the American Deflowering Delegation. When I tried to stop them, one of the A.D.D. members belted me in the gut. He mumbled something about fags when I dropped to my knees clutching my stomach. The weird part about the dream was that Emma didn't put up a fight. The guys took her inside the van and the side door slid shut. I heard her laughing as they pulled away. All that remained of Emma was her tassel from her graduation cap that had fallen into the gutter.

Jubajel and her brothers came for us when the day's first light showed through the spaces between the barn wall slats.

Hick Haywood gnashed his teeth and cursed the lot of them, even when they offered some cold gruel in wood spoons that tasted like honey and oats.

Fly put up a good show, but he didn't say no when Jubajel began feeding him.

One of the brothers fed me, shoveling the gruel into my mouth as fast as I could swallow. He let up when I started to choke and cough.

Plush Prince looked ill. He barely ate any of the gruel, despite Fly and me assuring him that he needed to eat something.

There were tears in Plush Prince's eyes. It was plain to see by his defeated expression that he considered himself nothing without his voice.

Water came next. I never thought I'd be so happy to taste it. Afterward, Jubajel's brothers untied us one by one and let us do our business in one of the harapanik stalls.

If anyone were going to make a break for it, I figured it would be Hick. Fly was too smart to risk getting killed when he understood that better chances of escape might await us in different circumstances. Hick did a lot of cursing under his breath, but, aside from spitting on the barn floor at one point, he didn't try to flee.

Plush Prince proved to be the odd man out. After he did his business in the harapanik stall, he took hold of what looked like a three-prong pitch fork with a short handle—well, short for our gargantuan captors. Jubajel and her brothers formed a horseshoe formation around Plush Prince. All it took was for Jubajel or one of her brothers to distract him and Plush Prince would be a goner.

That wasn't the voiceless man's intention at all. He stuck the handle end of the pitchfork where the stall wall and barn floor met. Then, pressing one of the sharp prongs against his neck, he pushed forward until the rusted prong pierced his skin.

If he thought he was going to die instantly, Plush Prince had another thing coming. He slumped and fell over on his side, the prong still stuck in his neck tore at the flesh, widening the wound. He bled out within a minute after that.

Fly, Hick, and I cried and cursed and pulled against our restraints, but it was no use.

One of Jubajel's brothers tore the prong loose from Plush Prince's neck, nearly decapitating my old cohort in the process. He hung up the pitchfork in its original place. Then he grabbed Plush Prince by his leg and pulled his body out of the barn, leaving a drag mark of blood for several feet before he reached the doors.

Beyond the barn doors the sky looked overcast. At first, I thought it was snowing, but the temperature was too warm. What fell from the sky were ashes from the destroyed city of Riengmarnoon. Jubajel and her brothers had no knowledge of such weapons. The bomb that had been Captain Prescott was a limited strike nuclear warhead with a one-mile blast radius and approximately two miles of collateral damage beyond that. If we stayed on the farm, everyone would have suffered radiation sickness. Some of us might have died from it.

That morning I became convinced that Jubajel and her brothers were going to dispatch Hick, Fly, and me in the same fashion Jody Pickett died. If they did, they would have been able to travel faster to avoid the radioactive waste, provided they knew what it was.

It turned out I had been wrong about Jubajel and her brothers. They had other plans for us.

Chapter 25: The Augurs of Spring

They took us to a place called *Zaphkarshuk*, which in Veknyrian meant Zaphkar's Seat. Jubajel told me in so many words that it was the place where Zaphkar dwelled. He would be angry, she revealed, scribbling furiously in broken Veknyrian so I could understand, over the destruction of the city. An offering needed to be made.

Zaphkarshuk was located north of the mesa where my group had last camped before everything fell apart. It was a two-day hike from the farmstead to get there.

On the second day, long caravans of other Veknyrians appeared heading north like we were. Two long lines of travelers, one from the west and one from the south converged a half-mile ahead of us. Before long, we joined the converging caravans.

Like Jubajel and her brothers, the other Veknyrians were armed with long javelins and a few bolt-action rifles. They carried the weapons for good reason.

Along a wash less than a quarter-mile away, several Veknyrians fought a full-on battle with a swarm of parupanoon that numbered one hundred or more. For every parupanoon that was brought down two more snatched up Veknyrian children, lifting them to great heights and dropping them against rock formations. The parupanoon already engaged in battle looked as if they were losing the upper hand against the ground forces when a second wave of the creatures flew in to join the battle.

"Hey, man," Hick said casually as we lay strapped to our x-shaped crosses on the backs of harapaniks.

"Hick?" I said, closing my eyes against the searing sunlight.

"I just wanted to say that if we don't survive this ordeal," he went on, "it's been a true pleasure. That goes for you too, Fly."

"Quit that morbid bullshit, you old country-ass hillbilly," Fly said. "Stay positive."

"Hey, Cal," said Hick.

"Yes?"

"You were an editor before the army got its claws back into you, right?"

"Yes, Hick," I replied. "That I was."

"Does Fly need the modifier 'country-ass' in front of hillbilly?" he asked. "I'm just a dumb boy from southern Georgia, but, in my opinion, it seems redundant. Wouldn't you agree, Cal?"

"Yes, Hick. I concur."

"Paladin," Fly cried, "you're supposed to look out for a fellow Jersey boy—"

"Also, Fly," Hick went on, "the word 'hillbilly,' while it dates back nearly two centuries, is most definitely a derogatory term."

"I'm sorry if I offended you, Hick."

"I'm free."

"How's that?"

"My hands are free," Hick said. "The straps must have been dry-rotted."

"Paladin, tell me that you didn't teach that Veknyrian bitch English," said Fly.

"No," I told him. "I did not."

One of Jubajel's brothers walked on the left side of the harapanik hauling Hick. In one fluid motion, Hick leaned forward, snatched a long knife from a scabbard the Veknyrian wore, and stuck him in the lower back.

Jubajel's brother screamed as he dropped to his knees.

Hick cut the straps that bound his feet. He slipped off the harapanik and finished the job on Jubajel's one brother.

Meanwhile, Jubajel and her other two brothers rushed toward us, hoping to save their fallen sibling. Hick threw the large knife at one of the remaining brothers. The blade pierced the giant's stomach and remained there, but it didn't slow him down. He kept charging. Hick ran toward the wounded Veknyrian at the same time. Just before he reached him, Hick dropped like he was sliding into home plate. He took hold of the knife handle as he slid beneath the Veknyrian's legs, dragging on the blade, and tore the wound wider before he wrenched it loose. Hick stood up behind his victim then and stabbed him in the lower back three times while the wounded Veknyrian tried to hold onto his guts that were slipping out of his lower abdomen.

With two brothers down, Jubajel and her remaining brother armed themselves with javelins. They advanced on Hick who looked exhausted already. Meanwhile, Fly and I pleaded with him to cut us loose.

A shadow blotted out the sun. One hundred feet overhead was a large rectangular craft painted flat black and spackled with various shades of hunter green, olive drab, and tan. It had to be a least a city block long. Suddenly, music shot out of an unseen speaker. I recognized it immediately from Stravinsky's *The Rite of Spring*, specifically the "Augurs of Spring." Veknyrians ran helter-skelter from the metal sky boat.

"Is that ours?" Fly shouted.

Hick didn't waste any time waiting around to find out. He cut Fly and me free while Jubajel and her remaining brother knelt down. Were they under the impression that the craft belonged to Zaphkar?

From somewhere on the belly of the craft a .50 caliber machine gun opened up, the rounds raining down and chewing up the scenery in concentric circles. Jubajel was screaming louder than her brother. Fly, Hick, and I dove beneath one of the harapaniks. The firing continued. Seconds later, Jubajel and her brother had quit screaming.

"Humans of United States Army," a voice with a thick Russian accent sounded from above. "Stay where you are. Spetsnaz

Regiment 47 will descend to extract you. Do not try to flee. We are here to help."

"Spetsnaz?" Hick cried. "What are the Russians doing here?"

Part III

For who shall reign over human beings if not those who reign over their consciences and in whose hands are the loaves?

~Fyodor Dostoevsky, *The Brothers Karamazov*

Chapter 26: Parables of Light and Salt

"Allow me to introduce myself," the Russian officer said once we disembarked from the Kamav Ka-60 helicopter that picked us up. "I am Polkóvnik Dimitri Yustonov Zamyenko. Polkóvnik in America would be colonel, no? Please address me as Colonel Zamyenko."

"Colonel," Fly was the first to speak. "Thank you for saving us."

"It is my pleasure," he replied in his thick accent, "to rescue you from such savagery."

Colonel Zamyenko stood five feet ten inches tall. Like his junior officers in tow and a few noncoms milling around the flight deck of the airship, they looked to be in fantastic physical shape. Unlike Fly, Hick, and me, Colonel Zamyenko and the others moved as if they had been born on Veknyria.

"The Stravinsky piece was a nice touch," I said.

"Yes," he said, proudly. "You Americans with your rock and roll and your tabloid newspapers. So much for the shining city on the hill. If not for Russian music and literature, the West would have descended into darkness long ago. But enough with parables of salt and light. You are not injured, yes?"

Fly, Hick, and I assured him that we were fine.

"How did you know we were here?" I asked.

"Seismograph picked up movement," the colonel said. "We come to investigate who nuked city in trees."

"Our captain," Hick said.

"We didn't know he had the bomb," Fly added.

"You men look terrible," said Colonel Zamyenko. "Kapitan Yorlovsky here will take you below deck to your quarters."

"Colonel," I said, "why didn't our army rescue us?"

"Your government officially doesn't recognize you," the colonel announced. "This I deduced because they did not send rescue party. Also, old men are expendable as well as young boys. The Nazis showed us that during the Great Patriotic War. It seems America got message loud and clear, yes?"

The junior officers and noncoms laughed along with Colonel Zamyenko when he did.

"How long have you been here?" Hick asked.

"In this desert?" the colonel asked.

"On Veknyria."

"We are the children of immigrants," Zamyenko said, raising his arms to his side and performing a short barynya. He straightened up after that, and he added, "everyone on this vessel was born on this planet."

"How long have our governments known about this place?" Hick asked.

"Since 1956," he replied. "Soviet Union put Sputnik into orbit the following year to deflect attention from real exploration. My mother and father were among the first wave of great Soviet colonists to land on Veknyria.

"The Soviet Union is the first country in the history of Earth to blaze trail toward communism for all people," he went on. "It is a testament to the people's struggle for peace, democratic freedoms, and social progress. Communism, as you may know, needs more than one continent to survive if you consider various resources alone. Now, we bring communism to a new world. Imagine the dream unfolding on two planets at once? Workers of the worlds unite!"

"He doesn't know," Fly said to me under his breath.

"What is it I do not know?" Zamyenko said to Fly.

It was hardly the time to explain the last thirty years of history back on Earth, specifically the collapse of the Soviet Union, to the colonel, given that he just rescued us.

"Hey, how did y'all keep this world a secret for so long?" Hick asked him.

"You might ask the same of your government and yourselves," he said, ignoring Fly for now. "A year ago, you were getting up in the middle of the night to pee and worrying if you'd ever have enough money to retire on. Now, you have traveled to planet in parallel universe, met another intelligent species, and killed them. I'm guessing you are the buckaroo of the bunch?"

"Shit," said Hick. "I guess so."

"Kapitan?" the colonel said. "If you will please take these men below deck now. They need to get clean and join us for dinner as our honored guests."

Kapitan Yorlovsky stepped forward, offering the colonel a salute. He rendered a mock bow at the three of us as he pointed to an open hatch a few yards to our left.

"How big is your colony?" I asked.

"Large enough to defend our people and our guests against the natives."

"Where is it?"

Colonel Zamyenko pointed in a northwesterly direction. "Out there," he said. "I'm surprised your giant girlfriend down there didn't tell you about us. I believe the natives refer to us as the *grexrid.*"

Kapitan Yorlovsky grilled the three of us about possible survivors from our unit. He lacked the sense of humor the colonel had, especially with regard to the limited nuclear strike against Riengmarnoon. Yorlovsky grimaced when Colonel Zamyenko started cracking jokes about the detonation.

"How many Veknyrians does it take to screw in lightbulb?" the colonel asked on the way down below the flight deck. He didn't wait for anyone to reply. "None. They have all been vaporized."

As the captain made his way ahead of us down a narrow corridor, the ship tilted and banked slowly to the left.

"What's going on?" Fly asked.

"We make turns to survey for survivors," said Kapitan Yorlovsky.

"There's no one left in our unit," Hick assured him.

"You watched them all die?"

"Well—"

Over the intercom came an announcement in Russian. In college, I had studied the language for three semesters. I had a scheme in my head that as Russia rebuilt herself after the fall of communism I might join up with a literary agency, or even form my own, and go over to find untapped or otherwise recently suppressed talented writers. As aspirations go, that one fell by the wayside. I still remembered enough of my Russian to figure out what человек (chelovek) meant. A human had been spotted on the ground.

"You were saying?" the captain said to Hick.

The steady hum of the .50 caliber gun on the underside of the ship sounded like a vacuum cleaner where I stood.

"If they hurry," Hick announced, "maybe they can wipe out the whole planet's population."

"Natives should not brandish javelins," Kapitan Yorlovsky announced, pronouncing the word javelin with a "y" instead of a "j" so it sounded like *yah-vul-eens*. "We give them chance to lay down arms. But then why am I explaining our actions to Americans who settle everything with nuclear bombs?"

"My communist brother has a point," said Fly.

We set politics aside when another announcement called us to the flight deck. Once there, Hick pulled Fly and me aside.

"You boys remember a few years back people were reporting rectangle-shaped UFOs?" he asked.

Fly said nothing, but I remembered. I gave Hick a conspiratorial nod to indicate that I knew the deal.

It was one of those things that Emma chided me about constantly when we were together. One night I thought I saw a craft similar to the one in which we were riding at present. I wasn't a complete nut. At the time, I convinced myself that it had been something experimental that the U.S. Government had developed. Still, to be safe, I reported it to MUFON (the Mutual UFO Network) on their website.

Emma found much humor in my knowing about such websites. She did not discount intelligent life out there among other stars, but my wife had always been a pragmatist. For her, the math involved in traveling such great distances did not add up. How little she knew.

"I saw one of these once," I told Hick.

"So did I," he said.

"Mine was over Princeton," I began.

"Gentlemen," the captain called to us as one of the helicopters started up. "I need volunteer to accompany me."

Fly and Hick took a step back, grinning like madmen when they did.

"Dicks," I said to them.

Hick gave me his giant knife to take with me. I jammed the sheathed knife under my arm.

"Mr. Paladin," Kapitan Yorlovsky gestured toward the bird. He pronounced my name Pal-yah-deen.

The pilot circled a small group of Veknyrians who brandished their long javelins, threatening to hurl them at the helicopter. In their midst a man wearing a collar with a thick chain affixed to it squatted within the circle of giants.

"Sergeant Popov," the captain said to a door gunner.

"Sir?" Popov replied.

"Aim high," he instructed him.

Sergeant Popov fired his GSh-23V 23mm cannon from the helicopter. It sounded like a series of drum rolls.

As the rounds chewed up the ground in front of them, the Veknyrians hurled their javelins. One of them had a rifle. He got off one shot before Popov adjusted his fire and gunned down better than half of the Veknyrians, including the rifleman. The remaining giants turned tail to run, dragging the man on the leash like a dog who didn't want to follow.

Popov fired a few more volleys. The man was free of his captor now. He turned and ran toward the helicopter as it set down on the desert floor.

Kapitan Yorlovsky slid open the door. He motioned to me, signaling that I should run out and assist the man. I did as the captain wished.

Through the fine sand that whirled around me like a red fog I recognized the man headed toward me. It was Sonny Keegan. He looked startled for a moment when I removed the knife and took hold of his collar. When I cut it away, Sonny looked relieved.

"Good to see you," I told him.

We took a few steps toward the helicopter and Sonny stopped.

"Wait," he said. "What side are you on?"

"I'm an American," I assured him, "just like you?"

"When did we get so friendly with the Russkies?"

"Times have changed. You should meet our current president."

"He's Russian?"

"In a manner of speaking," I said. "Come on, let's get out of here."

Sonny pointed at the distant ship in the air.

"Since when did aircraft carriers fly?" he cried.

"We'll talk about it later," I guided him back to the waiting helicopter.

Back on the main craft, upon hearing of Sonny Keegan's past, Colonel Zamyenko had one of his corporals pour vodka for all of us and offered a toast.

"To the second-most sought-after hero of Project Rainbow," the colonel said.

"Who's the first?" Hick asked, a little too loudly.

"That is classified," said Colonel Zamyenko. "But I can tell you he lives in American Southwest. Also, he's invisible. So you won't find him."

After that, Fly, Hick, Sonny, and I were shown separate quarters a few levels below deck.

I showered, put on the dull gray pants and shirt that were left on my bunk, and lay down after that. I dreamed that the Veknyrians were taking us to Zaphkar's Seat, which, it turned out, was a mountain in my dream and not a basin like in real life.

There were men and women dressed in red-tinted camouflage uniforms like the ones issued to me back at Fort Dix.

Jody Pickett, still very much alive in my dream, stood a little off to the side of a trail that wound its way up the mountain. From where we stood together, we could see soldiers leaping to their deaths from atop the mountain. No one said anything in my dream.

I had a feeling that eventually Jody's turn then mine would come. We took turns letting others go on ahead of us, telling them that it would be impolite to think only of ourselves first.

The sound of the intercom woke me up.

"Mr. Paladin," the announcer spoke, "please report to galley on level 2."

Chapter 27: The Ministry of Birth Control

Fly, Hick, and Sonny were already seated at Colonel Zamyenko's table along with the colonel himself when I arrived. Kapitan Yorlovsky looked dour when I passed his table to join my cohorts.

Colonel Zamyenko continued a story lauding the communist system, citing both planets as integral chips in the game of spreading Marx's legacy throughout the multiverse. Fly and Hick had sense enough not to comment. Sonny Keegan, however, countered each of the colonel's claims with a capitalist's viewpoint. Both men acted as if they had just come through a time tunnel of sorts. Colonel Zamyenko told us all about how he had been born on Veknyria.

"Do you have children?" Hick asked.

Rather than answer, the colonel went on to tell us about how the Veknyrians did not want them there. It was an old story, colonization always was, and from what I had seen so far the indigenous population wasn't about to embrace an absence of the state, such as they understood it, and common ownership.

Prior to dinner, Sonny provided me a crash course in time, space, and wormhole theory based on his unwitting participation in Project Rainbow. He told me that he'd been on the planet for four Veknyrian years now. That meant that when he departed Earth against his will—as a result of malfunctioning government equipment built specifically to bend light and to manipulate electromagnetic energy, which in turn altered gravity locally around the USS Eldridge—it was still a couple of days before Halloween in 1943.

"It could have been worse," Sonny informed me. "During the transition phase, that's what I call it, I saw guys plummet through the ship's structure and land on the moon. There's no atmosphere there so my guess is they died.

"It's hard to explain what happened to reality during the transition phase," he went on. "All I know is I ended up here. One minute, I was watching cargo get loaded onto the deck of the ship and the next the Eldridge and the dock went fluid then turned to static. That's the best way I can describe it. The military needs to recruit poets to find the right words to record specific events. I still can't find the correct ones to describe what I went through."

That Sonny Keegan was mad in the classic sense was no secret. I would be too if I had been catapulted through matter, space, and time seventy-seven years into the future.

As we stood there in the hall I smelled chlorine. At the time I didn't think anything of it. When I sat down next to him at dinner that evening, I detected the odor again. Only now the odor was closer to a burning wire than chlorine.

"Is it the smell?" he whispered when he thought the colonel wasn't looking our way.

"Excuse me?" I played dumb.

"Ever since I transitioned here," Sonny revealed, "it happens every time I get nervous. I'm surprised my head doesn't just pop off or something crazy like that."

There were numerous and wild theories associated with Project Rainbow, which became known by its more popular reference: The Philadelphia Experiment. Legend told of how some crew members were fused with the ship when it teleported from its place in the Philadelphia Naval Yard to Norfolk, Virginia and back again. Along the way, some of her crew allegedly went missing. Some people believed that the missing ended up in parallel places the way Sonny did. Others maintained that some crew members ended up on Europa. Never mind the ice crust there being nearly fifteen miles thick. My purpose here is not to chronicle the events of the so-called Philadelphia Experiment. I leave that to others.

What interested me about Sonny and whether or not he actually was from Earth's recent past was that in all probability he could not have witnessed such a thing. The U.S.S. Eldridge herself, the cannon-class destroyer purported to be the center of the Project Rainbow conspiracy theory, had been transferred in 1951, thanks to the Mutual Defense Assistance Act, to Greece where she became *Leon*. The ship remained in service until she was retired in 1992 and sold for scrap in 1999[10].

The story of the U.S.S. Eldridge was part of Delaware Valley lore, ranking up there with tales of the Jersey Devil. Such strange events my wife Emma had no patience for, owing to how dismissive she had always been of all things paranormal. According to her, every event in reality could be easily catalogued and categorized, if not now eventually once science caught up.

I grew up with parents who in their spare time read books like *Project Blue Book*. America's fascination with the unexplained transitioned from all things *Exorcist*-related to threats from outer space, especially after the shark in *Jaws* was blown to bits. Some societies were once obsessed with angels; others remain so. America replaced angels with aliens after the Roswell Incident and never looked back.

Presently, Sonny excused himself. Kapitan Yorlovsky and another officer followed him out.

"Mr. Paladin," Colonel Zamyenko said. "You look depressed."

"No, sir," I assured him, "I am fine."

"Such maudlin disposition is suitable for Russian like me," he said, "but it looks wrong on one so handsome from land of opportunity and bliss."

It struck me as odd that Zamyenko, and by extension the men that served under him, were closely aligned with their Cold War ancestors than they were with the present Russian federation. I didn't suspect that they went back to Earth often. It may have been

---

[10] One might think that some seaman or another, between November 1943 and November 1999, would have reported to his commanding officer a human tooth or bone embedded in one of the ship's surfaces. At the very least, perhaps some disgruntled sailor, in either the United States or the Hellenic Navy, might have sold his story to any number of tabloids if such a discovery were made.

by choice. A colony founded by fervent members of the old Soviet establishment may not have looked favorably on the collapse of communism. For all I knew, they may have been living out Lenin's Last Stand, an autonomous state that, given the marked differences in technology between the indigenous and invasive species, were determined to succeed where their Earth-bound comrades failed: turning an entire planet red.

"I am curious to know where you are taking us?" I asked.

"You are going home," Zamyenko announced. "You think America is the only one with Frulx gateway?"

"What about the one I used?"

"There are only four of you now," he pointed out. "Three and Mr. Keegan, to be more precise, who was not part of your unit."

"Why not let us use the one in the desert?"

"There are threats there beyond the giants who wanted to sacrifice you to their god," Colonel Zamyenko said. "You would never survive long enough to reach your gateway. Besides, reliable intelligence sources report that your gateway was found by Veknyrians and already compromised."

"I don't believe you," I told him.

"You can thank the ghost of your company commander," he said, "for martyring himself when he blew up Riengmarnoon with his tactical weapon. Farmers outside city have always known that the Frulx gateway was in the desert. Your captain's actions pushed survivors over the edge. Crops will be ruined, poisoned with radiation. Veknyrian farmers will retaliate."

"You have sources on the ground?" I asked.

"I am Soviet Spetsnaz officer, buckaroo," said the colonel. "We never reveal sources. Besides, I must show you and your comrades New Arkaim. She is the fourth Rome. Then you can tell your capitalist government all the good we are doing here. Soon, all workers from around the world on Earth will be welcome at New Arkaim."

New Arkaim, the Russian colony city, named for the Bronze Age fortified settlement discovered in the Ural Mountains, was located just over eight hundred miles due north of the desert where we had been rescued.

Colonel Zamyenko, in a show of Soviet aviation superiority, ordered his airship brought in low as we hugged the coastline of the continent so that we could glimpse one of the planet's oceans before sunset.

"We name it Hella after succubus in Bulgakov's *The Master and Margarita*," the colonel told us. We stood together at a floor-to-ceiling window on an observation deck. "First generation settlers brought many banned books with them. They meant to form a new society. The old Soviet regime, in the settlers' estimation, did not move fast enough from socialism to bona fide communal living. The first generation here wanted a utopia of common property as well as ideas, but the old guard among the first colonists suppressed rebellion in favor of continued socialist ideals. It is only in my generation that we see true communist utopia within reach.

"The Hella Ocean," he went on, "cares not about the affairs of men and giants. She has not been kind to the People's Republic of New Arkaim. Many irregularities in magnetic fields, not unlike Bermuda Triangle. We have lost a few craft over the years. Sadly, we don't have the technology to retrieve our waste from the ocean. This does not sit well with young comrades who have the planet's ecology in mind."

At the mere mention of ecology, Hick's face glazed over with indifference.

"Hey, Colonel," said Hicks. "Who thought up this square airplane?"

"You are student of aviation?" asked Colonel Zamyenko.

"Hell no. I flunked out of high school," he said, as if failing was a point of pride. "I did get me a GED later on. I just don't know how a box without wings or rotor blades on top stays in flight."

"In September 1977," he revealed, "a great celestial event took place in the skies that stretched from Petrozavodsk in USSR to Helsinki. Forty-eight unknown objects appeared, some of them emitting other luminescent objects, over a period of two hours. It is well-known in UFO lore, this Petrozavodsk Incident. One of the objects crashed near the village of Yanishevo in the Vurnasky District. Soviet aerospace engineers reverse-engineered the antigravity drive. With such a drive, any shape can fly. Square, rectangle, isosceles triangle—"

"I get it," said Hick.

"Where did it come from?" I asked.

Colonel Zamyenko shrugged.

"Who knows anything about the origin of such things," he said. "Only now, in recent decades, with travel to Veknyria open to both Soviet and American explorers, are we beginning to understand physics we did not know before."

"Is someone going to tell him," Fly whispered to me, "about how that Soviet shit collapsed decades ago."

"What is that you say?" the colonel asked.

"Nothing, sir," I said.

Hick shot me a look. Like most self-described patriots, he equated respect of a foreign officer's rank, regardless of what country that person served in, as an affront to the good old U.S. of A.

"Your friend is comedian," Colonel Zamyenko said.

"Not me, man," said Fly.

"In communist utopia of the People's Republic of New Arkaim," he said to him, "you would be treated as equal."

"I doubt that," he argued.

"It's true," the colonel said. "Once we get there, you will change your mind. New Arkaim is much closer than you think, but we must continue scheduled reconnaissance before we go back."

In the day's dying light, Fly, Hick, and I studied the ocean and a coastal front that lay far to the west. The waters which were several hundred feet below the craft appeared calm from that height. A flock of white birds flew beneath us as the craft descended toward the coastline. As quickly as they appeared, we lost sight of them.

A couple of hours after nightfall an announcement came over the intercom in Russian. When it finished, the speaker at the microphone exhaled, as if disappointed, and repeated the message in English.

"Please take seats and fasten seat belts, comrades," the voice said. "We are making our final approach to New Arkaim. Thank you for flying The People's Republic of New Arkaim Air. As always, tips are appreciated."

"Where the hell is Sonny?" I said.

"That crazy sailor?" Hick asked.

We were already seated in a common area on sofas that faced one another. Colonel Zamyenko laughed and elbowed his captain.

"Mr. Keegan has been quarantined in our sick bay," Yorlovsky announced. "He has radiation poisoning."

"Your comrade is in good hands," the colonel added. Then, addressing Yorlovsky, he asked. "Was that Uri on the radio?"

"It was," said the captain. "Always with the jokes. If he paid as much attention to keeping his quarters in order for inspections, who knows what rank he might achieve."

"That reminds me," Colonel Zamyenko said, unfastening his seat belt, "I wanted to have a word with you in private, Kapitan."

"But sir," he responded, "we will be landing soon."

"You doubt safety of Soviet technology?" he asked as he raised his hands from his side the way a conductor might the moment before a symphony begins.

Kapitan Yorlovsky followed Colonel Zamyenko through a door that slid open at their approach. Once they cleared the threshold, the door slid shut.

"I'm going to say it just this once," Fly announced. "I don't trust these dudes at all."

"I'm with you, brother," Hick said. Fly leaned back in his seat and shot him a look. "I meant like brothers in arms and all that."

"Uh-huh."

"I'm serious. Anyway, I just had to say what was on my mind."

The paranoid nutcase inside me kicked into high gear. I pointed at the ceiling and mouthed the words *they might be listening*.

Hick made a face. Fly threw his hands up in despair.

"I don't read lips," said Fly.

"Me neither," Hick added. "Unless they belong to some fine dish of a woman."

Fly shook his head. "How the fuck did you ever procreate?" he demanded.

"I don't know how you northern bucks do it up yonder," said Hick, "but banging my wife like a screen door in a windstorm always did the trick."

"Charming," Fly offered. To me, he said, "What were you saying?"

"They might be listening to us," I said.

"Shit," Hick said. "Ever since we got on this contraption I've been sweating like a pregnant nun at confession."

"You going to stand for this?" Fly asked.

"Me?" I asked. "Why?"

"You're Catholic, aren't you?"

"Lapsed is more like it."

"Didn't you and those other guys always go to chapel services every Sunday in basic training way back when?"

"You have a good memory."

"Thank you."

"I went to chapel services," I confessed, "because it got me out of shit details like KP duty."

"That's fucked up," Hick said. "Using Jesus like that."

"Why don't you pray on it, chucklehead?" Fly asked.

Before Hick could respond, the door to the common area slid open. Colonel Zamyenko entered alone. He settled onto the sofa next to Hick and fastened his seat belt.

"Weather is fair in New Arkaim as we make final approach," the voice on the intercom Zamyenko identified as Uri announced. "A special note for our American visitors: New Arkaim covers twenty-seven square kilometers. That's approximately seventeen square miles for our American guests. Population of New Arkaim is 69,872. It's going to be cold winter, so the Ministry of Birth Control forecasts an increased population soon. In all, sixty percent of population was born here on this trippy, far-out planet filled with monsters and giants. Thank you for flying The People's Republic Airlines. We hope to see you again soon."

"That Uri," Colonel Zamyenko said, proudly. "Always with the jokes. Far-out, trippy. Where does he get such stuff?"

Chapter 28: The Next New Party Member

The climate in The People's Republic of New Arkaim was considerably cooler than the desert of my unit's undoing. If I had to find a comparable place temperature-wise, I would say northern Michigan. Since the fractured moon Hiriruta had receded below the horizon that time of year, Destrayama, in the withering sister's absence, loomed large over the abundant tree line that bordered the airfield adjacent to the fortified city of New Arkaim.

The tallest structure in New Arkaim, save for some evenly spaced watched towers placed at different points around the walled city, was a building called The Ministry of Travel. It stood only four stories. Most houses, the colonel had informed us, stood only two stories high. The rooftops were all reinforced with a steel mesh meant to stop falling javelins thrown over the walls.

When we exited the airship, Colonel Zamyenko strode proudly across the field to a heavily guarded gate. The soldiers manning the post eyed us with the same suspicion that Kapitan Yorlovsky had throughout most of the flight. It may have had to do with some inane indoctrination, American capitalist pigs are all bad and that sort of thing, or the dirty looks may have been a direct reaction to Hick Haywood's distrust of the Russians that he proudly wore like an armed forces campaign badge.

One of the sergeants under Colonel Zamyenko's command with the unfortunate moniker of Pavel Ravel briefed Fly, Hick, and me about the particulars of New Arkaim. By his rehearsed enthusiasm, it was clear to the three of us that in addition to his regular duties as a noncommissioned officer in Spetsnaz, Pavel was also responsible for playing the part of cultural attaché and all-around utopian commune enthusiast.

"It is like nothing you have seen," Pavel said. "The city itself was designed by our founders before embarking on the journey that served as Soviet manifest destiny. In 1962, some six years following the discovery, after much consideration and long hours of arguing into the night, it was the daughter of one of the primary architects who settled the dispute over planning the city's layout. Her name is Sofia Dashkova. You will meet her, I am sure. It was Sofia who set the architects straight. Her father Romany Dashkova put the question to his only child: what shape appeals to you most? Sofia, who was seven years old at the time, told her father the city of our utopia should be shaped like a chambered nautilus shell.

"As you will soon see," he continued, "none of our streets are straight and all of the houses and buildings possess no right angles. In the early days, Veknyrian hordes tried to overrun New Arkaim, but the settlers triumphed thanks in part to Sofia's ingenuous design. You are military men. As such, you know that the soldier who is lost is the soldier who diminishes his chances of survival.

"And here," he said, halting at the gate so the guards stationed there could verify his identification along with ours, "just inside the walls, our chariots await."

I recognized them by their silhouettes in the dark. A long time ago, when I was an infantryman, all the units were issued playing cards with standard suits printed on one side and the silhouettes of enemy ground vehicles on the other. The jeeps awaiting us, Pavel's chariots, were UAZ-469s. Each one had to be at least thirty years old. The jeeps looked like they were made from equal parts painted over body fill and doubt. When the drivers in each of the four jeeps turned their ignitions, the sound of the aging engines did not inspire much hope.

"Cal," Fly said to me, "these dudes are single-handedly going to deplete this planet's ozone layer."

"You need not worry about ecological damage," Sergeant Pavel Ravel told us. "Converter kits have been placed on each vehicle." He pronounced the word "vehicle" as *wee-huckle*. "Combustible engines still, yes. But now, thanks to superior Soviet science, all conventional motors run on biofuel created from agricultural residue and wood waste."

"Couldn't you spring for electric motors?" Fly asked.

Pavel stared at him. A huge grin formed.

"You are the joker," he said, at last. "Colonel Zamyenko tells me this."

"Sergeant Ravel," Kapitan Yorlovsky shouted. He snapped his fingers on one hand and made a circular motion in the air with his other hand. "Load them into vehicles."

"Yes sir!" Pavel snapped. Then, he pointed to the jeep closest to me. "You will ride with Colonel Zamyenko. Your comrades will go in separate vehicles."

"Hell, buddy," Hick spoke up. "Why can't the three of us ride together?"

"There is danger," the sergeant informed him.

"What danger could exist in a utopia?" I asked.

"Partisan heathens of the Veknyrian Resistance sneak close to wall at night," Pavel announced, "and lob their javelins. Sometimes there are casualties. It's best to drive in separate vehicles spaced apart to avoid getting killed."

When we landed, I saw no signs of fixed structures outside the walls of New Arkaim. If there were Veknyrians in the woods surrounding the city, it made sense that they kept no lights or fires going.

"Resistance?" Hick said. "Sounds like we're with the wrong bunch."

"Please," Pavel said, gesturing to the jeep, "it is dangerous to stand still."

"I don't like it."

"Hick, come on," Fly said. "If these guys wanted us dead, why save us from the Veknyrians who were going to kill us anyway?"

"That may be," said Hick. "But I'm nervous as a cat in a roomful of rocking chairs."

"You will come with me," Kapitan Yorlovsky stepped up behind Hick and jammed a pistol into his kidneys.

"All right, all right," he said, putting his hands up in surrender. "Just put the gun away."

Pavel pointed to the jeep I was to board. "Mr. Paladin," he said. "If you please."

Fly and I looked at each other. It felt like several minutes passed in silence even though it was only a few scant seconds.

"Be cool, man," Fly spoke first. "We'll see each other soon."

"Of course," the sergeant said before I could respond. "We are not at war."

The jeep's interior smelled of cigarettes and rust. The driver, a private with no discernible neck beneath his big head, hunched his massive shoulders and put the jeep into gear. With a lurch, we were off to the interior of New Arkaim.

The outermost rim of the city, Sergeant Pavel Ravel explained to me, was reserved for military quarters. At the center of the fortified city lay the Ministry of Travel, he told me with a wink.

"You get a lot of vacation trade on this planet?" I asked.

"No one ever needs vacation from utopia," Pavel announced. "No, it's an inside joke. Actually, that was one too. You see, at the very most interior of the city lies the gateway off this world. It is also heavily guarded with soldiers who are authorized to shoot trespassers on sight. Even utopias have their limits."

I didn't say anything. Instead, I took in the sights as we rode through the curved streets of the city. Inside the perimeter of military quarters was a layer reserved for businesses of every sort from food stands to bars, from foundries to factories. The military quarters, the business section, and the houses that stood closer to the center were all connected, just as the chambers of a nautilus shell were, and they were constructed from stonework cultivated, Pavel informed me, from a nearby quarry. The edifice of the fortified city was colored red from the stone and mortar made from the planet's rich red soil.

It wasn't so much fitting as it was disturbing that the Soviet comrades lost in time built a city colored red. If the Veknyrian mind reacted to the color red anything like the human mind did, no wonder the indigenous people spent their days and nights hurling javelins over the walls.

I shared my revelation with Pavel.

"That is yerunda," said Pavel. "What you Americans call nonsense. The Veknyrians want to kill us because we are here. You are a learned man, so you will understand. Sometimes war is needed to make peace. They will come around or they will die clinging to their old ways."

The hulking driver nodded his approval, as if he were driving Vladimir Ilyich Ulyanov Lenin himself.

They put me in a house on a street with no name and a guard posted at the front door.

Where food was concerned, the first four days I spent in that house were eerily similar to my brief stay at Fort Dix. A cook showed up three times a day to whip up simple meals. Whenever I finished eating, whatever knife I was allowed to use, the cook took away. Stabbings must have been a thing in this utopia.

On the fifth day, one of the junior officers I recognized from Colonel Zamyenko's airship showed up bearing a dull grey nondescript uniform.

"The People's Couture," the lieutenant cried. His name was Isbalov. He was a short, stocky effete. I decided I didn't like him. "Everyone's wearing them."

"You're not," I pointed out his full Spetsnaz regalia.

Isbalov looked down at his government-issued attire. Then he straightened up and stared at me.

"I am on-duty," he declared. "Official business. I am to take you to meet Comrade Podrovsky, the politruk here in New Arkaim."

"What's a—"

"Our chief political officer," said Isbalov. "When in a foreign land, one must learn the local language."

"That doesn't sound like Veknyrian to me," I said.

"Yes, well, one should have a working knowledge of the savage's tongue," he said, "if only to subjugate them."

"When the hell am I going to see my friends?" I asked, tiring of the repartee.

"I can assure you that your comrades are quite safe," he assured me. "Now, please. Get dressed. We must not keep Comrade Podrovsky waiting."

I went upstairs to the closet that constituted a bedroom, changed, peeked out the window that had bars affixed to the frame outside, and saw the guard at my door smoking a cigarette. A relic of a jeep, slightly different in shape than the one that had brought me to my temporary quarters, idled in the road.

Descending the stairs, a feeling of desperation overcame me. I felt more removed from Emma than ever before. My knees buckled and I nearly toppled down the steps. The only thing that prevented me from doing so was how narrow the stairwell was. My footing remained precarious at best when I reached the bottom step. Like a good politruk in the making, Lieutenant Isbalov was there to stop my fall.

"Mr. Paladin," he said, catching me under the arms with his powerful hands. "You don't look so well. Do you need water? Shall I have your escort call for a medic?"

Escort, I thought. That was rich.

"No," I told him. "Just dizzy from high blood pressure."

Half of the statement was true. Given the amount of medication my cardiologist had me on before the army came calling, I didn't know how it came to be that I had not dropped dead yet.

"Then we go," the lieutenant let go of me and gestured to the door.

When we exited the house I noticed that nobody bothered to lock the front door. At first, I thought my "escort" was going to hang around in my absence. He didn't. No sooner than Isbalov and I climbed into the deathtrap of a Russian-manufactured jeep the guard faced right and marched away from the house.

"You keep your doors unlocked?" I asked.

"Mr. Paladin," said Isbalov. "You are in the People's Republic of New Arkaim. This is not your Chicago or Watts with dope fiends burning and looting everywhere."

"You know," I felt compelled to stand up for the homeland, "that happened decades ago, right?"

"It is the nature of every capitalist society to destroy itself," he looked out the side window as he spoke. "Your whole life has been one of glut and false remorse, comrade."

"Is this the part where you tell me I'm a sleeper agent who's come home to roost?" I asked.

"Perhaps you are," the lieutenant said.

The driver was the first to break character. He started laughing like a maniac. Isbalov's turn was next. He sounded worse once he got going with his jackal-like snigger. They kept on laughing until the driver reached the Ministry of Travel building.

Alexei Ivanovich Podrovsky, the politruk supreme, looked like someone had just pulled him from a crate crammed airtight with moth balls. And he smelled like that too. Alexei Podrovsky, squat of build like Lieutenant Isbalov, was much thinner than any of the other Russians I had encountered so far. Every breath he took was labored; each step could have been his last. He looked to be eighty years old, maybe older than that.

Colonel Zamyenko was in attendance along with Kapitan Yorlovsky who scowled at me the moment I entered the giant drawing room just inside the street entrance. Conspicuously absent were Fly and Hick.

"Thank you for joining us this evening," the old man said. "My name is Alexei Ivanovich Podrovsky. Welcome to the Ministry of Travel."

"Where are my friends?" I asked.

Podrovsky looked at Colonel Zamyenko. When he spoke, I didn't catch all of it, given how rusty my Russian was, but I definitely heard the words for "manners" and "goat."

"Mr. Paladin," Colonel Zamyenko spoke up now. "Please extend Comrade Podrovsky some respect. He is a revered hero of The Great Patriotic War. Without him and his vision, New Arkaim would not thrive."

"I meant no offense," I said.

"It is rare we get visitors here in our city," Podrovsky announced. "And then most of them are Veknyrian who wind up dead. If they were not such savages, perhaps they could embrace a true government for the people by the people, yes?"

"It sounds like you're pitching democracy."

"Why impose a form of government on the indigenous population that will create class struggle down the road?"

"That's a good question," I admitted.

"Come," he gestured to a set of double doors across the room. "Let us dispense with ideology and see that our stomachs get full."

I followed him and Colonel Zamyenko through the double doors. Lieutenant Isbalov took up the rear behind me. Kapitan Yorlovsky had slipped away already.

The bar on the other side of the double doors looked more like a mobsters' social club than it did a government-sponsored watering hole. The linoleum tiles on the floor were chipped and curled at the corners. The tables, a baker's dozen in all, were small round ones, the kind you'd see at church bingo. The bar itself was a series of haphazardly assembled planks, unstained, against a wall that offered a polished piece of sheet metal instead of a mirror.

To my relief, Fly Kidd sat at the bar drinking from a snifter as he smoked a cigar. Hick Haywood was still absent.

"Hey, Fly," I said, "how's it hanging?"

"It ain't nothing but a thing," he replied. "They gave me Courvoisier and a Cuban cigar. An actual Cuban cigar, Cal."

"Where's Hick?" I asked.

Fly averted my gaze.

"What is your poison, Mr. Paladin?" Colonel Zamyenko asked.

"Oh," I didn't feel like drinking, "I don't know—"

"Anatole!" he barked.

The bartender looked up from the book he was reading, a thick tome with a title printed in Russian on the spine. His hands were all wrong for his job. They were thick, the knuckles calloused. My guess was Anatole was either a soldier in plainclothes or part of Podrovsky's security detail.

"Yes, sir," Anatole dropped the book. "How may I be of service to you and your honored guests?"

"Vodka all around," the colonel instructed him.

"Where is Hick?" I asked no one in particular. "Why isn't he here?"

Anatole poured the vodka into large shot glasses. Colonel Zamyenko picked up a glass and handed it to me. Next, he gave Fly one even though Fly shook his head. The colonel insisted. Once everyone had a shot glass in hand, Colonel Zamyenko offered a toast.

"To old friends and new," said the colonel. "May the next new party member be you."

I looked at Fly. He shrugged and downed the vodka in his glass. I followed his example, slamming the glass down on the bar after I did.

"Smooth," I said, barely able to speak from the burning in my throat.

"And now we wait for poison to do its job," said Colonel Zamyenko.

"Dimitri!" Podrovsky admonished him.

"I was just having a bit of fun," he replied.

Behind Podrovsky, a door opened. On the threshold stood a beautiful, blue-eyed woman whose dark hair was graced with white gray streaks.

"Do you mean to leave me in the dining room alone all night?" the woman asked.

"Snap to it!" Podrovsky cried. "We must not keep Comrade Dashkova waiting."

"Goddamn," Fly muttered loud enough for only me to hear. "I didn't know they built brick houses in Russia like that."

He looked around for an ashtray for his cigar. Anatole slid one along the bar to him.

"Thanks, Ivan," said Fly.

"It's Anatole," the bartender corrected him.

"I'm just playing, man," he told him.

"We do not play in New Arkaim," said Anatole.

"Gentlemen," Colonel Zamyenko called out. "May I present the designer of New Arkaim, Comrade Sofia Dashkova."

Suddenly, the woman stood before me. Up close, her eyes were colored pale crystal blue, her oval face graced with full lips and a narrow nose.

"The credit goes to my father," she said.

I extended my hand, unsure of what to do. Sofia took it, gave it a good strong pump, and let it go. Fly shook her hand next.

Sofia held onto Fly's hand, turning it over this way and that.

"Forgive me," she said. "I have not seen a man of your complexion in decades."

"Not many brothers in New Arkaim?" Fly asked.

"Alas, I am an only child," she replied.

"Comrade Podrovsky beckons us," Colonel Zamyenko announced.

Sofia stood between Fly and me and threaded her arms through ours. She guided us to the dining room in that fashion. It felt like my feet barely touched the ground as she walked beside me.

Chapter 29: Operation Dry-Out

Dinner consisted of a fowl dish with native vegetables and wine made from a colony vineyard. I had never been a wine guy, but Emma, when we were still together, lauded wine as the only alcoholic beverage that went with dinner. Red wine, white wine, it didn't matter. One of the many things I admired about Emma when we first met was that she had always been repulsed by zinfandel. In the late 1980's, while I was still in college, many girls I knew were into zinfandel, but Emma never liked the taste. She wasn't much of a drinker at all. Around the holidays, if someone bought me a bottle of whiskey or bourbon, Emma often forced me to regift. She never wanted hard liquor in the house. In the early days after she first left me, you can bet I kept plenty of bottles around.

At some point during my story, Sofia excused herself and got up from the table. That's when Fly tapped me on the shoulder.

"Stop doing that," he said.

"What am I doing?" I asked.

"No woman wants to hear all that."

"What do you mean?"

"Stop talking about your ex-wife."

"I was talking about wine."

"The wine was anecdotal," said Fly. "You were talking about your ex. You think a woman like Sofia wants to go to bed with a guy who talks about his ex-wife like some saint?"

"What makes you think she wants to sleep with me?" I asked.

"You're stupider than I thought," he informed me.

We didn't get a chance to discuss it much further. Kapitan Yorlovsky entered the dining room. He stood behind Colonel Zamyenko and whispered into the colonel's right ear.

"Something's up," said Fly. "We have to get out of here."

"And go where?" I asked. "So far, everything on this planet, barring our hosts, wants us dead."

"We could use their gateway," he said.

"If we knew where it was."

"I'm going to piss," Fly informed me. "Maybe have a look around."

"Fly," I started to say, but he was already gone.

He made his way to the door Sofia had used to exit the dining hall. One of the colonel's sergeants followed him. So much for snooping around.

"Mr. Paladin," Sofia said when she returned to the table, "please tell me more about your home."

"What do you want to know?" I asked.

"You are reluctant to talk to me now," she said. "I'm gone for only a few seconds, and you have closed me off. What a pity."

"I'd rather not bore you with details of my working-class upbringing," I confessed.

"You read books?"

"They are better than television."

"Yes," she said. "I have vague memories of state-run television. Did America switch to such a set-up?"

"There's a conservative news agency our president *thinks* is his personal state-run broadcast news," I said.

"Like Pravda?"

"That's a good analogy."

"Who do you read?"

Pandering to Sofia's Russian sensibilities would have seemed transparent. She was smarter than that. Still, I had no idea how long she had lived on Veknyria. She was too old to have been born in New Arkaim. Besides, it wasn't like citizens of the fortified city were members of the Book-of-the-Month Club. Did they even have a library? I wondered. If they did, what titles from Earth were banned? Honesty, I decided, was the only way.

"I've always liked Kurt Vonnegut," I said.

"He doesn't sound familiar," she said slowly, as if searching for the right words. "No wait. Of course. He wrote *Player Piano*. My father had this book. He worried, my father, that is, about the Party's validity after such a time when machines replaced workers in factories. I remember this. Who else?"

"There are so many," I said, worried that Fly had gotten into trouble or arrested.

"Did you read Dostoevsky?"

"In college," I revealed. "A seminar. We read *Notes from Underground, Crime and Punishment, The Idiot,* and *The Brothers Karamazov.*"

"In the original Russian?"

"Sadly, no."

I left out the part about taking three semesters of Russian and my dream of going to Moscow after Communism's collapse to find writers and introduce their books to the free world.

Sofia patted my forearm. "Tell me who else," she said. "I don't get to talk about books that much."

"Don't your comrades read?" I asked.

"We have books," said Sofia. "But ultimately the Politburo decides what is for the good of the people."

"Do you still have the Vonnegut book?"

"I have many books," she said.

"I'd like to see them," I told her.

Fly returned to the dining hall with a fresh snifter of Courvoisier and a new cigar. He appeared chummy with the sergeant who had escorted him to the restroom.

"Everything good?" I asked Fly when he came back to the table.

Podrovsky, Colonel Zamyenko, and the officers stood up one by one and headed for the door that led to the bar. A couple of old waiters entered the dining room and began clearing plates.

"Fly," the sergeant called to him. "Let's go freshen our drinks."

When Fly protested, the sergeant hauled him to his feet. Fly went off with him, leaving me alone with Sofia.

"Should we join them?" I asked.

Sofia stood up, taking my hand as she did so.

"You want to see my books?" she asked.

I did.

We left the dining room and went into the foyer where the grand staircase was located. Sofia showed me to her rooms on the third floor. She had a lovely library with books from Russia, America, Europe, and South America. She had a first edition English version of Gabriel Garcia Marquez's *One Hundred Years of Solitude.*

"Gabo's one of my favorite writers," I said.

"Caleb," Sofia spoke softly as she stood behind me.

I turned to face her just as she pulled her dress over her head. For a moment, standing there with the Marquez book in my hands, I almost forgot what to do.

I am a world-class idiot when it comes to lovemaking. No sooner than Sofia of the soft pale skin and ample assets and I had finished, I began drifting in and out of sleep. She left me in her bed to go to the bathroom. I should have known better. The moment Sofia closed her bathroom door and locked it; her bedroom door swung open.

Kapitan Yorlovsky stood there with two noncommissioned officers, real salt of the earth meatheads who looked like they were itching for a fight.

"You will come with us," Kapitan Yorlovsky announced. When I looked toward the bathroom door, he added, "she's not coming out."

"Please don't hurt her," I told him.

"Comrade Dashkova has done the people and the party a service," the captain said. "She will be rewarded accordingly. Now, get dressed."

When he brandished a pistol, some old Russian-made firearm that looked like it had not been fired since the Bosnian War, it seemed at once cheap and comical. Nevertheless, I put some hustle into getting dressed.

Kapitan Yorlovsky and his two henchmen escorted me to a spiral stone stairwell at the far end of the hall. We had to move single-file down the winding stairs. The two bruisers were ahead of me, and the captain was behind me pressing the barrel of his pistol against the top of my head the whole time.

After passing the main floor we descended two more landings before reaching the bottom. The lead goon pounded his fist on a wood door. The thick door opened. A guard stood on the other side. Yorlovsky tapped me on the ear with the barrel of his pistol before waving the gun at the open door.

I wanted to grab his gun hand and force him to shoot his two goons before I elbowed the captain in his balls and turned the gun on him. The problem with my plan was that I was a fifty-four-year-old Earthling on a planet where the gravity was nearly twice as strong as it was at home. Fucking Sofia had proved more of a grueling chore than I first realized. I was exhausted. My martial prowess, as it turned out, had been severely diminished by time and gravity. I didn't feel much like heroics that night. One of the captain's goons grabbed me by the neck and pushed me through the open door.

I turned with what I hoped was a defiant look on my face. The expression I wore turned out to be a waste. The guard in the hallway behind the heavy wood door was joined by two others. They were armed with nightsticks. One of them pointed at a cell door at the opposite end of the hall.

A tall guard who looked like he hadn't seen the sun since the day he was born inserted a skeletal key into the door lock and turned it. The other two grabbed me and shoved me into the cell before the cell's occupants or I could react. The door was shut and locked behind me.

Fly sat on the floor with his back against one wall. There was no furniture in the room, not even a crude bunk. There was a small toilet, one of those old-fashioned jobs with the box on the wall about head level and a pull chain, along with the smallest sink I'd ever seen in my life. Hick Haywood lay on the floor opposite Fly. He looked worn out. The skin beneath his eyes was bruised and dried blood crusted his nostrils.

"They fucked him up," said Fly, nodding at our cohort.

"Should have seen the other guys," Hick grunted through his teeth.

Fly pointed to his jaw. "Broken," he said, nodding in Hick's direction.

"And some ribs too," Hick offered. "As long as I don't move or breathe, I'm fine."

"Back to normal," I said.

"Don't make me laugh."

"What did they want?"

"The usual," he said, keeping his teeth clenched. "Where are the rest of our troops? How far away was the main element? Are there plans for an invasion on New Arkaim?"

"Did you tell them we were it?"

"They didn't like that answer."

"I'm sorry, Hick."

"Someone's going to have to pinch hit for me," he mumbled. "I won't live through another beating."

They came for Fly next.

Meanwhile, Hick looked worse than he did the previous evening. I did my best to keep him still, but he insisted on getting to his feet and hobbling around the cell, pausing at the toilet to spit blood into the bowl.

"Does your head hurt?" I asked. Then, I thought better of such a stupid question. "Of course it does. Do me a favor when you stop walking."

"What's that?" Hick asked.

"Don't lay with your head on the ground," I said. "You should sit up."

"I'm fine," he said.

"No," I told him. "Chances are you have a concussion, maybe even a skull fracture."

"Christ, Paladin," said Hick. "You're worse than my old lady."

Hick and I didn't talk much after that. When we served in the 101st Airborne as young guys, he was a knucklehead of the highest order; a *good-time charlie*, he was, a term coined by some general for the army who in turn included it in a handbook about army life they issued to recruits during basic training.

Good-time charlies were the guys who went drinking to excess the night before the start of a big field exercise. They tried to sneak girls into the barracks which was not permitted for obvious reasons:

namely, the barracks belonging to infantry units the world over
were, from modern times dating back to the ancient Greeks, zones
of controlled lawlessness as opposed to a regimented lifestyle.
Good-time charlies were the stars of the military, the goofball
angels who kept the whole works glued together, the specter of the
Uniformed Code of Military Justice be damned.

I confess I was not above good-time charlie behavior in my days
as a young soldier. I drew the line with trying to lure women into
the barracks. The kind of girls who were up for such shenanigans
were not girlfriend material and the girls who were possible
girlfriend material would never be caught dead in an army infantry
barracks unless it was open for public tour[11].

Hick Haywood and his merry band of good old boys were a
different story. One of their favorite activities on a Friday or
Saturday night, if they had no luck with the local ladies at any
number of honky-tonk bars up and down the strip outside the army
base, was to adjourn to one club or another they normally refused to
frequent, mostly because those establishments didn't play country
music, and, having had their share of liquid courage, start fights
with other soldiers. Sometimes, depending on their state of
inebriation, they even got into brawls with guys from their own
unit. Sometimes they won; other times they got their asses handed
to them. When the latter happened, they begged off working on
Mondays by going to the medic station and sulking there long
enough for some medic to take pity on them and their blackened
eyes and issue them light-duty orders for a few days.

Hick and the other good-time charlies in our company were the
reason why we spent more time in the field than any other unit on

---

[11] In the army there were some good days. Those were outnumbered by
the bad days like when the post opened to veterans for a tour and your unit
was designated host. There was nothing worse than spending a week
making sure your boots were spit-shined, your uniforms were pressed, the
floor in your room and the hallway outside were highly waxed and buffed,
and all evidence of alcohol consumption and porn magazine perusal was
removed—all of which was preparation for what we used to call *the dog-
and-pony show*—and then having some geezer come through your room
and run his old trigger finger atop your wall locker, the one he had used to
kill countless Nazis during WWII, and come away with a speck of dust.

post. Our company commander used to refer to our field exercises collectively as Operation Dry-Out.

The absurd behaviors that proved acceptable for infantry soldiers had to be curtailed upon reentering civilian life, even Hick Haywood had to change his ways or eventually wind up in jail. What didn't change about him over the decades was his combative nature. Like him, it just got older. Hick either refused to acknowledge or simply could not comprehend that not every confrontation had to be settled with fists.

There was no place in the cell to get comfortable. I ended up sitting on the floor and leaning against the wall beside the door. A few times I dozed off, my head snapping forward when I did so. At one point, Hick was lying on his back again with his head beneath the small sink at the back of the cell. The first time I saw him like that I felt angry because he hadn't listened to me. Later, as I lingered between consciousness and sleep, I saw him roll over onto his side, grunt in pain, owing to his broken ribs, and turned onto his back once more.

"Hick," I said. "Sit up."

He ignored me.

I fell asleep again after that. I didn't know if it was only mere seconds or several minutes that passed after that, but I came to long enough to see that Hick looked like he was no longer breathing.

As soon as I got to my feet to go to him the cell door lock turned, and the door swung open. Someone shoved Fly into the cell and slammed the door shut. Fly caught himself against the rim of the sink and pushed back.

"Are you okay?" I asked him.

"My arms are killing me from how they chained me to the ceiling, but yeah I'm good," said Fly. He nodded at Hick. "Is he dead?"

"No, you goddamn moron," Hick muttered.

"Did they..." I started to say.

Fly shook his head and nodded at Hick who kept his eyes closed. "They wanted intelligence," he said.

"Then they should have killed you, you dumb son of a bitch," said Hick.

"Hey, Hick?"

"Yeah, Fly?"

"I will stomp on you until you die if you bring my momma into this, understood?"

Hick considered this a moment. "You're right, Fly," he said. "I apologize for that."

"That's more like it—"

"I was referencing your daddy," Hick told him. "Did you know him?"

"Tell us about what happened," I stepped between Fly and Hick now.

"They want to know about how we got here," he said.

"Name, rank, and serial number," said Hick. "That's all I gave them."

"Right," Fly said. "And look at where that got you."

"At least I didn't tell them anything."

"Is anyone going to remember you for that?"

"Listen," I said to Fly, "it's important to know what you told them."

"I told them about the gate on the reservation," he said. "Then I told them about how I shot Captain Prescott and he was back to work the next day like nothing happened."

"You sang like a canary," Hick said.

"They thought I was joking about the android," said Fly.

"And you didn't give up anything else?" I asked.

"No," he said. "How could I give them anything else if I don't know anything?"

"Did they ask about Riengmarnoon?" I asked Fly.

"They think we did them a favor in that respect," Fly told me. "Oh yeah, they should bring some food soon. I told them we're hungry."

Fly wasn't kidding. It wasn't long before the lock was disengaged, and the door opened. Two guards entered and stood on either side of the door. Three others came in behind them bearing trays with a plate of gruel on each of them, tin mugs filled with cold water, and utensils. One of the guards by the door nodded at Hick before all five of them exited.

Less than a minute later, the cell door opened again. Two guards entered bearing a litter. They hoisted Hick up rather unceremoniously and placed him on the litter. One of them warned him not to move. The guards hauled Hick out of the cell.

When they came for me I had already finished eating. To think that the slop they served may have been my last meal felt like I had been short-changed. In my interrogation fantasies during my first enlistment back in the 1980's I always pictured filet mignon done medium rare, grilled shrimp, and a baked potato with sour cream and chives as my last meal before they put the screws to me. It was sheer foolishness to consider such things. What was the point of a good meal if you were going to waste it by dying? I don't think we carried such memories with us after death and I told my guard escorts as much. They looked at me like I was crazy and did not respond.

Chapter 30: A Reasonable Facsimile

My arms had gone numb by the time Sofia entered the interrogation room. Once my interrogators started beating me, I knew why they had left Fly unscathed. They wanted us to be at odds over our mutual treatment.

Kapitan Yorlovsky conducted the interrogation. That is to say he took particular enjoyment in seeing me suffer while asking me questions. At one point, as I hung there from the ceiling, my shackled wrists chained to a metal rafter, he asked me if I had any questions for him.

"Where's Sonny Keegan?" I asked.

"Who?"

"The sailor."

It wasn't accurate to describe Sonny as such, but Colonel Zamyenko and his men did anyway.

"Oh, yes," the captain said. "A terrible thing, really. It seems your American sailor friend had a weak heart. He could not withstand the rigors of interrogation—"

"He's dead," I cut him off.

Yorlovsky laughed.

"You misunderstand," he said. "Keegan survived heart attack. He's being tended to as we speak."

"I don't believe you."

Yorlovsky waved a dismissive hand. "What you believe doesn't change facts, Mr. Paladin," he said. "Now, here's your situation: you must give us something we don't know in exchange for your freedom."

"A particle of light can be seen as either a point or a wave," I said, "but never both at the same time."

"Do you take me for a fool, Mr. Paladin?"

"That's a fact."

Yorlovsky nodded at his lackey. Popkov hit me in the gut with his cudgel.

"I meant physics," I grunted, clenching my teeth.

"I know that," he said. "Now you are wasting my time. More importantly, you're wasting Ladislav Popkov's time. And Ladislav hates to have his time wasted."

Popkov was a low-ranking noncom who administered state-sanctioned pain, a low-brow miscreant of the highest order, a torturer devoid of empathy toward the tortured. He'd spent too much time underground in the catacombs of the fortified city, judging by his gypsum complexion. Fortunately, thus far, he'd spent a great deal of time explaining in broken English how he preferred not to waste lit cigarettes on me. Ditto for using a rusted, imposing-looking hand drill on my kneecaps, as if I should be grateful he had decided against that particular form of pain management—as Kapitan Yorlovsky referred to the interrogation session.

One instrument that was as unrelenting as it was unavoidable was the torturer's breath. Popkov exhibited a penchant for invading personal space and exhaling his putrid breath on me.

"You like woman, yes?" Popkov asked.

"What woman?" I asked.

He jabbed me in the ribs with a cudgel.

"Maybe I make you woman like I did your comrade Hick," he said, pronouncing the Georgian's name as *heek*.

"Give me something, Mr. Paladin," Yorlovsky interjected, sounding as if he were bored of Popkov's threats. "The sooner you do, the sooner we can verify. It's that simple."

"Our company commander was an android," I said.

"Your other comrade gave that up already."

"Did he mention the bomb?"

Yorlovsky stepped close to me and swatted Popkov away, wrinkling his nose at the torturer's breath as he did so.

"We know a bomb destroyed Riengmarnoon," the captain said. "How did he transport it to this planet?"

"It was inside of him," I informed Yorlovsky. Despite Hick Haywood's undying and misguided love of country, I figured since Captain Prescott had self-detonated there was no harm in telling Yorlovsky about it. "He was pre-programmed to self-detonate if the need arose."

"Yes, we heard this tall tale from your black comrade," he said.

"It's true," I told him.

"How many stories tall was this Captain Prescott?" asked Yorlovsky. "A nuclear missile—"

"American scientists have made them small enough," I said, "to fit in a rucksack. The same kind that Captain Prescott carried inside himself. Look, I can't help you are stuck in the 1950's cut off from the rest of—"

Popkov, at Yorlovsky's nod, struck me with his cudgel several times in the small of my back.

"Try again," the captain said, and yawned.

"It's called a limited strike weapon," I explained. "It had a blast radius of a mile and a total kill radius of two and a half miles. Look it up on the internet, for Christ's sake."

"What is internet?"

"A wireless network...wait, you don't know what the web is?"

"This web you speak of," Yorlovsky said. "It is some form of surveillance?"

"It can be. Sure."

"I don't believe you," Kapitan Yorlovsky said.

"What you believe," I repeated what he had said earlier. "doesn't change facts."

Yorlovsky smirked. Then he snapped his fingers and jerked his thumb at me.

Popkov came at me with his cudgel again. He worked over my legs that time. My shin bones felt like they were fractured from the blows he administered. This went on for a couple of minutes. He tired easily, given his large frame, becoming winded which didn't sit well with Yorlovsky.

The captain mumbled something in Russian to Popkov. The torturer approached once more, raising his cudgel high into the air. He brought it down hard on my head.

The hand that led me out of the dark was lavender-scented and soft.

"Good morning, my little American," Sofia leaned close and whispered in my ear.

"What are you—" I started to say.

"Give Yorlovsky something we can use," she whispered as she kept her cheek close to mine. "He would like nothing more than to kill you."

"Enough," Kapitan Yorlovsky announced.

"You dare to speak to a cultural hero that way?" Sofia turned on him now.

"Please, Comrade Dashkova," he said, "You must understand I am only doing what is required."

He tried to grab her hand and kiss it, but Sofia slapped his hands aside.

"The American has something to tell you."

Don't leave, I thought. As long as Sofia remained in the interrogation room I knew that no more harm would come to me.

"What would you like to share?" Yorlovsky asked me.

"If it will benefit the people's republic," Sofia said, "you will be obliged to let him go."

"Of course, comrade," he said. Yorlovsky took a step closer to me and said, "Well, Mr. Paladin?"

I looked at Sofia. She nodded.

"My superiors told us that your moon, Destrayama we call it," I said, "is home to complex life."

"The withering sister?" Yorlovsky asked, ready to snap his fingers at Popkov.

"The other one," I said. "The intact one."

"Are they certain?"

"Satellite imagery shows fixed structures," I lied. "We have also picked up movement." Once the lie started, it was hard to stop. "The lifeforms in the northern hemisphere perform a mass migration every lunar year. Heat signatures confirm this."

"How do you know this is not animals moving?"

"Do you know of any animals on Earth or Veknyria that build fires? Thousands of them spread across flatlands?"

"We are at an impasse," Kapitan Yorlovsky said after some consideration.

"What would that be?" Sofia asked.

"We lack the technology to confirm such claims," he said. To me, he asked, "Are Americans that much more advanced than us?"

My instinct was to shrug, but that proved difficult to say the least since my arms were chained above my head and they had gone numb hours beforehand.

"We've made some advances in satellite imaging, yes," I told him.

"Extraordinary," Yorlovsky said as he turned to face Sofia. "Comrade Dashkova, I must report this to the Politburo at once."

"Set Mr. Paladin free," she advised him.

Yorlovsky snapped his fingers.

Popkov leaped into action. He unlocked the shackles around my wrists and let me fall to the stone floor without so much as trying to stop me from landing face-first.

Sofia came to me when Yorlovsky exited the interrogation room. She put one arm around my waist and lifted me effortlessly, supporting my weight with her one arm as she pushed Popkov out of the way.

In the corridor outside the interrogation room, Sofia passed me off to two guards.

"See that he does not sustain any more injuries," she warned them.

Before I could thank her she set off after Kapitan Yorlovsky. Someone sang a Russian folk song in falsetto. It took me a moment to realize that the singer was Popkov. He exited the interrogation room, passed me as he continued singing, and kept on going.

"You can walk," one of the guards said.

It was more like a command than a question.

It was slow-going at first. By the time we reached the tunnel that took me back to the cell, I was able to limp at a good a pace.

A third guard unlocked the cell door and stood by at the ready as I approached.

The cell was empty. A single bunk had been installed in my absence. When I turned to inquire about Fly and Hick the guard slammed the door shut in my face.

I spent several days alone in that cell, not knowing whether Fly and Hick were alive or dead. Guards brought meals that consisted of the same gruel and a bird dish that I did not touch. Water was the only liquid offered to me, and that came in an old-fashioned, wood pale with a wood ladle in it.

The day after the interrogation ended the pain set in and I could not move. On the second day, I was able to stand up. The day after that I started pacing the length of the cell. On the fourth day, I tried a few push-ups to an almost hilarious result.

Sofia visited me on the fifth day. She instructed the guard to take a break and give us some privacy. The guard rendered a lascivious grin and wandered off.

"Is this the part where you help me escape?" I asked.

"Don't be an imbecile," she said. "The ice I skate upon is razor thin already. My status among my comrades diminishes daily. It's been that way since before you and your friends arrived. Speaking of which, the crazy one—"

"Hick?" I asked.

"No," she said. "The other one. The sailor who thinks he's invisible—"

"He's not invisible."

"But he told Kapitan Yorlovsky that he can be when he wants to," Sofia informed me. "The captain found this so amusingly ludicrous that he ordered Popkov to beat the sailor to death. Your friend Keegan got so scared he suffered a heart attack."

"That's what Yorlovsky told me."

"And the captain was right," she informed me. "Shortly after he was admitted to the infirmary, Keegan vanished."

"How?"

"We don't know."

"What about Fly and Hick?"

"You are going home by yourself," she said. "It has been decided. Comrade Podrovsky says that without anyone to corroborate your story about us and this planet, you will be completely discredited. It is Comrade Podrovsky's wish that your own government put you away in an asylum."

"For what?"

"For telling your story too often," she said, "but mostly because it would reinforce Marx's claim."

"Are Fly and Hick dead?" I asked, wanting to avoid any more talk of communist ideology.

"I am sorry, Caleb."

"Did Yorlovsky do it himself?" I asked. "Or was it Popkov?"

"Neither," Sofia informed me. "We sent your friends ahead of you separately."

"So, they've gone back to Earth?"

"Comrade Podrovsky says that a reasonable facsimile was the best he could do," she said.

"What does that mean? A parallel Earth?"

"I must go," Sofia announced.

She exited the cell. I followed her, but I didn't get very far. A guard was waiting for me in the corridor.

"Please," the guard gestured at the open cell, "for your own safety."

Did everyone have a double on a reasonable facsimile of Earth? I wondered. Were there versions of me trying to get their Emmas back? Maybe there were subtle differences between each Earth. Perhaps there was some other version of me who never tried to get his wife back. On an even different Earth my double may have reconciled with his Emma. Another possibility came to mind. On yet another parallel Earth, my double's wife never left him in the first place. The longer I remained isolated, the worse such reasoning became. Podrovsky pulled strings to ensure the seeds of insanity took hold.

I promised myself that Podrovsky would not succeed. Cut off from the others, however, left me no alternative. What else would one do if they were incarcerated but think. Instead of all the Earths and their Emmas, I pictured Jody Pickett lying lifeless just below the surface of the creek near Jubajel's family farm. It did no good. The more I thought about something else, the more I came back to Emma. The cell with its walls, its floor, and its ceiling, the blanket on the narrow bunk that smelled of sour milk and iron, all of these distractions proved nothing next to the interior prison that my thoughts of Emma created. I needed once and for all to break free and put our marriage behind us. I kept repeating the phrase *she's never coming back* like a mantra.

"Shut up in there," a guard called out from the other side of the door. I wasn't aware that I had been repeating the phrase out loud. "If I have to come in, you will be sorry."

Chapter 31: Perpetual Celebrity

When it came time to be released, Sofia had to vouch for me. Part of the deal was that she took me to her rooms. When I got there, I insisted on sleeping alone. Sofia demanded that I sleep with her in her bed, anyway, using my health as an excuse.

"You can't die in your sleep on my divan," she said. "I just had it made."

Only after they let me out of jail did I see much of New Arkaim. Two armed soldiers escorted us to the Ministry of Travel where Sofia lived. They were cordial enough, the soldiers were, but in their eyes I could see the same discontent that most poor people had for those who were well off. Once, there was a time when Sofia's status as the daughter of the famed architect translated to special favor. The years passed. The younger generation born in New Arkaim eventually looked upon her with only mild curiosity.

Sofia told me that in New Arkaim schools a course on the People's History was a requirement. That class included the story of how her father had asked his daughter what design the city should take and she responded with her famous answer concerning the nautilus shell.

"There will come a day when they stop teaching that part of the city's history," she informed me.

One disturbing aspect of the city I discovered was that no college or university existed there. The education system was based on the old Soviet style dominated by Marxist-Leninist ideology. No track for college preparation existed in New Arkaim; mostly because the Ministry of Education, an extension of the state that

Alexei Podrovsky oversaw in addition to his role as chief political officer, deemed higher learning inessential.

Colony citizens on Veknyria learned any number of trades instead. Military service in the regular army which consisted of guarding the perimeter and the interior of the city was compulsory for both men and women. Spetsnaz troops, recruited from the ranks of the regular army, conducted direct actions against the indigenous population. A citizen of New Arkaim could choose the military as a career, provided the need was there. Despite the lack of higher education, citizens were strongly encouraged to read, especially as young adults once their school years ended. Books and other materials were controlled by the Ministry of Education.

"I have nightmares," Sofia confessed to me a few nights later, "that the dream had failed."

"It did," I said, knowing full well that all she had to do was pick up a phone and summon Podrovsky's heavies to silence me.

"What?" she sat up in bed.

In the dark, without her make-up, she looked much older.

"On Earth," I said. "The USSR is no more."

"But Alexei Podrovsky—"

"Has been lying to everyone."

"No," argued Sofia. "Just four years ago I traveled back there. The Kremlin is the same. Gorbachev's push for a democratic Russia had been deemed illegal and the opposition crushed the movement. It was a great victory for the Soviet Republic."

"That didn't happen," I said.

"Lev Ponomaryov, Sergei Kovalev, Viktor Sheinis, and the others who wrote the Declaration in 1990 were jailed—"

"Did Podrovsky tell you this?"

"We were there when it happened," she whispered.

"Has he been forcing you to travel to an alternate Earth," I said. "How did you say it? A reasonable facsimile?"

"Am I from your Earth?" Sofia wondered.

The answer was anyone's guess. She might have been born on an alternate Earth. Or Podrovsky may have figured out a way to alter the route back to a similar Soviet Union. He might have gone so far as to have that Podrovsky, his double in an alternate universe, disposed of as well as the alternate Sofia Dashkova, leaving them both to travel back and forth without raising suspicions.

"Come with me," I told her.

Sofia was only ten years older than me. She was beautiful. She was smart. She exuded an animal magnetism that made men and women attracted to her. The moment I saw her standing in the doorway between the bar and the dining room of the Ministry of Travel, it happened to me. Her presence stirred something in me I had not felt in years. Even so, she still was not Emma. I wanted to be in a place where that was a positive rather than a negative.

In New Arkaim, with her perpetual celebrity status as a pre-adolescent city planner, Sofia could have had the pick of any man. How many times did one of her alternate world comrades of high rank invite her to stay behind whenever she went there? Did they even know about Veknyria? I doubted it.

"I cannot," Sofia said, at last. "My home is here."

"This planet doesn't belong to you and your comrades," I said. "No more than it does to me and my American counterparts."

"I helped build something here."

"You're here to maintain a memory."

"Is that what you think?"

"Did you draw the plans for New Arkaim? Did you pour the foundations? Erect the watchtowers?"

Sofia got on top of me. The straps of her nightgown slipped off her shoulders.

"Take me there," she said, reaching for me. "I want to see a liberated Russia."

She pushed her hips against mine as she guided me into her. I pulled down her nightgown top exposing her breasts.

"That might be a problem," I said. "Even on my Earth Russia isn't exactly liberated."

Sofia arched her back now and took my hands in hers. As she ground her hips against mine, she gripped her breasts with my hands.

"Do you love me?" she asked. "Do you love the Party?"

I lied and told her yes I loved her and yes I loved the Communist Party.

Later we held each other before we fell asleep. I whispered in the dark of her room about how my government had let me down, about how it was pure democratic propaganda through television and movies that led me to join the military in the first place. I was fifty-four years old, and I was still telling women what I thought they wanted to hear rather than being honest with them.

It was still zero-dark-thirty when Colonel Zamyenko and his staff came to retrieve me. One moment, I slept soundly, dreaming of a field I knew as a boy that was bordered on one side by young oaks and maples, beyond which flowed a creek. It was the place my childhood friends and I played war, using sticks for machine guns and pine cones for grenades.

The imaginary enemy had always been the Nazis. The more inventive minds of my childhood gang used to prop themselves in the low-hanging branches of trees and declare themselves killed by enemy fire. It was meant to rally the remaining members of our platoon, even though in our heads we were greatly outnumbered.

Before long, the dream dissolved and in those first moments after I opened my eyes I couldn't understand why Soviet Army officers had surrounded the bed in which I slept.

A toilet flushed. In the dark the light from the bathroom in which Sofia stood formed a seam around the closed door.

"Comrade Dashkova," Colonel Zamyenko began.

"Isn't coming out," I said. "I know the drill."

The colonel nodded to one of his underlings. The lieutenant, one I didn't recognize, handed me my red camouflage uniform which had been cleaned and pressed.

"Do not attempt to escape," said Colonel Zamyenko. "Your friends tried that, and it didn't work out so well."

"Sofia Dashkova said she wanted to go with me," I said, ignoring his comment.

"Too much of a security risk," said Colonel Zamyenko. "Besides, how would it look if the Daughter of New Arkaim is seen with a capitalist spy? Now, get dressed."

When I was ready, the colonel and his men escorted me down the steps and through the foyer of the Ministry of Travel.

Outside, two jeeps idled. Colonel Zamyenko pointed to the one behind the first and his subordinates all piled into the second jeep while the colonel and I got into the first.

"I thought the gateway was under the Ministry of Travel?" I asked.

"Too far of a walk," Colonel Zamyenko said. "Many stairs. Too many, Comrade Paladin. Bad for an old soldier's knees."

The driver drove a couple of minutes down curved streets until he reached one that butted against the city's south wall. There he drove the jeep down a ramp that resembled one from an underground parking garage. A minute later, we were directly beneath the city. The driver went another thousand yards. He stopped in front of a cave opening.

"Get out," the colonel said. I did as he instructed me. "The gateway has already been programmed. All you need to do is step on the plate and walk through. Before you do, take this."

He handed me two gold coins, each one about the size of a silver dollar. I pocketed the coins without looking at them.

"What are they for?" I asked.

"Upon arrival, present one to the guard there," he said, "and he will take care of all your travel needs back to the United States."

"What's the second one for?"

"That's for when your longing for Sofia Dashkova and the People's Republic makes your heart too heavy and you want to return," Zamyenko said.

He turned his back on me and headed back to the jeep. I wasn't one of them, and I doubted I ever would be. When I walked through the cave entrance I didn't bother to turn around and wave to him. He did call me a spy, but it sounded so obvious that I wondered if it was for the benefit of someone listening in on the apartment.

The gateway inside the rock formation was similar to the one my unit had used on the Zuni reservation. I found the plate I had to step on easily enough. The machine came to life. When I stepped over the threshold, fog swirled around my feet and legs. Through the pale fog I glimpsed brilliant stars and colorful nebulae.

Part IV

You could tell by the way he talked, though, that he had gone to school a long time. That was probably what was wrong with him.

~John Kennedy Toole, *A Confederacy of Dunces*

Chapter 32: The Thirteenth Directorate

On the other side, two soldiers stood at parade rest. Their uniforms were impeccable, their boots spit-shined, and their hands, when they came to attention, were covered in white gloves.

The soldier on my left stepped forward with his gloved hand out. The other one remained standing at attention. I handed the first soldier one of the coins Colonel Zamyenko had given to me.

"I need to get to the States," I said.

"You speak English?" the soldier said.

"So do you," I replied.

"I also speak Spanish," the soldier said, "but it's not so good as my English."

"What happens if the person coming through the gate doesn't speak English or Russian?"

"It happened once in 1977," he admitted. "That's what our company commander told us. The traveler was not human."

"We weren't born yet," the second soldier spoke up now.

He directed me through a door leading to a windowless hallway that sloped upward.

At the top of the inclined floor, a black sedan with diplomatic plates waited. The driver was a tall, muscular guy with a bald head. He opened the driver's side rear door as I approached.

Seated in the back seat was a blonde in a dark pantsuit. She did not speak when I sat down beside her.

The driver closed the door behind me. Once the driver started the car, the woman said something in Russian. The driver turned on a radio. A country tune came on sung by a Russian in English.

My darlin' you are no more special than me,
Than I am more important than you.
Let's remember the Party first and not be mad
Because the collective needs us both, comrade,
So let's not turn a small spat into something big
Like a couple of self-centered capitalist pigs...

Six lines. That's all it took me to question whether I should have ever left New Arkaim.

"Catchy tune," I said.

"You need to go to the United States, yes?" the woman said.

She was all business. I liked that.

"That's my home," I said.

The woman gave me a side-long glance.

"You are a little old for a soldier," she remarked.

"That's what I told them," I said.

The country song played on. The driver glanced in his rearview mirror at me. It was hard to tell by his steely eyes if he was counting the minutes until he killed me or if he was trying to figure out whether I was human.

The woman removed a manila envelope from an attaché case. She handed it to me.

"You will depart from Chelyabinsk Airport tomorrow morning at 0600 hours," she said, "and arrive at John F. Kennedy International Airport eighteen hours later. Tonight, you will stay in a hotel one-half mile from airport. At 0420 hours, our driver Vasily here will meet you in lobby to take you to airport."

Vasily nodded as he looked at me in the rearview mirror again.

"My name is Tatyana Murov," the woman said. "I am an agent with The Thirteenth Directorate."

"Cal Paladin," I said.

"There are some rules, of course," Tatyana revealed.

Travel rules were standard fare in a country where surveillance coupled with disdain for foreigners made for a bad mix. Do go here, don't go there. Take no photos. The list went on and on. I was particularly interested in the part when Tatyana informed me that revealing my off-world origin to any citizen within Russia or the Soviet Union at large, would be grounds for expulsion.

"I'm sorry," I said. "Did you say—"

"Yes, Mr. Paladin," Tatyana replied. "You do know you are in the United Soviet Socialist Republics, yes?"

"Of course I do."

Which meant I did not until Tatyana told me.

Zamyenko had pulled a fast one on me.

"Remember," Tatyana advised me, "do not reveal your alien origin to anyone outside this vehicle."

"Even if I am an American?"

"If that's what they told you to say," she replied, "then Vasily and I are king and queen of England."

They dropped me off at the hotel. I used to think that hotels near airports and industrial parks in the States were dismal. The hotel next to Chelyabinsk Airport gave new meaning to that word.

Inside the envelope Tatyana had given me was a phony passport and a thousand dollars cash US. At the airport, I would be Jesus Christos born in Havana, Cuba, 25 December 1965. Subtle, I thought. I didn't know Spanish in case someone tried to call me out. I doubted I'd make it past the boarding gate.

I tried to sleep for a few hours. I did so in fits and starts. At some point, I wound up sitting in the shower stall balling my eyes out over all the guys from my old unit that had been killed over there in Veknyria. By the time I cleaned myself up it was after two in the morning. I went back to bed.

On the opposite side of the wall to which my headboard was bolted, somebody was giving it to a woman good in the next room. I stood up on my bed and pressed my ear to the wall. It sounded like more than one man was in the next room along with the woman.

At four in the morning, I washed up and went to wait in the lobby. Vasily showed up at exactly 0420 hours. He said nothing to me as he drove me to the airport and dropped me off.

Inside the airport, I expected to be pulled aside at any moment by a couple of Soviet agents and taken to some windowless room where they would interrogate me for hours. I pictured myself mentioning Tatyana and Vasily and The Thirteenth Directorate. *There is no such division,* the hard ass of the two agents would tell me. The other airport agent, the one playing good cop, at that point would volunteer to go fetch me a soda or a coffee while her partner kicked the snot out of me. None of that happened. My passport moved through many hands before I boarded the plane. No one so much as batted an eyelash.

Chapter 33: Kilgore Trout Never Did This

Once I arrived at JFK International, I figured the passport charade was surely over. Some crack pair of American customs officials would see the passport for what it was: a sloppy forgery. Nothing doing. The customs officials there showed the same lethargy over my passport as their Russian counterparts did.

Nearly a year earth-time had passed since I had first received my orders and drove to Fort Dix. In my uniform I carried my wallet with a credit card and an ATM card. I tried to book a flight to Las Vegas using my credit card, but it was declined. My cell phone, after all this time, still had some charge left in it. I don't know how Pulsargenix did it, but I was happy they did[12]. The problem was that the phone had no service, so I had to use a pay phone to find out what had happened to my card. They made me jump through several hoops by transferring me to this representative and that one. No one wanted to give me an answer until a woman with a long fancy title like Manager of Non-operational Accounts got on the line.

She told me her name was Jane and that the call was being monitored for training purposes.

"This account was closed ten years ago," Jane from NA told me.

"That's impossible," I said. "I'm Caleb Paladin."

---

[12] It was not beyond the realm of possibilities to have had my old battery replaced with one from Pulsargenix. The worry of course was what sort of damage such a strong battery might wreak to my body. Cancer? Hallucinations? Involuntary bilocation? The sky was always the limit on untested top-secret equipment.

"Sir, Non-operational Accounts manage accounts of deceased card members," she said. "The only reason I am speaking to you is because you provided me with the correct social security number linked to this account. So, either you are Caleb Paladin back from the dead or you will stop at nothing to commit fraud using a dead man's identity."

I assured her I was very much alive. Jane went through a laundry list of items I'd need to reply to get my account reinstated, including proof of my identity of course and a notarized letter from my wife stating that I was alive. All I needed to do was find her.

I walked around the airport for thirty minutes trying to find an ATM. At last, I found one inside a gift shop. If my math was right, and Uncle Sam was still paying me, I should have had over thirty-five thousand dollars in the bank. Even though my credit card was no longer valid, my bank card was. I withdrew twenty-five hundred dollars, the daily limit on my card, from the checking account I once shared with Emma. The balance I had anticipated did not match what was left in the account. There was less there than there should have been.

Dealing with the old checking account was something I did not have time for that day. My guess was that Uncle Sam had written me off as dead and stopped making direct deposits. From the ATM, I proceeded to the nearest ticket booth to purchase an airline ticket to the Reno-Tahoe International Airport.

My next flight didn't depart for another four hours. I had time to kill, but I needed a change of clothing. My red uniform with its pixelated pattern was drawing attention. It was time for some civilian clothes.

The only place in the airport that came close to fulfilling my needs in that department was a Hugo Boss travel store. Ordinarily, I didn't go in for brand names, but necessity dictated that I break with tradition.

I bought a small travel bag, two pairs of jeans, a couple of button-down casual shirts, sensible shoes, underwear, and socks.

When I asked the store clerk if I could use the store changing room and wear my new clothes out he regarded me with suspicion.

"There is a men's room in the concourse to the left when you exit the store," he said.

By the time I washed up in the restroom and changed, I still had a couple of hours until my flight.

I went into Hudson News to buy a paperback for the flight west. When I was young I used to read all the time. The more I tried my hand at the writing game over the years, the less time I had to read. It was as if someone had let me behind the curtain. I became obsessed with how an author worked the plot, developed characters, and structured the story. A famous actor once said in an interview that she never saw the completed version of any film she had worked on. She also admitted to never going to the movies once she had learned how the whole process works. The actor said it took all the magic out of the joy of movies.

For some writers, I suppose books can be monotonous. It was that way for me for many years. The work of composing a novel, unlike an actor who relies on a production team, is largely individual. If you are lucky enough to make it, you might be able to afford a research assistant, but that's about the extent of collaboration unless you are coauthoring a work with another writer.

Once you give over to the idea that you are a writer you open yourself to the chaos and dis-ease of the universe that one dupes themselves into believing is the muse herself. Writing is a racket like any other profession. Sure, you will read writing magazine articles in which various authors will claim that they are so blessed to be doing what they are doing. Luck and blessings have nothing to do with it.

The truth is no one sets out to be a writer. No conscious decision is made early on in one's life to pursue such a vocation. It is an affliction. True original creativity of any sort is a virus for which there is no cure.

By the time I turned forty-five, I started having serious doubts about making it as a writer. A few years after that, I gave up. At first, it was liberating. For a few years, I finally knew bliss. I even enjoyed reading again. Then the bug came back. The infection had never gone away. I found myself scribbling in notebooks. The ideas I wrote down never went anywhere. Then the army came calling. I started thinking I'd try my hand at recording these events. I wanted to be able to go back and make sense of it all, to let people know that it was all true.

Inside Hudson News, most of the book titles I didn't recognize. Toward the back of the store there were two spindles filled with paperbacks. The sight of them took me right back to my adolescence when I could walk into a five-and-dime store and buy a book plucked from such spindles. Those were glorious days of wonder when the magic still existed. At Hudson News, I purchased a pocket paperback copy of Kurt Vonnegut's *Breakfast of Champions*.

When I was a young teen, my father had an idea of what books I should read if I was ever going to make it in the world. While other dads taught their sons how to catch a ball or fish, my father laid books on me that he thought contained some kernel of truth. It was his contention, I think, that by gathering up enough fragments of truth someone could, in theory, find an answer to the meaning of life.

At thirteen years old, I wasn't interested in the meaning of life. I was only interested in discovering new innovations in masturbation while I marked time until the day I would lose my virginity.

No sooner than my flight departed I nodded off. I have always been able to sleep on flights. The thing that allowed me to do so was my anxiety about flying. Some people suffered legitimate anxiety attacks while on planes. That wasn't me, unless you count losing consciousness as having an anxiety attack.

I once met a famous self-help guru who popped valium tablets like Pez candy throughout a seven-hour flight to England. We sat next to each other the whole flight. We never once talked about work. He thanked me for that after the flight landed. I knew who he was as soon as he sat down beside me. The reason I didn't talk to him was because the moment the plane took off I passed out. Now and then I'd come out of it long enough to get a drink or snack on whatever sodium-riddled food the attendants served that flight. For the most part, though, I remained unconscious.

If I were to die in a plane crash, I preferred to sleep through my death. People put too much faith in experiencing everything until the last minute. The existential pain and horror of dying should never be romanticized. That was one of the sins of the world: our fascination with taking memories into the next place.

Anyway, the problem I had with passing out on flights was that I had always been a light sleeper. The first hint of panic in the cabin if there was ever a real emergency would be enough for my fair-weather Catholicism to kick into high gear as I joined everyone in praying—despite the physics involved in engine failure and gravity's promise, namely, guaranteeing that what goes up must come down—that God might not be too busy, that He may let me live another day of my insignificant and dismal life in which I was always late on bills, leered at women too long, practiced a maniacal form of defensive driving that bordered most days on road rage, took extensive lunches at work, cheated on taxes for as I have been eligible to file, and never once donated to a single charity. Yes, God. Please hear my prayer if you are listening because a guy like me needed to remain in the world.

No sooner than I closed my eyes after the plane lifted off I smelled the desert on Veknyria. It came back to me along with visions of Sergeant Romero getting pummeled to death by the giant woman. We had been wrong to approach her. Who were we as men to stop a woman, giant indigenous species of a faraway planet or not, from playing with herself? Wars have been started for less. If the paradigm ever truly shifted, men were doomed.

When I woke up, I started reading *Breakfast of Champions* again. Before the plane took off I had reached the part where Kilgore Trout crosses the Walt Whitman Bridge into Philadelphia in the cab of a truck named Pyramid. The sign Trout views, drawn by Vonnegut himself, reads: You Are Entering The City of Brotherly Love. I lived not far from that bridge on the New Jersey side of the Delaware River. That passage made me homesick.

Chapter 34: The Demise of Diego Bloom

In the main concourse of the Reno-Tahoe International Airport near baggage claim a wall mural depicted a cute little cherub bearing fangs and strangling an American bald eagle with a banner upon which the slogan *E Pluribus Mortem* was visible. Why would a vampire baby angel choke the symbol of America with a banner bearing the words *out of many, death*?

"Diego Bloom," a voice said behind me.

It belonged to a dapper elderly man who leaned on a black cane capped with a sterling silver ball. He looked familiar, like an older version of someone famous I could not place. Beneath his black fedora he wore his gray hair long. I suspected a wig, but without him removing his hat I had no way of knowing for sure.

"I beg your pardon?" I said to him.

"Well, you look good," said the man, "considering all the things that have come to pass. Not much of a disguise, I must say, but then you've nothing to fear. Still, no hard feelings, I hope."

"Do I know you?"

"Well-played," he countered as he looked around. I had no idea what he was talking about.

"You have me mistaken for someone else."

"The artist who painted that monstrosity," the old man said with a wink. "He was a Puerto Rican Jew from the Bronx who advocated for the wholesale deportation of non-Caucasian citizens. Imagine that? Being filled with so much self-hatred you'd literally sell your family down the river, or across the ocean as it were—"

"I'm not familiar with him," I admitted. "Is it new?"

"That's the kick in the pants," he said. "The painting was completed during the Warminster Hearings back in the 1950's."

"The Warminster—" I began.

"You young guys don't respect history," the gentleman said, shaking his cane at me. "Gerald Warminster, the Senator from Minnesota who wrote *The Benefits of Whitewashing*? People burned the book in the streets? Don't they teach this in school anymore?"

I shook my head and took a step back. Of all the travelers that day, I had to sidle up next to the one airport lunatic.

"Interesting," I said, and instantly regretted giving the man an opportunity for further discourse.

The problem with conversing with angels and mental cases, aside from often confusing one for the other, was that it was impossible to keep up with them.

"Diego Bloom was one of a handful of artists who came to Washington and supported Warminster," the old man went on. "He was so hated by the American people he ended up moving to Moscow."

"Warminster did?"

"No, Bloom," he said. "They hung Warminster from the gallows outside his home in Portwood Falls north of Renville."

My bag came down from the chute and ended up on the conveyor. I snatched it up as soon as it came around and left the elderly man waiting for his luggage and presumably his next victim.

I rented a car outside the airport and purchased a map of Nevada from the agent. He was skeptical at first of me not having a credit card, but one hundred dollars in the way of a tip fixed that.

It was a five-hour drive to Elko. From there it was another thirty minutes to The Radiant Angels of Zaphkar compound. My plan was to check into a hotel when I arrived in town. Then, once night fell, I'd take a ride out to the compound. I had a whole spiel worked out if someone was guarding the front gate. It turned out I didn't need it.

The main gate at the compound was chained and locked. A wood placard hung from the gate. An announcement for a property auction had been printed on the placard in big bold letters against a white background. The date for the auction had passed five months prior to my arrival.

The headlights from my rental car, an old Peugeot station wagon, illuminated a section of the property just one hundred yards behind the chain link gate. An asphalt road led into darkness. There was no moon that night, so even if I wanted to see the silhouettes of buildings on the compound I could not.

I turned the car around and drove back to the Holiday Inn Express in Elko where I was staying. When I asked about Tuscarora, a small town halfway between Elko and the Radiant Angels compound, the front desk clerk told me that of course people still lived there. Her name was Gloria.

"They even got themselves a town library," Gloria informed me.

"It just looked empty," was all I could think to say.

Gloria recommended that if I was out driving at night I stop on the side of the road and get out of my car just past Tuscarora.

"Somewhere in the sage brush and grass live the ghosts of the old miners, the prospectors, and the prostitutes that worked the mining town," she told me. "If you stand perfectly still, sometimes you can see them in the dark, going about their business just like they were still alive."

It was hard to tell whether or not Gloria was simply having some fun with me. Maybe she thought I was just another in a long string of ghost-hunting tourists.

When I got back that night Gloria was still on duty. She was busy checking in a young couple. I waited in the lobby, pretending to be interested in the pool area visible through a set of glass doors.

When she finished with the young couple I said, "I have another question, but you may not know the answer."

Gloria looked to be in her early forties. A person could grow old quickly on night shifts. The human body wasn't wired that way.

"What do you want to know?" inquired Gloria.

"Are you familiar with the Radiant Angels of Zaphkar?" I asked.

The smile on Gloria's face went away.

"We don't talk about them around these parts," she said. Then, "They're gone now. That's all you need to know."

"Gone where?" I pictured Emma involved in some punch-drinking mass suicide.

"You don't really know?"

"I wouldn't ask if I did."

"Did you lose someone?" Gloria came around the desk to stand facing me.

I cleared my throat, fighting back tears.

"I don't know," I admitted. "I've been away. Years ago my wife left me and joined up with them."

"No, that's not right," she cut me off. "Are you sure it was the Radiant Angels?"

"I'm positive."

"You see, Mr. Paladin, the Radiant Angels of Zaphkar allowed only men to join," said Gloria.

"The founder," I said. "His name was—"

"Bertrand Bauerfang," she announced, cutting me off. "He's the one they are after."

"Who's after?"

"Everyone," she said. "State police. FBI. The Initiate Supreme, that's what Bauerfang called himself, led his followers into the desert. They found all the men in one cave, all three-hundred-thirty-three of them. Or maybe it was three-hundred-thirty-two? All I know for sure is Bauerfang lit out after it was over, and he's wanted now."

"I read a few of his books," I told Gloria.

"Were you a member?"

"Me? No."

"That's too bad," she said. "I mean if you were and survived. Oh, my goodness. Listen to me. I meant only because you could stand to make some money if you sold the rights to your story."

"How do you know there were no women in the cult?" I asked.

"Everyone around here knew it," said Gloria. "They were all real alpha male types, former commandos, that sort of thing. Bauerfang made sure his followers were an even mix of different races—white, black, Asian, Native American. He didn't want government heat coming down on him if someone in Washington thought he was leading a white supremacist group."

"What was their deal?" I asked.

"We used to see them around town here now and again," she replied. "Bauerfang had them believing they were actual angels."

My head ached. I felt dizzy all of a sudden. When I reached out my right hand to steady myself against the back of an armchair, Gloria took hold of it.

"Are you all right, Mr. Paladin?" she asked.

"None of this makes sense," I mumbled.

"I'm sorry," Gloria said, "what was that?"

"It's nothing," I said. "I haven't eaten since earlier today."

"The dining room's closed," she said. "Should I order some Domino's or something for you?"

I closed my eyes. That made my head ache less, but it didn't help my dizziness at all.

"Maybe a steak sandwich or something," I said.

"You're a long way from Philadelphia," she reminded me. "I get off work in ten minutes. Would you like to go to Denny's with me and get some breakfast?"

Reluctantly, I agreed.

After a late-night meal with Gloria, and learning the ultimate outcome of Bauerfang's cult, I saw no point in going back out to the compound site the following morning. I had been so eager to get there, without much of a plan in mind except for what I would say to the person manning the gate[13], because all I cared about was a chance to see Emma, even if it was from a distance.

---

[13] After Emma left me to join The Radiant Angels of Zaphkar, I played over and over in my head various scenarios regarding the compound where she had volunteered to be ultimately imprisoned. Over the years, the confrontation fantasy that involved me against those who would keep me from seeing and talking to my estranged wife changed very little. The Plan with a capital P, as I came to refer to it, involved a match of wits against the proverbial gatekeeper. My adversary would be an incarnation of Janus, Roman god of doorways and dualities, time and transition, and I would outfox him with my intellect, naïve as he may be of the outside world since he'd been cooped up in his desert retreat for too long. Part B of the Plan involved a tire iron, a baseball bat, or even a simple rock in which I would bash the all-knowing god of new beginnings in his all too human head, perhaps not killing him, but giving him a headache he would remember me by for eternity. The Plan beyond this point was not complete. I blame myself. In real life I got caught up in small victories and

In a parallel world, people you think you know see you as a stranger and sometimes the opposite happens. It was my fear after arriving back in the States, that I would see someone I knew who had no clue as to my identity. The shock of finding the USSR still intact when I emerged from the Frulx gateway still lingered. I wondered if the Emma in this world would even know who I was if I did meet her.

After finding out that The Radiant Angels were no more, I doubted that I'd ever see Emma again. Gloria seemed like a nice woman. Perhaps she wasn't as well-informed about The Radiant Angels of Zaphkar as she thought. My wife had been a member, and my sister-in-law as well. Still, Gloria remained adamant about an all-male membership. Now, there was nothing left of the place. The buildings on the property had been bulldozed by the county before the land was put up for sale.

I have always been something of a paranoid case. I saw patterns in events that weren't there. The conflict within me, so far as Dr. Strauss once helped me to understand, was that I did not know why I connected dots that weren't there. Emma used to joke that I'd end up institutionalized if I didn't cool it. She never wanted to hear about how I thought I knew a little about what was going on.

Given my innate paranoia, when I arrived at The Reno-Tahoe International Airport that morning my suspicion kicked into overdrive. At the time I couldn't say why, but it happened, nevertheless. And the reason soon became apparent.

---

failed to see the whole struggle. That was at least what I confided to Dr. Strauss during one therapy session. As you, dear Reader, may have guessed, Dr. Strauss did not have a kind response. I think, as I consider my therapist with the benefit of hindsight, he had his own baggage. I doubted he had his own Plan. He always struck me as conceited in that respect. When I think of Dr. Strauss and how his life was spent, I wonder if I missed my calling, having figured out the chink in his armor. I might have used the aforementioned soliloquy about my therapist to render whatever Janus incarnate manning the gate at The Radiant Angels of Zaphkar compound into a stupor long enough so I could bash his brains out—metaphorically speaking—before making a mad dash for what I took to be living quarters on the compound all the while screaming, "Emma!" in my best Marlon Brando version of Stanley Kowalski in *A Streetcar Named Desire*. This last portion would be catalogued under Part A of the Plan.

"Well, if it isn't the Diego Bloom fan?" a familiar voice said.

The elderly man with the black cane from the other day approached me as I looked over departure times.

It couldn't have been a coincidence, could it? My fear was that he was flying east on the same flight I was. I hedged around it a bit, without revealing my ultimate destination.

"I have business in Seattle," the old man said. "Then onto Moscow."

"Russia?" I asked.

"Heavens, no. Too much leftover Cold War angst for me," he said. Then he puts his fingers to the side of his mouth like he was about to tell me a secret. "Though I should consider it, given that the U.S. has no extradition treaty with Mother Russia."

He's certifiable, that was my first thought. My next thought was that he was actually one of those fugitives you read about who thought they were smarter than everyone else.

"Where's there another Moscow?" I asked, playing it cool.

"Idaho, of course. I'm to give a lecture at the library there."

I could tell he wanted me to ask what his lecture was about, but I didn't take the bait. Instead, I abruptly bid him a good morning and headed for my boarding gate.

"Mum's the word," he called out as I walked away.

Goodbye whacko, I thought.

Three hours after arriving at the JFK International Airport, I made it home.

Chapter 35: Wild Wilkey & the Pleiadeans

I kept a spare key to the house hidden inside a rather ghastly garden gnome's head in the backyard. The key was right where I had left it. I took it as a good omen. Things were beginning to look up. Maybe I didn't have anything to be paranoid about.

When I entered the house through the back door, I did not expect to find my wife Emma there. Judging by the expression on her face, one of both disbelief and awe, I knew she was not expecting me. Her mouth slackened. Her eyes widened a moment, and then she fainted.

"You're dead," Emma managed after I helped her come around a minute or so later. "Oh my God. Did I die? Is this the afterlife?"

"Don't be ridiculous," I told her. "I can't believe you're home. When did you get back?"

"I didn't," she started to say. Then she changed gears. "Have you been watching the house?"

"What? No."

"It's the shed, isn't it?"

"I wasn't hiding in the shed."

"Are you camped out in there like some kind of homeless person?"

"Now you're being hysterical," I told her.

"I hate when men say that," said Emma. "What are you doing here?"

"We haven't seen each other in how long?" I asked. "And this is the greeting I get?"

"I'm sorry," she said. "It's just a shock, that's all."

"You never answered my question."

"Which was?"

"When did you get back?"

"Me? I never left."

"What about the Radiant Angels of Zaphkar?"

"They're gone," my wife said. "You were too. Or so I thought. How did you survive?"

"I have heard this story about corpses in a cave," I said. "How did they die?"

"Poison," Emma replied. "That was the official word. Why? Do you know something else?"

"I don't."

Emma kept the kitchen island between herself and me.

"Were you in cahoots with that Initiate Supreme guy?"

"Bauerfang? How could I be?"

"I don't know," she said. "There must have been money laid aside. They say he absconded with it all. Ten years now and nobody can find him. You left me to join the Radiant Angels fourteen years ago. Then there was the mass suicide in the news about four years after you were gone. I have lived my life for the past decade believing you were dead."

"Did they prove positive identification?"

"Not exactly," she said. "Bauerfang attempted to burn some of the bodies. They managed to gather some of your DNA. Don't ask me how. I had your remains cremated and spread in the ocean off Cape May Point, just like you always wanted."

That much was true, in this universe or otherwise. I never wanted to be buried[14].

---

[14] Like many human beings, I obsessed for a long time over what should be done with my body once I finished using it. When I grew up adults had only two options: a coffin burial or cremation. These days, however, you can do any number of options. Well, *you* can't. But you can plan ahead of time. You can become fertilizer for a fresh sapling that gets planted. If you have the dough, I suppose you could even persuade NASA or some private company to jettison your ashes into space. I wanted to be cremated and have mine spread over the Atlantic Ocean off Cape May Point because I didn't believe in burdening others with visiting a cemetery. What was the point? The dead didn't know you were there. Let people go to the beach

I went to a cabinet over the sink and took down a drinking glass. Emma slid toward the refrigerator when I went to get some water from the cold filtered dispenser.

"What do you think you're doing, Cal?" she asked.

"I'm thirsty," I said.

"Stop acting like you still live here," my estranged wife said.

"But I do," I told her.

Emma stepped aside. "Get your water," she said. "And then come out to the living room. I have something to tell you."

"Give me a sec."

"Wait. Did you take money out of my account?"

"Our account, Emma."

"But you were dead."

"You didn't cancel the card," I said.

"Just come out to the living room," Emma insisted. "We'll deal with the money issue later on."

The news she had to tell me was not good. In the early days after I disappeared (it still hadn't dawned on me that she was referring to a facsimile of me in this parallel place), she found solace in none other than my old boss Herb Kaufman.

"His wife died shortly after the news out of the Radiant Angels compound gained international attention," Emma said. "I guess you can say that we helped each other grieve. It took so long after that because we both wanted to be sure."

"Sure of what?"

"Whether we wanted to marry."

"You and Herb Kaufman? Married?"

"Not yet," she said. "This coming fall. We're going to Antigua. The waters there are so blue, like something out of a sci-fi movie on another planet—"

"You can't be serious?"

"I can show you a brochure—"

"I meant about Herb?"

---

and maybe stand by the old pill box, look out at the Atlantic, and say, "This is where that universe-hopping, crazy son of a bitch Paladin wanted his ashes scattered."

"Of course, I am. We're in love. And his boys accept me."

"Avner and Eli? You're going to have to move out of this place."

"Why?"

"Not enough bathrooms," I said, clutching my stomach the way Herb used to.

"You are not a good man," she said.

"So the three of them are still *afflicted*?"

"As it turns out I will live with Herb and Avner," Emma informed me, ignoring my last comment. "Eli made Aliyah and lives in Jerusalem now. He's a staff sergeant in the IDF. Herb's so proud—"

"I'm going to need a place to stay," I said.

"No."

"Only for a little while," I assured her.

"Cal," she said, "you can't. Herb thinks you're dead."

"He was supposed to hold my job at the journal," I said.

"You quit the journal to join The Radiant Angels."

"What? No," I said. "The army called me back. Can you believe it? I didn't know they could do that."

"The army? You're a decade away from retirement age," Emma reminded me.

"More like thirteen years," I corrected her.

"Right, listen. Don't take this the wrong way," she said, "but what would the army want with someone your age?"

"They said the armed services were stretched too thin around the world," I told her.

"Who did?"

"It's not important right now."

"Well," she said, after an awkward moment of silence, "finish your water. Then you can go."

"This is my home."

"Are you sure you didn't survive the poisoning?" she asked.

"What's that supposed to mean?"

"I think your brain has been damaged," said Emma. "You don't remember what it was like, do you?"

Before I could answer Emma catalogued all of the shortcomings our relationship had accumulated. She lay most of the blame at my feet. If I was responsible for half of what she told me, I didn't blame her.

"Tell Herb you don't want to marry him," I said.

"Why would I do that?" Emma asked.

"Because you're going to give me a second chance," I said.

"I'll do no such thing, Cal," she said. "Besides, I've already converted. It would be such a waste now."

"Mazel tov."

"Don't get cute."

"You don't even believe in God," I reminded her.

"People change, Cal," she argued.

"How about your parents?" I asked. "How'd they take your converting to Judaism? I bet that went over well at the Quaker meeting house."

"My parents are dead," Emma said. "They died within six months of each other back in 2014. You were a full-fledged member of The Radiant Angels of Zaphkar, remember?"

I told her I did not. The world I returned to was not mine. Even if I didn't land in the Soviet Union after crossing through the Frulx gateway under The Ministry of Travel, the truth would have been made apparent in that hour. When I started crying Emma moved closer to me on the sofa and put her arm around me. She assured me that I would be ok. We sat like that for some time before I tried to kiss her. She pushed me to the floor.

"Now, you have to go before Herb gets home."

"I'm staying. We're staying together. I mean, I know I'm not the Cal you knew—"

"There is no 'we,' Cal," Emma said. "I'm sorry you pissed your life away with a cult. Maybe I should have staged an intervention. Not to save our marriage because that was rotten from the beginning, but to keep you from running off."

"That's not fair," I told her.

"The truth rarely is, Cal."

A key turned the dead bolt lock in the front door.

"That's Herb," Emma announced. "Get up from the floor, Cal."

Herb Kaufman entered my house like he'd lived there for years. He put his briefcase down on a small hutch by the door and shrugged off his coat. Herb looked at me, attempting to process the scene before him.

"What the hell is this?" asked Herb. "Back from the dead already?"

"I never died," I said.

"Sure, you and Jesus both," he said just before he fainted.

"Both of you fainting like that," I said. "What are the chances? Maybe you are meant for each other."

"Goddamnit, Cal," Emma rushed to Herb's aid. "Look at what you did."

Herb regained consciousness soon enough. Emma gave him a glass of water as the three of us sat in the living room. I told them all about the gateways, the separate universes, Veknyria, New Arkaim, the whole thing.

"You, my friend," said Herb, "need a shrink. I never heard something so crazy as that in my whole life."

"I agree," Emma said. "He needs to be committed."

"Let's not be hasty," he said. "This is your ex-husband you're talking about."

"Ex?" I asked.

"In the state of New Jersey either spouse needs only to show separation via different addresses for so many years in order for a no-fault divorce to take hold," Herb said. "You met that requirement a few years into your stay with Bauerfang the huckster and his magnificent henchmen. No offense."

"None taken," I said.

"Just level with us, Cal," Emma said. "How did you pull it off?"

"Yes," Herb said. "Tell us the truth. We won't tell anyone."

"They sent my old unit to another planet," I said.

"Ok," said Herb. "Enough of this absurdity. I'm calling the police."

"No!" Emma and I said at the same time.

"What? You want to further indulge this fantasy?"

"It's true."

Herb regarded me with suspicion. "Let me guess," he said, plopping down on the couch. "You boarded a flying saucer and little gray aliens took you there?"

"Don't be ridiculous," I said. "We used a portal on the Zuni Reservation under the Dowa Yalanne."

"Oh, well then. That clears it up," Herb said. Then, to Emma he said, "He's a lunatic! Hand me the phone."

"Here," I handed him my cell phone. Everywhere I went no bars showed. "Try this, but it won't work."

Herb leaned back on the sofa, as if my cell phone were laced with extraterrestrial contaminants.

"What is that thing?" he asked. "Your Star Trek communicator?"

"It's a cell phone," I said. "Everyone has one."

"Let me see that," Emma said. I handed her my phone. She looked at the flat screen, opened a few apps, and held it out in front of Herb. "Look, Herb. It's like a mini-computer—"

"I don't want that gadget near me," said Herb. "It could be radioactive. I got enough problems without my balls glowing in the dark."

"Don't be crass, Herb."

"Emma, please. The man needs help. No offense, Cal."

"Why don't we all just calm down for a moment," Emma said, handing me back my cell phone. "Cal, are you hungry?"

"Now we're going to break bread together?" Herb remarked.

"I'll go," I said.

"What will you do for money?" Emma asked.

"I have money," I told her.

"That's right," she said. "My money."

"What's this?" Herb asked.

"I'll pay it back," I assured them both. "I have nearly a year's army salary—"

"Not this army fantasy again," Herb began.

"Stop it," Emma said.

"Fine," he replied. Then, "If you've been dead—"

"He's clearly not dead."

"Missing," Herb clarified. "How is it that you have pay from the army when your last known address was a cult compound in Nevada?"

"This place is a facsimile," I said.

"A facsimile is an exact copy," Herb announced. "How can our world be a copy of yours if you're walking around with a Star Trek communicator?"

"It's not...Look," I said. "Both worlds are *mostly* the same, but there are, I admit, subtle differences."

"You see the nature of his psychosis?" Herb said to Emma.

"Herbert," she snapped. "You're not a psychiatrist."

"I read," he defended himself.

"In my world," I told them, "Emma was the one who joined The Radiant Angels of Zaphkar."

"Hah!" she cried.

"Bertrand Bauerfang allowed men and women to join the group," I said.

Herb looked at Emma. "He doesn't know?" he asked.

"No," replied Emma.

"What am I missing?" I asked.

"You talk about Bauerfang like he's still alive," Herb said.

"He's not?"

"It's been on all the news channels," he said.

Herb got up and turned on the television. Did they not have remote controls? I wondered, but I didn't pursue it.

A CNN reporter stood in front of the SeaTac Airport in Washington. He was dressed in full body armor and a helmet. Someone threw an open milk carton at him. Milk splashed everywhere, dotting the camera lens.

"CNN sucks!" someone shouted off-camera.

"Did you get that?" the reporter inquired.

"How could I miss it?" the cameraman said.

The reporter looked left and right. A half-dozen of Seattle's finest tackled the milk carton quarterback.

"Oh," the reporter looked surprised. "We're live. Ok."

"Journalists have become something of an endangered species," Herb noted, "since they elected that goose-stepping flunky from New York. We have had a crippled president. We have had a Catholic president. We even elected that black kid—"

"Barack Obama?"

"Who the hell is Barack Obama?"

"Never mind."

"I'm talking about Wilkey Stallworth," Herb said. "He played for the Philadelphia 76ers. They called him Wild Wilkey. He had that crazy three-pointer shot—"

"I don't know him," I said.

"It doesn't matter," he told me. "The current guy? What a doozy. He's like Himmler on Adderall—"

"Let me hear this," I said.

"This is Adam Ross live from the Seattle-Tacoma International Airport in Washington," the reporter on television said. "In case you're just joining us, authorities have confirmed that Bertrand Bauerfang, the self-described Initiate Supreme of The Radiant Angels of Zaphkar whose three-hundred-thirty-three members committed mass suicide in the Nevada desert ten years ago, was indeed on Red Arrow Airlines flight 524 that crash-landed on a runway here just a few hours ago. Surveillance footage from Reno-Tahoe Airport in Nevada from earlier today showed who many experts believe is Bertrand Bauerfang, a fugitive wanted for tax evasion, orchestrating the mass suicide that ended his cult, and the desecration of corpses, waiting for his luggage before making a connecting flight to Seattle. Bauerfang, the FBI has confirmed, did have his appearance surgically altered shortly after the atrocity at The Radiant Angels compound, which has allowed him to go about the country largely unnoticed."

The footage that aired was a loop of a dapper-looking elderly man with long gray hair wearing a black fedora and holding a black cane capped with a silver ball in his hand. Bauerfang held his fingers to the side of his mouth with one hand as he held onto his cane with the other while speaking to the pixelated face of another traveler. A good thing CNN blocked out the other man's face because the other traveler in the shot was me.

"The NTSB has not ruled out landing gear sabotage," the reporter Adam Ross appeared on the screen once more, "in an accident that injured ninety passengers and killed eleven, including fugitive Bertrand Bauerfang. The FBI declined to comment on how Bauerfang got back into the country some months before the fatal flight today and was presumably using his own identity to book flights and travel domestically—"

Herb went to turn off the television, but I stopped him.

"Wait," I said.

"After a while it all becomes white noise," he said. "So, there you have it. The one who caused so much trauma in your life it caused you to break with reality—"

"Shut up," I told him.

The CNN anchor in the studio offered a teaser before a commercial break.

"At the top of the hour," he said, "we will visit with our White House correspondent Amelia Mutti and find out why the president refuses to accept Soviet Premiere Ompromchev's apology over what the Soviet State has called quote 'a military blunder and a grave mistake' unquote when the Oceania Blue Resort in Guam was carpet-bombed."

Footage of an obliterated resort on Ipao Beach showed buildings that had been reduced to rubble. Here and there Red Cross members searched for survivors while soldiers carried body bags to awaiting deuce-and-a-half trucks.

"Ompromchev says it was a training accident," the news anchor said when his face filled the screen once more. "The president is calling the action a prelude to war. We'll have more on this developing story with Amelia Mutti when we come right back."

Herb turned off the television. "Satisfied?" he asked.

"Stay for dinner?" Emma offered, ignoring her fiancée.

"Not a chance," he said.

"Herb, come on," she cried. "Cal's a veteran, for Christ's sake."

"Hey, I'm as patriotic as the next imbecile," said Herb. "But I won't hear of any more psychotic fantasies."

"We'll order Chinese," Emma announced in a sing-song voice as if Herb were a toddler.

"Fine," he said, "but none of that brown rice. That stuff goes right through me."

"Did the Russians really bomb a resort in Guam?" I asked.

"CNN does not lie, Cal."

"And the president wants to go to war?"

"Of course," Herb said. "That neo-Nazi's been itching to be a war-time president ever since he took office. He thinks it will help his ratings. That bastard's crazier than you are."

Twenty minutes before the Chinese takeout was delivered, Herb's son Avner came through the door. He was older, maybe eighteen from the looks of him. He was starting to look a lot like his father, the poor kid.

"You remember Mr. Paladin?" Herb said to his son.

"Aren't you dead?" Avner asked.

"The stories of my demise," I told him, "have been greatly exaggerated. And please call me Cal."

"Ok, Cal. Well, you look good. You've been working out?"

"Cal's been to a distant planet," Herb informed him.

"Is that a new gym?"

"Avi," Emma said.

"Don't call me that," he snapped at her. "My mother used to call me that when I was little."

"I'm sorry," she said.

"It's not right," he continued.

"Avner, I apologize," said Emma.

Herb's son looked at me. "So, what?" he asked. "Can you come and go as you please? Or do you need permission from the Pleiadeans?"

Herb guffawed. "Good one," he muttered when he was able to recover.

"I'll probably head out west in a couple of days," I announced.

"Oh," Avner said, "like in *Close Encounters of the Third Kind*?"

"Cal," Emma said, "I do wish you would go see Dr. Strauss."

"It's been..." I started to say, unsure of how long ago my double had seen a therapist.

"He's still in practice."

"I don't know, Emma," I said. "And I don't appreciate you talking about therapy in front of Avner."

"Dude, I'm a vault—" Avner began.

"Shut up, Avner," said Herb, clutching his stomach now.

"Herb, stop it," Emma said to him. "We're all family, sort of."

"No we're not," Avner declared.

"Well, not literally family—"

"Not figuratively either," the young man said. "Mister...I mean Cal is not related to me."

"Damn it, Avner—"

"Don't curse at my son."

"Anyway," Emma rolled her eyes, "you should call him tomorrow. Dr. Strauss, I mean."

"If it will make you happy," I told her.

"It would."

"Wonderful," said Herb. "Maybe on my wedding night you can come around and shtup my wife, you know, for old time's sake."

"That kind of talk is beneath you, Herb," I said.

"This coming from the man who abandoned his wife fourteen years ago and led everyone, including his employer, to believe that he was dead?" Herb shook his index finger at me to stress his point. "That is the very definition of irony."

Avner stood up now, leaned across the table, and poked me in the arm. Then he shrugged and sat back down.

"I just wanted to see if he was real," said Avner of me.

"Moron," I said to him.

"No one calls my son a moron," Herb looked like he was ready for a fist fight now.

"You tell him, Papa," said Avner.

"Shut up, you moron," he admonished his son now.

Emma put her elbows on the table and rested her face in the crescent shape of her upturned palms.

"Aren't you glad you stayed?" she asked. When I didn't answer, Emma pressed me. "What's wrong?"

Herb and Avner were distracted with an argument having to do with the limitations of foul language in parenting. I was about to answer Emma when Herb threw his arms up in despair.

"Calling your own flesh and blood a moron is not the same as cursing at him," said Herb.

"In my book," Avner argued, "it is."

"Well, then, you're a goddamn moron," his father told him.

"I should be going," I said, standing up as I did so.

"What?" Herb cried. "Sit down. We haven't even opened the fortune cookies."

"Yeah," Avner said. "Stay, Cal. I want to hear all about The Planet of the Apes."

Father and son started cackling like a couple of old hens who had just shared a dirty joke.

"What are you grinning about?" Emma asked me.

I pushed my chair back and stood up. "I am going," I announced.

"You said you need a place to stay," she reminded me.

"I'll figure something out," I told her.

Herb and Avner were still yukking it up at my expense when I left the house.

Chapter 36: My Double's Ashes

The next morning, after staying in a motel near Emma's house, I drove over to the office complex where Dr. Kyle Strauss had his practice. Why I was still doing what Emma suggested—to be more precise, Emma's double suggested—baffled me. Maybe I just wanted someone trained to hold no personal opinion about the recent events in my life, off-world and otherwise, someone who could remain objective, to hear my story.

The office complex was a series of one-story buildings connected in fours with narrow tinted floor-to-ceiling windows, faux cabin exteriors the color of rust, oversized cast iron nautical anchors placed like objet d'art on gravel yards in front of each cluster of buildings, and rope fences that called to mind people who lived in shore towns that tried too hard to embrace the salty life of the sea.

The receptionist in Dr. Strauss's practice did not look familiar. She was blond, tanned, and green-eyed. A tiny constellation of freckles appeared on her chest like stars at nightfall thanks to the open collar on her shirt. A business card tray held a stack of the receptionist's cards. Strauss Psychiatric Care was emblazoned across the top of the business card with her name beneath it: Kym Woods, Executive Assistant. Kym with a Y struck me, upon first impression, as the kind of woman who never outgrew dotting all of her i's with little hearts.

"Do you have an appointment, sir?" Kym asked. No *hello, how may I help you?* She was all business.

"No," I said. "I used to be—"

"You need an appointment in advance," she advised me. "Would you like to make one now?"

"If you could let Dr. Strauss know that Caleb Paladin is here to see him," I told her. "I would appreciate it."

"He's with a patient right now," Kym countered. "We can make an appointment for you for a later date. If you would just give me your insurance information—"

"I don't have insurance."

"Ok, well. The fee is two hundred dollars an hour," she said. "If the cost is an issue, I can put you in touch with free services through the county."

"No," I said, "nothing like that. I will wait until he's finished with his current client."

"Suit yourself," said Kym.

I sat there in the waiting area stewing and avoiding Kym's glance when she looked my way. The hour drew close to eleven that morning. Finally, the door to Dr. Strauss's office opened.

"Thank you, doctor," a young woman said as she exited the office without looking my way. She walked right past the receptionist and exited the building.

"Dr. Strauss," Kym began.

I was already on my feet.

"Son of a bitch," Dr. Strauss cried.

"He insisted on waiting," his receptionist informed him.

"Get in here, Cal," he cried. Then, as I walked toward him, he added, "now hold on. A hug's in order, I think."

We hugged briefly. It wasn't really my thing.

"Kym," Dr. Strauss said, "this man right here was presumed dead. Now, like Lazarus from the tomb, he's come back."

"I won't take up much of your time," I started to say.

"Kym," he called out. "Hold my calls."

Dr. Strauss and I entered his office. He told me to sit down. I did. The furniture was new, but the set-up was just the same. Dr. Strauss wasn't big on sofas. He opted instead for armchairs in which the doctor and his patient faced each other. Patients, by his estimation, should never lay down when work needed to be done. That's how he put it: work to be done, as if therapy was simply an occupation. For him, it may have been, but for those who suffered it was anything but that.

I told him everything that morning. He scribbled some notes on a pad as I spoke. It wasn't supposed to be an official therapy session, but it turned into one quick enough. I told him about the army orders, about the secret gateway on the Zuni Reservation, the Veknyrians who could kill me with a single blow, and the Soviet colonists, some of whom had been there from the beginning in 1956. I left out the part about falling in love with Sofia Dashkova, mostly because I would just want to deny that I had done so despite her setting me up, twice.

Even though I had no recollection of belonging to The Radiant Angels of Zaphkar (mostly because I never did, though, evidently, my late double had), I admitted that I was not sad to learn of Bertrand Bauerfang's death. I told him that Emma held a funeral service for me and afterward she scattered my ashes in the water at Cape May Point. I even told him about how she planned to marry my former boss Herb Kaufman. Then I dropped the bomb on him. I told Dr. Strauss that I hailed from a facsimile Earth where the Soviet Union had dissolved more than twenty years ago.

"That is some fucking tale," Dr. Strauss said when I finished.

So much for objectivity.

"What's your prognosis?" I asked.

"Truth?"

"Yes."

"You're not going to like it," said Dr. Strauss.

"Tell me anyway."

"Your tale of another world inhabited by giants and Soviet-era colonists," he said, "are sure signs of masking some deeper trauma."

"At least I'm not crazy," I said.

"Not so fast," said Dr. Strauss. "Before I get to that let's talk some more about the deeper trauma—"

"There's none, doc," I told him. "I was never a member of The Radiant Angels."

"Sure, sure," he said. "But in my professional opinion that denial is just another mask. Clearly, you have experienced profound guilt over the other members killing themselves. Would you deny this?"

"Of course, I would," I told him, "if I was there and survived, but I wasn't."

"I knew you were going to say that," Dr. Strauss announced. "Listen, Cal. I'm going to recommend that you go in for seventy-two-hour observation down at Ancora—"

"Are you crazy?" I shouted.

"That's a good one," he said. "Classic. Deflection and shifting blame."

"I'm not crazy."

"Oh, I don't think you are either."

"Thank you."

"But I am serious about the trauma," he told me. "I know a guy at Ancora. He's phenomenal at breakthroughs. You have to want it though."

"Can I talk it over with my wife?" I asked.

He wrote something down on a form and handed it to me.

"Just show this to the admissions coordinator when you check in at Ancora," Dr. Strauss said. "They'll know what to do."

My old therapist wanted to have me committed for telling him something true. What was the world coming to? I wondered. This world, any world. It didn't matter.

Chapter 37: A Shirt Full of Bees

I left New Jersey that afternoon and drove into Philadelphia. My plan was

a) avoid the authorities if Dr. Strauss sicked them on me with some sort of warrant, and

b) try to get into the building where I used to work at *Morley's Health Guide*.

I doubted he had that authority, Strauss I mean, but then I never thought my former boss would help himself to my wife either, in this world or any other. Did I say wife? Why do I keep doing that? Ex-wife. You know what I mean.

Years ago, and this is the part where I failed miserably as a man and as a husband, guys like Herb Kaufman made Emma feel valued while I took her for granted. The publisher where I worked as an editor used to have a holiday party. Actually, it had been a Christmas party until the majority of the staff eventually became non-Christian. Of the fifteen people who worked in editing, the break down was as follows:

Agnostic	4
Atheist	4
Buddhist	2^{15}

---

[15] Technically, it was 1 Buddhist and 1 Jubu who wanted desperately to be a full-fledged Buddhist but couldn't dispense with 5,000 years of tradition dating back to Aaron, brother of Moses and Miriam, to say nothing of a lineage he claimed to trace back to Abigail, the prophetess who became a wife of King David. His name was Ira Roth. He counted himself in both

Christian	0
Jewish	5

I counted myself among the agnostics. The Christmas party that Bentley Gilbert Morley envisioned when he started his company in 1922 on Washington Square did not last into perpetuity, as he had originally planned. By the late twentieth century, it had been replaced by a non-denominational winter party.

"It's the stupidest thing I ever heard," Herb Kaufman had said when the board, fearful of a discrimination lawsuit, handed down the edict. "Who celebrates ice and snow?"

Even so, when I brought Emma to the party year after year, old Herb never failed to ogle my wife, allowing his gaze to linger a bit too long. Typically, there was music. In lean years, when the publisher wasn't doing so well, the powers that be trimmed back the winter party, opting for decorating the employee cafeteria rather than renting out an entire restaurant in center city Philadelphia.

Anyway, Herb would get half a load on and go around asking women to dance, even when his wife was there. Herb's wife Adele had always appeared sickly, so it came as no surprise to any of us when she became stricken with cancer. Poor Adele. Every winter at the company party it was understood, given her frail condition, that she could not dance. That left her husband to prey on other women.

It mattered little to Herb if a woman was married or not. He did not take no for an answer. Of all the wives and girlfriends at the party, year after year, Emma was the only one who indulged him. Herb danced like a genuine clodhopper with a shirt full of bees, a regular rhythmless and spastic Herman Munster. That didn't stop Emma from taking pity on him. And in this universe she'd gone one better. She was going to marry the guy since, until I showed up, they shared a commonality in losing spouses.

---

the aforementioned Buddhist category as well as the Jewish one. There was a rumor around the office that Ira was actually a Jew for Jesus, but that could never be substantiated, despite our collective best efforts. When pressed about the Messiah, Ira resorted to denial, just like Judas in the Garden of Gethsemane.

Facsimile Philadelphia turned out to be nothing like the original city of brotherly love. For one, on almost every corner in center city there was someone or another standing on a crate or a ladder, armed with a bullhorn, spouting nonsense from the effect the entropic universe had on free trade to advocating for militancy in recruiting for such groups as The Flat Earth Society, the Jehovah Witnesses, the Back to Lemuria Movement[16], The Neo-Neanderthal Separatists[17], and a host of other causes too numerous to catalogue here. My only respite that morning was when I crossed Washington Square and came across a statue of Muhammed Kenyatta who, in the parallel world I was trapped in for the time being, beat Philadelphia's most ardent advocate for police brutality Frank Rizzo for the Democratic nomination and ended up serving two terms as mayor of Philadelphia. The plaque affixed to the base

---

[16] A small yet powerful lobby that raised funds to build a floating city in the Indian Ocean where the lost land of Lemuria was believed to have once existed.

[17] Believing that nature had given early humans an upper hand which meant the end of Neanderthals, distant descendants of the extinct species, showing two percent or better Neanderthal DNA in their genes, established a foundation to raise money in order to purchase large tracts of land in Europe so that they might establish their own sovereignty. Dickie Joe Bryant, oil tycoon and movie industry mogul, founded the Neo-Neanderthal Separatist movement to ensure that precious DNA could not only be preserved, but increased through generational close inbreeding. Bryant's old classmates at Moishe Levy High School in Leopard, Louisiana and later at Princeton are on record detailing how young Dickie Joe Bryant, champion of the preservation of Neanderthal DNA, often fell asleep during biology class. Had he remained awake Bryant might have learned that inbreeding was never the answer. Despite a willful ignorance of biological outcomes between closely related offspring Bryant and his separatist group sold baseball caps bearing catch-phrases like *Stone Age Lyfe* and t-shirts with slogans like *Gone Clubbing* and *Fire Good* to off-set the cost of purchasing land. Every year the Neo-Neanderthal Separatists held conventions in which members were issued foam clubs and faux bone necklaces which only served to further propagate erroneous myths about the original Neanderthals.

of the ten feet tall statue read: *On this spot in 1976, Mayor Kenyatta gave his speech, "No More, No Less," during the city's Bicentennial celebration. The contents of the speech, calling for true equality, became the backbone of The New Declaration ratified by Congress in 1989.*

"Hey man," I said to a young guy passing by. "What's The New Declaration?"

"Yo cuz, what planet are you from?" he inquired, rhetorically. Or at least I hope he did. Then, before he continued on his way, he remarked, "Fucking foreigners, man. I swear to God."

Inside the lobby of the building where I worked I studied the directory on the wall near the elevator bank. A lethargic security guard gave me the once-over as he read a horse racing form. The closest thing I saw to *Morley's Health Guide* on the directory was *A.G. Morley Publishers.*

"Is this the publisher that puts out the health guide?" I asked the guard at his desk.

"Sure," he said without looking up from his racing form. "The health guide and a bunch of other things. Books, mostly, on paranormal bullshit and quack science concerning, get this, parallel worlds."

"Do you know Herb Kaufman?"

"Yes, sir. And his wife-to-be. Sweet girl. Easy on the eyes if you don't mind my saying so," he announced. Then, checking himself, he added, "Say, you're not family, are you?"

Whenever anyone said *if you don't mind my saying so*, it really meant the speaker didn't give two shits about your feelings.

I decided against going up to the offices. For one, if I ran into Ira Roth or anyone then I'd have to explain how I came to be not so legally dead. Worse, Herb was probably in the office.

By now, just shy of the noon lunch hour, I'm sure he had already shared the story of how I came back telling stories of other planets and interdimensional travel.

I sat in the square and watched the people pass by during lunch hour. After spending fifteen minutes watching women, young and old, walk through the square in their office attire, I felt hungry. I had a few hours to kill before I could officially check into the hotel

I was going to stay in until my flight left, so I decided that I'd walk up Walnut Street and pop into the first restaurant that looked like it served a decent hamburger.

"Jesus, Cal," a voice said. "Is that really you?"

I looked around. There was no one close enough for their voice to have reached me like that.

"Don't bother trying to find me, Cal," said the voice. "I'm not there in the sense that you know."

I knew that voice. "Sonny Keegan?" I asked.

"In the flesh, so to speak," he replied. "You can't see me. No one can. Hazards of Project Rainbow."

"I don't know how you are doing this," I said, "but I am stumped."

He swatted me gently in the back of the head.

"Don't be a chowderhead," he said. "I'm invisible."

"What? How?"

"Ever since that Ruskie sent me through that gateway," said Sonny. "I should have known to check the settings. Obviously, you didn't either."

"No," I said, "I guess not."

"I think it's a way for the whole goddamn system to ensure that we look like crazy chumps," he said.

"The system?"

"Yeah, you know. The secret shadow one-world government run by The Illuminati."

Oh boy, I thought. Then, I said, " When did you turn invisible?"

"The first time?" Sonny asked. "About three weeks after the incident at the navy yard."

"I meant more recently."

"Oh, well, it happened as I came through the gateway," he said. "I just knew something was up. I'm scared, Cal."

"I'd be too."

"No," he said. "I meant about being here. Nothing looks the same. All my relatives are dead and buried. I feel like a lost ghost."

"I'm thinking about going to Russia," I said. "I know there's a gateway there. I used it to get here."

"So did I," Sonny told me.

"Listen," I said. "Why don't you come with me? If money's an issue, I can pay for your plane ticket."

"Thanks, but no," he told me. "I saw what happened to your buddies. The spade and the hillbilly."

"Nobody uses those words anymore, Sonny," I informed him.

"Yeah," he said. "I'm sensing the whole world's gone to hell in a handbasket."

"I meant it's offensive."

"To you?"

"Never mind," I told him. "Are you sure you don't want to go with me?"

Nothing. Not even a heavy breath.

"Sonny?" I called out.

He was gone.

Chapter 38: A Proclamation for the Three

I didn't start to feel better until my flight was over Nova Scotia. Somewhere around twenty-thousand feet during the departure from Philadelphia International Airport, a panic attack set in when it became clear that I wasn't going to pass out the way I normally did when flying on a passenger jet. During my original army days, when I was much younger, helicopter rides never bothered me, cruising at sixty or seventy miles an hour with the doors open just above the treetops. The same went for Zamyenko's flying aircraft carrier. That didn't bother me at all. Planes, as you know by now, were a different matter. Anyway, my thoughts soon turned to other matters like whether or not other units had been called back from inactive reserve status to visit Veknyria like my unit did.

Clouds blocked my view of the coastline as my flight continued. That didn't help my anxiety at all. I liked being able to see the ground, even if it was from great heights. Something about it made me feel locked into the world, as if losing sight of land or the sea might cause the airplane I was in to break with Earth's gravity and drift into space. It was ridiculous. Commercial airlines weren't built for such things. That didn't stop me from considering it. I tried to fall asleep anyway, counting sheep and all that stuff people recommend, but nothing worked.

Two airline attendants made their way down the aisle, passing out drinks and snacks. I wasn't much of a drinker anymore (doctor's orders), but I made an exception that night. I asked one of the attendants for a vodka on the rocks. He was skimpy with his pour, but I didn't cause a fuss. It was his job.

"Make it two," I told him.

He frowned at me. His name tag read: Olaf. I wondered if he knew just how many known universes there were. It was probably enough to navigate the world he knew without considering that possibility. I know it was for me even before they let me behind the proverbial curtain.

Olaf, meanwhile, set down my two plastic cups of vodka with ice. I handed him a twenty-dollar bill and told him to keep the change. It was weird to me that monetary denominations remained the same, of all things. A paranoid case might think that someone orchestrated the *illusion* of interdimensional travel, like those rubes who considered the moon landing a fake, going so far as to plant a statue of an activist-turned-mayor of Philadelphia in Washington Square to further bolster said illusion. When it came to conspiracies, the questions to ask were: why bother and who benefits? I doubted that tricking me into thinking I had traveled to a parallel world had benefited anyone, which, in turn, took care of the first question. Then there was the obvious to consider, the fact that many who believed in conspiracy theories never acknowledged, lest their world come down around them. People harbored too much selfishness to keep a secret for too long. Sooner or later, someone would want bragging rights.

It was Dr. Strauss in his infinitely snide way that came close to getting me to crack. For a moment, he nearly had me convinced that what I was experiencing was indeed a break with reality. Even when I offered to take him to the Ural Mountains to visit Arkaim, the national heritage site there, and show him the gateway itself underground, he balked at the idea.

"How far are you willing to go to support this delusion, Cal?" Dr. Strauss had asked.

"Come with me," I said. It wasn't until that moment that I realized his not having a gold coin like mine might present another set of problems. "Of course, you'll need proof for permission to pass."

"Let me guess," he said. "A series of tests to prove I'm worthy?"

"No," I said. "It's a gold coin. About the size of a half-dollar."

"And do you have this coin on you?"

"I sure do."

"May I see this coin?"

What did I have to lose? I reached into my pocket, held the coin in my fist, and I was about to pull it out to show Dr. Strauss when I had second thoughts. And by second thoughts I mean my paranoia went into overdrive. For all I knew, facsimile Dr. Strauss might have been part of some enemy faction that absconded gold coins from travelers to prevent them from ever escaping this world. Maybe he was part of a cabal that perpetuated the myth of one universe, that Earth was the only planet suitable for human habitation.

I left the coin in my pocket. Then I told the good doctor that I had another appointment and I had to go.

"You come from a different universe," said Dr. Strauss, "just the other day and you're already making appointments that you have to keep? I am impressed, Cal."

He was still congratulating himself for being so damned witty when I walked out of his office. In the waiting area were three other patients waiting to see him.

"Take it for what it's worth," I announced to the three, "but if you happened to be from the universe next door, Dr. Strauss will never believe you."

Each of the three pushed themselves back into their seats, as if my condition were highly contagious. One of them even gasped like I had just goosed her on the subway.

After putting away my second vodka I finally dozed off. It wasn't until someone tapped me on the shoulder that I woke up. It was Olaf. He informed me that we were about to begin our descent toward Chelyabinsk Airport in Russia.

Chapter 39: In the Land of Eshyol

My taxi driver's name was Oleg Strakhov. As soon as we left the airport, it began to snow.

In the Kilzilsky District, we ran into a cordon of soldiers setting up camp. I promised Oleg a healthy tip if we could get past them without having my papers checked.

Oleg told me that he had been in the Soviet army. He had guessed that I was a former soldier as well. It was a thing among prior service people. No matter where you went in the world you could always tell a veteran.

"Why did you leave?" I asked him.

"Priorities change," he said. "Not for me. I liked being a soldier, but the State had other ideas. Many of us were separated from service as a cost-saving measure. Some of the old-timers, the *lifers* you call them, they become upset. Army life is all they know. Even now when I'm not driving taxi I run into them. They talk about army days like it was the best time of their lives. These are men with wives and families, some even have grandchildren. Yet, the best part of their lives happened when we wore a uniform and we were told what to do, when to do it, how to do it almost every hour of the day except for when we were asleep. And when we slept we dreamed about being told what to do."

"I know the feeling," I told him. "I'm still having that dream."

We drove in silence for a time as the wipers whooshed back and forth. The farther we got from the airport, the more snow that fell. Before long, it was all darkness and snowfall.

My thoughts soon shifted to Sofia Dashkova and her celebrated status among the citizens of New Arkaim. It did not occur to me during my time in the fortified city that Sofia, the politruk Podrovsky, and the rest were not from the Soviet Union I knew in my reality.

Sonny Keegan had been right. Like him I should have checked the settings on the gateway before leaving New Arkaim.

"Have you ever heard of Sofia Dashkova?" I asked.

"No," he said. "Her name means nothing to me. Why? Is she a singer?"

"No."

"Girlfriend?"

"It's not important," I said. "I was just curious."

Another mile down the road red lights turned and arced in chaotic patterns. The closer we got to the source, the more the lights became visible through the falling snow. I thought Oleg might slow down, but he did not. When we saw a soldier waving frantically at the oncoming taxi, Oleg jerked his steering wheel to the right to avoid striking the man.

Suddenly, the red glow from the flashlights were all far to the left and then behind the taxi as we slid down an embankment. I remember mumbling *no, no, no* as I envisioned Oleg's Vulga sedan, a vehicle that was at least ten years old, slamming into a tree and bursting into flames like in a bad espionage movie. In my death fantasy I ended up trapped in the vehicle, of course, while my bumbling Russian driver, survivor of countless crashes, escaped and lived to tell how he watched his American fare get slow-cooked inside a burning taxi.

There would be no fire. The Vulga did smash into a row of saplings, however, and got stuck there. No airbags deployed. The vehicle didn't have any. The passenger window beside me shattered on impact, but I did not get cut. By the time Oleg and I gathered our wits, a handful of soldiers had already come down the embankment to assist in extricating us from the vehicle. Oleg was first. The passenger side of the taxi had crashed into the young grove. I had to climb out the rear door on the driver's side. A couple of the soldiers excitedly pointed out how the front axle had broken off from the vehicle.

"Can you radio your dispatch for help?" I asked.

Oleg and the soldiers looked at one another for a moment before they erupted in laughter.

"You must be American," said Oleg.

"No dispatch?" I asked. It was doublespeak for *fuck, I'm going to freeze to death*.

Someone up on the road shouted at the lot of us beside the car. One of the soldiers saluted and took me by the arm.

"We must not keep Colonel Puchenko waiting," he said.

The snow was a foot deep in places. I did not wear the right shoes. Come to think of it, I did not wear the right clothes either. My jacket was too light for the Russian winter. I had an idea that I'd fly to the Chelyabinsk Airport, catch a taxi to the Arkaim site, and traverse the ramp below the small museum there, and present my coin to whatever soldier approached me first. I never once thought of snow. Otherwise, I would have worn something more suitable than sneakers.

When we reached the road someone took pity on me and draped a long wool olive drab coat over my shoulders. The soldier who still had me by the arm saluted an officer and let go.

"Papers?" the officer said. "Passport?"

Oleg and I coughed up our paperwork. The officer, a short fat man with a bulbous nose, scrutinized my passport for nearly a minute before handing it back to me.

"That is your name?" the officer said.

I reached casually into my pocket and produced the gold coin I carried with me.

"I need to get to Arkaim," I said.

One of the soldiers shined his red light on the coin as the officer took it from me and examined it.

"Forgive me, Comrade Christos," the officer's mood lightened. "I am Colonel Yuri Puchenko, Commander of the 287th Motor Rifle Division."

"We can't be more than thirty minutes from Arkaim—" I started to say.

"The road is closed," said Puchenko. "Perhaps in the morning it will be passable. In the interim, we will find you some suitable footwear and you can bivouac with my unit tonight."

I looked at Oleg. He shrugged his shoulders.

Puchenko shouted at one of his NCOs. The NCO in turn dogged a private who stood in the road stamping his feet. The private protested at first, but when Puchenko's gaze fell on him he moved into action.

A few minutes later, the private came back with a pair of cold weather boots and a few pairs of wool socks. I sat on the bumper of a jeep, removed my old shoes and socks, and donned the new gear. The boots fit perfectly.

"Do they always do maneuvers this close to the airport?" I asked Oleg when no one was listening.

"Best not to ask questions," he said with a wink. "They might take you for a spy."

Soldiers sat around campfires. One group, six in all, started a rousing rendition of Bruce Springsteen's "Born in the U.S.A." One of the NCOs shouted something in Russian from a separate campfire. The singing stopped. The soldier who knew most of the words to the song, even though I doubted he understood half of what it meant, continued to hum the tune while others warned him: *Budet!* He would not. The soldier kept repeating the line "There still there. He's long gone."

A sergeant descended on the group then and started kicking them as they sat around the fire. Other NCOs joined the fray, dragging these young boys off into the dark while admonishing them.

"What's all that about?" I asked Oleg Strakhov.

"Colonel Puchenko hates the West," he said. "He no doubt heard them from his heated tent."

"These boys are hardly twenty years old," I said. "What harm can come from singing?"

"This is the irony," Oleg explained. "Your Bruce Springsteen sings about the shortcomings and tribulations of a capitalist system, and boys here think his songs are pro-democracy. They want the

Soviet Union to change, but they are too young to see the long game."

"What does that mean?"

"Democratic leaders only plan a few years ahead," said Oleg. "Central Committee plans for one hundred years ahead."

"I need to get to Arkaim," I told him. "Like tonight."

"It is treacherous."

"It's a snowstorm," I reminded him. "I thought you people were born in this shit?"

"That may be so," he said. "But you were not. You would be no good if you fall and break ankle or worse. No, we move at first light. Besides, soldiers keep us safe."

A sergeant accompanied by two privates distributed field rations. They dumped a small box each for Oleg and me, said not one word, and trudged on through the snow.

My meal that night consisted of crackers, beef porridge, which wasn't bad once I heated the can over the fire, and sausage stuffing. If my cardiologist could have seen me eating this stuff with its high salt content (for preservation purposes), he would have had a fit. There were little packets of Russian chocolate and a couple of tea bags and a pack of sugar in the kit as well. I took Oleg's cue and let nothing go to waste. There was no telling when I might eat again.

I'm not sure what time I fell asleep after eating, but after I awoke to soldiers' shouts I saw that the snow had stopped. The more aware I became of my surroundings, the more I realized that there was something serious about to go down.

I stood up and grabbed one young soldier as he hurried past. He struggled to free himself when I shouted the Russian word for "invasion" in his face. My Russian was so rusty I might have used the word for "infestation" instead.

"Nyet," the soldier responded and shook himself loose from my grasp.

He muttered something I didn't understand.

"Summary field execution," Oleg announced.

We followed the small crowd into a clearing. The day's first light broke in the east like a seam of white gold.

Five soldiers were tied to posts stuck in the ground. I recognized one of them as the one who was singing the Springsteen song. Five privates in uniforms and coats too big for them stood facing those tied to the posts. The firing squad remained at parade rest with rifles at their sides while Colonel Puchenko spoke.

Oleg translated in hushed, hurried whispers.

"The traitors before you have sought to undermine my authority," Oleg said while Puchenko raved like Khrushchev once did. "Insubordination and democratic sympathies are the cancer which erodes the people's army and the Soviet Republics at large. Such crimes will not be tolerated."

Colonel Puchenko handed it over to a senior sergeant. He waved at his jeep driver to start the engine.

As Puchenko drove off, his senior NCO shouted the order.

The members of the firing squad readied themselves, took aim against their comrades, and waited for the order. Just as the senior sergeant told them to fire, the soldier who had sung the Springsteen song the previous evening started singing again. It was surreal to hear him sing "Born in the U.S.A." as the bullets tore into him and the others. None of the condemned died on the first volley. That's something they don't teach in school or show in the movies.

The firing squad was ordered to fire again. One bullet from the second volley caught the singing soldier in the right cheek just below his eye and exited through the back of his skull, taking better than half his head with it when it did.

"Let's pack and get out of here," Oleg suggested.

It was the best advice I'd heard since landing in the Ural Mountains. The only problem I had was getting Puchenko who just had five of his own soldiers executed to provide me transportation. Did he assume that, despite my American accent, I was a Russian too? I doubted it. Still, the gold coin gave me some leverage. At least, I hope it did.

Oleg and I moved through a copse to head back to where we had camped for the night. We didn't have anything to pack, but Oleg insisted that we dismantle the tent they gave us and roll up the sleeping bags they had loaned us.

"Old habits," said Oleg.

Colonel Puchenko sat in the rear of the jeep as it came to a skidding halt beside us.

"Leave that alone," the colonel said. "It's time."

"After you drop off our visitor at Arkaim," Oleg said, "you will bring me to airport?"

The colonel lashed at him in Russian. I didn't understand a word of it, but if I had to summarize all the same it had something to do with not running a taxi stand.

"You," he pointed at me, "In the back with me."

Oleg climbed into the front of the jeep with the driver. By then the sun had risen and the snow was already beginning to melt beneath the long rays.

At the bottom of the ramp beneath the Arkaim museum, two Spetsnaz soldiers greeted me as I presented the gold coin once more. One of them escorted me into the room where the gateway was in operation.

Two guys in lab coats stood on either side of the massive gate jotting notes down on tablets. The special forces soldier made a big show of taking the coin from me, enough for the scientists to take note. Then he exited the room, leaving me alone with the guys in lab coats.

I asked if they spoke English. They both nodded.

"Can this thing be programmed to travel time?" I asked.

"No time travel," said the lab coat on the right side. "Only station to station."

"It would be cool, right?"

They both looked at me.

"Relative motion can dilate time," the other lab coat announced, "and of course gravity can slow it down. Any other manipulation could prove disastrous."

"So, if I wanted to go back and witness the crucifixion—" I started to say.

"Who are you?" the lab coat on the right asked. "CIA?"

"MI6?" the other one inquired.

"Please don't tell us you are with the West Germans."

"That's classified," I said.

"West Germans," the lab coats said in unison.

The first one spat.

The other one said, "If you are going, do it now. We have to shut the gateway down for scheduled maintenance."

"How will I know from the other side when it's running again?"

"You won't," the second one said. "Comrade Podrovsky will. And he will inform you."

"If you shut down the gateway as I cross over," I asked, "do I blink out of existence?"

"Just go," said the second lab coat, annoyed.

I had a plan. It wasn't a good one. It wasn't necessarily bad either, but it was a long shot all the same.

In the fog between universes, something that Bertrand Bauerfang had written in *The Book of Ziyarae*, the revelation of the angel Zaphkar, came back to me. It was a parable concerning *Prumashvallu*, the notion that in any universe something is always given for something else. The parable went like this:

> *In the land of Eshyol lived King Rak who had a daughter that refused to marry the prince from a neighboring kingdom.*
>
> *Awni was King Rak's daughter. The reason she did not want to marry the prince from the neighboring kingdom was that her father was a widower, and she feared that her father would wither and die the moment she moved from Eshyol to Nexdor, the neighboring kingdom.*
>
> *"A marriage like this would surely bring peace between our two kingdoms," King Rak told his daughter.*
>
> *"A marriage like this would bring me only misery," Princess Awni argued.*
>
> *"You will wed the prince," her father the king demanded.*
>
> *"I would rather have war," she countered.*

Ultimately, Princess Awni relented and married the prince of Nexdor. After one year's time, Awni led an army across the border to invade her old country. Her victories, as she crossed the land of Eshyol, were swift; her armies ruthless as they laid waste to all in their path. When she at last confronted her father King Rak on the battlefield in front of his castle, the king demanded to know what drove her to such arrogance.

"I told you I would rather have war," Princess Awni said.

She took a bolt from her quiver, loaded it into her crossbow, and shot her father threw his heart as he stood defiantly facing her.

"Why?" came her father's last word.

"To establish peace between the kingdoms on my terms," his daughter said. "And now you will be reunited with mother in the forever after."

The principle of something for something else was not new. In physics we learn that matter can never be destroyed, that for every action there's an equal and opposite reaction. I could only hope my actions would create the reaction I wanted.

Part V

The city, beloved by me since childhood,
Seemed to me today
In its December silence
Like my squandered inheritance.

~Anna Akhmatova

Chapter 40: Talk of Tombs

When Sofia opened her door, her expression told me that I was the last person she expected to see. My birthday had passed on the day I flew from Philadelphia to Russia. At fifty-five years old, I still fantasized about the great homecoming that included a passionate embrace and kiss before she pulled me into her apartment where we moved room to room pulling each other's clothes off without error or tripping just like couples did in the movies.

"Caleb!" Sofia cried.

We didn't make it through every room. Right inside her door I pushed her up against the wall. She fumbled with my coat. I told her to leave it as I raised her skirt. Sofia went for the buckle on my pants. It was all very rushed and chaotic. She raised one leg which I took hold of while I tried, unsuccessfully, to ram it home. We ended up on the floor after that. That's probably when I pulled a muscle in my back. I didn't let that deter me. I got in a half-dozen strokes before I came inside her. She kept going until she caught up with me.

"How did you get back here?" she asked, breathing in my ear when we had finished. She pushed herself up then, straddling me as her breasts hung bare beneath the sweater that I had earlier pushed up around her neck. "Did you go to Comrade Podrovsky?"

"No," I said. "There were soldiers at the gate when I came through. Let them tell him."

"Oh, Caleb," Sofia said, "no. You must see him. He will want to know your purpose. Just why are you here? I thought I would never see you again."

"You," I said. "You are my purpose."

"Caleb," she said, "such sentiment is expected in your society. But here, in New Arkaim, where the dream of a communistic reality continuously unfolds, such fancies are not prudent or practical."

"People don't fall in love in the People's Republic of New Arkaim?"

"Is that you, Caleb?" asked Sofia before she pulled the sweater over her head and tossed it aside. "Are you in love with me?"

"I think you are beautiful," I confessed.

"The Cathedral of Vasily the Blessed in Red Square is beautiful," she countered, "but you cannot lay with it every night. Besides, you left here to go to your wife. What happened?"

"It was Colonel Zamyenko's fault," I said.

"Comrade Zamyenko stole your wife?" Sofia sounded alarmed.

"No, nothing like that."

"Then what?"

"The gateway," I said. "It only goes in two directions: to here on Veknyria and back to Arkaim in the Urals."

"Yes," she replied. "Why? Did you think the machine generated wormholes that allowed you to travel wherever you wish? The Frulx gateway is a closed system linked by two portals."

"Your Russia, *your Earth* is not the same from which I came," I told her.

"What? I assumed that your CIA had either stolen the technology to build a gateway similar to ours," Sofia said, "or that Americans stole the technology directly from the Frulx who shared the technology with Soviet scientists."

"My superiors told me that the Frulx shared the gateway generators with the Veknyrians first," I argued, "and the Veknyrians shared the knowledge with both of our nations."

"That is ridiculous," she said. "Everyone knows Soviet science is superior."

Sofia climbed off me, picked up the sweater she had earlier tossed on the floor, and put it back on. Then she crossed her arms and stared at me. I knew that look. It was the expression of a woman who had had her fill of intimacy. It was time for me to get dressed as well.

"Sofia," I said, "I'm not here to argue about which country's science is better."

"Good," she told me. "I never understood why you Americans are so full of yourselves—"

"And what about you Russians? Why does everything have to be so goddamn tragic with you people?"

"Take that back!"

"You deny that suffering is an intrinsic aspect of Russian life?"

"Americans read Dostoevsky in English and think they are experts on our culture," Sofia proclaimed.

"Come on," I said, "I don't want to argue."

She took a step backward. I stayed with her, nearly stepping on her toes as she backed up to a sofa. I was about to offer an apology when she pulled me down on top of her.

Sofia hummed some little song in Russian, a lullaby from the sound of it. I said nothing for fear that I might break the spell.

"What am I going to do with you, Caleb?" she asked.

"We should talk about that," I said.

"Yes, let's do that."

"Not here," I said. Then, I whispered, ""Is there somewhere private we can go?"

"In the people's republic?" Sofia asked then laughed. "You must be out of your democracy-poisoned mind."

Later, Sofia took me to her kitchen to prepare some eggs for me to eat. She made a great show of banging around utensils as she took out a pad of paper and a pencil. Sofia tore off a sheet from the pad and placed it on the kitchen table. As she talked about her limited cooking skills, she scribbled on the sheet of paper.

> *Listening ever since you left.*
> *Maybe even before.*
> *Must be careful.*

I took the pencil from her. Now, it was my turn to communicate without saying a word.

I really do need to talk to you.

Sofia snatched the pencil out of my hands.

After we see Podrovsky.

She handed me the pencil. I paused a moment, then I wrote:

I can go alone.

As I handed her the pencil back, Sofia shook her head.

No leverage, she wrote. *With me, he would never make you disappear.*
Podrovsky does not trust you.

After that, she hesitated before giving me back the pencil.

He thinks I'm a danger? I wrote.

Sofia shook her head.

"It is a human trait that does not know ideologies or boundaries," Sofia said. "Fear of the unknown, the unfamiliar, the strange. It's a throwback to our days in the cave. When someone approached who was a stranger, there were but three responses: eye them with suspicion and scare them off or kill them, invite them into your cave, or flee the cave and give it over to the stranger. Podrovsky and his secret police would never flee New Arkaim. He plans to die here. The stone masons are hard at work on his tomb already."

"What about you?" I asked.

"I'm too young for talk of tombs," she replied. Then, pointing to the light fixture in her kitchen ceiling, she added, "Let us visit Comrade Podrovsky to inform him of your return." Sofia picked up the pencil once more. "If you love me, you will renounce your

American citizenship and become a member of the People's Republic of New Arkaim."

She held the index finger of one hand to her lips while she used her other hand to write:

Don't be too hasty. Let Podrovsky promise you things.

I love you, Caleb. I would never let them hurt you.

She put the pencil down and quietly balled up the piece of paper. Then she took a match and burned the sheet over the kitchen sink.

Chapter 41: All Things Americana

In my absence, Podrovsky had added another face to his ranks of personal bodyguards. Ladislav Popkov looked out of place in his dull gray suit and black turtleneck, as if he'd worn his torturer's get-up for so long he'd forgotten what normal clothing felt like.

As far as the old man was concerned, it was hard to get a read on him. In the winter of his life, Podrovsky may have been appointed as a high-ranking member of the Politburo, but his stone face and noncommittal responses to Sofia's questions concerning my well-being told me where his loyalties rested, namely with the KGB where, Sofia had informed me, he rose through the ranks after his compulsory service in the Red Army.

"Sofia," said Podrovsky, "your father and I go back to the old days. I would never allow any harm to come to you."

"My father is dead," she reminded him.

"All the more reason to honor the promise I made to him," he said.

"Which was what exactly?"

"To ensure your safety, always."

"And what about Comrade Paladin?"

"Comrade is it now?" said Podrovsky. When he chuckled, his bodyguards did too. When he stopped, his thugs turned tight-lipped once more. "Has Mr. Paladin finally seen the international workers' light?"

"I am prepared—" I started to say.

"Comrade Paladin has become very dear to me, Comrade Podrovsky," Sofia cut me off. "If you must know, we are in love."

"Do you intend to marry?" Podrovsky asked.

"I am sixty-four years old. I have never been married—"

"If it pleases you, I can officiate? By the power invested in me by the People's Republic."

"A kind offer."

"We can do it right now. Comrade Popkov here, recently promoted from the ministry of interrogation and pain management, could stand as, how do the Americans say? Best man, yes. That is it."

Popkov, at the mention of his name, snapped to attention.

"Who needs marriage," Sofia announced, "when love is enough?"

"A very progressive view."

"Not at all, comrade," she countered. "Marriage by design entitles a woman rights where property is concerned should her husband meet his end. In the People's Republic, property is a crime."

"Well," Podrovsky circled his desk and sat down behind it, "if you should ever change your mind."

"You have my gratitude, comrade."

"Anything else?"

"Comrade Paladin needs work."

"What did you do in the other world, Mr. Paladin?" Podrovsky asked.

"I was an editor," I told him. "for a medical publisher."

"How is your Russian?"

"Ne khorosho," I told him. Not good.

Podrovsky spread his fragile hands out, as if he were fresh out of ideas.

"The Republic always needs beet farmers," he said.

"Comrade Podrovsky," Sofia said.

"Relax," the old man told her. "We will find him something soon. In the meantime, help your love with his Russian. I won't have him going around speaking English and extolling all things Americana. It's bad for morale, even for those most committed to the cause."

"Of course, comrade."

"Perhaps we can put him in a factory."

An exchange developed now between Sofia and Podrovsky in Russian. It became so heated at one point, that Popkov and the other bodyguards looked as if they didn't know whether to eject us from Podrovsky's office or erupt into cheers for Sofia. Podrovsky flew into a renewed frenzy after that. When the argument ended, he looked winded, his face pale.

Once things quieted down, Podrovsky waved his slender hand, dismissing Sofia and me.

Popkov snapped to once more and opened the office door for us. He offered Sofia an awkward smile.

In the corridor outside the office, Sofia and I stood and listened for a moment as Podrovsky shouted orders at his men.

"Are we in danger?" I asked.

"New Arkaim is a Soviet colony on an alien planet, Caleb," she said. "It is better to ask: when are we *not* in danger?"

"Can we talk now?"

"Not here," Sofia waved her index finger, indicating that someone was no doubt listening.

Just then the door opened. Sofia threw her arms around my neck and pressed me against the wall, kissing me as she did so.

"Like horny adolescents," Popkov commented when he spotted us upon exiting Podrovsky's office along with another bodyguard.

"How dare you speak to a cultural hero like that," Sofia shouted.

I took her by the arm and led her in the opposite direction. When I turned back to look at Popkov, he stuck two fingers on either side of his throat.

"Let go of me," Sofia broke free from my grip.

"Can we go now?" I asked.

"Did you see that gesture?"

"Yes. Can we—"

"Who is he to threaten me?"

"Nobody. He's just following orders."

"I'm going back into that office to speak to Comrade Podrovsky," Sofia announced.

I stood between her and the office door now. "Don't do this," I whispered.

Sofia's expression changed at that moment. It was somewhere between a pout and one of pity.

"Oh, Caleb," she said. "You do stir my heart so."

"The feeling's mutual," I said. "Can we go now?"

She put her hands on my face as if she were going to kiss me again, but instead she shoved me aside and opened Podrovsky's door. By the time I could react Sofia had already shut the door and locked it.

I knew better than to knock.

Sofia exited the office less than thirty seconds later.

"Come," she said. "We go."

I followed her down the corridor. She didn't speak a word until we exited the Ministry of Travel.

Chapter 42: The Tip of an Imaginary Hat

We ended up at a beer bar near the southern half of the city's outer wall. New Arkaim offered three types of public transportation: short buses (long, full-sized ones could not negotiate the curved streets of the city designed after a nautilus shell) which often had to be pushed by patrons when they broke down, taxis which were supposed to be free, thanks to the dream of The People's Republic, but the drivers extorted fares anyway (they were all armed to the teeth like taxi worker union Rambos, half of them former soldiers, and they were not afraid to use deadly force), carriages drawn by a local beast of burden the Russians named *snaryadski*—a tongue-in-cheek reference to the Russian word for missile. The snaryadski was a four-legged beast with a silver-gray coat like a wolf, elbows and wrists on the forelegs and knees and ankles on the back legs like a cat, and a head similar to a horse. They were also notoriously slow.

The snaryadski, I learned from Sofia, were slow to mate in captivity. In the early days of New Arkaim, carriage drivers tried to beat the animals into performing well. The snaryadski often turned on their aggressors, but more times than not the beasts were killed. Given their reluctance to mate while held in captivity, a law was enacted that forbade carriage drivers from inflicting harm on the animals.

In the decades since the law was put into place, the care and treatment of the snaryadski improved greatly. That didn't motivate the animals at all, however. They were creatures of mysterious habit and often quit halfway between one point and the next. It didn't matter if the driver had a passenger or not. When they were done, the snaryadski were done. It was not uncommon for a carriage driver to leave their snaryadski in the street overnight with a bucket of government-supplied oats. A passenger, owing to the havoc the oats wrought on the snaryadski, was advised to wear a scented surgical mask in case the animal became flatulent.

"Why don't they just retire the snaryadski?" I asked Sofia after a server brought us two bottles of government beer.

"I hate that man," said Sofia when the server moved on to the next table to take an order.

"He's just doing his job," I said.

"I meant Podrovsky," she said, quietly.

In New Arkaim, like any other police state, one never knew who a legitimate citizen was, and who was a stoolie looking for a handout from the Politburo. Though I had been back for a whole day by then, I still found it unsettling that everyone wore the same dull gray fabric. Occasionally, I'd spot black like the turtleneck Popkov had worn.

I leaned across the small table and took Sofia's hand in mine.

"He won't be an issue for much longer," I whispered.

"Don't say such things," she said as she casually looked around.

"I don't mean assassination."

A few faces looked our way. They were not seated close enough to hear what I was saying. No doubt they recognized the cultural hero Sofia Dashkova. I sensed that such celebrity, in the neighborhood called, unimaginatively enough, the South Wall, meant little to the people who lived there and worked the factories, foundries, and mills.

"What do you mean?" asked Sofia.

"An escape," I told her.

"Such talk is dangerous."

"More than plotting to murder the *politruk*?"

"He's well-protected," she said. "But there are chinks in any armor."

"You know this how?"

"Let's just say there is a group of committed citizens," she whispered, "who are tired of Podrovsky's iron grip."

"I just want to go home."

"Why can't we do both?"

"You would leave the dream?"

"You joke," Sofia said, "but there's nothing funny about a life of common ownership and the absence of social classes—"

"I don't need the manifesto defense."

"Fair enough."

Two men stumbled toward our table on their way to the exit. One of them mumbled something to the other and gave him a shove. The second man fell into me and landed on his knees. He apologized as he palmed the tabletop. I held the table steady as the man got to his feet. He apologized a second time, tipping an imaginary hat to Sofia, and followed his friend out of the establishment.

"Give me that," Sofia pointed at a small, folded piece of paper that sat where the man's palm just touched.

I slipped it toward her. Sofia took the paper slip and opened it in her lap as she looked out a window facing the road. In one swift movement she glanced at the message on the paper scrap and crumpled it in her fist. Next, she dropped the paper into her beer glass and drank it down as it dissolved.

"We're being watched," she said.

"Maybe it's time to go," I told her.

"Leaving now would only confirm their suspicions."

"What should we do?"

"What else? Dance."

Sofia called out in Russian to the bartender. The man ducked down and stood up with a violin in hand. As soon as he started playing, a few other couples stood up. I joined Sofia.

"What is this song called?" I asked.

"It is old," said Sofia. "It's called 'Dark Eyes.' The original lyrics were written by Yehven Hrebinka in the 19th century. The melody was originally by Sindo Garay, a Cuban trova musician, and it was brought back to Russia. Enough history. Just dance and listen."

When the bartender finished playing, everyone except two men erupted in applause. The two men sat grim-faced at the end of the bar.

"Podrovsky's men," Sofia whispered as she hugged me close. "Let's go."

After we exited the bar a taxi pulled up to the curb. The driver jumped out, pouring praise on Sofia when he recognized her. He kept gesturing to his cab. I was about to open the door for her when Sofia stepped into the road and flagged down a second taxi.

"This one," she called to me as she climbed inside.

The first taxi driver approached the second vehicle. Our driver leaned across the front seat, rolled down the passenger window, and pointed a pistol at the first driver.

"*Otvali!*" our driver shouted. Fuck off.

The first driver went scurrying back to his taxi.

As we drove away, Sofia grabbed my arm and pulled it over her shoulder. She nestled against me like we were a couple of newlyweds on our honeymoon.

"Don't look to see if we are followed," she said. "They expect that. It's how they start to break you."

The pilot's name was Igor Smelchak. He was not married. He had no surviving family members or even distant relatives at New Arkaim. His situation back in the Motherland was the same. Podrovsky and his henchmen could only go after Smelchak, if it came to that, for helping Sofia and me.

"Don't worry about Igor," Smelchak said, referring to himself in the third person. "He knows how to handle himself."

When I was in the infantry decades ago, pilots held themselves in high regard. For a grunt, however, a pilot's only job was to ensure that the aircraft he flew did not plummet out of control and explode when it crashed to the ground. Smelchak was rather proud of himself. And like most combat[18] pilots, he came off as

---

[18] The fight on Veknyria was decidedly one-sided since it was Smelchak in his flying fortress airship and a dozen gunners against javelin-throwing, bolt-action-rifle-firing indigenous people who, like most aboriginals, just wanted to preserve their way of life, limit outside influence, and not get into a protracted war they could not possibly win. Of course, the U.S. Government felt the same way about the Viet Cong and for invading forces that didn't turn out well. The same goes for the Soviets in

completely neurotic whenever he found himself on terra firma, a regular Soviet Yossarian if ever there was one.

"Igor is not the only airship pilot," he told us. Sofia, of course, had done her homework. "I guess you know who the best is. That's why you come to Igor."

"We need to count on your cooperation," Sofia told him.

"Yes, but what is in it for Igor?"

He stared lasciviously at Sofia's shirt, licking his lips.

"I don't know if Comrade Paladin would approve," Sofia said.

"Igor is kidding," he said. "I already have *malishka*. My baby girl works in shirt factory. Inspector 78. That is her."

We stood in a reinforced bunker just outside the wall on the airfield. Two soldiers on a tower on the wall took turns firing their Kalashnikovs into the tree line, hoping to entice Veknyrians into a fight. The giants did not take the bait that day, but I was grateful for the sporadic gunfire because it masked the words that passed between Sofia and Smelchak.

"Have you been together a long time?" Sofia asked, her voice cracked at this new development. She was convinced until the day of the meeting, about a week after I had come back, that Smelchak had no ties that Podrovsky and his secret police could exploit. A girlfriend changed everything, provided Smelchak was telling the truth. "It is quite extraordinary to be young and in love—"

"Love is a pain in my ass," Smelchak said. "I'm a lowly pilot who could get killed any day. But all Svetlana cares about is what I can buy her. I tell her: baby, this is New Arkaim. What can I buy you on food and clothing rations—"

"They may use her against you," I blurted.

I knew my interjection did not sit well with Sofia. She was the master spy. I was not. For years, her secret group had plotted to assassinate Podrovsky and destroy the dream for an even better one.

Afghanistan. What the Veknyrians were missing was backing from a separate sovereign entity—the North Vietnamese had China and the Mujahedeen had Uncle Sam's anti-aircraft guns courtesy the CIA. America would no doubt side with Veknyrians, but it was anyone's guess in those early days which America from what universe would provide the Veknyrians such aid.

"What my comrade means," Sofia said, "is if you are having second thoughts, now is the time to voice them."

"Igor wants to go to his world," Smelchak pointed his stubby, hairy finger at me. "I would very much like to see the Motherland. I only know USSR from history books."

"Comrade Paladin lives in America," she said. "The land of opportunity and bliss. That's where we will end up."

"I cannot go to Soviet Union?"

"That may be difficult," I said.

"What Comrade Paladin means is that you will have to defect," Sofia announced. "I don't know if they will let you leave America to visit Russia."

"What will become of airship?"

"Someone will retrieve it," she assured him.

"Then America it is."

"Comrade Smelchak," Sofia said. "You must ensure this remains a secret. If the wrong people find out, I will say that you devised the plan and blemished my good name."

"Igor will say nothing," the pilot said.

"When is the next flight check for the airship?"

"It's too bad for you. Igor just took her up the other day. We go every month."

"What date is the next flight check scheduled for?"

"In twenty-eight days."

"You should bring Svetlana," Sofia offered.

She had saved the coup de grace for the end of the conversation.

"Igor can do this?" he asked.

"Igor can, if he pleases," said Sofia.

"In America," he said, "they have..." Smelchak looked at Sofia and mumbled something in Russian. Sofia answered, though I didn't know the meaning of the phrase with which she had responded. "Yes, shopping malls. No?"

"We do," I assured him.

"Then no," Smelchak said. "A girl like Svetlana in a capitalist society becomes bad news."

"Think about it," Sofia advised him.

"Igor has a bad feeling," he shouted over a volley of automatic gunfire from the tower overhead. "We should get back behind the wall."

Sofia and I followed him back into the city. Smelchak walked several yards ahead of us like we were not there. I wasn't sure at the time what good it did. A member of the secret police, one of the two at the bar when Sofia and I danced to the bartender's violin, pretended to repair the engine of a jeep parked at a curb across the road from us.

"Comrade Koltsov," Sofia called to the not-so-secret policeman. "How is your mother these days?"

Koltsov slammed the engine hood closed, climbed into the jeep, started the engine, and drove off.

"The fall of every society," Sofia remarked, "begins when people forget their manners."

"Do you know everyone in this city?" I asked.

"Almost," she weaved her arm through mine as we continued along the curved street.

Chapter 43: The Facsimile Influence

It was a big risk waiting nearly a month to board the airship when Smelchak made his next flight test. After we talked about it, however, Sofia decided that a greater risk would be returning to Podrovsky and feeding him some lie about my wanting to fly out to the sight where my American cohorts had fallen in battle against the Veknyrians. For one, it wasn't much of a battle since we were not armed. Podrovsky would know that. He would also see my efforts for nothing more than they were: a blatant escape attempt. Reluctantly, I agreed to stick to the plan.

"You should get work," Sofia said. "Maintain a cover."

"Podrovsky didn't want a debrief?" I asked.

"He got all the information he needed about your unit from your cohorts."

That was Sofia's kind way of saying they ultimately tortured Fly and Hick until they both died. Podrovsky never had any intention of ever letting anyone go. He was convinced that our purpose had been to act as a reconnaissance party for an invading force. No doubt the planet was rich with natural resources. And with a Frulx gateway it would be easy to exploit natural gas, minerals, and crude oil if it were there for the taking. Podrovsky, however, knew full well what he was doing when he directed Colonel Zamyenko to let me pass through the gateway. What he had not counted on was my return.

The Earth facsimile I had returned to, the one in which Emma was set to marry Herb Kaufman, the one in which my double took part in a mass suicide, may have been easier to contend with. I had no doubts that I could have proven that I survived the suicide ordeal, even if they had buried my double. I had no family left. Presumably, if my double's life followed my own, timewise at least, since the lab coats under Arkaim said it could not be altered or tampered with, then his parents and brother were dead. It may not have been easy at first, proving my identity[19]. That much was true. It was the quality of life that concerned me. How well would I function knowing I was once removed from my world? How long would it be before I was overcome with longing for my real home? I wondered. No, returning to Veknyria had been my only option. It was the only chance I had of getting to the Frulx gateway that would return me to my Earth.

The waiting game began. Sofia found me a position at a book printer. I wasn't able to engage in editing work since my Russian, even with Sofia tutoring me and speaking to me in her mother tongue, remained rudimentary at best. My job was more like factory work. I basically ran a machine that dispensed an equal amount of glue for binding the printed matter to the book spine. The first week on the job there were orders for the following school year. I could only imagine what propaganda filled the pages of those primers that came off the presses. During that first week, I worked six days from seven in the morning until five in the afternoon. The workers at the bindery were all given one hour for lunch. Since my job was clear across the city in the West Wall neighborhood, I couldn't go home to Sofia's for lunch. So, I packed what I could in a metal lunch box.

The bindery workers spent their lunch hour complaining about the bosses. Sometimes, for my benefit, some of them spoke English. At my job, I learned that every colonist learned English in

---

[19] There was the question of DNA. Granted, intelligent lifeforms on Earth and its facsimile where Sofia, Podrovsky, Zamyenko, and the other colonists originated from were carbon-based, but given the subtle differences between both worlds, perhaps our DNA varied as well. For all of my efforts, had I chosen to stay on facsimile Earth, I may have been first deemed an imposter and then become a medical curiosity when people realized I could pass for my double's twin but not share the same DNA.

order to know the language of the enemy that sought to destroy the utopian dream. The bindery workers were disillusioned. The destruction of the utopia by the nebulous albeit ever-lurking enemy boiled down to a simple question among the workers: *what's taking them so long?*

Some of my coworkers quizzed me about why I had come back. I was honest. I told them that I was in love with Comrade Dashkova. They started calling me Romeo and much worse. Most of the guys were younger than me and cut from a rough cloth. I let them have their fun.

Of the few women who worked at the bindery, they exhibited more sympathy for my position. It would be false to say that they revered Sofia and her celebrity status as a cultural hero. What they understood, however, was that for several years Sofia had fought off the advances of powerful men like Podrovsky. Some of those women flirted openly with me, seeing something in me that I never understood. The men made fun of me for that, too. My public declaration of love was seen as a portent that the great cultural hero Sofia Dashkova had chosen a commoner like me, and a foreigner to boot, as her partner.

When they thought I wasn't paying attention I heard them call me *Tupoy* because I smiled at people. They thought I was stupid. Only mental defects and naïve people, in their estimation, smiled at someone they didn't know. I suspected that any day they would turn on me, but they never did. One afternoon when talk of the gateway in the bowels of the Ministry of Travel came up the workers talked about how the machine was cursed.

"They say every time you pass through," one of my fellow workers said one day, "you leave a little bit of yourself in it."

I didn't disagree with him, but I wasn't about to go into detail about the three trips I'd made between the universes. I also had the luxury of pretending I didn't know any Russian at all which helped me, despite my comprehension slightly improving each day.

The conspiracy theorist's name was Boris Velikan. He was a hulk with massive arms and shoulders who never packed a lunch but went around bumming food from his coworkers in the breakroom. One of the old men warned me about Boris on my first day. Fighting was grounds for dismissal and possible arrest, so I didn't worry that it would come to that.

When Boris approached me I played dumb. He reached for my bread. We got into a shoving match as I tried to keep what was mine. He punched me in the chest at that point. It felt like someone had set my lungs on fire. I worried that the blow might induce another heart attack. I got so angry that I punted him right in the balls. Everyone cheered. I kept my bread.

Boris left me alone after that. In order to save face, he started bringing his own lunch to work. He had the diet of a child. His lunch consisted mostly of sweets. By three in the afternoon he would saunter off the floor to take a nap in the locker room. In a society where everything and everyone was equal, performance-related discipline was unheard of. The bosses left him alone.

On the third day of my second week at the bindery everyone went outside to take their lunch since it was unseasonably warm. A siren went off somewhere along the wall. It was the first time I had heard it.

"The giants are just probing us," one of my coworkers assured me.

Her name was Sonya. Those were the last words she ever spoke. Several javelins came over the wall. One of them struck Sonya in her back and the steel tip exited through her chest.

Bindery workers ran helter-skelter after that, seeking cover as the javelins continued to come down. Suddenly, a shadow passed over the city. The airship that had wreaked so much havoc in the desert flew over and the forward guns began spraying the field and the woods beyond the Western Wall.

When the attack ended, it was Boris who picked up Sonya's corpse and brought her inside to the bindery floor. One of the bosses came out of his office, took one look at the dead woman, and ordered her body removed. Boris came forward, scooped up the corpse, and walked out.

I learned later that Boris brought Sonya to her parents' house. A week later, Sonya was given a hero's burial. All of the bindery workers were ordered to appear at her funeral where party officials extolled the young woman's virtues. After the burial, Sonya's likeness was flown on flags and banners all over the city.

The following week, I asked one of the old men at the bindery what became of Boris. He refused to talk about it. We were standing near the bosses' offices outside the breakroom. Sofia had told me to remain under the radar while at the job.

"Comrade Velikan has gone for re-education," a voice called out. It belonged to Anton Chesnokov, the floor boss. "Sometimes a great tragedy like the senseless death of a New Arkaimian daughter like Sonya Alexey Rebikov makes even strong men question the dream, Comrade Paladin."

"Thank you, Comrade Chesnokov," I told him. "You have been most helpful."

He lit a cigarette and waved me off, indicating that I should return to work. The odor was pungent. In New Arkaim, tobacco was one of the crops that never quite took. People resorted to growing their own on rooftops. Some argued that the acidic quality of the soil had to do with the tobacco's sour taste. Others maintained that it was all in the curing, that the wood burned in the process tainted the tobacco leaves as it dried them out. Then there were those who firmly believed that the leaves weren't aged long enough before curing and significant amounts of ammonia were left over in them. Finally, though their numbers were few, a smattering of the people believed that the spirits of dead Veknyrians flew over the city and poisoned the tobacco before it was even harvested.

No one liked to get close to Chesnokov because his breath had been turned rancid from his cigarettes. I was more than happy to get back to the machine I worked at. It gave me time to consider all the different means the Politburo used to "re-educate" a worker who had blown a gasket like Boris Velikan.

Four nights out of the week after work I reported to a local party meeting house to receive instruction on the utopian dream. The people of New Arkaim, Sofia had informed me, were reluctant to use the word *communism* because stories had reached the fortified city from the Motherland that some of the Soviet campaigns to liberate the workers in various countries on Earth had not gone according to plan. It didn't matter that better than half the citizens of New Arkaim had been born in the colonial city. Such knowledge was not good for the Republic. The hardest chain to break in liberating a people was collective memory.

"Podrovsky knows this," Sofia told me. "But even the Politburo isn't that strong. KGB, on the other hand, can be."

"He's both," I said.

"In the Motherland, no one serves in the Politburo full-time," she told me. "The members are appointed during plenary sessions. Prior to joining the Political Bureau, Podrovsky served in the Central Control Commission. It wasn't until he became Chairman of the Party Control Committee that Podrovsky was appointed to the Politburo. Some say he never left KGB, but there are not many of them left. Those who know for sure are all dead now."

"And how long did he serve as chairman?"

"His methods were extreme, even for the most committed Party members," Sofia explained. "When I was twenty-two years old, I went back to the Motherland to meet with the Central Control Commission on my father's behalf. He was quite ill by then, and he could not make the trip. Only the commission knew about New Arkaim. It was the best kept secret in all of Moscow, which meant it was the best kept secret throughout the Soviet Union.

"Of course, Comrade Podrovsky returned with me," she went on. "There was no way he was going to let me have all the Party glory. He was very pompous. And he was used to getting his way. In Moscow, I was received by the Commission as a cultural hero. To the rest of Moscow, I was simply the daughter of an architect whose name would eventually be lost in time.

"Podrovsky was madly in love with me then," said Sofia. She blushed when she made the admission. "He was already in his mid-forties, forty-four, I think, and he fancied himself a regular Don Juan who, in New Arkaim, away from the Central Control Commission, conducted himself like a king exercising the practice of jus primae noctis. Through the 1970's into the early 1980's the running joke in New Arkaim was that a man did not have to support his children since they were all fathered by Podrovsky. Rumors circulated widely that there was a Podrovsky sex cult, one in which female comrades were willing to knock each other over just to get into the man's bed. It was all propaganda started by Podrovsky himself, of course.

"When the talk turned from heterosexual relationships," she continued, "to homosexual trysts, Podrovsky lost his mind. He started rounding up random people and hanging them from lamp posts. Sometimes he would have signs pinned to their coats. Libelous Scum. Agitator. You name it, he used it."

"He conducted a purge," I said, "because someone started a rumor that he was queer?"

"Podrovsky never got his hands dirty," Sofia informed me. "A good political leader never does. There were interrogations followed by hangings. For the accused, there was no defense. And there was no trial. The secret police here is quite a small contingent, but very powerful, thanks to Podrovsky. The goal was originally to out the person or persons who started the rumors about Podrovsky being homosexual. They never found the one who started the rumor."

I took a piece of paper from the pad on the kitchen table and wrote: *It was you?*

Sofia nodded.

"People under duress will confess to almost anything," I said when I got up to burn the piece of paper in the kitchen sink.

"True," she said. Then, "There is something else you should know."

"What's that?" I asked, returning to the table once the note was gone.

"Podrovsky made several advances when I came of age," she said. "He was very powerful. Not physically, of course. I had nightmares that he would have members of the secret police hold me down while he raped me, but it never came to that. He wanted me as his wife. My father was in no position to disagree. In the Party I could have done much worse. Then my father died. I told Podrovsky that I would rather join my father in the grave than give myself to him. He relented. I am not sure why. If I had to guess, I think he feared I might kill myself. Losing me was not the issue for him. Having his name associated with my suicide would, in his mind, cause harm to his reputation as a Party leader."

"Why tell me all this?" I asked.

"If our plan fails," said Sofia, "they will tell you lies about me in order to break you. Then they will kill you. And by the time that happens you will wish you never knew this forsaken planet."

Even though I learned more about the Party from Sofia as we talked into the night, I was expected to show my face at Party meetings. Many aspects of the version of communism practiced in New Arkaim diverged from the original ideology set forth by Marx and later implemented by Lenin. Of course, I had to allow for the facsimile influence, those subtle differences that occurred even though the copy, for all intents and purposes, resembled the world I knew.

They ran the political education meetings the same each night. Minutes of a previous meeting were read after singing the Soviet national anthem (the louder you sang the less likely you were to be harassed by low-ranking political officers when the meeting ended). Then the floor was open for questions before that night's lesson got underway. This was the part where people around the room asked questions ranging from workers' rights to more complex ones concerning Marxist and Leninist ideologies. Then a speaker from the Party, some office head or another, read a prepared paper concerning any number of topics from the inception of the Comintern to Political Economy. The meetings ended with participants reciting the Oath of New Arkaim, which was pretty much a rip-off of the oath Stalin devised for those joining the Red Army, penned, no doubt, by Podrovsky himself:

> I, _____ (fill in the blank with your name), a citizen of New Arkaim, colonial city of the Union of Soviet Socialist Republics, joining the ranks of Workers' everywhere, do hereby take this oath of allegiance and do solemnly vow to be an honest and disciplined worker, to protect to the best of my ability State secrets, and to obey implicitly all Party laws and regulations.
>
> I vow to study the works of our founders, to safeguard shared property in every way possible and to be true to

my People, my city of New Arkaim, my Soviet Motherland, and the Workers' and Peasants' Government to my last breath.

I am always prepared at the order of the Party to share the dream of a true utopia to the inhabitants of this host planet, and I vow that if our way of life should ever be endangered I will take up arms against those who wish to destroy the dream.

And if through evil intent I break this solemn oath, then let the stern punishment of the Party, and the universal hatred and contempt of the working people, fall upon me.

Those were long days during that month before Sofia and I rendezvoused with the pilot Igor Smelchak. I found some of the philosophy discussed interesting, but ultimately only a surveillance state can ensure that everyone in a utopia is doing exactly what they are told to do in the interest of the Party. It only reinforced my desire to return home. After all, if I was going to live in a surveillance state at least it should be one in which the illusion of voting rights existed.

Chapter 44: The People's Hero

Sofia and I had two days until we were to meet Igor Smelchak. That's when we were visited by Kapitan Yorlovsky and two rather grim-looking goons who looked like they spent their free time using their bare knuckles to make gravel out of cinderblock. They were not in uniform, which is to say they wore the standard gray pants and shirt issued to citizens of New Arkaim. This Sofia took as a bad omen. Army members remained in uniform at all times, shedding it only when their time in service officially ended. Even during off-hours they were required to wear uniforms in case the city was overrun by Veknyrians. The only time an army officer or an NCO would be out of uniform, like Yorlovsky and his goons, was when they were moonlighting for the secret police.

"The secret police force is of a certain size," Sofia had told me one day. "If they got any larger, they'd draw attention to themselves. To remedy this, Podrovsky often recruits temporary operatives from the army to conduct unofficial raids and arrests."

It was this last morsel of information that made my stomach turn after I opened the door. Unlike America, there was no such thing as a search warrant in New Arkaim. Since property ownership didn't exist, and everything belonged to The State, the sole of a secret policeman's boot served as such notification. It was better, economically speaking, to open the door before they kicked it down. The cost of replacing a door kicked off its hinges was theoretically absorbed by the State, but workers somewhere within the city made up the deficit, usually the party living in the space where the door was damaged.

"Comrades Dashkova and Paladin," Yorlovsky said, snapping his fingers at his two goons as he did so. "It is so very nice to see you again."

The captain made small talk with us about the weather and the crop yield from the fall harvest while his muscle set about rummaging through the apartment, searching for anything that could be brought to Podrovsky's attention. For all their efforts, they found only my Party meeting homework. One of the goons presented my completed assignments to Yorlovsky.

"I know these questions," Yorlovsky exclaimed. "They are from Comrade Joffe, yes?"

Maxim Joffe was one of the party members who had taught a class at a Party Meeting my first week there. He congratulated me on my knowledge of the Party system when he handed back my homework the following week.

"Yes," I started to say.

"Joffe is thorough," said Yorlovsky. "He was a lousy officer while he was in the army. But the Party embraced him all the same once he left military service."

"He is a teacher committed to the cause," I told him.

Yorlovsky wasn't stupid. He knew that to say anything questionable about Maxim Joffe would result in an investigation into his Party commitment. I wasn't about to jeopardize the life of a guy I didn't know. Yorlovsky knew that.

"You will come with us," he announced, tossing aside my paperwork.

"Where are you taking Comrade Paladin?" Sofia demanded.

"The great cultural hero deems to address the lowly captain," said Yorlovsky. "Worry not, Comrade Dashkova. You are to accompany us as well."

"Is this Podrovsky's work?"

"Please," he gestured to the door.

The goon who had found my homework took Sofia by the arm. When I advanced on him the second goon stepped between us and punched me in the ribs. I dropped to one knee. The second goon gripped me by my hair and pulled me to my feet.

"Careful, Ivan," said Yorlovsky. "They are to remain unharmed."

They took us that night by jeep to a small warehouse located near the army barracks. Several secret police types with scarves around their lower faces like train robbers stood in a semi-circle behind a chair bolted to the floor. Bound to the chair was a man I didn't recognize. Sofia's expression remained neutral. She would have never given away if she knew him. If she had, the game was over.

"Do you know Comrade Igor Smelchak?" Yorlovsky asked.

The man bound to the chair looked incoherent. One side of his face was swollen. Blood and spit were caked to his chin. Broken teeth lay at his bare swollen feet. His hands looked wrong, as if all the bones had been pulverized. How he was still conscious was beyond me.

"What have you done?" Sofia asked.

"So, you do know him?" Yorlovsky said.

"Of course not," I said.

"There is an interesting rumor going around certain circles within the Party," he said. "Talk of sabotage and assassination. Do you know this talk?"

"This man needs medical attention," Sofia said.

"Fine," Yorlovsky nodded at one of the masked secret policemen.

The masked policeman pulled out a pistol and pressed it against the side of the injured victim's head.

"Wait," I said.

"Caleb," Sofia hissed.

"You wish to tell us something, Comrade Paladin?" Yorlovsky asked.

"We don't know this man," I said.

"When we picked him up," the captain announced, "he was carrying identification that named him as Igor Smelchak. Naturally, Comrade Smelchak denied being the man his papers say he was. So we implemented some pain management to help him recall his true identity. Admittedly, he was drunk when we picked him up, so it took an extra amount of convincing. Would you like to know what he told us?"

"Every man has a breaking point," I said. "This proves nothing. If you beat me long enough I might admit to being Leon Trotsky."

Yorlovsky and the secret policemen laughed.

"What's so funny?" Sofia asked.

Yorlovsky mimicked killing one of the masked men with an imaginary ice axe. The other men laughed again. The victim in the chair lifted his head to expose a mouth of broken teeth. The captain nodded. The policeman with the gun shot the tortured man through the head.

"Comrade Podrovsky is the heart of New Arkaim," Yorlovsky announced. "We are well aware of the clandestine movement that seeks to topple the old man and dismantle the utopia. When the hammer falls, and believe me it will, don't be on the wrong side of history like this worker who violated his oath."

The captain dismissed us with a wave. His two goons grabbed Sofia and me and shuffled us outside.

The Vulga sedan driver whipped through the curved streets of the city. He slowed down to five maybe ten miles an hour when we reached the circle in the center of which the Ministry of Travel complex was located. Car doors flung open. Sofia was pushed out first. The goon in the back seat backhanded me in the mouth and shoved me out.

I hit the ground and rolled a couple of times. The sedan sped off into the night. By the time I got to my knees Sofia was already on her feet. She had a cut over her left eye, and she cradled her left elbow like it was broken.

All around the circle, banners hung from lamp posts bearing the likeness of Sonya Rebikov, the bindery worker killed by a Veknyrian javelin. Beneath her face on each banner the phrase *The People's Hero* had been rendered in Russian.

"We should leave this place before we get killed," I told Sofia as I stood up.

"Abandoning my home will be an admission of guilt, Caleb," she told me. "Soon, we will leave for good. For now, we conduct ourselves accordingly and let's not give Podrovsky any reason to think he has won."

"We could pack food," I said. "From here it's probably seven or eight hundred miles. We could make it to the other gateway in—"

"Caleb, listen to yourself," said Sofia. "If the Veknyrians didn't kill us we'd surely die of starvation. Plus, we're far from having catalogued every single predator that lives in the wild of this planet. And Podrovsky would send soldiers after us. We wouldn't get far."

We made it to Sofia's rooms without seeing anyone else. When she removed her shirt I cleaned the scrapes on her back. Sofia was reluctant to use ice on her elbow, but the skin there had turned deep purple with a bruise. The cut on her forehead proved more problematic. The wound would not stop bleeding, no matter the pressure I applied.

"Do you have a needle and a thread?" I asked.

Sofia sat on the edge of the tub. I had fashioned a sling from an old pillow case that cradled a bag of ice against her injured elbow.

"You work in a bindery," she reminded me. "And before that you were an editor. Giving you a needle and thread to stitch me up is like asking a grave digger to perform brain surgery."

"What do you propose?" I asked. "Perhaps a trip to a medical facility?"

"There's rubber cement in the desk drawer," she replied. "Use that."

I went to the desk in the living room. There I retrieved the rubber cement and returned to the bathroom.

"It's going to sting."

"They will come for you again," Sofia announced when I began working on the cut over her eye. "When they want you gone for good, they will use someone you know, someone unassuming, someone you would never expect."

"Why are you telling me this?"

"Because you should know."

"That sounds a little paranoid," I said.

"It's not paranoia, Caleb," she told me. "It's how we live and die here in New Arkaim."

Chapter 45: Grab-ass in Gilgamesh's Day

The next morning, Sofia looked like a losing boxer with a terrible corner man. For starters, she couldn't close her left eye over which I had applied the rubber cement. My less-than-stellar handiwork made it appear as if she was in a perpetual state of arching her eyebrow in alarm.

When I woke up beside her I thought she was awake already. Then I heard her snoring.

Since she could not shut her left eyelid I feared her eye would become irritated. In a worst-case scenario, she might even go blind in her left eye.

"I'm not going to go blind," she assured me when I posited the scenario.

After that she kicked me out of the bathroom. I heard water running.

Sofia and I had less than twenty-four hours until we were to meet Igor Smelchak on the airfield for his airship maintenance run. All we needed to do was to lay low and avoid Podrovsky's long arm of secret police goons. I wanted to play hooky from work, but Sofia thought it might raise suspicions. We argued about that before finally falling asleep. I was in no mood to deal with the bindery. She worried that even calling out sick would be out of the ordinary.

"We cannot let them think they got to us with their theater last night," said Sofia.

"We're never coming back," I told her. "I run a machine that any worker monkey can—"

"Is this what you think of the utopia? That we are monkeys?"

"We watched an army captain moonlighting for Podrovsky's secret police kill an innocent man last night," I said. "That's not very utopian to me."

"Caleb, don't be obtuse. It doesn't suit you."

My other option that I considered was leaving Sofia's place and pretending to go to work. The problem with that plan was that in New Arkaim there existed a small cadre of auxiliary police officers, some of them no more than mere teens, whose sole purpose was to check papers of citizens. They were called the United Workers Militia. They weren't armed with guns, but they did carry clubs which, rumor had it, they were quite liberal with if they felt like using them. The Workers Militia made certain that citizens were not loitering where loitering was not allowed (in New Arkaim that was everywhere except designated government beer bars). The only exception was made for soldiers who, in a long tradition of playing grab-ass and fucking off when the duty day ended, dating all the way back to the Sumerians in Gilgamesh's day, often hung out on street corners chewing the fat until late into the night. If I ran into one of the Workers Militia zealots out on the streets, they'd know that I wasn't where I was supposed to be since my papers stated the times from Monday through Saturday when I was supposed to work at the bindery. If I ran into one or two of the little teenaged bullies, I wasn't worried. The problem, as Sofia explained it to me before I began working at the bindery, was that the UWM were all issued whistles.

"One toot," she warned, "and they will swarm on you like fire ants."

Playing hooky while pretending to go to work was out. Getting beaten by a gang of club-wielding uniformed young thugs was one thing, getting hauled into jail was something else entirely. I could not risk missing the opportunity to depart New Arkaim with Sofia courtesy the pilot Smelchak.

I was looking around Sofia's apartment, debating about what to pack for my work lunch, when a knock sounded at the door.

"Answer that," Sofia called from the bathroom. "Then come see me."

"What if they want to come in?" I asked at the bathroom door.

"Of course they will want to come in," she replied. "They always want to come into your home, if only to remind you that your home and you belong to the State."

I opened the door expecting to see Yorlovsky again flanked by two or more goons.

"Comrade Popkov," I said, loud enough for Sofia to hear.

"It's a personal matter," he pushed past me and entered the apartment. "I must speak to Comrade Dashkova at once."

"Wait here," I told him.

I went to the bathroom door and knocked. Sofia let me in. She held a wad of toilet paper against her forehead.

"I can close it now," she winked at me with her left eye. "But I need more rubber cement."

"Ladislav Popkov is here to see you," I told her.

"I blame myself."

"For Popkov?"

"No," she said. "Last night, I kept my eye open when you applied the glue."

"Stay here," I said. "Let me tell Popkov you will be with him directly. Then I'll come back."

"Do I know this Popkov?"

"One of Podrovsky's bodyguards?"

"I need more."

"The torture flunky?"

"Ah," she beamed. "I wonder what he wants."

I went back to the living room. Popkov was pacing in front of the door. He must have checked the lock three times before he realized I was standing there.

"Comrade Dashkova will be here momentarily," I told him. "Why don't you have a seat? Or better yet, help yourself to a drink."

"It's six in the morning," he said, as if that meant something.

"I should be on my way to work soon," I said. "But I must help Comrade Dashkova. She's not well this morning."

"Nothing serious I hope?"

"Nothing I can't patch up for her."

Back in the bathroom, I found Sofia still holding the tissue to her forehead. Her robe was open. I marveled at her for only a moment before applying the rubber cement after she closed her eyes.

Sofia joined Popkov and I in the living room. She was dressed in her government-issued pants and shirt with a matching kerchief tied over her head to hide the wound above her eye.

"Comrade Popkov," she said with all the aplomb of an elder statesman. "How may we be of service to Comrade Podrovsky this morning?"

"The old man didn't send me," he said. "I'm here on my own."

Sofia arched her eyebrow as she looked at me. I worried the rubber cement on her skin might crack and her wound would bleed through, but it did not. Her simple gesture told me what I suspected already. Popkov was lying.

"Comrade Paladin is due to work at the bindery soon," Sofia informed him.

"Yes, well," said Popkov, pausing long enough to listen at the door for a moment, "I have it on good authority that Comrade Paladin intends to go back home."

"Comrade Paladin and I," Sofia said, "with Comrade Podrovsky's blessing, intend to wed. Why would he want to leave?"

"Then..."

"No, Ladislav," I said. "It is not true."

"So, it is first names now?" he asked. "Caleb?"

"We're all friends here."

"Even though I beat you?"

"You were doing your job," I said. "How's the new one? You like being Comrade Podrovsky's bodyguard?"

"It is trying," he admitted. Then, he asked Sofia, "If I were in trouble, would you help me?"

"What is the trouble?" she asked.

"I fear the old man wants me dead," he replied. "I must leave this place, if I am to survive at all."

"Would you like me to talk to Comrade Podrovsky?" she asked.

"No," he said. "He must not know I came to you."

Popkov didn't look worried. That was the tell in his charade. He was in no way smart enough to pull off what Podrovsky had sent him to do.

"I should probably leave soon," I said, "if I'm to catch my bus."

"Yes, to work," said Popkov. "I'm sorry to have troubled you."

He unlocked the door and let himself out.

I waited a minute or two before I opened the door and stepped into the hall.

"Forgot my lunch," I said, loudly and stepped back into the apartment.

I didn't see Popkov in the hallway, but that didn't mean he might have been hiding on the stairs nearby.

"Why send Popkov?" Sofia whispered.

"He knows us both," I told her. "The other bodyguards saw me only once."

Sofia pointed at the ceiling, her signal for *they are probably listening*.

"Imagine being that desperate to think we plan to leave New Arkaim?" she said loudly for the eavesdroppers' benefit. "Why would he think that Podrovsky moved him to his personal detail just to kill him?"

Ten minutes later, I sat in a crowded bus headed for the bindery. Standing in the aisle by the driver were two members of the Workers Militia. One of them rubbed his club against his cheek as he stared in my direction. When the bus reached my stop I got off. To do so I had to pass between the militia members. They couldn't have been no more than twenty years old. The one on the right, the taller one, tried to look hard but his expression came off like he was constipated.

The Workers Militia boys followed me off the bus. At least, I thought it was me until they cornered one of my coworkers on the street just outside the bindery. Her name was Irina Kurkova. She had short blond hair and blue eyes. The shorter militia bully rubbed his club along her collarbone and down her chest. Irina presented her papers and pointed at the bindery entrance. The two young men scrutinized her papers. The tall one took out a small notepad and wrote down her address. Then the short one with the wandering club handed Irina's papers back to her, thanking her sarcastically for her cooperation.

"*Svin'i*," she said and spat as she approached the entrance. Pigs.

Irina marched defiantly through the bindery entrance, pushing past a few other coworkers just to put as much distance between herself and the Workers Militia tools as she could.

A few male workers liked to loiter by the entrance before the work day began. They divided their time between smoking sour-smelling cigarettes and watching female workers pass along the sidewalk. None of them made a move to aid Irina. They knew better. The United Workers Militia was just the start of a prolonged and well-executed pattern of harassment. If they tried to do the stoic thing and stand up for Irina, whistles would have blown. Papers would have been pulled from their pockets after they were beaten senseless. Once they were known, then the real harassment would start. Irina was on her own in Podrovsky's utopia. No one was coming to her rescue when those boys would eventually show up at her home.

A bell rang deep in the recesses of the bindery, signaling the start of yet another work day. I shuffled to the clock inside the entrance and punched in. I did my best to mask my elation regarding my escape. It was then I remembered that after work I had to attend yet another Party meeting.

The meeting house was packed that night. Even with all the windows open, it wasn't enough to dispense with the sour smoke from cigarettes that filled the large room.

The speaker that night was Marina Tolkalina. Her talk had to do with Hegel's Theory of the Modern State by Shlomo Aveniri, specifically with labor being the essence of modern man.

In a philosophy course I took in college we read portions of Bertrand Russell's *A History of Western Philosophy*. Russell pointed out that Hegel thought that if enough was known about a thing then its properties can be inferred by logic. Russell pointed out that if one's reasoning was flawed or otherwise worse than others, the consequences, in his words, would be interesting. He did not say they would be correct. Russell did not have to. It was an important point I learned all those years ago, one that could be applied to almost any endeavor.

Comrade Tolkalina knew her material but quoting Aveniri who quoted Hegel was a rabbit hole I'd just as soon avoid. The problem was I could not just get up and leave without arousing suspicion. So I had to sit there along with everyone else.

Having spent her take on Aveniri, Comrade Tolkalina shifted gears. Like any good public speaker, she saw that interest in her lecture was waning. A joke or anecdote would have sufficed to bring her audience around, but there were too many minor party bosses in the audience. Comrade Tolkalina needed to up her game.

"Let us not lose sight of our collective purpose, comrades," she said. "We are creating here in New Arkaim a prototype not only for all mankind but other intelligent species as well. The Communists back on Earth uphold a peaceful coexistence, and they struggle relentlessly to prevent war.

"The Statement of 81 Communists and Workers Parties from the Moscow Meeting in 1960 tells us this much," continued Comrade Tolkalina. "New Arkaim stands as the vanguard to continue the good work of our Communist brothers and sisters on Earth. You, comrades, are living history which can never be erased."

Stirred by a few strategically placed Party cheerleaders, everyone started applauding. The meeting attendees hooted, hollered, and shouted gibberish like it was a regular old Pentecostal tent revival. If religion was the opium of the masses, as Marx once wrote, Comrade Tolkalina's oratory served as the People's methamphetamine. The meeting hall erupted into a frenzy of favored workers' songs and squat dancing. A few people even fainted.

I didn't need the low-level Party bosses in attendance taking notes about my lack of enthusiasm. If they reported as much to Podrovsky, my chances of escape lessened even more. So, I clapped and stomped my foot until the frenzy quieted down.

As Comrade Tolkalina began her closing remarks, I looked around the room, never letting my gaze linger too long, and made up stories about the attendees. Most of the men sat there with wide-eyed, slack-jawed expressions, owing to Comrade Tolkalina's black high-heeled pumps and gray skirt, and a few of the women did as well.

When the lecture ended we all stood up and recited our oath. Mine of course was interspersed with English since I still didn't know enough Russian to recite the whole thing in its native language. Afterward, the crowd exited the hall into the street.

I had just stepped out to the sidewalk when a familiar voice called my name.

"Comrade Paladin," said Irina Kurkova. "I didn't know you attended Party meetings?"

"I'm the new kid in town," I told her. "Call it my crash course in utopian living."

"You must be careful of what you say, comrade," Irina warned. "You never know who is with the secret police."

We made small talk after that. From what Sofia had told me, people attended Party meetings for one of three reasons:

1) they had made some minor offense and the powers that be decreed that the offender needed some fine-tuning (philosophically speaking, of course),
2) they were there to spy or otherwise keep tabs on a fellow comrade, or
3) they genuinely sought to better understand the system that masqueraded as liberation.

Of the three categories, the last were always small in number. I couldn't make up my mind as to which category Irina belonged.

"I have a taxi waiting for me across the street," she said. "Maybe you want to come to the beer bar with me and my brother?"

She waved to a brutish fellow with wide shoulders, a bull neck, and a cap pulled down low over his Neanderthal mug who stood beside a Vulga sedan taxi. The taxi driver seated behind the wheel looked like he could have been the caveman's brother. Sofia's words came back to me in that instant: *When they want you gone for good, they will use someone you know.*

"I am expected home," I told her.

"A kept man," said Irina, "by the cultural hero herself, Sofia Dashkova."

"Her reputation often precedes her."

Irina stepped closer to me. When she turned to look over her shoulder at her brother standing in the street I smelled a whiff of perfume. It wasn't the usual government-issued kind. She waved to the brute beside the taxi. He didn't wave back.

"Gregor is shy," she said. "He looks scary, but he's nice once you get to know him. Are you sure I can't change your mind?"

I had to be twice her age, maybe even a few years more.

"I'm not feeling well," I said. It was a half-truth, at least.

The longer I stood there, the more I became convinced that if I left with Irina and her "brother" then that would be my last car ride.

That didn't keep her from pouring it on by leaning against me so I could feel the swell of her breasts against my arm.

"You are sure?" Irina inquired. "I do like older men. They know exactly what they are doing when it comes to intimacy."

I wasn't sure where she got that information. Did they teach female operatives this sort of thing at a Ministry of Ineffective Flirting? It was apparent that a man had coached her. No self-respecting woman would ever teach another woman to be so blatant if they wanted to catch unawares a world-weary, learned target like me.

"Maybe some other time," I started to back away.

"Comrade Paladin," she said. "Wait."

I didn't. When I looked back the caveman in the street was jogging around to the passenger side of the sedan. On the next block I flagged down a taxi and climbed inside. I told the driver to keep his light on while I ducked below window level in the back seat. A moment later, as I peeked over the back seat. I saw the taxi occupied by the two cavemen barrel down the curved road and turn left.

"The Ministry of Travel," I said in Russian.

"They are closed," the driver said.

"I live there," I said. Then I thought to add, "With Comrade Sofia Dashkova."

The driver spat on the floor of his own taxi when I mentioned her name. He slammed on the brakes. Then he launched into a litany, all in Russian, that sounded like he had composed it prior to that evening.

He was still going off when I exited the taxi and darted across the street for the cover of a dark alley.

"What did the men look like?" Sofia demanded.

"Muscular missing links," I said, "with wool fiddler's caps pulled low over their faces."

It took me over an hour to get back to Sofia's apartment. I rode the bus for part of the way, expecting any minute for Irina's goons to get on at the next stop.

"If we weren't leaving tomorrow," Sofia announced, "I'd have this Irina girl arrested."

"I think she's with the secret police," I said.

"How can you be so sure?"

"There was an incident this morning," I replied. "I'm certain I was meant to witness it."

I told her about the Workers Militia boys stopping Irina in front of the bindery.

"Was she on your bus?"

"I don't think so. Why?"

"But the boys from the Workers Militia were?"

"Yes."

"Do you get off in front of the bindery?"

"No, the stop is just before it."

"She was waiting this morning," Sofia said, "until your bus pulled up. Then she started walking ahead and the militia boys pursued her."

"Why do they make it so difficult?"

"What do you mean?"

"Why not just come here and kill us both?"

"It's craft practice," Sofia explained. "Every operation serves two purposes. One is an actual objective, and the other is a training one. It's also a question of optics. What the public perceives is just as important as the goal itself."

Sofia pointed at the ceiling. She quietly took a piece of paper and a pencil from the desk.

This is no time to panic, she wrote.

"Please forgive me," I practically shouted for the benefit of the surveillance team who had bugged Sofia's apartment. "I am tired from a long day."

"Thinking only of yourself does not benefit the collective," Sofia shouted back at me.

She wrote:

> *We are not staying here. Take only what you*
> *need to get back to your country.*

We snuck past the night watchman in the building lobby and emerged on the square. No sooner than Sofia raised her hand a taxi pulled up to the curb. She took one look at the driver and told me to climb inside.

"Where are you headed?" the driver asked.

She gave him an address.

"Where are you taking me?" I whispered.

"To an old friend," she said.

"Care to elaborate?"

"I don't know," Sofia said. "You seem like the jealous type."

"An old boyfriend?"

"It's ancient history."

"That's cool."

"We weren't really a couple," she clarified.

"Sort of a friends with benefits thing?"

"This I don't know," confessed Sofia. Then, "We used to fuck. That is all."

"Oh, ok," I said. "What happened?"

"It stopped," she replied.

"You found someone else?"

"What business is my past to you?" Sofia said. "Do I ask the details of your sordid American life?"

"No, but you can feel free to do so."

"Just let it go," she advised me. "It is of no consequence."

"He found someone else," I said. "Do you know her?"

"You will see."

"Sofia, you sound like you're not over this guy," I told her.

"Don't do that," she said. "Men always act like they are hurt when a woman has a past whereas a man can brag, and his friends put him on a pedestal and worship him like a god for his sexual liaisons. When a woman sleeps with someone for the sheer sake of sex men say she is a—"

"*Svin'i?*"

The taxi driver kept his eyes on the road.

"What? Pig?" Sofia cried. "I will show you pig. I meant...what is the word?"

"Whore?"

"You should stop," she told me. Then, "What is the American idiom? Quit while you are ahead?"

"Fine," I said. "I get your point. And for the record, I don't think that way about you."

Sofia swung her leg over mine and pulled me close to her. She took my hand and placed it on her chest as she kissed me.

The taxi pulled to a stop. The driver recited the address.

After the taxi departed, Sofia took my hand and led me across the street. She knocked on the door of a house opposite the address she had given the taxi driver. It was a smart move. If someone questioned the driver and then followed up with whomever lived at that address it would prove a dead-end.

The knock Sofia used was a patterned one. I recognized it. Three quick knocks followed by three more with a brief pause between each and then three more fast knocks. SOS. The Morse code signal for distress.

"Well, well," Polkóvnik Dimitri Yustonov Zamyenko said as he stood there in a smoking jacket and slippers like some kind of Bolshevik Hugh Hefner. "If it isn't the Lost Yankee and his sponsor, Cultural Hero Comrade Sofia Dashkova."

"Knock it off," Sofia said. "Podrovsky wants us dead."

Colonel Zamyenko looked up and down the street. He waved us inside.

"*Kotik,*" a male voice cried out from somewhere inside the house, "*kto u dveri?*" Kitten, who is at the door?

The colonel blushed. "*Lyubov' redka,*" he said. Love is rare.

"Indeed," I said.

A spry, middle-aged man appeared in the living room now where the three of us stood. He wore a matching smoking jacket and brandished an identical homemade pipe.

Colonel Zamyenko cleared his throat. "May I present to you," he said, gesturing at the man, "my attaché—"

"Dimitri," the man said, stomping his foot.

"Sorry," said Zamyenko. "This is my common-law husband, Uri Kozlovsky."

"Charmed," said Uri, extending his hand to shake mine.

"Cal," I told him. "Hey, I know that voice. You're—"

"Thank you for flying The People's Republic Airline. Yes," he said. "It's a pleasure to meet you in person, finally."

He gave Zamyenko a sideways glance.

"Do you know Comrade Sofia—"

"Ugh," he exclaimed. "Let's dispense with the Party formalities. Of course I know Sofia Dashkova. We share," his gaze fell on Zamyenko now, "common tastes."

"Uri," Zamyenko said, "will be assisting with your escape."

"How did you know—" I started to say before Zamyenko cut me off.

"Honestly, honey," the colonel said to me. "The odds were against you since we picked you up. We're surprised you lasted this long. But you did. That's important. So much so, in fact, that you have become an inspiration to the movement."

"Movement?" I asked.

"After tomorrow," the colonel said, "things will never be the same."

Chapter 46: Without Igor

For months, a network that included Sofia, Zamyenko, and others planned for revolution. A general strike was to commence at the start of the morning work whistle. Political bosses sympathetic to the cause were charged with organizing strategic flare-ups of violence and vandalism in order to occupy the police. The army, under Zamyenko's command, was to participate in the strike, calling for freedom and the abolishment of Party rule. Colonel Zamyenko's own Spetsnaz unit was scheduled to storm the Ministry of Travel and take Podrovsky into custody.

"Or kill the old trick," Uri said the following morning while it was still dark. "I am all for his execution, but kitten here has a heart."

"There is much he knows," Zamyenko decreed. "Podrovsky lives as long as he is useful."

"Resistance?" I asked.

"Count on it," the colonel replied. "But it will be dealt with accordingly."

"Wouldn't it go faster if the airship stayed here?" I asked.

"Cal," Sofia said.

"I'm just curious."

"In Podrovsky's secret police," said Uri, "are several ex-pilots of the airship. It's better to put as much distance as possible between them and the aircraft."

As for Sofia and me, we were to adjourn to the airfield where we would meet Igor Smelchak before sunrise.

We opted to stay awake.

An hour before sunrise, a sedan from the Colonel's outfit pulled up in front of the house and took us to the airfield. The driver transported us all the way out to the strip where the behemoth airship sat idling as it prepared for take-off.

"Igor is brilliant, no?" the pilot Igor Smelchak said to Sofia and me when we visited the cockpit. "What is phrase in America? Yes. I threw off the scent."

"You got an innocent man killed," I said.

"Not so innocent," he countered. "He was secret police."

"How do you know that?" Sofia asked.

"How did he die?"

"Answer Sofia's question first," I said.

"You and Comrade Dashkova are on a first name basis now?" Smelchak said. "Igor never stood a chance against the buckaroo, yes?"

"Comrade Smelchak," Sofia began.

"Did the revolution kick off without Igor?" the pilot interrupted.

"The man they killed—" I started to say.

"Sure," he cut me off. "I have uncle inside the Ministry of Travel. He is recruiter for secret police. That's how I know."

"Are you certain?" Sofia asked.

"Uncle Vanya gave me file," he said. "Happy?"

"I'd like to see it," I said.

"You need to take seats now," Smelchak said. "Igor is about to get this big hump into sky."

Sofia and I left the cockpit and took our seats.

"Attention comrades and our special guest, the Yankee son of a bitch," Smelchak's voice came over the intercom. "Please fasten seat belts. And thank you for flying Air Revolution. Also, I'm kidding about the Yankee son of a bitch. I'm sure Yankee's mother was a fine woman."

After the initial take off, Smelchak banked the airship to his left and circled wide over the forest to the north of the city before continuing his loop and heading south. He flew directly over New Arkaim.

"Please prepare for target practice," Smelchak said over the intercom.

"What is he doing?" Sofia asked.

The rapid burp of .50 caliber machine gunfire sounded.

"Thank you for dying in bed this morning," Smelchak's voice sounded once more over the intercom. "Igor for Podrovsky kill!"

Sofia rushed to a window.

"He shot at the Ministry of Travel," she said.

"Was that part of the plan?" I asked.

"No," she cried. "That crazy bastard."

I followed Sofia back to the cockpit door. She tried to open it, but the door was locked.

"Open this door, Smelchak," she shouted. "Right now."

"I'm terribly sorry, Comrade Dashkova," the pilot's voice came over the intercom system. "As a safety precaution, cockpit door remains locked for duration of flight."

"You fired on your own people!"

"Correction. I fired on enemy."

"Someone will follow," she pounded on the door with both fists now. "Don't you get it? Someone will come after us!"

"None of the helicopters can fly this fast," Smelchak shouted, "and they cannot travel farther than 1200 kilometers."

"That's not true," Sofia said.

"What do you mean?" I asked.

"The army has one MI-26 helicopter," she said. "The original model could fly twelve hundred kilometers using regular and auxiliary fuel reserve. They retrofitted the helicopter with a larger fuel tank. It can make the trip to the desert mesa."

"But no return without refueling?"

Sofia looked at me. "Podrovsky's men don't care about returning," she said. "They only care about becoming heroes of the Party."

Chapter 47: Pineapple Grenade

Igor Smelchak kept the cabin door locked until we reached our destination.

Colonel Zamyenko had plotted Smelchak's course prior to take off after I showed him on a map the location from which my unit had first emerged. Smelchak put us down within a couple of hundred yards of the cave entrance.

Toward the rear of the craft there was a bay door which he opened after we landed. Aside from Smelchak, there was a team of six onboard that was responsible for manning the guns and providing security. They were armed with pistols, so when Sofia confronted Smelchak at last about shooting the Ministry of Travel back in New Arkaim she did it in a brief, non-threatening manner.

"What gives you the right to fire on innocent people?" Sofia demanded.

"Listen to the cultural hero of New Arkaim," Smelchak said. "She's promoted herself from city planner to insurrection expert."

No one laughed. We stood on the ramp that protruded from the bay door.

"You had no right," said Sofia. "The actions for the revolution were carefully planned."

"You think Igor is an idiot?" the pilot asked.

"Yes," she replied. "And a dangerous one."

"I think it's time you leave my craft," he said. Smelchak looked at me, "take your lady with you and get out."

"You're going to wait, right?" I asked.

"For what?"

"If the Frulx gateway is compromised in any way," I said. "We'll have to return with you."

"Take radio," said Smelchak.

He pointed to a shelf on the wall of the fuselage where several two-way radios were stored in chargers. As he gestured, the sound of rotor blades echoed against the low mountain where the cave entrance was located.

I grabbed a radio and clipped it to my belt. As I reached for one to hand to Smelchak the pilot in the Soviet-made Mi-26 helicopter came in low toward the rear of the airship. The helicopter's machine gun fired directly at us. Several rounds struck Smelchak, sending pieces of him flying in a cloud of blood mist and bone splinters as I pulled Sofia to the bay floor. Rounds ricocheted everywhere. Sofia screamed when one of the crew fell dead beside her.

We high-crawled toward a door through which Smelchak had led us to the bay area only minutes beforehand. Sofia made it through the doorway first. I followed. Before I did I stole one look back and watched as another member of the crew kneeled on the ramp as rounds from the helicopter machine gun whizzed and banged all around him. He had an FIM-43 Redeye surface-to-air missile launcher. The crew member fired the launcher. The helicopter returned fire and killed him. Sofia kept pulling at my shirt as I watched the helicopter pull up, but not before the Redeye missile struck the rear of the helicopter and exploded upon impact.

"Caleb!" Sofia screamed. She kept pulling me deeper into the airship. "We'll use another exit."

"No," I took hold of her arm. "This way is the fastest."

"Are you crazy?"

"They took out the helicopter."

We made a dash for the ramp while the remaining members of the airship crew tried to assess the extent of the downed helicopter's damage.

Outside the airship, the desert's heat felt like an invisible wall.

Something whizzed past my ear. I thought for a moment that it was just an insect. When I turned to look back, I saw someone chasing us on foot. He had a pistol out and was shooting as he ran.

Small arms fire erupted in the distance behind me. I didn't look back. I knew it was the remaining crew shooting at our pursuer.

Sofia reached the cave entrance first. Once I got there I turned and saw our assailant. He was perhaps fifty yards from us now. It was Kapitan Yorlovsky. He reloaded his pistol as he sprinted toward us.

Once Sofia and I entered the cave I knew it wouldn't be long before Yorlovsky would catch up to us. I looked around for a rock to throw at him. From over the mountain behind us a band of Parupanoon flew. Two of the winged creatures broke off and dove for Yorlovsky. One moment he was there, the next he was gone.

I turned to say something to Sofia, grinning as I did so until I heard Yorlovsky slam against the rocks just outside the cave. Sofia turned away. Yorlovsky's pistol skidded to a halt just inside the cave entrance. His mangled body of broken bones lay like an abstract art installation. Two Parupanoon landed with their backs to the cave entrance. They went to work on Yorlovsky, smashing his head against the rocks before tearing at his flesh.

My radio came to life.

"Comrade Paladin," a voice said, "come in, Paladin."

The two Parupanoons turned to face the cave at the sound of the staticky voice.

"What?" I responded to the radio as I slowly backed up to where Sofia stood.

"Another soldier from the helicopter—"

The radio went dead. I tossed it aside, distracting the Parupanoon who had stepped into the cave to see what all the noise was.

Sofia and I retreated into the deeper recesses of the cave. We found the Frulx gateway. I stepped on the plate on the cave floor. The gateway revved up, the lights on its frame flashed in a counterclockwise motion, and the spinning fog appeared.

"Come on," I said.

Sofia remained hesitant. She was no stranger to the Frulx gateway the Russians had used, but it had been years since she last transported back to her world.

Over the soft hum of the machine came the sound of automatic small arms fire.

"Go now," I told Sofia.

"Not without you," she said.

I picked up a rock from the cave floor and took up position in a blind spot beside the chamber entrance.

"Lieutenant Isbalov?" Sofia cried.

It was the stocky effete who had hand-delivered my government-issued clothes before he took me to my very first meeting with Podrovsky.

"The People's Couture," I said.

Isbalov turned on me, holding a Kirapis machine gun, as I swung on him with the rock in my hand. The weapon fired as I struck him in the side of the head, rendering him unconscious. Isbalov spun as he fell, spraying rounds in an arc as he did so.

A few of the bullets narrowly missed me. Sofia was not so lucky. A stray round struck her in the left cheek. The bullet exited the back of her head, taking with it a good portion of the crown of her skull. She fell to the cave floor in a crumpled heap.

Isbalov had a utility belt around his waist with two hand grenades attached. I dragged him close to the Frulx gateway and propped him up against the chamber wall beside it. Then I removed the hand grenades from his utility belt. I pulled the pin on one of them and held onto the lever, wedging the whole works under his ass. It was a risky move. The grenade was a Soviet-made F1 that resembled the old "pineapple" grenades American troops used in WWII. With ordinance that old, the fuse may not have lasted thirteen seconds which was standard for that model. As long Isbalov did not move I would be ok. If the fuse was bad or he regained consciousness and shifted his weight, it would be another story.

I went to Sofia and straightened her, so she lay on her back. Her eyes were still open. Her left eye, resulting from her fatal injury, looked down along the length of her body while the right one stared straight ahead. I tried to close Sofia's eyes, just like they did to dead people in the movies, but they would not stay shut.

Part VI

A happy present is not something we can always take for granted.

~Thomas Mann, *Buddenbrooks*

Chapter 48: The Hollowman Experiment

I came through the fog and emerged from the other Frulx gateway in the underbelly of Dowa Yalanne. It was dark inside the chamber when I arrived. The slightest hint of light came from an opening ten or fifteen yards from where I stood.

I held up the remaining hand grenade and pulled the pin. Then, holding the lever against the grenade with one hand, I felt along the wall until I reached the chamber opening.

As I stepped over the threshold I tossed the hand grenade behind me, hearing it clank against the Frulx gateway. By the time it exploded I had already moved fifteen yards down a tunnel toward an opening that led out of the mesa cave.

I made it about twenty yards down a slope along the mesa exterior when they made their presence known. Ten of them stood up at once with their weapons trained on me. They wore clumps of scrub brush on their backs and helmets to further camouflage their uniforms that matched the red earth.

"Caleb Paladin?" Captain Prescott approached me, his weapon at the ready.

Of course, it wasn't *the* Captain Prescott. The android I knew had vaporized himself back on Veknyria.

"Yes, sir," I responded.

"You are alone?" the facsimile Prescott asked.

"Yes," I said.

"Welcome back," he said. "Did you witness the detonation at Riengmarnoon?"

"How did you know?" I asked. It seemed so long ago. I acknowledged that I did serve as witness. "Did any of the other guys make it through here?"

"That information is classified," he replied.

"Do you know about the Russians?"

"Yes," he said. "Any survivors left behind?"

"Fly and Hick," I said.

"Who?"

"Sorry," I told him. "Bartholomew Kidd and Silas Haywood. They may have been eliminated by the Russians. Or maybe sent to an alternate Earth."

Prescott nodded at a staff sergeant. The sergeant signaled his radio man who produced a handset.

"No one else?" Prescott asked as the sergeant radioed the information about Fly and Hick.

"Why didn't you tell us the Russians were there first?" I asked.

"That's classified," he said.

"There's a whole city," I said. "They're from an alternate Earth where the Soviet Union is still intact."

"That's classified, too," said Prescott.

"I went there."

"You'd do well not to repeat that."

"So, what happens now?"

Prescott nodded to two soldiers on his right.

"Cuff him," he said, "and put him on the truck."

They brought me back to Kirtland Air Base and kept me there for three months for debriefing. The first four weeks they kept me in an attic space with no light and no ventilation. I was given water, MREs, protein bars, and a bucket in which to relieve myself. Every day the bucket was removed and a new one replaced it. When I wasn't busy eating or pissing and shitting into a bucket in the dark they took me out for questioning. Every time they did they tried to trip me up. Each time they did my story remained the same.

After the first month ended, they moved me to a barracks slated for demolition. They put two members of the Air Force Security Forces at the front door leading in and out of the one-story building that was an old-fashioned WWII-era open bay room. There was a back door to the barracks, but it was blocked by stacked metal framing from old bunks. On my first night there, I thought I might try to escape by moving some of the bunks out of the way. Someone had painstakingly tack-welded the bed frames together that were haphazardly stacked there. In some places the frames appeared to have melted together and cooled.

"Weird, isn't it?" a Security Forces airman said one evening when they escorted a food service worker in with my dinner.

"The bedframes?" I said. "Who would weld them together like that? Was it a prank?"

"It's not welded," the security airman said.

"They look that way to me."

"Something happened here," he said. "We're not really supposed to talk about it."

Any time anyone said they didn't want to talk about something, they really meant that they did. The airman was no different than any other person in that respect. He wanted me to press him. So, I did.

"Please do," I told him. "It will break up the monotony."

"The rumor around the base is that they did experiments all the way down in White Sands," he blurted, relieved to share what he knew. "Teleportation. They were going to transport a team of twelve from Holloman to here. Something went wrong."

"You think?" I tapped on the melded bunk frames.

"That's the legend," he said. "Anyway, we're going to leave you to your meal now."

He held the door open for the food service worker.

"What happened to the team of twelve?" I asked.

"Did you ever hear of the Philadelphia Experiment?" the security forces airman replied.

"Something similar happened here?" I asked.

"The government's into all kinds of shit," he said.

"And yet here we are," I told him, "serving their interests."

The airman tapped his index finger on the trigger guard of his assault rifle.

"Is it true that you came from another planet?"

"I'm from New Jersey," I replied. "That may seem like another planet to the likes of some corn husker from Nebraska..." He winced when I said that. "You from there?"

"Ashland, born and raised," he said. He started tapping the trigger guard on his rifle again. "Are you psychic?"

"Not at all."

"Well, enjoy your meal."

"You didn't answer my question."

"What was it again?"

"The twelve they tried to teleport," I said. "What happened to them?"

His name was Naylor. Or at least that was the moniker on the name tag velcroed to his uniform. Nervous Naylor with the itchy trigger finger. I wondered if this was his first gig like this. All I knew was that at his age I would have been scared shitless to talk to a guy placed under house arrest who was rumored to have come from another planet. The times sure do change.

"Down at Holloman they had twelve guys lying in bunks," said Naylor. "This one website? CodeBlackWhiteSands.com it's called. They talked about how scientists thought it best that the subjects lay perfectly still. When they kicked on the machines—"

"What type?" I asked.

"I don't know," he answered. "I didn't study teleportation in high school."

"Fair enough. Continue."

"When they flipped the switch," Naylor concluded, "the twelve guys zapped out of view. They were supposed to end up in bunks here, but somebody messed up."

"What do you mean?"

"The story goes that all twelve guys, army soldiers they were," he said, "died because they ended up here in one tangled mess of twisted bunks, bone, and flesh."

"Fused to that monstrosity right there?" I asked.

"That's the story," Naylor said. "Anyway, my relief will be here soon."

Nervous Naylor had his M-16 trigger setting on auto. I know this because his finger slipped as he tapped his trigger guard. He fired seven rounds into the wall to his left.

At the sound of the gunfire, the other guard came through the front door. He was a dullard named Bromsky. He had the butt of his M-16 rifle against his cheek as he squinted along the sights of his weapon.

"Put your weapon on safety," he told Naylor.

"But I...I didn't mean to," Bromsky's trigger-happy partner pleaded.

"Put it on safety right now," he told Naylor, "or I'll blow you away!"

"Fellas," I said. "Let's just take a breath and relax. It was an accident."

"I thought you killed the guy," Bromsky said to Naylor like I wasn't there. He lowered his weapon. "That was intense."

Naylor put his weapon on safety and slung it on his shoulder, the muzzle facing the floor.

"Were you really going to blow me away?"

"Shit yeah," said Bromsky. "I was totally going to blow you away."

"That's not right," Naylor said.

"Are you injured, sir?" Bromsky asked me.

"I'm fine," I assured him.

"I thought for sure Naylor here was trying to blow you away," he said.

"Stop saying that," I told him.

"Hey, Bromsky," Naylor spoke up. "Are you going to report this incident?"

"No," he said. "Come on, let's get the fuck out of here."

The following day when Captain Prescott 2.0 came around to check on me I told him all about Nervous Naylor and the dullard Bromsky. I didn't want to get the poor boys in trouble, but Nervous Naylor and his itchy trigger finger made me uneasy. To bring home the point, I showed Prescott the bullet holes in the wall. Captain Prescott 2.0 assured me he'd take care of it.

Nervous Naylor didn't make the rotation of guards outside my door after that. Neither did Bromsky. The day after that they didn't return either. They were replaced by a couple of real sticks in the mud named Smith and Tanner who didn't speak two words to me.

It took all kinds. One day I told Smith the truth about Captain Prescott 2.0, that the officer was indeed not human.

"You see," I told him, "the old captain is an android with a limited strike nuclear weapon built into his torso. Imagine lugging that around all day every day. Robot or not, it would wear my ass out."

Smith didn't respond, not even the slightest perturbation showed in his expression. He was well-trained.

Chapter 49: Uncle Sam Takes A Bite

Once a week they sent an interrogation specialist to interview me further about my experiences. She was by the book, as that type tends to be on the job, but she was easy on the eyes. Sergeant Basso was her name. She looked like a younger version of Sofia Dashkova. This was purposely done, I was sure, since I had described Sofia to my interrogators during my four-week attic stay.

They also sent me a shrink once a week to make sure I hadn't blown a gasket. The psychiatrist's name was Dr. Rand. He seemed concerned primarily with the year or two leading up to the day I received my orders to report back to duty. I told him everything about my job, Emma's joining a cult, my non-existent life that ensued following my wife's departure, and even some stuff about my childhood.

"So you would say the media influenced your decision to join the army after high school?" Dr. Rand asked.

"Isn't it that way for everyone who signs up?"

"Elaborate." That was his favorite word. It made me wonder if he came from the same mold Captain Prescott 2.0 did.

"We see movies," I said. "We see commercials on television. Hell, we even see commercials at the movie theater now. We hear them on the radio—"

"Elaborate."

"We're bombarded by such imagery," I told him. "From a young age boys are slowly brainwashed into thinking that the greatest thing they can do for their country is serve it. It's usually the working class and the poor. The whole thing is positioned as the only way out for certain kids in low-income areas. It's the military or claw your way up to managing some fast-food joint. The poor are programmed to become part of a system that holds the potential to kill them.

"When's the last time," I went on, "when you heard someone on television, or the radio say, 'build free housing,' 'shelter the homeless,' or 'feed the poor.' Imagine what the Peace Corps could do with half the annual defense budget? The way it is, it's a disgrace. These days we advertise the military like it's the backbone of democracy."

"What do you think is this nation's backbone?" asked Dr. Strand.

"We can start with empathy," I said. "In school they only teach us subjects that are meant to make us more efficient workers. We don't teach people how to be empathetic. We don't teach them to think for themselves. Instead of promoting the study of science all the time maybe we should stress literature or art instead.

"Imagine taking just one-eighth of the U.S. Defense budget," I went on since he didn't interrupt me, "and use it to finance free workshops for citizens to learn to be more empathetic. Imagine reallocating those billions of dollars every year to promote peace with other nations rather than preparing for war all the time."

"You would have made good officer material," Dr. Rand said.

I wanted to strangle him.

"Do you have anything to do with getting me out of here?" I asked him instead. "Or are they just going to extract as much information from me as they can before they put a bullet in my head while we stand over a shallow grave?"

"The United States Government is not in the business of assassination," the psychiatrist said.

"Maybe you're the one who needs a shrink."

"I'd like to discuss the woman you met over there," said Dr. Rand. "Sofia was her name, wasn't it?"

"I met her," I said, feeling like a broken record playing the same lyrics over and over again. "I fell in love. She got killed trying to get back here with me. I came back alone. That's all I care to share."

On the night of my eighty-ninth day of captivity, an army captain from the JAG Corps came to the barracks bearing a sheaf of paperwork I had to sign in the way of non-disclosure agreements for the work I had completed. His name was Jack Wolverton. Captain Jack Wolverton of the JAG Corps. He spent four hours that night reading each line of every document I was supposed to sign.

When he finished at last, Captain Wolverton handed me a ballpoint pen to sign the papers on the lines where little yellow Post-it notes with red arrows had been attached.

I ended up signing my name and writing the date thirteen times. When I finished, I considered the pen a moment. Then I stabbed Captain Wolverton in his left hand just to see if he was human or not.

He was human, all-right. I must have pierced a vein because he bled a lot. When I stabbed him he began screaming. A whole hullabaloo ensued when guards came through the door and knocked me to the floor.

Had Captain Jack Wolverton of the JAG Corps not fainted, things would have gone much worse for me. Luckily, the guards turned their focus on saving the officer rather than breaking every bone in my body. I never got to thank the captain for the distraction.

I was scheduled to leave the following morning. They kept me for an additional thirty days. They said it was for further observation, but I knew it was really punishment for stabbing screaming Jack Wolverton in the hand.

On day one-hundred-nineteen, another captain visited me. He was from the Army Finance Office. Spencer was his name. He wanted me to sign for my final check since my end of time in service or ETS date had arrived. The document detailed how I had been hired as a "consultant."

"Do I sign for it?" I asked.

It was a test of trust. Captain Spencer produced a government-issued ballpoint and handed it to me along with a single-page form. The trust test was made easier for the captain since he was flanked by two Security Forces airmen I'd never seen before. Judging by their stern looks, they no doubt had heard all about my time with Captain Wolverton.

"Congratulations, Mr. Paladin," said Captain Spencer. "On behalf of the United States Government, I want to thank you for your special service to the country."

"Pack your shit," one of the airmen advised me. "You're out of here first light tomorrow."

"I have no money, no resources, and no hope," I quoted Henry Miller. "I am the happiest man alive."

Judging by the blank stares, neither the captain nor the airmen had ever read *Tropic of Cancer*.

"Whatever," the other airman said. "Just be ready."

"Before I leave," said Captain Spencer, "you should review the check and attached deductions."

"Deductions?" I asked.

"Your attempt to destroy military property did extensive damage," he said.

"No one should have the capability to travel between—"

"That's not for you to decide, Mr. Paladin," he cut me off. "Open the envelope and read."

I opened the manila envelope containing the government check. A memo marked *Consulting Fee* had been included on the check itself. Below a perforated line were two sheets. The first one itemized repairs for the damage I had caused to the Frulx gateway. The original amount of the check paid to me totaled $1,200,000. The itemized repair cost list with labor included, deducted before taxes, looked like this:

Tervalum Alloy Outer Casing:	*$95,000*
Gyrohydrolic Accelerator:	*$85,000*
Fiber Optic Tanner Drive:	*$67,000*
Phase Shift Assembly:	*$43,500*
Ionized Water (300 gal):	*$6,000*
Ring Assembly Sealant:	*$3,500*
Subtotal:	*$300,000*

Uncle Sam also deducted a donation to the Zuni Reservation Dowa Yalanne Preservation & Education Fund to the tune of an additional $850,000. This amount was also deducted before taxes, leaving me with $50,000.

"The donation to the Zuni Reservation I can live with," I said. "But that little Russian grenade did all this damage?"

"It's not like you bent a tent peg," Captain Spencer noted, "or lost an ammo pouch. You damaged highly classified extraterrestrial technology. You're lucky they didn't send you to Leavenworth."

I would have felt better if he told me, *We're the United States government. Of course we're going to fuck you on the deal.*

On the second sheet, an addendum had been attached to the aforementioned charges. The government charged me $135 a day to off-set the cost of room, board, meals, and around-the-clock security.

"It was more of a goodwill gesture," Captain Spencer explained. "The actual fees were much higher."

For what? I wondered. Stupid Philadelphia Experiment rip-off stories from a trigger-happy half-wit and constipation-inducing meals?

"Anything else?" I asked.

"On behalf of the United States Government and the Elders of the Zuni Nation," he went on, "you are forever barred from stepping foot on their reservation. Should you be found there you will be arrested and charged with—"

"You think I'm ever going to leave New Jersey again?" I asked him. "After all this?"

"You're free to roam the country like any citizen," the captain assured me. "You just can't ever visit the Zuni Nation ever again."

For my one-hundred-nineteen-day stay, the total came to $16,065, leaving me with $33,935. The government took a fifteen percent consulting fee tax from that final amount. That left me with a grand total of $28,844.25.

"Not bad," Captain Spencer said, doing his best Groucho Marx impression with his eyebrows.

"Are you nuts?" I asked. "All of my old buddies are dead or exiled to some parallel universe."

"We all make sacrifices for our country," he said.

"With all due respect, sir," I told him. "You're an asshole."

"If by asshole you mean patriot then—"

"What's the difference?"

Captain Spencer didn't stick around for any more verbal jousting. He snapped his fingers and his two escorts from the Security Forces followed him out.

Chapter 50: The Federal Geniuses

I stayed at a Motel 6 outside the airbase until the check from Uncle Sam cleared. Once it did, I bought a used pick-up truck, a 1978 Dodge Power Wagon complete with a roll bar in the back and a ram's head hood ornament, for $2500.00.

The used car salesman who sold me the truck said that it had belonged to his nephew. He offered no other information except to assure me that the truck ran well enough for its age. The salesman forgot to tell me that the truck devoured gasoline like fossil fuel was going out of style.

I left New Mexico and drove to Nevada. There I checked into the same Holiday Inn Express in Elko identical to the one on facsimile Earth.

The clerk behind the desk looked around my age, but he moved like he was much older. His name tag read: Kirby Joe Johnston.

"Do you know the best way to get out to The Radiant Angels of Zaphkar compound?" I asked him.

He stared at me, jowls turning red.

"You some kind of reporter?" he asked, suspiciously.

"No," I told him.

"You got kin out there?"

I didn't want to give too much away. So, I lied.

"Thinking about writing a book," I told him.

"Well, I don't know how much there's left to tell," Kirby Joe said.

"How do you mean?"

"You're sure you're not a reporter?"

"I'd be obligated to tell you if I was."

"Seriously?"

"I'm pretty sure they have to identify themselves," I told him, "and the organization they represent. It's not a law, but more a question of ethics—"

"Mainstream media ain't got no ethics," he announced. "At least, not anymore."

"I hear you," I said, for lack of anything else to say while I thought: *of all the kooks I had to meet in the American Southwest...*

"What's your book going to be about?" asked Kirby Joe.

"I've been corresponding with the founder of the Radiant Angels," I lied again, "Bertrand Bauerfang—"

"I know who that Eurotrash son of a bitch is."

"He was born in Canada."

"Same difference," his eyes widened with rage now. "And I don't mean no offense by this, but did you know he's half a Jew?"

"What happened to the other half?"

"Are you mocking me?"

"Not at all."

Kirby Joe took a deep breath. Then he said, "I promised the misses I wouldn't get worked up on account of my heart disease, but you got to be a fool not to think they the ones who are what really running—"

"I had a heart attack a couple of years ago."

"What do you want? A medal?"

"Do they still give them out?"

Kirby Joe grinned. "You're a crazy son of a gun," he said.

"I've been called worse," I told him.

"Well," he said, "I doubt you'll have much chance of talking to him, Bauerfang I mean, after what happened this morning."

"What happened?"

"You haven't heard?"

He was one of those guys, the kind who answered every question with a question.

"No," I replied. "I've been traveling all morning."

Kirby Joe frowned. He fidgeted with a pile of papers behind the desk.

"It's in the hands of the State Police now," he said. "They're all dead. Every last one of them so-called angels."

"Thanks," I grabbed my key off the desk and headed to my room.

I paused long enough to use the bathroom and splash some water on my face.

On the way out of the lobby, the desk clerk waved me over.

"I have to get out there," I said.

"If any of them state troopers give you any grief," he said, "tell him Kirby Joe Johnston says you're all right. I used to be police chief in Elko."

I thanked him and made a dash for my truck.

The roadside opposite the compound's main gate was filled with buttinskies, gawkers, lookie-loos, peepers, rubberneckers, and snoopers of every stripe watching the spectacle as they sat on beach chairs in the beds of their pick-up trucks, leaned against their cars, or straddled motorcycles. I had to drive a quarter-mile up the road just to find a parking spot and then hoof it back to the main gate.

A gaggle of troopers stood with their captain as I approached. The captain stepped toward me.

"You with the press?" he asked.

"No," I said and told him my name. "My wife is in there."

"I'm Captain Randolph," he told me. "Let's take a walk."

"Do you know Kirby Joe Johnston?"

"Yeah, I know him."

"I need to get in there," I said.

"No one is going into the compound," Randolph announced. "What did you say your wife's name was?" I told him. "We're putting together a list."

"What happened? Can you tell me that?"

"It's a mess in there," said the state trooper captain. "FBI just got here an hour ago. It's not our show anymore."

"I might have a photo," I reached for my wallet.

Randolph held out a cautionary hand as he placed his other hand on my right shoulder.

"That's not going to help us right now," he said. He looked me over for a second. "You're in the military?"

"Prior service," I said.

"Branch?"

"Army."

"I was in the Corps. M-O-S?"

Would he let me in if I told him I'd been to a parallel universe where a bunch of out-of-touch Soviets were trying to establish a utopia despite the animosities offered, and rightly so, by the indigenous population whose average height was ten feet? I doubted it.

"Infantry," I said.

"Listen," Captain Randolph said. "Trooper Barnes over there is collecting information from people related to members. He'll take your information. The FBI also has a hotline—"

"I still don't know what happened."

"Oh, that. Preliminary findings point to a highly toxic beverage."

"What about Bertrand Bauerfang?"

"Like I said," the trooper captain told me. "We're still working on positive identification—"

"He's not here," I said.

"We're not commenting on that until everyone inside has been positively identified," he puffed out his chest as he hooked his thumbs in his police utility belt.

After my stay at Kirtland Air Base, the last thing I needed was to get arrested for disturbing the peace or whatever bullshit charge the captain wanted to slap on me if I pushed too hard. I asked him for a business card. He produced one from his shirt pocket.

I walked the quarter-mile back to my truck. I thought about slipping through the wire fence that bordered the compound property, but sooner or later I'd run into a uniformed trooper or an FBI agent. Instead, I headed back to the Holiday Inn Express.

After three days, all of the dead had been positively identified. It turned out that Bauerfang kept detailed files on his cult members, including collecting their drivers' licenses which the Nevada State Police discovered during an initial search of the group's offices.

My former wife Emma was not among the dead. My dead brother's wife Marianne, however, was listed among the victims.

I called Captain Randolph just to grill him and make sure.

"Emma Paladin," Randolph read from a report and recited my address. "Her license was one of two that did not match the bodies found at the compound."

"Who was the other one?" I asked.

"Bertrand Bauerfang," he replied. There followed a palpable pause. "Cal, I probably shouldn't tell you this but the FBI agents out of the Las Vegas office are working an angle that Emma Paladin—"

"Emma Bartram," I corrected him, not quite understanding that a chapter in my life had indeed closed.

"Right," Randolph said. "Emma Bartram and Bauerfang lit out together for points unknown. How did the federal geniuses deduce such a theory? They're the only two left alive. And they are presently unaccounted for."

"Nothing else?" I asked.

Randolph hesitated for so long that I thought the call had disconnected. I was ready to replace the receiver in its cradle atop the nightstand when he spoke again.

"There's the matter of the journal," the trooper captain said at last. "It's in FBI possession now, evidence in an ongoing case and all that."

"Who's journal?"

"Your, I mean, Ms. Bartram's."

"Did you see this journal yourself?"

"No," he replied, "but they're using it to build up a psych eval on Ms. Bartram."

"Do they think she had a hand in all of this?"

"I am unable to comment, Cal. Not now, at any rate."

"You never really know anyone, do you?"

"I wish I could say I had cases like this in the past," Randolph said, " but I haven't. I can say that I agree. Sometimes we don't really know anyone."

I thanked Captain Randolph and hung up the phone. Suddenly, the room in which I had been staying appeared smaller than I remembered, claustrophobic almost.

The next day I checked out, drove my truck to Reno, and pulled into the first used car lot near the airport that I could find. There was much tire kicking and consideration on the part of the salesman I dealt with named Jimmy Frizzell.

In his large sunglasses, embroidered wide-collar shirt, slacks, cowboy boots, and oversized belt buckle, one engraved with flying ducks over a pond, that looked like it was ready to give way to the pressure of his big gut, Jimmy Frizzell looked like an aging, down-on-his-luck Elvis impersonator. It was part of his sales schtick. He even sounded like The King.

"Uh...I don't know, man," Jimmy rubbed his giant chin. "I already got me a couple of Dodge trucks in inventory."

"I am going to abandon it on the street and take the keys with me," I said.

"Oh don't do that, man," he said. "I guess I could offer you something."

What Jimmy Frizzell meant to say was he'd offer me next to nothing. He paid me eight hundred dollars cash for the truck. He licked his fat thumb each time he counted off a fifty-dollar bill from a stack he kept in a safe inside his trailer office. When he finished, he scooped up the eight hundred dollars and handed me the damp bills.

"Counting money makes me thirsty, man," Frizzell said.

"No kidding," I told him. "I wonder why that is?"

He didn't even let me call for a taxi from his place to the airport.

Chapter 51: Déjà vu Airlines

All the food in my house had gone bad. I threw it all away.

Since I had automatic payment set up for my utilities the power company took money from my bank account every month like I was still there. On my old laptop I checked bank statements. The army paid me my warrant officer pay every two weeks without fail, even up until the time they let me leave Kirtland after I had been apprehended by Prescott 2.0.

The prospect of doing something remotely normal like going to the supermarket to buy fresh food left me feeling uneasy. The last thing I wanted to do was turn into some kind of shut-in, but I couldn't bring myself to leave the house once I got there. I went online to a supermarket website and used their delivery service.

The guy who delivered my groceries looked familiar, at least he did through the front door peephole, but I couldn't place him. That made me nervous. I shouted at him through the door to leave the bags on my porch.

I got it into my head the moment I thought I recognized him that he had been sent to kill me. It was ridiculous. If the government wanted me dead, they wouldn't have let me leave Kirtland Air Base. The poor delivery guy probably thought I was a paranoid kook. I prefer extra careful, but we can't have everything.

The paranoia didn't end with the supermarket delivery guy. Every day, at different intervals, I found myself looking out windows from behind drawn curtains. I stood off to the side to do so, pushing the edge of a curtain out of the way just an inch or two to glimpse outside.

A woman walked her dog past my house every day. Her name was Lynne Something-or-Another. She and her husband Bill lived around the block from me. On summer holidays like July 4th, Emma and I used to attend the block parties they held. That was a long time ago. Lynne passed my house each day at the same time in the morning. In the past, sometimes I'd go out and talk to her. Not this time. I convinced myself that maybe she was an operative, a sleeper agent of some kind or another.

Other people walked past my house. They were teens and kids mostly on their way to and from school.

Sometimes a car or a pick-up truck would pull to a stop on the other side of the street. The drivers of these vehicles were always scrolling through their phones or looking over paperwork once they parked. Eventually, they always moved on.

One day I got fed up. I decided to confront a guy who parked across the street from my house. On the way down the porch steps that chestnut about kindness Emma used to say came to mind: *You attract more flies with honey than vinegar.* My ex-wife always encouraged me to be nice to people.

"What the fuck are you doing here?" I said to the guy.

"You a cop?" he said with a cocky assuredness.

"State your business?" I said. "Did Prescott send you?"

"I don't know anyone with that name."

"Who are you with?"

Rather than answer, the guy pointed to the company logo on his truck. Polinsky & Sons Sewage Systems Repair. The motto beneath it read: *If Things Get Stinky, Call Bob Polinsky.*

"Are you with the NSA?" I pressed him some more. "CIA?"

"Dude," the guy said. "Take your meds, man."

He started his truck and drove away.

The other thing I did in those early days after I returned home was keep my television on tuned to a cable news channel. Sometimes an hour or more would pass. If there wasn't any mention of The Radiant Angels of Zaphkar, I'd change to another station hoping to catch a story update.

There was other news, of course. None of it interested me, but I left the television on anyway, even when I slept.

I had gotten used to having no cell phone. When I was brought to Kirtland Air Force Base after my return to Dowa Yalanne they took my cell phone and never gave it back. I didn't think to ask for it or my other personal effects. I just wanted to get out of there. It did not occur to me at the time that somehow the Pulsargenix platform on all the phones in my unit were used to eavesdrop on our mission. Did data get transmitted wirelessly every time the gateway opened? Was there a relay station of some kind near the Frulx gateway on Veknyria they didn't disclose to us? I would never know. Whatever the case, I would have to buy another phone. That meant going outside, which I did not want to do just yet.

Eight days after I returned home I experienced a nervous breakdown thinking about Sofia Dashkova. I remembered her voice, the way she looked at me, how she made me feel wanted. Everywhere I turned in my house that day I kept seeing her with the fatal bullet wound in her face.

There was of course no way of confirming if the grenade I left under Isbalov killed him. If it did not, and he made it out of that cave, I doubted he survived the desert.

Such thoughts, however, were no consolation when it came to losing Sofia. I ran it over in my head repeatedly that day. What could I have done differently? Why didn't I try to wrestle the machine gun from Isbalov's grip instead of trying to bash his head in with a rock? I had many questions, but they would all remain unanswered.

On the ninth day I woke up overwhelmed by a certain calm. I even went out and purchased a new cell phone. The clerk was accommodating, even when I asked to keep my old number.

I thought if I were ever to get on with my life, I couldn't hide from people anymore.

No one followed me to the store or back to my house.

My phone rang at eleven the next morning.

"Turn on your television right now," a voice instructed me when I answered the call.

"What? It is on," I said.

"Sad news coming from SeaTac," the voice said.

I sat up straight. "Who is this?" I asked.

"It's Captain Randolph," he replied. "Nevada State Police."

"Oh, I didn't recognize your voice."

"Are you watching? Turn on Fox."

"I don't watch Fox."

"One of those guys, huh?"

"What do you mean?"

"No disrespect," the trooper captain said. "The country is divided these days into assholes and patriots—"

Not this again, I thought. Then, I told him, "Is there a difference?"

"What?"

"You heard me."

"Are you watching the news?"

"CNN, yes."

"Communist News Network? What are you? One of them socialists?"

I hung up on him.

On the television a female reporter stood near a baggage claim area at Seattle-Tacoma International Airport.

"This is Morena Valdez for CNN," the reporter said. "The end of a two-week old mystery has come to an end for Nevada law enforcement and the FBI. In the early pre-dawn hours here just a few miles from this busy airport, Red Arrow Airlines Flight 524 crashed after engine failure. All seventy-seven passengers onboard were killed. Authorities just confirmed that Bertrand Bauerfang, the self-described Initiate Supreme of The Radiant Angels of Zaphkar, was among the dead on Red Arrow Airlines Flight 524. Surveillance footage from Reno-Tahoe Airport in Nevada from early this morning showed Bertrand Bauerfang waiting for his luggage before making a connecting flight to Seattle. A fugitive wanted for tax evasion, Bauerfang was also being sought for questioning regarding a mass suicide of three-hundred-thirty-two members of his cult and the desecration of a number of corpses at his compound outside Elko, Nevada. CNN has obtained exclusive footage of Bertrand Bauerfang inside the Reno-Tahoe Airport prior to boarding Red Arrow Airlines Flight 524."

On my television screen a loop showed Bertrand Bauerfang with a red ellipse drawn around the dapper-looking elderly man who gestured with a black cane capped with a silver ball as he spoke to two people with their faces pixelated to obscure their identities.

Bauerfang was dead. None of the news stations mentioned if he was traveling alone. Emma didn't appear in the short loop that depicted Bauerfang at the Reno-Tahoe Airport.

For several minutes I just sat there, stunned by the fact that I still didn't know of my ex-wife's fate. I telephoned Red Arrow Airlines. Ultimately, I was connected to an automated response system. A computer-generated voice instructed me to say the name of the person I was looking for and to spell it afterward.

"Emma Paladin," I said, before I provided the spelling.

"That name was not on the passenger manifest," the automated voice said. "If you'd like to search for another name, press 1 now."

I pressed 1 and used Emma's maiden name.

"That name was not on the passenger manifest," the automated voice said. "If you'd like—"

I hung up. It was hard to decide which was worse: finding out that my ex-wife had died or that she was a possible fugitive out there somewhere in the world.

An hour after the story of Bertrand Bauerfang's death broke, a knock sounded on the door. It was an authoritative one, the knock of a cop or an overzealous Jesus huckster running low on conversion quotas.

"Who's there?" I barked as I stood behind my locked front door.

"Mr. Caleb Paladin?" a man on the other side of the door asked.

"Who wants to know?"

"Sergeant First Class Alfonzo Fabrizio," he replied. "I have some paperwork for you."

"Just leave it on the porch."

"You have to sign for it, sir."

Reluctantly, I unlocked the front door and opened it.

"What kind of paperwork?" I asked.

Sergeant Fabrizio stood there in class A's with a green beret on his head. He had more ribbons and citations than any three generals.

"It's a sealed packet, sir," he told me.

"So you don't know what it is?" I asked.

"The operative word just then was *sealed*."

"You're a regular smart-ass."

"That's what my mother used to tell me," said Fabrizio. He produced a smart pad and stylus. "Sign on the line at the bottom and press the red X."

I took the pad and stylus from him, signed where he told me, and touched the X with the stylus. Fabrizio handed me the packet he held after I turned over his smart pad and stylus.

"Thank you for your service, sir," the sergeant said before he performed a perfect about-face and descended the porch steps.

Back inside the house, I had no luck cutting open the extra thick manila envelope. It was no easy thing since all four sides were taped over with a reinforced tape the likes of which I'd never seen. I tried scissors on one corner of the folder-sized envelope. That didn't work. I went to the basement and came back upstairs with wire cutters. No sooner than I snipped through a portion of the tape my house phone rang.

"Hello?" I answered.

"You have to use the pull tab," Fabrizio said over the phone.

"What are you talking about?" I asked.

"The reinforced tape sends a tamper alarm," he explained.

"Are you serious?"

"Yes sir," Fabrizio responded. "It's the latest thing. Isn't technology grand?"

"Where's the pull tab?"

"You see the seal on the back?"

I turned the envelope over. There was a seal with the official U.S. Army emblem complete with the Roman cuirass, the Phrygian red cap, the sword, the cannon, and all the rest rendered in fine detail. A band bordering the circumference of the round seal was marked *United States of America* on the top half and the bottom rendered in two lines read *Board of Off-World Operations & Resource Appropriation Established MMI.*

"I see it," I told Fabrizio.

"Pull the snakehead over the Phrygian cap," he instructed me.

"What's the roman number MMI?"

"2001," he said.

"What does 'Resource Appropriation' mean?"

"Just pull the snakehead to open the packet, sir," he said.

I did so, expecting the whole packet to explode. It did not, even when I finished unsealing the packet all the way.

"Got it," I said, "now—"

Son of a bitch. Sergeant Fabrizio had hung up on me.

Inside the packet were photocopies of all my termination of consultation paperwork (they didn't ever think to refer to it as a discharge, honorable or otherwise). The photocopies also included signatures of others who were absent during my detention—mostly colonels and generals. The copy of the non-disclosure agreement had a thick red border all the way around it, no doubt to call my attention to it and to serve as a reminder of all the things that could happen to me if I ever told the story. I put the paperwork in a file cabinet in my office off the kitchen where I kept my original discharge papers.

The open packet envelope I took into the kitchen to throw out. When I did I looked over the broken seal one last time. On the spot over the space that the snake had occupied before I broke the seal was the Latin phrase *A Terra Ad Novum Mundi*. I had to look it up. It meant "From Earth to New Worlds."

A subsequent Google search for "Off-World Operations & Resource Appropriation" turned up little except for a podcast recorded in May 2011. The podcast had been hosted by a guy who called himself Ezekiel Lev. In it, he went on for nearly thirty agonizing minutes trying to connect dots that were not there between the disappearance of large sums of money just prior to the terror attacks of September 11th and secret government space exploration.

Ezekiel Lev had a cohost named Jubal who read comments from listeners logged onto their website. The consensus that took shape over the course of the thirty-minute podcast was that it was Ezekiel Lev's worst one yet.

Despite the feelings of his hardcore fans, Ezekiel Lev's mention of a secret branch of the army tasked with visiting new worlds via shared alien technology may have been meaningless to anyone else, but not to me. I decided to find Ezekiel Lev and ask him the name of the anonymous government source who allegedly had given him his information.

The search, sadly, was short-lived. Ezekiel Lev, whose real name was Lev Povich, the son of Russian immigrants, died in a car wreck just one month after his May 2011 podcast aired. The fatal accident took place on Dale Mabry Road in Tampa, Florida, not far from MacDill Air Force Base. Much had been made over the years about Lev Povich's accident occurring in such close proximity to the headquarters of the United States Special Operations Command.

Lev Povich's autopsy revealed that his blood alcohol content was more than three times the legal limit in the state of Florida. It was hard to imagine someone like that being able to operate a vehicle. Ezekiel Lev's most ardent fans maintained that he was killed for what he knew. It was always that way. Lone investigative journalists of varying credibility were always getting killed under strange circumstances. I often wondered if the U.S. Government had a special branch of operatives whose sole function was to go around dispatching independent journalists who got too close to the truth, but I never looked that far into it for fear of them coming after me.

Of Ezekiel Lev's podcast cohost nicknamed Jubal, I found nothing.

Chapter 52: The Ugly Gnome

It was late in the day when I heard the key in the back door. I turned off the television and headed through the dining room. By the time I reached the kitchen Emma was already inside.

My ex-wife looked like she had gained a few pounds since the last time I saw her. She looked good. She looked healthy, which was something our relationship toward the end had prevented her from doing. Gone were the dark circles under her eyes. The desert had been good to her.

"The key was still inside that ugly gnome's head," she said by way of greeting. "I wasn't even sure if you still lived here."

The one thing about The Radiant Angels of Zaphkar was that they took their privacy seriously. It helped that Bauerfang managed to recruit the mercenaries sent to retrieve the twin daughters of Judge Silas Bowery. The soldiers of fortune may have buried their weapons in the desert, but they knew more than Bauerfang ever would about maintaining security. Since privacy remained such a high priority, no one ever gained admittance to the compound. Photographs of members were rare for that reason. Of the few photographs of Radiant Angels that existed, women were dressed like their everyday counterparts.

In daydreams and off moments when I thought of Emma's return, my visions became increasingly troublesome because the more time had passed the more in my mind she started to look like some high queen of desert-dwelling doomsday preppers.

To my surprise, Emma was dressed like a normal woman for her age. No weird tattoos, no crystals strung around her neck or woven into her hair. No silver wristbands with blue turquoise taken from

Iran or Northwest China and passed off as the genuine article from the American Southwest. In fact, she had on no jewelry at all.

"Say something, Cal," she pleaded.

"I'm not even sure where to start," I said.

"A simple hello may work."

"Hello."

She wore a faded pair of jeans and button collar shirt colored light blue. The Initiate Supreme considered the strict dress codes of other religious orders, like The Blessed Sons and Daughters of the Lost Conquistador whose female members wore long dresses and headscarves and the men donned tunics and pantaloons[20], excessive since such attire only drew attention to the members of a given order. More than that, Bauerfang considered such fashion a distraction that kept followers further enmeshed in the prison of matter Zaphkar had warned the Supreme Initiate about. It stood to reason that Bauerfang no doubt thought drawing attention to one's self would not help his angels assimilate in town whenever they had

---

[20] The attire adopted by The Blessed Sons and Daughters of The Lost Conquistador, founded in 1988 by Fausto de Azara, a group that numbered three-hundred-strong until an ATF raid in 2009 on their compound not far from Amboy, California. The Blessed Sons and Daughters accepted de Azara as they living incarnation of the last conquistador to set foot in California, one who abandoned the search for gold and, according to Fausto de Azara, followed an angel named Rama-El who promised to share the secret wisdom of heaven. Fausto de Azara told his followers that in his former life when he told his brothers-in-arms about the angel Rama-El they did what any well-armed good Catholic boys would do in the name of King Philip II of Spain. They crucified the blasphemer in the desert. The Blessed Sons and Daughters of the Lost Conquistador believed that Fausto de Azara would reveal all the secrets of heaven given to him by the angel Rama-El. They believed, that is, until the ATF showed up with a search warrant targeting illegally purchased firearms and explosives. When de Azara ordered his followers to fight, the ATF did what any well-trained and well-armed government law enforcement agency would do. Fausto de Azara, celebrating his sixty-fifth birthday the day of the raid, was shot multiple times while trying to flee the compound in a Humvee and run over several agents in the process. The Blessed Sons and Daughters, feeling a little embarrassed over their sixteenth century garb in the blistering Mojave Desert heat, laid down their arms and surrendered.

to leave the compound for supplies or to pick up a new convert freshly arrived in Elko. Hence, my ex-wife's casual wear.

"How are you doing, Cal?" Emma asked.

"You walked out nearly a decade ago," I said, "and that's your first question?"

"What should I ask?"

"Why don't you tell me why you are the sole survivor of one of the biggest mass suicides in recent history?"

"Over the past couple of years," said Emma, "things started going bad for The Radiant Angels. Well, actually, we were good. But the Supreme, I mean Bauerfang was in serious financial trouble."

"Speaking of," I started to say.

"I know, I know," she said. "I'm going to pay you back."

"Don't," I said. "Tell me what happened."

"At the compound? From the beginning?"

"Let's stick to the days leading up to the final exit."

"Mine or everyone else's?"

"The latter."

"I had nothing to do with it," Emma said. "I wouldn't lie about that."

"So the cult grandee had tax troubles and he decides to convince everyone to kill themselves?"

"It wasn't suicide," she said. "I can tell you that."

"Sure, Bauerfang force-fed poison to three-hundred-thirty-two people, including my former sister-in-law, until they died."

"You mock us," she said, "but it was beautiful."

"Not beautiful enough for you and Bauerfang," I said.

"They started mixing up Kool-Aid and cyanide," Emma told me. "Bauerfang, I mean the Initiate Supreme had a vision."

"One that did not include you?"

"The others were going to meet Zaphkar," Emma announced.

"But not you."

"I was the messenger's bride," she said. "Zaphkar was to tell the Initiate Supreme when the others arrived safely—"

"That's enough," I said. Then, "Are you staying?"

"I don't think it's a good idea," she said.

"Why wouldn't it be? You only left seven years ago—"

"Eight," she corrected me.

"Closer to nine now. I just wanted to see if you counted."

"While I was gone," Emma said, "I thought about our vows."

"Oh?"

"Yes."

"There are worse things to do in this world than break marriage vows, Cal."

"You don't get to do this," I told her.

She looked as if she might cry.

"I need a place to stay for a day or two—" she began.

I'd known estranged couples who had been through this. Well, not the running away to join a cult part but the old "I need a place to stay for a few days" routine. If it happened around Christmas, the estranged spouse was still there come Labor Day.

"One day," I said. "Hungry?"

"That's it?"

"You can leave now if you want?"

"I thought we might try to iron things out," said Emma.

"Because you have nowhere to go?"

"I deserve that."

I ended up ordering from a local restaurant that we used to like. Emma wanted to go to the diner together like nothing ever happened. Her nonchalance about the events in Nevada spoke volumes about the pain it was causing her. Indifference of that sort did little to mask the trauma. She might have been fooling herself, but she wasn't fooling me. She needed to be deprogrammed, for starters. That wasn't within the realm of responsibilities for former husbands.

"Did you love him?" I asked.

"The Sup...I mean Bertrand?" she asked. "I guess so. But not the way you think."

"Were you with other men there?" I pressed on.

"Yes, Cal," she said. "There were other men. We tried to create a new reality devoid of former constructs. What about you?"

"I didn't run away with my sister-in-law to join a cult."

"You know it wasn't like that."

"My life turned upside down when you left," I said.

"Mine was suffocating while I was here with you," Emma countered. It wasn't a lie. She'd been unhappy for years.

We sat there not really looking at each other after that. I cleaned up the dishes and put away the leftovers. It was already ten o'clock by the time I finished.

"I'm going to bed," I said. "I'll get you a pillow and a blanket for down here. If you are here in the morning, we can talk."

I went and got her a pillow and blanket. Emma was already undressing. She turned her back on me as she did so.

"You mind?" Emma said, looking over her shoulder.

Her skin had been such familiar territory once. Now it was foreign and treacherous for all the wrong reasons.

I left her in the living room and went upstairs. For the first time in I can't remember how long I locked the bedroom door. At some point, I thought I heard Emma try the door and whisper my name. Or maybe I dreamed it.

The next morning I woke up early. I had a good quiet cry over Sofia's passing. Afterward, I did my thing in the bathroom, washed up, brushed my teeth, and went downstairs.

The blanket was folded neatly at the far end of the sofa with the pillow placed on top.

Emma was long gone. No note, just like last time. The difference now was that her absence no longer weighed on me.

Later that morning I called Herb Kaufman. He sounded like his old self.

"You're back?" he asked, gruffly.

"I am," I told him. "Hey, are you going to marry Emma?"

"What the hell is wrong with you?" asked Herb. "Why would I put myself through the pain of marriage again?"

"Didn't you love your wife?"

"With all my heart and soul," he shouted. "I'll never find another like her, thank God. You want to come back to work soon? Or what?"

"I got some stuff to work out, Herb."

"I know the feeling."

For a moment, I thought old Herb might have been a fellow traveler. Then I came to my senses.

"Is that right?" was all I could think to say.

"When Adele died I was a basket case," Herb confessed. "You got to remember we'd known each other since middle school."

"I never knew that," I said.

"We were the only Jews in the whole school," he said. "We used to call it WASP Junior High. Every other kid there was a Sloane, or a Tilly, or a Todd, or a Whitaker. There was a boy in math class named Whitaker. They called him Whit. He was as dumb as a rock. What were his parents thinking?"

"That whole experience really traumatized you," I said.

"Imagine being uprooted and sent to some alien planet you know nothing about—"

"I know what that's like—" I cut him off.

"Bullshit," he wasn't having it. "You're just like them."

"I'm hardly a WASP."

"Fine," he said, "I'll concede that you are a mensch. You should wear that like a badge of honor."

"Thanks."

"What's got you down?" asked Herb. "I can hear it in your voice."

"I met someone," I told him, "but she died suddenly."

"Did you love her?"

"I did."

"What's to lament? Carry her around forever in your heart," he advised me. "It's the only way the departed get a taste of immortality."

"That's it?"

"Sure," he said. "You should also write it down in a notebook. When you think you've finished, take it out in the backyard and burn that shit. That's what I did after Adele died."

"Did it work?"

"How the hell should I know? Some nights I still cry in the dark and she's been dead for years."

"I'll come by Monday," I promised.

"It's good you're home," he said. "Now, let me fire somebody so you can get your old job back."

"Don't do that," I said.

"It was a joke," he said. "I've been doing your job for the past year or so."

"Thanks, Herb."

"Not because I wanted to, you rube," he quipped. "Remember the notebook. It'll work wonders for you."

I took Herb's advice. I bought a notebook and wrote in it every night when I got home from work. When the first notebook was filled, I bought another.

I wrote it all down. I didn't mean for it to turn into a confession or a memoir for others to read. I wrote it because I missed Sofia. I was afraid that I would forget who I am, what I'd gone through. I wanted a reminder that love can be found late in life in the most unlikely places.

When I finished, I took the notebooks into my backyard, threw them in the firepit, and burned them.

Once the deed was done I called Herb to let him know the news. I barely got two words out before he started carrying on like a maniac.

"What do you want from me?" Herb shouted into the phone before I could tell him anything. "Go live your life, you sorry bastard. Stop bothering me every ten seconds. Just be at work on Monday. And no more of this army business. You're too damned old for all that crap—"

He was still shouting when I hung up.